THE
MEDLAR TREE

Michael Adams

First published in Great Britain in 1997 by Halsgrove

Copyright © 1997 Michael Adams

*All rights reserved. No part of this publication may be reproduced,
stored in a retrieval system, or transmitted in any form
or by any means without the prior permission
of the copyright holder.*

ISBN 1 874448 77 9

British Library Cataloguing in Publication Data

A CIP record for this title is available from the British Library

HALSGROVE
PUBLISHING, MEDIA AND DISTRIBUTION
Halsgrove House
Lower Moor Way
Tiverton
Devon EX16 6SS
Tel: 01884 243242
Fax: 01884 243325

Printed in Great Britain by Short Run Press Ltd, Exeter

CONTENTS

Chapter 1	5
Chapter 2	15
Chapter 3	17
Chapter 4	26
Chapter 5	39
Chapter 6	47
Chapter 7	52
Chapter 8	59
Chapter 9	126
Chapter 10	134
Chapter 11	163
Chapter 12	186
Chapter 13	192
Chapter 14	196
Chapter 15	201
Chapter 16	203
Chapter 17	213
Chapter 17	260
Chapter 19	297
Chapter 20	304
Chapter 21	312
Chapter 22	329
Chapter 23	363
Chapter 24	391
Chapter 25	397
Chapter 26	399
Chapter 27	419
Chapter 28	423

Scenes from the novel, set in Paignton of years gone by. The top picture shows Well Street, scene of Willy's upbringing, 1 shows the gate to the dairy and 2 the open stream that ran down the street. The picture below shows the grander side of Paignton, Dellers Cafe in the 1930s. Sadly, it was demolished in 1965.

Chapter 1

It was one of those hot, breathless days that happen sometimes during a long dry spell of weather in August. Willy pulled himself up by the window sill, his toes scraping against the wall, and looked out through the aspidistra leaves and the looped net curtains, on to the white road that ran immediately against the cottage wall.

White lime dust, rising in clouds with the passing of every vehicle, lay thick upon the ivy and valerian that grew on the high wall opposite the window.

At the moment, the road was quiet, in fact the whole town seemed to sleep in the afternoon heat. Only the goldfinch, in its cage by the side of the front door, kept up its constant hop from perch to perch, calling, calling. Then, distantly, came the sound of a cow lowing, and Willy dropped to the ground and quietly opened the street door. At once, the silence in the cottage was somehow given another dimension, less cloistered, and with little stirrings that whispered around the walls. Willy's mother, sitting in the kitchen with her feet up, and the week's darning in her lap, sensed the change.

"Willy, where y'going?"

"T'see the cows."

"Well, keep away from the fountain."

The door closed, and Willy ran the twenty yards or so down the road, and sat himself down on the step of the little general shop. He hugged his knees and with half-closed eyes, watched the dust motes dancing in the sun. Presently, the slow, soft, plodding sound of many cloven hoofs drew his gaze to the end of the school wall, further down the hill.

"Now!" he said to himself, judging when the first cow would appear, wriggle with pleasure as the head of the first beast appeared. He'd been nearly right. Sometimes he was exactly right, but this time he was nearly right. There were times when the whole herd would stop, and he would have to say "Now" twenty times.

It was a lovely place for a small boy to sit. The shop at his back smelled of bread and bacon and liquorice, and before him, set in the crotch of a Y-shaped road junction was the fountain, a centre of activity at all times of the day and year. There, the passing tradesmens' vans were drawn to a halt for the horses to drink. The great drays of the brewery and railway pulled up too, and massive shires drawing the high, two-wheeled dust carts, thrust their soft mouths into the welcome water. Best of all though, were the twenty or so cows that came down from the fields twice a day to be milked in the shippen below the quarry in Well Street. These paused, coming and going, each time, to be watered. Sometimes they would spend a quarter of an hour milling around, and dropping their dung with rattling splats all over the area.

The whole place was like a farmyard and on that hot afternoon, the air was heavy with the smell of cattle and dust and the lovely aromas from the little shop. Willy wriggled his bottom on the step, hugged his knees and peered against the sun from under the protection of the broken brim of an over-big cloth cap. A bicycle on whispering wheels, wound its way through the last stragglers of the herd. The sun beat down, the dung flies buzzed, the day dreamed.

"Yah!"

In a split second Willy was awakened in frightened dismay. His cap was being whirled around on the end of a stick, and he stood in numbed terror as he saw his arch enemy, Bill Gurney, cavorting amongst the cattle, calling him, daring him, to come and get it back.

"Yah! Windy! Cry baby! Bet you won't get it! I'm gunna put it in the fountain!"

Every nerve in Willy's skinny little body was willing him to run home and fetch his mum, but something wouldn't let him.

"Give me back."

"Shan't. "Give me back."

"Come and get it then."

The early arrivals in the herd were now moving off up the hill towards their pasture, and some of the others were standing, just gazing, at the boy waving a stick with something impaled on it. Bill came closer, tantalizing Willy by holding the cap just out of reach. Then, as he circled one cow, the animal suddenly lowered its head and made a warning gesture with its bright, curved horns. Bill jumped aside, and in so doing, let the cap fall from the stick, and in a moment, Willy, driven by desperation, dived for it and got it. Next moment, hard fingers gripped his arm and a tug of war started for the cap.

"Gimme."

"No."

"Gimme. I'll stick your head in the fountain! Got it!"

The cap gone again, Willy dissolved into tears, to the jeers and delight of his tormentor, who, holding the mishapen article by its broken brim, skimmed it away in the direction of the fountain, leaping after it with delighted laughter, while the blubbering Willy stood by the school wall in misery.

Suddenly, a third figure had appeared. This was a boy of about ten years, big for his age, who was earning the fourth penny of the day by taking the cows back to the field on the last of their two double journeys.

This lad materialised from behind the fountain, and put his hobnailed boot on the cap, just as Bill stooped to pick it up. At the same time, he grabbed Bill by the neck of his guernsey and held him easily.

"What you tryin' to do?"

"Lemme go. I'm only playing."

"No you're not, you're bullyin."

"Lemme go!"

"Now look 'ere, Bill Gurney, I'm giving you fair warning - if I ever catch you going for that boy again, I'll - (with dreadful insistence) - put your 'ead in the fountain 'til you're drowned."

Bill looked up at the fierce face above him, squirmed against the grip on his neck, and suddenly released, tore away to one of two cottages on the lowerside of the Y, where reaching sanctuary, he hurled abuse before darting indoors.

" 'ere y' are."

Willy took the cap, and gazed in awe at his saviour.

"'Oo are you?"

"Willy Churchward."

7

"Where d'you live?"

"Over there."

"Well, I'm Jerry Wilkins, and if ever Bill Gurney goes for you again, let me know, and I'll get him - see?"

"Yes, thank you,"

The last of the cows were now well ahead, on their way back up the hill, and the boy ran after them.

Willy tried to put some shape back into his cap and went back to his cottage.

The small westcountry town of Paignton was little more than a collection of villages in those days. Following the Great War, the rapid changes caused by so many developments of industrial skill and modes of life, occasioned by the war, had not yet made any impact on life.

Where Willy lived, with his mother, was a little village within the town and was still referred to by old-timers as 'The Green'. This must have harked back to when there was only the thatched cottages on Barn's Hill, and four more on the other side of the fountain. Doubtless, there must have been a green at the road junction then, and the name survived, as had the name Barns Hill, although there had been no barn on the green in living memory. It was bounded by country lanes on two sides, the town on another, and the steep hill roads leading to the monastery on the fourth.

Willy's cottage sat beside the road leading into town on the right hand branch of the Y. Actually, it was on the top of a quarry, but this was screened by a wall, some ten feet high, the top of which wore a wig of red valerian and branching ivy. On this road, besides the two cottages, was a blacksmith's shop, some barns and a small triangular piece of grass dividing the town road and the steep ascent to the monastery. Beyond this triangle was Winner Street and the town. Below the cottages, were the road junctions and the fountain. This was a circular cattle trough, about six feet across, with a lamp post in the middle. The trough was about three feet high, and because of the slope of the road, it stood on a plinth about twenty-five feet across, that was level with the road on one side and about two feet high on the other. Every Friday, a council employee would come with a bucket and broom, empty the water, remove the stones and rubbish, which he placed in the gutter, scrub out the trough and turn on the water again. As soon as he had departed, the boys came out of school and replaced the stones, some throwing from a distance, others deriving pleasure from standing on the rim of the trough, and dropping stones in with satisfying plonks.

There were houses climbing the hill on one side, the road leading off to the country at its end. Cottages and the little chapel on the other. Across the width of the Y was the school and shop, and at the end of the left hand branch of the Y was the Big House "Effords". Beyond that the road wandered off to the country.

Behind the school and shop the ground fell away, and at the foot of the quarry was Well Street, with its cottages, farmyard, and the brook that burst out from a conduit, chortled amongst the assorted rubbish that constantly found its way there, gave a last wink to the sun, and dived again into darkness on its way to the sea. It was a small world, where each one's business was fairly common property and people tended to group together, in terraces, or roads, each one wary of the other, somewhat reminiscent of the territorial claims made by creatures of the wild, and all ready to defy the advance of anyone from beyond its boundaries.

Willy's cottage had no name. It was officially No. 3 Barns Hill, but wore no number on its door, after all, there were only two cottages and everyone knew who lived in them. From the outside it was picturesque. The walls had been whitewashed in some bygone age and were now peeling and grey. The windows were small and many paned and the rotting thatch sprouted moss and even a seedling sycamore or two, that were the result of the flight of seeds from a garden on the next contour, a hundred feet above. An ash tree had grown in a crack near the road and then raised its spindly height nearly to the eaves.

Two steps led up to the front door and large boulders leant against the wall at six feat intervals to discourage wagoners from crowding the cottage windows. Over the door was a little arch and under this, all summer long, hung a bird cage with a goldfinch fretting against the wires.

Inside it was dark and airless, the cottage backed into rock that towered upwards no more than six feet from its windows. The kitchen and bedroom above it were always damp.

Willy's mother had been sitting in the kitchen when we first took note of her. She was having a "bit of a sit down" while she darned the many times darned, articles of essential wear. Sometimes she sat on the front step, but after such a long, hot spell, the dust from the road filtered into everything, and for once the cool of the back of the house was welcome. She was a handsome woman, not yet thirty years old, but already showing some signs of the constant battle to keep herself and Willy "decent".

Willy was now eight, and it was six years since that dreadful, shattering day when the telegram had come to tell her that her husband, "my Dave", would never come home again.

Dave Churchward had been a saddler, serving his time, and continuing to work for a firm of saddlers in the town. In those days, it seemed as secure a trade as a blacksmith, for whom there seemed no possibility of lack of work. He was a dreamer and reader of books. As his awl probed the leather and the twin needles pushed through, his mind was, like as not, on a journey to some romantic place or remembering the magic of some moment when bird song, or flower scent, or flashing dragonfly brought the miracle of nature into his very being. At such moments, although the awl never stopped, the needles pushed in and out and his body stooped and rose as the threads were pulled; it needed a deftly thrown wad of tow, or something heavier, to bring him back to reality. His old master would look over his glasses at him and say that he'd never get on if he didn't pay attention

Dave had met Gwen, who was a maid at the Big House, and they had fallen in love, and when the cottage on Barns Hill fell vacant, they had married and moved in. Gwen was an orphan and had gone into service as soon as she was fourteen. She did not know her parentage and the nuns who had brought her up from infancy, had been all the family she had known; they, and the thirty or so girls that made up the crocodile that wound its way between orphanage and school. At the Big House she was well fed and warm, both luxuries to her. The kitchen and an attic bedroom were her home. She was happy. To have a room of her own was wonderful and a real delight. She seldom went out. Ogling delivery boys were kept well at bay by a large and masterful cook. She had been there more than two years and had grown into a pretty, well-developed girl, when Dave was sent to repair a strap on Gwen's master's dog cart. That was the beginning, and many a subterfuge had to be invented to contrive the meetings that followed.

So they were married. Gwen had an artistic flair inherited from someone never to be known, and she took delight in making the cottage as elegant as she could. Dave's parents gave them some very dilapidated furniture and Gwen's mistress gave her some of her oldest linen and a china jardiniere that was at once given pride of place on the windowsill, where it sported a truly magnificent aspidistra, given to her by Dave's employer. The cottage was washed and polished, brushed and dusted until, even in the dark rooms at the back, light was reflected wherever one looked.

War came like a bolt from the blue. First it was not fully comprehended. Willy was on the way, and life in the town seemed to go on as usual. But after a year, people began telling Dave that he should enlist, and gradually he began to feel ashamed not to be in khaki. The local territorials had gone to India to relieve regular soldiers. There were soldiers billeted in the town who were marching and training down by the harbour. So Dave joined up. Gwen hugged Willy and wept, laying on the bed engulfed in misery long after she had heard the train pull out in the distance. Dave came back twice on leave, in ill-fitting uniform and bright buttons. It took Gwen a long time to accept that he would never come home again.

Gwen never learned how Dave died. The numbing telegram was a month old before she got the letter from his Company Officer - "...a good soldier, who was conscientious in his duties and popular with his Company. His sacrifice has been made, that we may all live in justice and freedom...". Nothing to remember him by, no one to tell her how he plied his trade amongst the gun carriages and transport wagons, much of which were horse-drawn.

A saddler was in great demand to keep the harness in working order, and Dave had his own wagon, drawn by a huge black mule, brought, with hundreds more, from Argentina. A vicious brute, that wreaked vengeance on mankind with hoof and teeth whenever opportunity offered.

Dave was content with his lot, counting himself lucky by the standard of the Infantry, the Sappers and even the Gunners. He was able to ply his trade in relative safety, and was to some extent self-sufficient.

It was a cold, rain-sodden day in February, the guns had moved up over shell-pitted roads, and one had got bogged down. In an effort to haul it free, a leather collar had been damaged and at first stop, Dave had set about the urgent repair He had the shelter of his wagon to work in, and he sat hunched over the clamp holding the leather. The awl pushed in and was withdrawn in a neat row, leaving tiny holes, as regular as if punched by a precision machine; then the two needles, one from the front, the other from the back, took the waxed threads through and Dave bobbed forward as he pulled them tight. There was a smile on his face, the sewing was almost automatic, and his mind was far away, away in Devon, with the wife he had left at home. He thought of her, with the fire glow on her face and their child sucking contentedly at her breast. Then some errant thought took him to the market square in a nearby town where, every two weeks, he set up his bench and mended the broken harness brought in by farmers. His thoughts drifted to the soft, blossom-filled days of May, and he saw himself with his arm girdling Gwen's waist, as they wandered through the hazel tunnels of Shorton lanes, while close by the cuckoo called and called. If Gwen could have known of that happy thought, reflected in the dreaming eye and half smile, she would have been comforted a little. The stray shell found Dave's wagon as if predestined to do so. The cuckoo must have gone on calling into eternity.

Gwen went back to work at the Big House. Girls were hard to get now that more money could be earned in factories and on the trams, and they allowed her to bring Willy to work with her. His little world became the kitchen and back yard. He was too young to remember his father, and Gwen poured all the love of her poor bruised heart into the care of him, in spite of which he grew into a skinny child, small for his age and given to long silences. Gwen sighed over him, "You'm just like your Dad" she used to say, half knowing, half guessing, that, though his body was still and he hardly spoke, his mind was leaping joyously in some delightful daydream world. "You'm a dreamer too," she would say, looking at the miniature of her dead Dave.

So Willy grew up and went to the church school that was handily placed between the cottage and the Big House. Gwen still watched him with a fierce care. He was not permitted to go down Well Street. "They'm too rough down there," she would say. Nor was Willy allowed past the triangle of grass by the blacksmith's shop - that was Winner Street and into the town; the town was another place, only to be visited when accompanied by mother. Nor did she dress him like other boys. This was partly because his clothes were always bequeathed to him by Gwen's mistress who had a growing family. Instead of the "father's cutdowns" usually worn by the very poor, or the knickerbockers and stockings worn with a fisherman's guernsey, Willy was dressed in proper short trousers, together with roll top stockings, shirt and tie, jacket or jersey. Usually he wore shoes, whereas the other boys at school wore hobnailed boots. Gwen cut his hair so that it parted on one side, while all other boys had their heads shaven except for a tuft over the forehead - the forelock of old. This had its disadvantages, for as soon as he started school, Gwen had to perform a nightly ritual with a fine comb, with Willy's head bent over a sheet of newspaper and from time to time the lice would rattle out on to the paper. Willy would then delightedly crack them with his thumbnail and Gwen would soak his hair in Sassafras Oil.

All the children at school were lousy - some always, some, even the best cared for, from time to time. No houses had bathrooms, baths were taken before the kitchen fire, in a tin bath that spent most of the week hanging on the wall in the back yard. Water had to be heated on the kitchen range and though there might be a gas light in the living room of some newer houses, the normal lighting was a paraffin lamp on the table and candles elsewhere. It was not easy to keep clean, and some houses were truly filthy. There were children at school who really stank, and who passed on their lice and ringworm to any who might have to sit next to them.

Living on Barns Hill, in one of two cottages, Willy had no neighbours to play with. An old couple lived in the cottage next door. They earned pennies where they could to eke out the man's minute naval pension, and staved off the workhouse from week to week. So Willy took to hanging around the fountain after school, until his mother came home. He felt safe there, for he had two lines of retreat, one up the hill to his home - only yards away, the other to the Big House that was just around the corner. This was very necessary, for each street had its gang and any of them would descend on Willy, who was a sort of stray, and with boisterous horseplay, terrify him with their roughness. Boys are very cruel, and sometimes Willy used to say to himself "I wish I had a big brother, he'd show 'em." He never wished for a dad. Having a dad was beyond his comprehension. Dad, to him, was a picture on the mantleshelf, of a soldier wearing a crumpled cap and a sad looking moustache. That, and a jackknife, that his mother said he could have when he was twelve years old. That had been Dad's. His mother said he used to wear it on his belt.

The Big House.

Chapter 2

Down in Well Street, life really teemed. There was a terrace of houses, at the top end, that had bow windows. Each with its Aspidistra and net curtains, and an air of respectability. Then, in the middle of the street stood a row of cottages, some thatched, some slated. Opposite these was the farmyard, with milking shed, pig sties and dung heaps. The brook appeared in front of this for a few yards. From there the street climbed up to the church and pubs. Cottages flanked this little hill and from them emerged swarms of children who held this, their own world, in fee, and woe betide strangers. From one of these cottages also came two ladies, too flashily dressed for the normal dwellers, and to this home, came strangers, some furtive, some well gone in drink. From the dip in the middle of the street ran two cul-de-sacs of tiny houses with a communal yard at the rear, and a row of stables where tradesmen stabled their ponies and traps. At the apex of the triangle made by these two rows, was a general store. At the end of one cul-de-sac, in the last cottage, lived Effie Wilkins and her son Jerry.

Jerry was a boy of dauntless spirit. On the day that he had met and championed Willy Churchward, he was as carefree as he had ever been in his ten years of life. It was school holidays and life was full of opportunities for such as he. Although he lived in Well Street, he was, somehow, not of it. Probably because he had only recently lived there full time, and had not established his place in the rough and tumble of the scrummage of boys who lived around him. Being big and strong meant that he would have had to fight for a niche in the tribe. This he had avoided doing, and because of his size and strength, the other boys tolerated him, but did not include him in their games and fights, nor in their forays into other parts of the town.

This day he was spending in the farmyard, mucking out, bringing the cows in, taking them back to the pasture, half a mile away, and generally enjoying himself, earning a few pence.

He adopted a rolling gait, pitchfork on shoulder, in imitation of the dairyman, scattering the hens and spitting on the dung heap. The dairyman was kind to him, and, appreciative of the work he was capable of doing, encouraged him to hang around the yard. If Jerry had thought of it, he might have decided that this was the first time that he had ever been really happy.

Chapter 3

People forget, or have never been told, what that Great War was like. Tragedy was so commonplace it hardly caused concern except to the victims.

Jerry's father, Bert Wilkins, was a fisherman, working for a skipper who owned a small boat that was used in the bay for crabbing, long lining, and for netting the mackerel shoals that swept around the coast in the summer. He earned about two pounds a week, and a few cheap fish, like whiting, when the weather was good. Nothing when the boat was unable to leave harbour. When long storms kept him ashore for days or weeks, he turned his hand to anything, like cattle droving or gardening. During the winter he sometimes spent days mending and tarring nets, or making crab pots. One way or another he kept himself and his wife, Effie, in frugal decency.

Effie was only nineteen when he married her. She was in service, and he delivered fish to the tradesman's door of the little villa where she worked. She "lived in" and Bert used to meet her in the darkness of the garden, when her day's work was done. He was not really upset when she told him that she was "in the way". He liked her, and took it for granted that he would "get caught" sooner or later.

They rented one of the cottages off Well Street and settled happily to the hard, rough existence that both expected marriage would bring. There were bonds of family, and a rough affection between most people in the street, but romance was not expected or known. When possible, most husbands came home drunk on Saturday nights, and liberal use of the buckle end of the wide leather belt that supported their corduroys, brought reluctant wives to bed when the constant childbearing made them wary. Bert and Effie accepted the arrival of Jerry as a fact of life and Bert had to search that much harder for odd jobs to support them. Effie earned a little, cleaning one of the public houses at the top of the hill.

Jerry was four, and happily tumbling in the dusty gutter outside his house, when Bert came home and told Effie that he had heard that war had broken out. It was a Sunday, the church bells were ringing and everything seemed as usual. Later he came back from the pub with beer on his breath and excitement in his voice. Someone had told him that he could join the navy, Effie would get a regular allowance for herself and Jerry and he would be able to do his bit for the country. Effie heard this with some satisfaction. A regular wage and Bert out of the way had a considerable appeal She said little, but did not dissuade him. As for Bert, a whole new world opened up. He saw himself as free again in the camaraderie of a boisterous ship's company, no money worries and the delights of a "Jack ashore" when available.

It took Bert some time to enlist. He was surprised he could not just walk aboard some waiting ship, but within three months of the outbreak, he was gone. When Effie received her separation and child allowances, small though they were, she was delighted with herself. Only Jerry was a nuisance. Without him, she could have got work in one of the big houses.

Bert came home on leave and Effie was quick to claim her inability to meet his needs, and felt only relief when he took himself off to the house on the hill, where for the sum of two shillings, he was given what he wanted. Effie was thankful that somehow she had managed to avoid any more pregnancies, and did not intend to risk her new found freedom again.

She never found out what ship, or where Bert was, and did not really care. The day came when the licensee of the pub where she did her scrubbing each morning, looked at her frizzy red hair, her strong body and large bust, and suggested that she should serve behind the bar instead of doing the cleaning. This, Effie would have liked to do, but she had no relations in the town, nor had Bert, so she did not know what to do with Jerry. The publican solved that problem by finding someone who would look after him for a small sum. So Effie became a much admired barmaid while little Jerry was handed over to the ministrations of an old crone who kept the "dratted kid" in order as if he had been a wilful pup.

It was 1916 when Bert was reported "killed in action". Jerry was six years old by then, and was getting too strong for the old lady to handle. She used to come to Effie's house each morning to allow Effie to be at work at 11 o'clock, give the child a meal at midday, when he came home from school; reappearing for Effie's evening working hours, when she put the child to bed and stayed until 10 o'clock.

Jerry detested his minder, and never ceased to keep close to his mother while she was at home. She treated him with a rough kindness that showed scant affection and little patience.

When Bert's death left her a completely free woman again, she found Jerry an encumbrance, and began to look around for a solution to the problem he caused. It was then that she remembered that she had been to a Catholic day school in the next town, and had gone to church with the other children whenever a Saint's day or something occurred. She was not sure if she was a Catholic. She had been brought up by a foster parent, and her own ancestry was scarcely known to her. But with that upbringing behind her she presented herself to a Catholic orphanage and told a tearful tale of war widowhood, old parents to support, and desperate need to have her child cared for.

The nuns took Jerry and Effie returned with great satisfaction to her bar and the chaff and admiration of the servicemen who made up most of her customers.

A bewildered Jerry found himself in the tumultuous company of about fifty boys, from babies to fourteen year olds, who were cared for in the spartan surroundings of the orphanage. He was lost. Tears were of no avail, but gradually the natural demands for survival worked and he settled down, woebegone at times and very naughty often. The nuns were as kind as their situation allowed, but discipline was harsh, and soon Jerry shut himself within himself, only emerging on demand, as it were. He would join in rough games but bullied those smaller than himself, and took to hiding when called. His unhappy little mind was full of spite for others. Often he thought of his mother and longed for her warm, familiar presence. He accepted that he had been banished from his home and could not think why. He was at the orphanage for two years. He went home several times, but Effie was busy, and the boy was an embarrassment. He wept and refused to go back, which meant she had to have time off to take him. She was hurt too, she hated taking him - even though she did not want him. The sad reproach in his eyes as he watched her go and leave him, troubled her, so that she was sharp with her customers and got into trouble with her boss. Then, somehow, through her pension, some naval association found her, and Jerry was suddenly transferred from the care of the nuns to another orphanage for seamens' children. He was further away from home. The life, based on the lower deck of an old fashioned training ,ship,was even more spartan. He hated it, and felt a particular hatred for the Bosun, who was apt to communicate with his young charges with a rope's end.

Effie meanwhile, found that her job gave her ample opportunity to excite the interest of her customers, and the time came when in the celebrations of the armistice, she was persuaded to bring a little gladness to a returned seaman with money to spend. After that she chose her clients carefully, never allowed any indiscretions to show while behind the bar, but found herself with a source of income undreamed of. Her tiny house down by the stables became comfortably furnished. She dressed well, and, tossing her head at the neighbours' abuse, did not care a damn what anybody thought or said.

She had been there about four years when the publican sold out. He had reaped the harvest of the brief post-war boom and was retiring to a farm. The new landlord was a different type and took little time in summing up Effie for what she was. The old one had always maintained, when pressed, "She's a hard worker, knows her job, never upsets a customer, and as far as I know, never does anything improper on my premises - what she does in her own time is her business." But this new man had no wish to nurture a dubious reputation and decided to get rid of Effie as soon as an opportunity occurred.

This soon happened, for, being jealous of his licence, he had to take heed of his customers' complaints, and complaints there were for, generally, the town folk were law-abiding and decent living, and Effie's reputation was an affront to their families.

So Effie left and went up the road to the other house. The publican there had had his eye on her considerable charms for some time, and installed her behind his bar with the agreement that she should extend her favours to him when opportunity occurred. The opportunity was not long delayed. His wife always attended the weekly meetings of the Mothers' Union on Wednesday afternoons; so on the first Wednesday, Effie was required to stay after the midday opening hours, to unpack and wash a case of new glasses that had just arrived.

The publican's wife was no fool however, and half an hour after leaving, she returned quietly and walked in on the couple. Her husband was caught at a great disadvantage and she lashed his bare rump with a walking stick caught up in the hall as she entered. By the time he could disengage himself and climb off the bed, the stick had caught him a dozen times, in all his tender places. She worked ferociously and in complete silence no neighbours of her's were to spread tales of screams and fighting and the poor man, struggling into his clothing, was virtually defenceless. Meantime, Effie was quick in gathering up her things and getting out of the room. She was standing before a mirror in the empty bar, making sure that she looked presentable by the time the woman reached her. Effie was big and the woman was small and thirty years older, but that did not deter her. Her shrewd mind had decided, even in the heat of her fury, that she must not give Effie any excuse to make a scene, even have her charged with assault, thereby exposing her shame to the neighbourhood. She advanced on Effie in grim silence, looked at her very slowly from head to foot, letting her eyes linger while her lips curled in disgust. Then turning, she spat into one of the bar cuspidors. Effie felt the shock and shame of that wordless appraisal and sidled towards the door. The woman stood aside for her to pass and watched her go in silence.

Back in her cottage, Effie raged in futile fury, but she knew that she was guilty. She was an outcast in the street. A wave of gossip and abuse followed her passage up and down the narrow paths and she was ashamed. She had never felt that she was a whore, not like the two at the top end, who sauntered between the pubs, and ventured as far as the seafront in the summer, making do with the bushes in the park if the custom was urgent. She told herself again and again that she was as decent as anyone. How many of the back-biting neighbours - lined, thin and ragged, worn almost beyond endurance by work and childbearing, would not have swapped places with her, instead of submitting to their drunken husbands? But it was no use; that woman's scorn had bitten deep and Effie discovered that she did care, and hated herself. Rage had given way to self-pity, and the tears had come in floods, so much so, that she was hardly aware that she was really seeing Jerry, when he materialised before her, a figure in naval uniform, his face white with fright. Effie sat up.

"What you doin' 'ere?"

"I runned away."

The boy stood there, expecting he knew not what, and Effie looked at him in bewilderment. She'd almost forgotten he existed, but here he was, grown quite big, but with despairing, frightened eyes.

"Don't send me back. Please Mum, please. I'll be good, I will. I'll be ever so good. Don't send me back."

Effie just sat, saying nothing. Suddenly this boy had come back into her life, needing her, pleading to stay. He wanted her, his mother. He was her son, and he wanted her. Effie wasn't very bright really, and she wasn't used to having to sort out her emotions, and they certainly needed sorting then. Something was amiss. A sort of turmoil was going on somewhere inside her. She had never loved his father, but when they had made their clandestine love, she had felt tenderness, and now here was their son, and his ears stuck out just like his fathers

"Why did you run away?"

"I kicked the Bosun.'

Silence. The boy was trembling.

"Are you hungry?"

"Yes 'm."

She got up, cut a couple of inches off the loaf, spread it with dripping and gave it to him, watching while he munched it. Then she made tea and poured a mug for him, and one for herself. Still nothing more was said. Jerry finished the bread and tea. The trembling was gone and some colour had come back to his cheeks. His eyelids drooped: and he was nearly asleep. Effie watched him, her tea mug cradled in both hands, her eyes peering over the rim.

"When did you run away?"
"Last night."
"How did you get here."
"Got a lift on a fish cart."
"Where did you sleep?"
"I didn't. I was walking."

Silence again. What was she to do - send him back? Yes, She'd have to. They'd make her. But something seemed to be saying "No. Why?" She could work, and if she didn't work at the pub they'd be company. Yes, but he'd be a nuisance too. What about that traveller who called on her every other Tuesday, and the Grocer who did his accounts, with her help, every Sunday morning? She could do with the groceries too. And there were some others. All right to say she was a decent woman, as good as any other, just a bit more generous and free to be so. But it would be hard to give it all up and go into service or something instead. The problem went round and round in her head. The shock of the afternoon's encounter was wearing off. The shame was receding with it and something like indignation was taking its place. And now Jerry was there to make life more and more complicated - a little Jack Tar, falling asleep as he sat across the table.

"Oh Gawd!" said Effie. The boy's eyes blinked. He sensed a softening in her voice and gave a timid smile.

"Can I stay, Mum?"

"Oh Gawd!" said his mother again. Still she sat in bemused silence, until jolted from it by a resounding banging on her front door. Jerry quietly slipped around the table and stood behind her, his face white again and fear on his trembling lips.

"Don't send me back, please Mum."

Effie crossed the room and opened the door that led on to the narrow street. The Bosun stood there, an authoritative figure in semi-naval uniform. A big man, ex-Chief Petty Officer, used to making people jump to orders.

"Is Wilkins 'ere?"

For the moment Effie wondered who "Wilkins" was, and in the moment it took her to realise that it was Jerry, the Bosun had been able to take stock of the woman standing before him, and he liked what he saw. He made swift judgement of the comfortable looking room behind her, her clothes, her appearance. He had expected to see someone wearing a sacking apron, with a man's cap secured with a long hat pin, and with a tired, care-worn face.

"A bloody tart." He concluded. Just as swiftly, Effie saw the familiar gleam in his eyes. Another time, it might have been welcome, but not then. This was not the day to pander. Effie was on the defensive and a strange joy seemed to be bolstering her courage.

"Oo wants to know?" Arms akimbo and the doorway blocked. "Oo the 'ell are you."

"I'm the Bosun from the seaman's orphanage, and the governor has sent me to fetch young Wilkins back."

Effie eyed him. "Gawd! Men," how she hated them all.

"E's been insubordinate. Kicked me, 'e did, jest because I was smacking the arse of one of the lads for wetting his bed. Took the skin off me shin 'e did. 'es got to be disciplined, so if e' s 'ere, as I think, 'and 'im over."

Effie had no idea of what conditions Jerry lived in. She had not thought much about them. On the few occasions when she had seen him, he had looked smart and well-scrubbed in his bellbottoms and blouse. For all she knew, he might be a real hooligan, but he was hers, and here was this man with his bullying manner and leering eyes.

"Well, 'e aint going back - so you can clear off!"

Jerry, crouched behind the table at her rear, heard the words as though a voice had spoken from heaven.

"I'm keeping 'im 'ome now - so you can tell the Superintendent."

"You can't do that."

"Oh no? Well I'm goin' to, and you try and stop me."

She'd burnt her boats then, and stuck it out against all the Bosun's demands and threats, and the more he demanded the more it became obvious that if she surrendered, Jerry would suffer for her opposition.

Finally, the Bosun decided to let matters be taken up by higher authority, only warning that he could return with a policeman. As a last thought, he demanded that he should take back Jerry's uniform.

"Certainly," said Effie. "Take it off son."

Jerry stripped, shyly trying to hide his nakedness. Effie took a towel from beside the sink and wrapped it around him, stopping with shock as she saw three red weals across his back.

"What's this?"

"Rope's end." said Jerry, flinching from her touch.

With nothing more said, Effie took the clothes, opened the door and looked at the Bosun who had waited outside.

"You swine. You rotten swine!" With each furious word, Effie threw a garment - hat, blouse, trousers, vest and then, harder, and well-aimed, the boots. It gave her some pleasure to see the man ducking and weaving amid the laughter of an appreciative audience that had gathered. She slammed the door and put her back against it.

Jerry moved towards her, burying himself in her warmth and softness. "Oh Mum!" he said. "Oh Mum!"

In the days that followed, various people came. She had an official looking letter that she couldn't understand. Then a stern, old gentleman came and lectured her on the folly of taking Jerry from such a fine, character-building institution, then gave her a form to sign and cautioned her to take good care of Jerry's morals, as well as his health. Effie saw him off with some of her old, professional warmth and laughed to herself as she saw his colour heighten and knew that he was going away in haste, when the old 'Adam' within him was saying stay.

It was late July, so Jerry had no need to attend a school until after the holidays. Effie got a job as chambermaid-cum-waitress in a small hotel on the sea front. She started at seven in the morning and got home again about three in the afternoon. Jerry's confidence grew. He touched her sometimes with a devoted longing, but she was brusque with him, and was relieved when he found the dairyman's farmyard and occupied himself there.

Chapter 4

When the little school at Colly End opened again after the summer holidays, Jerry was presented by his mother and accepted by the Headmaster, Mr Fox, who remembered him from his infant days. This man had taught in the school for many years and was well informed concerning all the families that lived around the Green. Jerry was not new to him, nor was his mother, but he was impressed by the boy's appearance, and his mother's explanations of his past history. He was a kind man who lived according to the code of his day. Discipline was good, and maintained by generous use of the cane; a punishment easily accepted by most of his scholars who were well used to beatings at home and bore him no grudges, for he was always just.

Jerry, at ten, went into Standard 3, taking his seat on the long bench near the back of the row. He looked across the room and saw that Willy was turning towards him from the front bench of Standard 2. Willy smiled a welcome and Jerry gave a little flick of his eyebrows and head in acknowledgement, but inside he felt a little glow of pleasure.

When playtime came, Willy, feeling rather important, like a patronising squire welcoming a stranger to his estate, went up to Jerry. "'ello Jerry, fancy you being 'ere."

"'ello young Will," replied the older boy, and turning away dived into a scrum of lads fighting for the possession of a rubber ball.

"I know Jerry Wilkins, he's my friend." Willy confided to another urchin who had emerged from the scrum. "He's from Well Street." This information was ignored by the other boy, and Willy felt a bit let down. Nevertheless, he felt pleased that he had this big boy as a champion. He watched as Jerry overcame most of the opposition, even the older boys, and was suddenly electrified when Jerry reared out of the melee and yelled "Catch Willy" and the ball came to him. He missed it, and diving to catch it again, was immediately engulfed by about ten struggling forms who flattened him to the concrete, trod on him, tore at him and shouted at him in shrill screams. He got to his feet eventually, and Jerry shouted to him to catch it next time. Willy did try, not very effectively, to join in, but his skinny, little body was tossed about as if he were the ball. When the bell went for end of play, Willy went back to his class with a bleeding knee, dirty face and hands, and a torn collar.

"Willy Churchward. What have you been doing? What will your mother say?"

Miss Blake was the middle teacher, who had charge of Standards 1 and 2, and Willy was a star pupil of hers, always clean, well-dressed, quiet and well-behaved. He was interested in his lessons, though given to daydreaming, and now suddenly appearing much as all the other ragamuffins looked. Miss Blake was shocked.

Willy felt pleased, he felt he was one of the boys, tough, even becoming a heroic character.

Miss Blake retreated, as she always did when nonplussed, behind a large, white handkerchief, into which she blew her nose with stentorian effect. Mr Fox frowned and sighed. That foghorn sound was a cause of constant irritation to him. He did so wish she wouldn't do it. It made the children titter and whisper behind their hands. Not good for discipline. He rapped on his high desk and warned "No talking!" He constantly recalled the unpleasantness that had occurred some terms ago when a cow, passing on its way to pasture, had bellowed as cows will, at the precise moment that Miss Blake had blown her nose. The volume of sound she made had completely deafened her to the sound of the cow, and only as the trumpeting died, she heard one of the girls say "Hark at the old cow!" Without questioning the child, Miss Blake had called her out in front of the class and punished the imagined insult with a swift "two-hander" with the cane. The child, as it happened, was no spiritless waif, and for the next few minutes, there was an unseemly "No I didn't..." "Yes you did..." argy bargy, with all the class hugging themselves with delight.

Mr Fox had to leave his high desk and cross the room to settle the matter. As it happened, he was so used to hearing the sounds of cattle passing, and for that matter, of Miss Blake blowing her nose, that on that occasion he had not noticed either, having set his classes work to keep them quiet and then being engrossed in *T.P.'s Weekly*, his favourite extravagance.

He got no further in resolving the truth of the matter, so with a solemn warning to the girl "not to be impertinent," he awarded her one more stroke with the cane for causing such a commotion, and sent her back to her seat. There she wept, and at playtime ran home to Well Street to tell her mother. The next thing to happen was the eruption into the classroom of a very virago of a woman, who raged and shouted and, had not Miss Blake taken refuge in the babies classroom, would have wrecked dire vengeance on her.

Mr Fox was not unused to dealing with abusive mothers, and eventually, by sheer weight of authoritative personality, had persuaded her to go home. Halfway to the door, however, the woman stopped, walked over to the blackboard easel on which hung two canes, and, taking them, she broke them into pieces, fighting the pliant fibres with grim intensity until they were a fuzzy wreck.

Mr Fox wisely let her continue her destruction, knowing the difficulty would put her into an embarrassing position from which she would be glad to escape. The children loved it.

When Willy went home that day, torn, dirty and bleeding, his mother was as shocked as Miss Blake had been.

"Who were the bullies who did this to you? I'll go and complain."

"No Mum, please. I only been playing. I like it."

Gwen tidied him up and warned him to keep away from "them Well Street boys". Willy nodded, but he thought to himself "Not from Jerry, I won't."

When Jerry had rescued Willy from his tormentor at the fountain, he had been moved by some strand of his character that came through from time to time. He was at heart, a rebel, hating authority , because he blamed it for its cruelty to him in taking him from his home, and for all its harshness and lovelessness. Because of that he did inexplicable things, like turning on taps that flooded washrooms; pulled up plants from gardens; defaced walls with chalk; anything that occurred to him. As a result of this he suffered much in punishment, yet he had on several occasions stood between blubbering weaklings and bullies, and, as he had flown in rage at the Bosun when a wretched little bedwetter was being thrashed, he had done so knowing the dire consequences to himself. His protective role towards Willy was probably an unconscious release of his need to give affection and a way of obtaining the response of someone to whom he could appear strong and big-brotherly.

Willy certainly responded. It was an instant response. Despite the love and comfort Gwen had given him - so in contrast to Jerry's bleak upbringing - he had never been a "mother's boy", always seeking some strong character to follow into a boys' world, but always timorous and frustrated by his mother's watchfulness.

With Jerry's arrival at the school, 'young Will', as Jerry dubbed him, took to hanging around the fountain more than ever, and often during the early evening, when he would sit on the shop doorstep, watching the horses being watered at the end of the day, Jerry would arrive, sitting sideways on the dairyman's big horse, and with studied nonchalance, would nod in the direction of the younger boy. "Will", he would say in acknowledgement, spitting from the side of his mouth, like a man who chewed tobacco, and thumping the mare's ribs with his heels to start her on her way up to the fields. Willy usually stayed until Jerry came trudging back, rolling along with big strides with a hazel stick in his hand. "See you tomorrow" they called, or sometimes Jerry would stop and fish about in the fountain with his stick, hitching out tin cans and other rubbish. Willy joined him then, for other boys appeared whenever a game seemed to be on, and with Jerry there, Willy dared to join in. Mostly they were boys from the Green who accepted Jerry because he had the confident air of one who could take good care of himself. Even the odious Bill Gurney confined himself to pulling faces instead of his old tricks. Willy hopped about, dodging the splashes and the cow dabs as best he could. Then, like as not, Gwen would come to the cottage door and call him in. He always seemed to be called in just as the fun started.

One Saturday, Willy, without thought, said "Come and see our Goldfinch, Jerry", and Jerry stood on the top step and lifted the birdcage down. They both inspected it.

"Shall I let it out?" said Jerry teasingly.

"No, no!" said Willy, in alarm.

Then followed a scuffle as Jerry held the cage high, pretending to open the door and the finch fluttered against the wires in panic. It was then that Gwen appeared on the scene and rescued the bird.

"Who are you?" she demanded.

"It's Jerry. He's my friend" said Willy.

Gwen looked at Jerry, seeing his shaven head with its bunch of a forelock. His guernsey, knickerbockers, stockings and heavy hobnailed boots. Both knees of his knickerbockers were a disc of tar (where he had inadvertently knelt on a freshly-tarred pigsty roof) to which had adhered bits of hay and various other rubbish. She was not pleased with what she saw.

"Where d'you live."

"Well Street."

Gwen's worst fears were confirmed. "One of them boys," she thought. "Well, you'd better get back there," she said.

Then Jerry smiled, a thing he had only lately taken to and Gwen suddenly felt that this boy, with his grubby clothes and face, his stick-out ears and bullet head, had some attraction - like a misused puppy, all paws and wriggling body, that begs for kindness. Jerry, in his short life, had become adept in judging adults' reactions to him. Sensing her indecision, he said "Can Will come up the field with me tomorrow?"

"Up the field?"

"When I take the mare up. I'll look after 'im - I do at school."

"Yes he does. Oh please Mum, can I go?"

The suggestion, coming so unexpectedly had sounded to Willy like an invitation to explore an unknown world, and the excitement showing in his eager little face quite shocked Gwen. She had never known Willy to want to go anywhere without her, and the idea alarmed her. "I'll see" she said, and took Willy indoors. "I'll see" was tantamount to approval to Willy - not instant, but eventual, if persisted in. And Willy was a very persistent child.

In the few remaining weeks of Autumn, Willy discovered a blissful happiness in the companionship of Jerry. At school they planned evening and Saturday adventures. Willy rode the mare behind Jerry, finding the rank horse smell, the bobbing gait and noisy nostril cracking, something to fantasize on. Sometimes as a knight of old riding to battle, or other times a whooping red Indian. The mare was always anxious to get to the meadow with its lush grass, new grown after the early summer hay, and by the time the field was. reached, she was blowing like a pair of bellows, and Willy's thin legs were tired of stretching across the broad back. Nonetheless, he rode through the gate with lance upraised, plume flying and shield at the ready.

Jerry loved animals. When he managed to ingratiate himself into the dairyman's yard, he immediately absorbed himself in the animals. The mare he loved, and each cow and pig became a special friend. The aging dairyman, who had lost both his sons in the war, saw the boy's interest and responded to it, telling him how to do this and that, explaining the feeding and handling of the cattle, letting him do some grooming and mucking out. He began to look out for the boy and the companionship he offered. It seemed such a short time since he had done the same for his own two boys. He had long since given up saying to himself "Well, they'm gone, they'm gone, naught I can do about it" and he began to feel some pleasure in having this boy, with his bright smile and stick-cut ears, around the place. He taught him something about the birds that foraged in the yard. 'The different finches, the blackbirds, tits and wrens and how to recognise their call notes. Jerry absorbed it all.

Later, when Spring arrived again, the quarry face, that stood a hundred feet above the yard, became a wild garden that Jerry was drawn to. Many small trees had managed to grow in cracks and hollows, particularly Sycamore and Ash from the winged seeds floating down from the higher ground above. Hawthorns, wild roses and blackberry brambles sprouted from seeds dropped by birds and ivy, wall daisies and ivy-leaved toadflax climbed and cascaded. Every ledge with a crack in it, capable of absorbing a tiny, floating seed, was covered with valerian, the 'drunkard's nose', that poured its red plumes down the whole rock face. In this little wilderness a multitude of birds found refuge; from the wheeling jackdaws to the busy chattering wren; and Jerry brought Willy there to climb and explore.

Before then was the winter with its long, dark evenings, when Willy had to go straight home, or to the Big House, lest he came to some harm, likely or imagined, that Gwen feared for him.

She had allowed the friendship with Jerry to continue for a while as Willy seemed so happy with it, but came the day when alarming rumours reached her concerning his mother.

Gwen went straight to the school and saw Miss Blake, who pursed her lips and looked knowingly at Gwen, saying that it wasn't for her to judge, but she had heard tales, and Willy had certainly got rougher in his manner and less tidy in appearance since the advent of Jerry. She really didn't think that Jerry was a suitable companion.

The children had left, and Mr Fox was sitting at his high desk tidying up some forms, while Gwen and Miss Blake raked over the bones of the Wilkins' skeletal cupboard. He had one ear cocked to the conversation and when he heard Gwen Churchward being persuaded to break off the boys' friendship, he half turned in his chair, leaned forward so that he presented a bald pate, wrinkled brow above raised eyebrows, and stern yet kindly eyes looking above his glasses that were positioned on the end of his nose. His mouth and chin seemed to have disappeared into his chest.

"Miss Blake. Mrs Churchward," he said in his schoolmaster's voice. "I have noticed that Willy and the Wilkins boy are on good terms. Pals, I suppose you would call them, and I'm very pleased to see it. Willy needs an older boy to follow and Jerry needs a friend. God knows he has had few so far. I know all about him and his mother, and his father - who died, as did your own good man, so that we could be saved from the enemy. I do not think that harm will come to Willy, and I hope much good will come to both. I will keep an eye on them, and, have no fear, I will see to it you are not deceived. I advise you to let matters remain as they are and allow the boys to find their own interests."

There was such an air of judicial finality about the statement that Gwen accepted it without question. Miss Blake, a little high in colour, and features set in disapproval, sought solace in her handkerchief.

Although Gwen accepted the schoolmaster's advice, she stipulated that Willy should never go home with Jerry. This was not likely to happen, had she known it, for Effie had put a complete ban on Jerry bringing anyone home. Jerry didn't want to anyway, because his mum seemed to have friends to entertain sometimes and she would tell him to go out to play and come back later. With the coming of winter he used to go straight from school to the farmyard where he 'made down' the mare's stall and rubbed her down with loving care when she came in from her day's work. The cows still went up to the fields after the milking, but they were milked a little earlier now and the dairyman drove them. They grew thick coats and sometimes Jerry tried to curry them, but the comb lost itself in the warm, springy hair, red as the earth they ploughed up with their huge, splayed feet.

On Saturdays and Sundays there were things to do when the weather was good. Gwen would not allow Willy to go far, always fearful for his skinny, little body, but Jerry roamed the town, even down to the harbour, where he found and was welcomed by his father's old employer. He delivered milk with the dairyman too, fetching and delivering the jugs that the dairyman filled from tin measures of foaming milk, drawn from the big churns, with their brass tops and taps.

The dairyman called a tuneful "Milko!" and the mare moved, without being told, from door to door. Jerry got paid sixpence for each Saturday and Sunday round and sixpence a day for delivering milk from a big can carried from door to door, up and down Well Street. He was saving up, and derived great satisfaction in counting his little hoard as it grew. He wanted to buy a bicycle. Nobody in Well Street, or the Green, had one. One or two men used to cycle off to work, but it was affluence, almost undreamed of, for a boy to have one. Most of the boys earned small sums in one way of another, but this was always contributed to the common purse. None kept any, the lucky ones had a copper or two returned for sweets or the front of 'The Bughouse' as the primitive cinema was known.

Effie made no such calls on Jerry. She could afford not to. Jerry sometimes bought sweets and gave them to his mother. There was little show of affection between them, but he adored her as his shield and saviour, and got great pleasure in the warmth of her presence, the pleasant fragrance that was about her, the flashing trinkets and the gleam of the red hair that topped her strong body. His home was cosy and warm and he was well fed. Sometimes he shivered inside himself, when he dared to think what might happen to him if his mother should die. The nightmare life that was his in the cold, grey building on the river bank, seemed suddenly very near again.

So the year rolled on. Christmas was anticipated at the school with paper-chains hung from the pendant gas brackets to the window frames. Holly crowned the cuckoo clock that ruled the spells of lessons, and carols were rehearsed in half moons around Miss Blake's piano. The girls' voices pealing prettily against the accompaniment of Miss Blake's "'ooter." (as the boys called her voice).

The boys stood in the semi-circle with the girls. A few of the youngest, in Standards 1 and 2, added their trebles to the choir, but once in Standard 3, it was the accepted thing that no boy sang. Any that did would have been 'cissy'. Miss Blake had often tried to persuade, more often had recourse to threats, but to no avail. Once, Mr Fox, who knew his boys, had half-heartedly added his appeal, but the only result was to have one boy start 'singing in his boots', as a gesture of obedience, but an assertion of his manhood. In the end, Miss Blake had given up asking and now the boys stood in token response to her efforts - annoying the girls by tweaking their hair, trying to make them giggle, and making nasty smells that they blamed on one another. Willy liked singing, and would have joined in, but Miss Blake noted that he had joined his friend and was silent.

At the end of the term, some ladies from the church provided a tea for the children. The long benches were lined up, face-to-face in rows, and home-made cakes and buns were displayed on them with various other offerings that the good souls had provided. There were crackers and balloons and afterwards songs, carols and recitations. The tortoise stove grew almost red hot, making life most uncomfortable for those trapped close to it. Even those on the other side of the room, who normally dwelt in a near frozen state, with numbed fingers and chilblained toes, felt warm. To close the party, the Vicar made a speech. Mr Fox,

Miss Blake and the young woman who was in charge of the 'babies room', stood up and bowed. The ladies clapped and the children followed suit, though none of them had attempted to listen to what had been said.

During the winter months it was too cold or wet for Willy to spend much time at the fountain, but instead he would go up the hill to where the blacksmith had his forge, by the stables and the little triangle of grass. Here there were always people idly watching the horses being shod, and the smith hammering out the intricate pieces of broken ploughs and harrows. It was dark in the smithy, and the smith was a silhouette against the red glow of his fire as he plied the bellows with one hand, and stirred the coals with the other. Willy loved the smell of the burning hoof as the red hot shoe was tried for fit, the smell of horse and the sulphurous reek of dowsed iron.

On a cold day, he could slip right inside and feel the warmth of the fire and when it was wet he could stand with the inevitable group of old men and young boys, who sheltered under the lean-to roof with the horses waiting to be shod.

There were other things to see too, besides the blacksmith. Gypsies made the grass triangle their headquarters when they came to town. The men used to take ponies and traps around the stables and yards, doing trade with the tradesmen, buying, selling and swapping, while the women hawked clothes pegs around the streets. They were a tough, fierce lot, mistrusted and feared for their dishonesty and ability to cast spells, or at least bring bad luck. Few would cross them, and though they caused obstruction and were a nuisance on the triangle, no one tried to move them. A market gardener, who kept his horse and cart in the stables next to the smithy, had been known to protest when he found a bag of oats missing. He did so in the high, piping voice that an unkind providence had given him, and had been shocked and humiliated by a screaming woman who had cast loud doubts upon the development of his genitals.

Even the local police kept their distance. There were only three. A sergeant who lived at the police station and two constables who lived one at either end of the town. The sergeant had once been prevailed upon to go to attempt to redress some grievance, and his experiences of that day taught him to be busy elsewhere when gypsies were in town.

On that occasion they had been hawking strawberries, and there was a stormy encounter, that finished by one of the women crowning the sergeant with a basket of fruit. The shrieks and screams of laughter turned to abuse when the woman was arrested and led off to the police station. There she was put in a cell and had to remain there all that day and overnight, before appearing before the magistrates next day. The sergeant's wife had to double as wardress on the very rare occasions that a female prisoner was there, and the gypsy kept the poor woman running between her house and the cell, demanding to go to the lavatory every few minutes. By the time the case was dealt with the sergeant's wife was worn out, the sergeant was in a state bordering on homicide, and the entire gypsy tribe were driving the two constables demented.

Gwen did not approve of Willy hanging about the smithy, and would reprove him gently when she smelt the reek of burnt hoof in his clothes and hair, but she was at the Big House all day, and could not keep the boy housebound. She used to say "When them gypsies is there, you come straight 'ome. They'm a bad lot." She had little hope that he would though.

There was one, never to be forgotten day, when Willy saw the gypsies pass his cottage, with their horse and trap, laden with big rush 'fish baskets', and with a couple of horses roped to the back. During the midday break from school, he hurried over his dinner in the Big House kitchen, and made his way to the smithy to see whatever was to be seen. Several women were sitting on the patch of grass. There were small children with them and one woman was feeding her baby, in a natural uninhibited manner - this to the shocked "brazen hussy" exclamations of passing womenfolk of the town. Willy looked these strange folk over from a distance, in a sort of awesome fear. Their dress and behaviour was quite foreign to the local people and they had a peculiar attraction for him. Standing there with a gaggle of spectators, he began to edge himself into the Smithy.

The blacksmith was busy shoeing and the hot sparks were flying from the red hot metal as he shaped it on the anvil. "Thump, thump" went the heavy hammer on the soft, red iron - "thump, thump, ring-ading-ding, thump, thump, ring-a-ding-ding." He turned the hot iron between each pair of "thumps", letting his hammer ring on the anvil between blows. Willy loved to watch, he used to count the "thumps" and the "rings", but they never varied and the iron took shape as he watched. The hammering getting sharper as the iron cooled, when the smith thrust it back into the coals and plied the bellows again.

He was a tall man, permanently stooped, his face, hands and arms as black as his leather apron. What teeth he had were black too, for he chewed tobacco, and, whether he was half hidden in a cloud of smoke against the massive rump of a dray horse, or was busy at the anvil, every little while a thin stream of black spittle was squirted out of his mouth.

That day was memorable because of the appearance of one of the gypsy men, who went over to a grey horse, standing tied to a ring in the wall. He began to untie the cord, saying "All done then Maister?"

"Yer! 'ang on" said the smith, leaving his bellows and moving quickly to the front of the forge. "That's six shillin' you owe me. You pay me first, then you can 'ave 'un." Then came an argument: the gypsy maintaining that he had overpaid the last time, and the smith swearing he hadn't and so on.

The man got the horse untied and the two of them held its bridal shouting and abusing one another. Shrill voices entering into the argument announced the arrival of the women, as reinforcements. The spectators grew in number. One of the women flicked a stick on the horse, causing it to stamp and wheel. Another put her high-laced boot against a pile of miscellaneous iron, causing a clattering avalanche to roll over the floor, and they all shouted and screamed at the smith who, badly outnumbered, still hung on the horse's halter, demanding his money before he would let go.

A moment later, to Willy's astonishment, one of the women put her hand inside her dress and produced a large, white mass of flesh that squirted a stream of milk into the smith's face. He, poor man, was still rubbing his wet face with the back of his hand, as the gypsy was galloping off down the road and away. Ribald laughter from the women drowned the curses of the smith.

Willy hurried back to school and spent the playtime recounting these happenings to Jerry. Neither he, nor Jerry, had any experience of living with mothers nursing babies, though most of the other boys were from crowded homes and accepted it as a part of everyday life. They soon enlightened Willy on the subject, and Willy privately notched up another item of knowledge that made life so curious.

Chapter 5

Willy was growing up, and growing up in a rapidly changing world. More and more cars were to be seen. The roads were being surfaced with tarmac so that the water sprinkler was not needed in the summer, while the mud scraper had no need to be used after heavy rain. There were still more horse-drawn vehicles than motors, but the pace of life was quickening. There was more work and better pay. People could eat better and dress better, but life was still very tough, and most people had to work extremely hard for little reward. Many who had no specialist skills turned their hands to all sorts of jobs, and gradually built up a reputation as being pliable as, say, a drover, a wagoner, or a carpet beater. One such occasionally earned a few shillings in the Well Street farmyard, carting dung and spreading it on a couple of fields that the dairyman kept for hay making. He used to go to market and get paid for driving sheep, or bullocks to the farms of their purchasers. This required him taking the railway bus the six miles into market and then driving the animals any distance up to ten miles or so. Jerry discovered this and when he was able to do so he prevailed upon this man to let him accompany him. In fact, he was very useful, as a long drive needed either a dog, which the man lacked, or another man to go ahead and "stop" side roads and so on.

Jerry's ambition to own a bike became reality in the course of time. The machine was old and too big for him to ride in comfort, but it was his pride and joy. He doubled a paper round that he had added to his milk round, setting out with the handle bars and crossbar laden, and swooping home when all had been disposed of.

Willy was envious, as were all the local boys, and Jerry often allowed him to ride on the step over the rear wheel. It was in that fashion that he and Jerry went to market.

Jerry had been thinking of this enterprise for some time, and had suggested to Willy that they might go together. Willy had no idea how far it was to the market town, or what was entailed, but he immediately agreed, and after telling Gwen that he was going for a ride in the country with Jerry, he set off with a cheese sandwich in one pocket and a bottle of cold tea in the other. His jacket was weighed down, and opening like a pair of broken wings as the wind got under it.

A great part of the journey had to be walked, as the road was an undulating ribbon of hills and valleys. By the time they had reached the outskirts of the town, Willy's leg was already bruised from where he knelt on the bracket over the rear mudguard, and it seemed to him that they had been travelling for hours. It was a weary little figure that eventually trailed up the ancient high street of Totnes to the market at the top. Jerry was tired, but Willy was exhausted and was glad enough to be sat on a doorstep and told to wait there. It was hot and dusty, flies were a constant worry and his battered leg ached, so that he was glad that Jerry took himself off to a corner of the market, and he could cry without Jerry seeing him.

Willy had never been to a market before, and though he had often seen wild-eyed bullocks jostling for a place to drink at the fountain, he had always, there, had a safe retreat to turn to. Here the animals, frightened and confused, ran through the narrow streets, harried by dogs, beaten by drovers, liable to charge into any opening or doorway that seemed to offer a sanctuary from the noise and tumult of the market.

Willy flattened himself into a niche behind a farm cart, and thought, a dozen times, that he'd lost sight of Jerry and wouldn't know how to find him. Jerry, who had not wasted his time on previous visits, and had got some idea of how the market worked, came back to Willy and with a nonchalant "Cum'on", retrieved his cycle from the nook he had found for it, and with Willy trailing, regained the High Street. There they mounted and wobbled off through the maze of farm wagons, gigs, traps and the occasional motor car, down towards the river.

"'s too early for the sheep," he informed Willy. "Us'll go down the island, and come back when they'm selling." This meant little to Willy, who wished once again that he had never come, but when they got to the island he cheered up. They sat beside the water and watched the ducks tacking across the current.' 'There was a paddle steamer just leaving the landing stage, and this, with its paddles foaming on either side, was a marvel to gaze on and remember. Both boys were hungry, for although it was only little more than mid-morning, they had used up a lot of energy in getting to the market. If the clock on the arch over the High Street had not belied it, Willy might well have believed it was mid-afternoon. Jerry, having some money in his pocket, had not brought any food, so when Willy unwrapped his crushed and broken sandwich, Jerry said "You stay 'ere, I'll be back", and rode off into the town.

It was very peaceful there on the island. Several family parties were making little territories for themselves, spreading out bags and parcels, sometimes a blanket too, so that their little area would not be encroached upon. The farmers' daughters looked after their younger brothers and sisters, while their parents bought and sold, met old friends and sampled the cider of the many inns, open all day for the benefit of the market.

There was a cider store fronting the river in one place, and the racks of barrels could be seen behind the wooden-barred windows. The sweet smell of crushed apples was heavy in the air. Willy finished his bread and cheese, took a last swig of tea from the bottle, carefully keeping half for Jerry, then lay on his chest looking down into the water. Some flotsam had made a little pool below him, and he watched the pond skaters playing their intricate games.

" 'ere y'are," said Jerry, appearing suddenly to wake Willy from his daydreams. Willy sat up to see Jerry with his face half hidden behind a huge pasty. Another one, much smaller, was on a paper bag by his side.

"That's yours," said Jerry, munching. "Cor! Thanks." Willy said. 'The pasties were hot and full of meat and potato, the pastry flaky, full of hot fat that made long finger licking much pleasure when every crumb was eaten. Willy gave Jerry the half bottle of tea, which he drank, and then threw the bottle at a swan that had paddled hopefully towards them. The pasties had cost sixpence and threepence.

"That'll have to come out of your share of the drive," Jerry warned. They both then lay face down on the bank watching the fascinating movement of the river.

The sun, shining on the water, dazzled Willy's eyes and he was soon near to sleep. Jerry spent his time spitting into the water in an effort to sink the pond skaters, without success. After about an hour, Jerry declared it was time to return to the market. Though refreshed by the rest, Willy felt that he had two strange appendages attached to his knees, instead of his lower legs, and trailed slowly behind Jerry, who wheeled his bike back up the steep street to the market. Arriving, he told Wily to stay in a doorway and mind his bike, while he went off to look for the chance of some droving. Beasts were already being driven away, frightened, thirsty and bewildered, lowering threatening horns at anything that obstructed them, or seemed to threaten. The drovers, one in front, and one behind, kept them from stampeding and steered them through the narrow streets to the open country roads. Some would have several miles to walk, others went to the railway station, where whole trains of cattle trucks waited to take the cattle to more distant towns. Willy barricaded himself into the doorway with Jerry's bike, till Jerry returned. When this happened he was given a curt "c'mon" and followed Jerry, pushing his bike, into the market itself, among the sheep pens. Here he met a big, red-faced man, smart in polished leggings, tweed suit and bowler hat.

"Us is 'ere,' said Jerry to him. "Where's the ship?"

The farmer looked the boys over.

"You can manage 'em, can you? You know where to go?"

"Yes 'ir, I bin there," said,Jerry drawing on a hazy memory of a previous trip with the Well Street drover. "Us'll be all right."

"Right then," said the farmer. "Get on with it, and when you arrive, the missus will pay'ee two shillin', and 'er'll tell 'e where to put 'em". Then waving vaguely with his stick. "This way, and dawnt'ee let 'em get away from 'ee this side of the bridge."

The boys followed the farmer to a row of pens, where sheep stood panting with heat and distress. Jerry immediately took charge. He gave Willy a hazel stick, that he had acquired from somewhere and sent him to the end of the aisle between the pens. "Don't you let'em pass," he warned Willy, "till I tell 'ee."

There was then much clanging of metal gates and cries of "Come on, get out, ow, ow, ow!" and in a moment a flock of twenty sheep were milling around, looking for a way out, turning, stumbling, bleating, standing as if transfixed, then plunging into a short rush, stopping, trying to go back again, all confused. To Willy, standing and waving his stick and arms, more in terror than in purpose, they looked a huge, menacing flock of hundreds.

"Right," called Jerry, "us'll go down the back lane, down to the island, then over the bridge - you keep in front, don't let 'em go into any side roads, and don't let 'em pass' ee. Fortunately for Willy, his novice journey as a drover was with sheep that keep together. Cattle are another thing altogether, and pigs are purgatory.

Leaving the market, there was a hold up as another flock emerged. This lot was driven easily by two crafty-looking dogs and an old man who seemed to do nothing but clump along in the rear just giving an occasional call or whistle. While they waited, Jerry shouted above the din of their baa'ing' flock: "Make a noise like a dog when you want to drive' em - like this - arf, arf - they'll go!" He then demonstrated getting the flock under way by wheeling his bike from side to side and "arf, arfing".

The sheep moved forward, and Willy, caught between the twin terrors of having them catch up with him and undoubtedly trampling him to death, and losing them in byroads or yards, even forgot his tiredness, and was soon relieved to find that the sheep moved along between him and Jerry, in an orderly way, as if only too pleased to do so, even with a touching sort of trust. Jerry did most of the work; standing on one pedal of his bike, he anticipated any intention of the flock to break, and by running first on one side, then the other, he did the work of a sheepdog. They soon reached the island where they had eaten their pasties, and found themselves in the busy traffic of the town, all being bottle-necked to cross the bridge over the river. There was no other way to get cattle in and out of the town, except on the hoof (other than calves and pigs carried under a net in a farm cart) and the townsfolk and farmers were all understanding; many a brandished stick, or cuffing hat, helped the boys to keep the flock together.

Once over the bridge, the bustle of the town died away, and all that had to be done was to keep the sheep moving. Willy was sent ahead to stop each side. road, standing spreadeagled and arf, arf'ing' as instructed , while Jerry, leaning on his bike, wove from side to side in the rear, doing his sheepdog impersonation rather better than Willy, whose dry throat was producing a sound reminiscent of a Yorkshire terrier.

It was a long, long climb up the hill from the bridge, and the panting sheep kept trying to rest under overhanging trees. The hedges were white with lime dust, and this dust, stirred up by the pattering hooves of the flock, and passing traffic, got into the boys' eyes and throats. Willy began to wonder if he would ever see home again. Jerry seemed tireless and continued to herd the flock from the rear. Farm carts and gigs passed them slowly, the horses blowing heavily and thumping their hooves into the dust. Most drivers were walking beside the carts to ease the load, those with laden vehicles often had the farmer's wife walking too. Sometimes they both pulled on the shafts to help a little.

The boys reached the top at last, and for half a mile or so the road was level, then started a slight decline that permitted Jerry to stand on one pedal and do his dog act without so much effort. Some two miles from the bridge the road divided, and an old toll gate cottage stood at the junction. Here, Jerry herded the sheep into a gateway and put Willy on guard to keep them there while he knocked on the cottage door. This produced a wildly barking lurcher dog from the rear of the cottage that spread panic amongst the sheep, who tried to break both ways. Jerry managed to stop the few that had run backwards and they immediately galloped off after the others that had run on ahead.

"Stop' em! After 'em!" yelled Jerry. But Willy sat in the gateway in tears.

"I can't. I'm too tired, I can't run."

Meanwhile a woman had come into the garden, shouting at the dog to "Get een out o'it."

Jerry asked her where the farm was, and was told that it was a mile or so ahead down a side lane by a barn.

Jerry gave little sympathy to Willy, but he knew that the little boy was exhausted and experienced once again the strange protective emotion that he always felt towards him. " 'ere, you get up on the bike and I'll push'ee," he suggested. The sheep had bunched farther ahead downalong the road and were drinking from a tiny wayside stream, and grazing on the verge. Jerry arf-arfed at them and they went on again. It was all downhill, and Willy sat across the crossbar while Jerry rode a pedal.

The barn came in sight, and a lane running steeply into a valley turned off beside it. Willy was left with the bike and Jerry went ahead and turned the sheep down the lane. It was narrow and rough and too steep for riding, so Willy had to limp along in the rear while the flock, seeming to sense an end to their journey, moved sedately forward without trouble. The farm appeared, and from it came a collie who, without any instructions, side-tracked the flock, and without any apparent effort, induced them to enter the yard into a dead end occupied by a rusty roller. The dog then lay down with lolling tongue and eyed the bleating animals with a look that said so clearly "Now stay there, there's no way out."

The farmer's wife had appeared also, and took the boys into the kitchen where she gave them milk and a slab of cake. She looked askance at Willy, with his cheeks tear-marked in the lime dust,

"You'm come too far. Where be gwain now?"

Jerry told her, adding "It's all right, I got me bike."

She considered this, then went to the door and called. "Albert! Be'ee gwain up the field presently?" The distant voice of Albert replied, and he was told to come into the yard first. When he appeared, driving a horse and wagon, the woman told the boys to get up with the bike. She gave Jerry a two-shilling piece and warned him "Don bring'ee so far 'nether time." The boys sank gratefully into bundles of straw and the long steep climb up the rutted lane to the road was, to them, a blessed journey, all too short.

The lane to the farm had taken them a mile or more from the road home, but unemcumbered by the sheep they made better time of it. The hills had to be climbed, but each one surmounted, meant a good run down the other side. Jerry straddled the cross bar, mounting from some convenient bank, while Willy sat on the rear bracket. Many false starts and spills accompanied this manoeuvre, but, once away, they spun off, sometimes at perilous speed. Willy's bruised shin was now extended beside Jerry's straining legs, but he soon found that his bottom and other tender parts were receiving a dreadful hammering. He was glad when the next hill set him afoot again. It was late, early evening, and long after Willy's usual mealtime when he arrived home. Gwen, anxious at his absence, was about to give him a scolding, when she saw the grey exhaustion showing in his face, she took him indoors, her hand across his thin shoulders. "Wherever 'ave 'ee bin?"

"Market," he replied. She asked no more then, biding her time for later questioning.

"Take your boots off" was all she said. Then she gave him a thick slice of bread and dripping, well-salted, and a mug of cocoa. "Now off to bed, you've bin too far," she told him.

A couple of minutes later Willy was in bed, grime and all, and fast asleep. "'They Well Street lot!" said Gwen to herself. "I'll give that Jerry somethin' when I see 'im!"

Chapter 6

As the boys grew up, they grew into a changing world. The motor car was transforming life and the tempo quickened, but still Colley End and the fountain were unaltered. The town streets still changed into country lanes once the fountain was passed. The dairyman still drove his cows up and down from milking to pasture, twice a day. Store cattle came in a wild stampeding mob down from the waterless fields on the hills to slake their thirst at the fountain and, though cars, lorries and steam traction-engines were quite common, most of the traffic was still horse drawn, and the fountain was seldom without some beast drinking there. With so much traffic, there was ample opportunity for the boys of the area to get up to mischief and nobody was safe from their pranks, sometimes cruel, but done without malice.

The little church, opposite the school, was occasionally the scene of a funeral and this always provided entertainment for the Gurney tribe. There were two gateposts standing at the bottom of the steps leading up to the church door, and it was the habit of the funeral bearers (who, dressed in black frock coats and top hats, flanked the hearse on its progress to the cemetery), to place their top hats upon these pillars when they carried the coffin into the church for the service before burial. It was then that the wretched Bill Gurney would quickly rearrange the hats from one pillar to the other, retire to his home doorway, or to a vantage point somewhere out of reach, and watch with glee as the six bearers spent time swapping hats, trying to find their own.

On one occasion, he went further in search of devilment. There was a well-attended funeral with more than the usual number of cabs to convey the mourners, so much so that cabs from the next town had been enlisted. Bill Gurney, prowling this ostentatious sign of wealth, or importance, discovered that the last cab was parked well down the road, and that the cabby had gone up the line to confer with his colleagues. Hopping about with the excitement of a brilliant idea, Bill ran home and reappeared in haste with a rope hidden under his guernsey. This he tied to the axle of the cab, and to the iron grid over a drain in the gutter. When the service was over, the mourners entered the procession of cabs, the bearers took up position, three on each side of the hearse and, at a sign from the undertaker, the whole cortége moved off in solemn splendour - all except the last cab. This moved about six feet until the rope tightened, then came to an abrupt halt. The horse immediately crouched his hindquarters, dug in his hooves and threw himself into his collar, heaving in a staccato of stamping feet. For perhaps ten seconds there was a tremendous tug-of-war, with the bewildered cabby looking about him to find the cause. Then the rope broke, the horse went down on its knees, the cabby was catapulted on to its rump and the passengers were flung about the inside of the cab like persons caught in a storm at sea. Bill Gurney was not to be seen, but the story of his awesome wickedness was to be heard for years to come.

Willy never got himself involved in these escapades. Gwen kept a close eye on him and was strict with him about his behaviour, but in any case, his was not the nature that could indulge in extrovert mischief. As he grew older, Gwen saw his father appearing in him more and more, in his gentleness and neatness, but most of all in his quiet, secretive life. His daydreaming with wide eyes that saw beyond the natural happiness in his own imagined world. Gwen would look at him, see that look, and her throat ached with the contraction of her whole being. "Dave! Dave!" her body would yearn. Sometimes it was hard to remember, after so many years, just how Dave had looked or spoken, but as his boy grew, some sudden turn of the head, or gesture, would take her back to the few, lovely months of their love, and she would reach out to Willy with a sudden tenderness.

Jerry was a big boy, almost man sized. His head was no longer shaven, but was an unruly mass of hair that corkscrewed into tight curls when it was wet. He was the undoubted champion of the school, and of all the school-aged boys of Well Street and the area. He never bullied, he seldom fought, but there was something in his bearing apart from his size, that awarded him top-dog status without effort on his part. Mr Fox saw his character blossom and loved him like a son. It wasn't until years later that Jerry realised the guidance and help the old man had given him, without him ever being aware of it. In those innocent years, he was still unaware of his mother's reputation, and never thought to question the origin of her relative affluence amongst the still very poor neighbours. He loved her, and though they seldom displayed any affection, she was proud of her big son, and would have fought tigerishly for him if need be.

Jerry was no scholar. He struggled through the elementary school curriculum because he was made to, but his interests lay elsewhere, in the down-to-earth life of the neighbourhood and always in the wonderful world of living things. He kept rabbits and pigeons in the little back yard behind his home, a little yard that had an intriguing door leading into another road, parallel with his own, but otherwise a quarter mile's walk away for other means of entry. This door had once given entrance to a wash house, with its copper boiler and drainpipe chimney, and the reason for its connection with the otherwise remote road, had been forgotten before Effie and her husband had moved in. Now, however, it contributed in no small way to Effie's affluence. She had a very well-to-do friend, who found it convenient to slip into the cottage in Well Street by the anonymity of the back door. Jerry kept his rabbits in the shed and made a sort of den of it.

Mr Fox had hopes for Willy. He saw him gaining a scholarship to secondary school, but in spite of patient teaching, Willy never managed to do so. He read avidly. There was a cupboard full of all manner of books donated by friends of the school and augmented by 'left overs' of church jumble sales, and Willy read them all. He surprised Mr Fox one day by producing a short poem as a 'free' composition, (Mr Fox sometimes filled an unconsidered English period, by telling the children to write a composition, on a subject of their own choosing). A poem that not only scanned, but opened a window, however small, into that world that beckoned Willy away when other duties waited, and left the pages blank before his secret, smiling face. Mr Fox despaired, and encouraged his reading and writing but his other subjects floundered.

When Jerry reached the age of fourteen, he had to leave school. This he did without regret and immediately set about earning his living, doing a variety of jobs, but mostly assisting his friend, the dairyman, who gladly loaded him with a full man's share of work. He decided for himself what he wanted to be in life, and that was a woodworker. He had somehow acquired an affinity with timber, with its smell and texture, and he knew that his hands could take it, and shape it to his will. But that was two years away. You had to be sixteen to be apprenticed, so Jerry strove happily with the cattle in the Well Street yard, milking, grooming, feeding, doing the milk rounds, often on his own, and taking the cows up and down to pasture. He did not see so much of Willy now, but Willy often appeared in the yard, or would waylay him on his way to fetch the cows, and Jerry would greet him with the usual upward jerk of the head and the greeting that just left the final "… Will!" Willy replied in the same way, adding "Can I come?"

Willy discovered that Jerry was known down at the harbour and once or twice he was taken out into the bay in a rowing boat, to fish. They even caught some mackerel once. Jerry, young though he was then, had been taught something of handling a boat when at the orphanage on the river bank, and he was proud to show off his prowess. To Willy he was displaying yet another of his incredible skills, somewhat taken for granted though, because, to Willy, it was just inconceivable that there was anything that Jerry could not do.

When Willy approached fourteen, Mr Fox pondered long on what to advise. He guessed that his mother would want him to go into some 'safe' trade as soon as he was old enough, she meanwhile, depriving herself of all but necessities until the five-year apprenticeship was done, and Willy would receive a man's wage. Mr Fox thought of that bright intellect dreaming away the hours as his hands went about the job of plumbing, painting or whatever he drifted into. He saw Gwen and told her to send the boy to night-school, at fourteen he was just beginning to learn and must not be deprived. He also saw a solicitor friend, and persuaded him to find a place as an office boy for Willy, until he should develop his talents. Gwen was pleased to think of Willy as being something other than a manual labourer, and, as it all seemed arranged, Willy accepted it, though he thought wistfully of summer days cutting hay and stalking the raucous corncrake in the wheat. To his fanciful thoughts, life should always be summer, and work a pleasure. When he finished school, he had never known hardship, worry or grief, so well had Gwen sheltered him. It was not the best preparation for a poor boy to face life, but it was fourteen idyllic years.

Chapter 7

Jerry became acquainted with other delivery men while on his milk rounds and also when, occasionally, he took the dairyman's mare to be shod, and as he grew older he was accepted as someone who could handle a horse. In this way, he became an admirer of a little stallion pony, owned by a furnisher, who had a small workshop at Colley End, and used the pony to draw a light wagon upon which he collected and delivered the furniture that he renovated for his customers.

This pony, Dancer, had been bought from the gypsies when a mere yearling and was a handsome sight now that it had matured, with its thick, arched neck and powerful quarters. Its owner, having had it when so young, could do anything with it, but other people trod with care. Dancer had a boisterous nature, and would bolt at any opportunity just for the sheer joy of movement. He was driven on a straight bit, but he had long since worked out an answer to that, lulling his driver into carelessness with slack reins, and his attention elsewhere, then having shaken his bridle and got the bit where he could bite it hard, he would take a wild plunge, and be off. There was never a dull moment for his driver, especially if there was a mare about who was advertising her attractions.

Jerry had managed to get permission to drive Dancer up to the cemetery to collect mown grass. This was the pony's main diet all summer, as he was never turned out to grass, and the almost daily chore was passed on to Jerry with relief by the furnisher. Jerry delighted in the quick action of the pony, the controlled power of the shining body, sleek from grass, the constantly questing ears, and the proud, bright eyes. He contrasted so with the heavy mare that drew the milk float. She was aged now, and lackadaisical. Compared to her, this high stepping stallion was like a tensed up spring, and delight to drive. So it was that Jerry invited Willy to join him, in what he called 'a bit of fun', with Dancer.

There was an elderly lady, stout, red faced from being out in all weathers, and gifted with a repartee that had been known to leave loose-mouthed louts in abashed confusion. She had a greengrocery business; a small shop near the church, that was tended by some ancient relative, while she hawked her goods from street to street. This woman, a widow of many years, had one great delight and that was to decorate her little cart and herself, dressed in some form of theatrical finery, to enter for the annual carnival. This assembled on the sea front and then wound its way through the town, collecting funds for the cottage hospital.

In those days that was an event that the whole town entered into with gusto, and crowds collected to watch the procession. This lady, Mrs Molly Bellcott was well known for her colourful entry, and people from the area were always agog to know what her theme would be. This was always a secret until she drove out in all her glory from the yard where she stabled her patient, old, droop-headed mare.

This year, tragedy had struck. The mare had developed an abscess on its neck that prevented it wearing a collar and poor old Molly was distraught. She took the mare to the smith, who also acted as vet to many of his customers, and he opened the boil and dressed it with tar, but gave no hope of it being recovered in time for the carnival. By chance, the furnisher happened to bring in his pony for shoeing, and he entered into the debate. Suddenly taking leave of his senses, he offered to lend his pony.

"My Dancer would set your wagon off a treat," he said.

Molly quailed at the thought. She remembered when Dancer had got out of his stable and, cornered in the pub yard, had held all the stablemen from the neighbourhood at bay with his yellow teeth and flashing forehooves. He had surrendered quietly when his owner had arrived, but Molly, for one, did not see herself as a rodeo artist. The furnisher declined to take part in the turn-out and after much discussion the smith suggested a solution.

"Let young Jerry Wilkins lead 'un. 'es goodiwi'un."

So Molly sought out Jerry in the cowshed and Jerry accepted with delight.

On the day, the greengrocery cart was adapted for a great and colourful display of fruit and vegetables, with ribbons and bunting and bells. The wheels were entwined with coloured crêpe paper and the driving seat had become a throne. Over all was rigged a streamer with the words 'Eat British Empire Fruit'. Willy had already been co-opted to assist with the decorations, and had been given a particoloured costume and wide-brimmed hat to wear. He was to ride on the back, supposedly a footman, but in fact to stop any of the fruit from rolling off. Jerry was given a beefeater's costume. It had no bearing on the theme, but was colourful. Finally, Molly emerged from the loft over the stable clothed as Britannia, complete with shield and trident. She took her seat, Willy got on the back, and the beefeater led Dancer into the street. A few neighbours had gathered and there was a ragged cheer and a pattering of hand claps. Dancer did a little cavort, but settled down when Jerry spoke in his ear and tightened his grip on the bridle. The reins were tied to the brake handle. Molly had enough to do with her trident and shield that kept her more or less immobile on her throne. Willy, perched on the back between vegetable marrows, tomatoes and apples, watched, fascinated, as the great cone of oranges, the centre piece of the display, trembled at Dancer's uneven pull. Once on the street though, all seemed well and in due course they arrived at the assembly point on the Green, down by the harbour.

They were in good time for the judging. In fact, as it turned out, too early. Both sides of the road leading to the lawns, were already occupied by early arrivals, determined not to miss any part of the spectacle, and the little tableau was given a cheer that rippled along the road to accompany it all the way to the gate. Dancer had behaved so well that Jerry had risked perching one half of his bottom on the back of the shaft and, taking the reins, allowed the pony to proceed along the level in his most attractive manner, nimble hooves tap-tapping, gleaming neck arched, ears a-twitch and eyes roving. Britannia ruled her imaginary waves with a regal authority that convulsed many of her 'subjects' who were used to seeing her in her workaday role.

Several other decorated horse drawn vehicles were already lined up on the Green and Jerry, going to Dancer's head, began to lead him along to a place at the end. Dancer had been born wild on the moor (how the gypsies had got hold of him was anyone's guess), but since his yearling days, he had never been turned out to grass, and now feeling turf under his hoofs, he began to get excited, tucking his rump in and starting his characteristic dance that had suggested his name. Jerry hung on to his head and spoke soothing words, but Dancer was an opportunist, his powerful little body contracted like a spring. Britannia shouted in alarm to Willy to go and help Jerry. Willy ran around the cart and took the other side of Dancer's head and the two boys fairly dragged the pony forward. After the initial flurry of excitement, he calmed down and was put in position without trouble. He was next to a coal cart, drawn by a horse that dwarfed him in size. There were about twenty entries in the class and all the time newcomers were arriving. Dancer created great interest among the spectators by constantly 'testing the wind' for scents that only a virile young stallion could appreciate. This he did by raising and curling up his upper lip and moving his head in a questing motion

"Oh look, that pony's laughing," people said.

The inevitable happened, and Dancer's high pitched squeal went across the Green. Jerry hung on to his head for dear life, but a mare's deep-throated whickering had acknowledged his call, and Dancer was not to be pacified. Anxious stewards milled around him.

"Keep him in line. Keep control of him," they demanded, and the knowledgeable said things like "Shouldn't ever have been entered. Entires b'aint safe ," and so on.

Meanwhile Britannia was having her work cut out to preserve the display of fruit behind and under her, especially the pyramid of oranges, which, although built on an ingenious frame, was in imminent danger of collapse. Every time the pony plunged or backed, the whole display was in jeopardy and Molly's instructions to Jerry and Willy got more urgent and wild.

A senior official arrived and ordered Jerry to take the cart to the extreme end of the line, behind a steam lorry owned by a corn and forage merchant. This position was achieved without more trouble and, after a while, Dancer lowered his head and started to nibble the grass.

Molly rearranged her display, put her crested helmet on again and awaited the judges.

The judging went on for ever, and Willy was sent every few moments to scout its progress. The spectators, three or four deep, behind a wire fence, were close enough to enter into Molly's anxiety, and to add to it.

"Yer! Missus. They've forgot you!" they told her with wicked delight.

"You bin disqualified," others opined.

Molly raged inwardly. "That bloody 'oss," she kept saying.

Dancer's composure soon lulled them into a false sense of security. His head drooped, his eyes closed and he appeared to sleep, but who knows the mind of a horse, especially an 'entire' that had his ardour roused, even so temporarily. There were some guffaws from a bunch of youths in the crowd and Britannia and company, had they noticed, would have seen a small child point excitedly, and seen its mother shushing its embarrassing question. Other ladies were taking an exaggerated interest in some seagulls flying over, others turned away and spoke of the weather. Jerry, in response to some lewd comment from the youths, turned to find that Dancer had lowered a good foot and a half of obscenely piebald masculinity and was swinging it about in tune with, no doubt, happy day dreams. Then Jerry did a silly thing.

"Put it away!" he growled at Dancer, at the same time giving the offending organ a tap with the butt of the whip. The effect was instantaneous. Dancer reared and plunged backwards, the cart jack-knifed and Britannia flew backwards on to the piled oranges, at the same time, grabbing at anything to save herself. She grasped the reins and all her considerable weight was transferred to Dancer's head at the moment that he stood tall on his hind legs. Nobody knew exactly what happened next, but certainly the rearing pony almost fell across Molly who was on her back amid oranges and pineapples in the cart.

Jerry managed to grab Dancer's head when he came down on all fours again, and all might have been well had not the steam engine, (which till then had been immobile within its polished brass and bunting, making little hissing and cooking noises) suddenly reached a head of steam and blown its safety valve'. The roar of noise and the clouds of steam enveloped the little cart, and the pony, until then merely fractious, was terrified. With one great plunge he was off, the cart jerking forward so suddenly that Britannia and half of her fruit was thrown out, and only the opportune arrival of a "horsey" gentleman, who grabbed the pony's head and virtually smothered him, prevented Dancer from bolting.

Held as he was though, he still had the ability to kick, which he did most violently. The cart had been made for a much larger horse, and Dancer had too much room between the shafts. Again and again, his hind legs thrashed out, then, trying to slew around to free himself, he managed to get one hind leg over the shaft. When a horse does this and feels the shaft between its legs, it usually goes berserk, but this cart was so big that the shaft effectively hobbled the pony, who was frightened and hurt.

Quite a crowd of spectators had gathered by then. "Runaway horse," had been called along the road, and plenty of men were milling around giving advice of all kinds. Amongst them appeared the pony's owner, the furnisher, who had come to see the show. He took Dancer's head and when the pony heard the familiar voice, and smelt the well-known hands, he quietened down and stood, sweating and trembling, while they unhitched the traces and breeching, lowered the shafts and freed him. Then he was re-hitched. The furnisher stayed with him, demanding what the devil they had done to him and why!

Britannia had picked herself up, and with Jerry and Willy was collecting fruit and vegetables, and throwing them back in the cart. The chief marshall arrived and ordered her to take the pony and cart away, and retire from the competition, before some serious damage was done.

Poor Molly had not had a chance to express her feelings adequately until then, so she took the opportunity of visiting on the marshall a fury, expressed in such a wealth of colloquial abuse, that the man behaved much as the pony had done, backing off in shocked surprise, then retreating in abashed alarm.

Once the harnessing was done and the fruit collected, Britannia, the beefeater and harlequin were all loaded on to the cart, the furnisher ascended the throne, took the reins and with a chirrup from him, Dancer trotted off through the gate and back to the stable yard. The streets had by then been closed to traffic to allow the procession to pass, so the little tableau, somewhat disarrayed, had it all to themselves, and the crowds, bored with waiting, gave them a rousing cheer all the way.

Molly said no word until the yard door was closed, then she turned on the three males, and fairly hissed her hate and anger. The boys got out of their fancy dress while the furnisher took the pony out of the shafts. He did not remonstrate with Molly, contenting himself with saying "Well it's a good job he's not hurt, that's all I can say!" Molly said much more, all the way to the stable yard gate most of which seemed to be a string of curses on "That bloody 'oss."

Chapter 8

Willy started work in the solicitor's office, arriving on the first morning in his first suit with long trousers. He gave no thought to the cost to Gwen, who had so little. She did as most people of her class did, buying through a "tally man", for one shilling a week. The cheap suit of tweed had cost her one pound ten shillings, and she looked with pride on her son, so suddenly a man. He had grown tall in the last year, and his bony body and sharp-featured face was so like his father's, that Gwen was near to tears to see him.

At the office, Willy found himself responsible for sweeping and dusting the three rooms, emptying the wastepaper baskets and generally tidying up before his employer arrived. There were two clerks: the senior was a middle-aged man who had a small room to himself, and the other was a young woman typist, who sat at a desk in the larger room. This had filing cabinets, a table piled with bundles of paper with pink tape, and three chairs ranged along one wall for clients to sit on when waiting to see the solicitor, who had the third room at the rear of the building. Below, on the ground floor, was a florist's shop. Willy had a cautious welcome from the typist, who was quick to see that his arrival relieved her of several menial chores. The clerk introduced Willy to the filing system and decided, privately, that if Willy proved intelligent, he could gradually pass on to him several of his more boring tasks. The solicitor, on seeing him for the first time, told him: "Be on time, be clean, be polite, and be on hand any time that I need you."

Willy found life entirely boring. There was little that he was capable of doing, and what there was had scarce interest for him. He spent a lot of time looking out of the window on to the street where various carts and vans made deliveries to the shops below.

This seemed a far more attractive life, and he looked with envy at the van boys carrying sacks, rolling barrels and wheeling cases. His favourite job was hand-delivering letters to other offices. He liked that because he could loiter a little and look in the shop windows and generally observe the street going about its business.

When he returned to the office through the passageway beside the florist's shop, he would stop and look at all the potted plants, the great sheaves of flowers and, sometimes, the funeral wreaths, or the wedding bouquets awaiting delivery. He loved the scent of the flowers and the clean smell of freshly watered vegetation.

Gwen had taken Mr Fox's advice, and enroled Willy at night-school. He found himself committed to learning typing, shorthand, book-keeping, mathematics and English. This occupied four evenings each week, and also entailed homework. This Willy accepted. There was little for a fourteen year old to do in the evenings, especially one with just a shilling a week pocket money. He was paid seven shillings and sixpence by his employer. One shilling and sixpence was put away for clothes, and five shillings was given to Gwen towards his keep. He felt very manly to be, as he fondly imagined, "earning his own living".

Gwen smiled at his self-importance when he handed it to her, and gave him a little hug; but she was very glad of the money, and was happy to see Willy at his books doing mysterious signs over and over again.

"It's a sort of alphabet, Mum, only you write down sounds, instead of letters."

For some reason, shorthand appealed to him and he decided to write everything in it, as a code. The book-keeping was way beyond him. He could scarcely comprehend its purpose. Figures were a blank spot in his brain, so that the mathematics class simply stunned him. At day school he had floundered as far as long-division and there surrendered. Logarithms and algebra had never even reached the horizon of his mind, so after sitting doing nothing for several weeks, he decided that he would quietly skip the class. The frustrated master was careful not to enquire why.

English was another matter. In that class he shone, and the English master, delighted with his ability and enthusiasm, went home one night and told his wife, "At long last I've got a pupil who knows the magic of the written word." He made a mental note of the authors and poets that he would introduce to the boy and looked forward to sharing his many loves with this fresh young mind. After a while the typist allowed Willy to tap out addresses on envelopes, and sometimes, when she had no work to do on the machine, Willy would be allowed to do some practice. He would take a paper covered in elementary shorthand from his pocket, and type out some of his English homework. He was enthusiastic when doing something he enjoyed, but otherwise he mooned over his work, daydreaming of more pleasant things.

A couple of years passed, and Willy was now styled a junior clerk. He took some dictation, and typed when he could. He also, having been discovered capable of writing a fair hand, was gradually allowed to engross documents, and began copying out tax claims and other work done in the office. At sixteen, he was tall, still thin, and a bit awkward in his manner, but a young man who was generally smiled upon by ladies met in the course of business, and thought to be a "nice, polite boy".

At seventeen, when the typist left to get married, he was promoted to her place, and he and the senior clerk worked as a happy team. He then received thirty-five shillings a week and felt himself rich. Gwen was so proud of him, in his dark suit and trilby hat. She loved him, and agonised over him when she saw some new evidence of his maturity. "Oh Gawd!" she would think. "'e'll be getting married before I know what!" And she hated some unknown, unthought of, woman, who even then was probably growing up into buxom womanhood, fated to take her son.

Jerry, two years older than Willy, duly became indentured as a joiner with a local firm of builders. There was a post-war building boom then, and Jerry was kept hard at work assisting a craftsman on the building site. As his skill increased, he was promoted to more intricate work, making stairways and window frames, learning to turn newel posts and baluster rails, even to coffin making, for the firm had a wide range of activities. He still spent time in the cowsheds and yard, often helping out with the animals at the weekends and during the long summer evenings. He continued to live at home with Effie, with whom he had had a confrontation over her way of life.

When he was sixteen, he had been obliged to face her with the knowledge, unhappily gained, when neighbours cruelly sneered. Effie was angry. The shame, in the face of the boy, making her bitter and abusive. Jerry heard her out, then, with all the years of her care and kindness crouching in his aching throat, he took her into his arms and whispered "You're me mum, you never let the Bosun 'ave me - I don't care, you're me mum!" Effie ran into her bedroom, (her 'office', as her clients had been known to call it), and wept as she had not done for years.

Jerry and Willy were still bosom pals, Willy tagging along wherever the adventurous Jerry led. He was seventeen before Jerry introduced him to the society of girls. Jerry had the happy, assured manner, that made meeting people an easy and natural art. He could strike up an acquaintance that was instantly reciprocated, and then, he would just as graciously drop it, as his wide smile and engaging manner was welcomed elsewhere. He never got involved very deeply with friends, only Willy, and the milkman, had his affection.

Willy was just the opposite, shy and diffident. He was always on the edge of a crowd, a follower, never a leader.

One day, in early summer, Jerry met Willy on his way home. "How about going to the church hall tomorrow, Will?" It's pretty good, there's a lot go."

"Dancing?" asked Willy.

"Yes, it's fun."

"I can't dance."

"Don't matter. You just pick it up. I do, it's easy."

Willy felt some excitement at the idea.

"O.K.? See you at the fountain, 'bout eight?" continued Jerry, knowing Willy would agree.

"I'm going to a dance tonight, Mum," Willy told Gwen the next morning. "Could you iron my suit for me." Gwen heard the request like the voice of a malignant fate speaking from the years of his babyhood.

"Where you going?" she asked, sawing desperately at the loaf she was cutting for breakfast, and trying to sound nonchalant.

"Church hall. I'm going with Jerry."

Some relief found its way into her dismay. At least he was not going with a girl. She never knew, she told herself, what Willy was thinking, or doing, he was so secretive; but that Jerry Wilkins, she had never trusted him. And his mother! Jerry must know! What sort of influence was she on him? What sort of girls would Jerry hobnob with, and introduce her Willy to? The bright morning suddenly seemed black with clouds of worry.

Willy ate his fried egg and fried bread and later departed for business, a gentleman, starting work at nine, while all the world had been busy since seven-thirty. Gwen had to start at the Big House at eight and, as usual, waved from the kitchen window to her tall son as he passed on his way. Willy waved back, never for a moment imagining the mental turmoil behind the worried eyes of his mother.

Willy's introduction to the social life was not very impressive. The hall was very full, most of the people were young, but to Willy's eyes they were middle-aged, being in their twenties and thirties. Some of the girls were "Eton cropped", most had the fashionable hairstyle called a "shingle", all were wearing very short skirts, and Willy was uncomfortable in such sophisticated company. They were the young shop assistants, typists and hairdressers of the town, with many a maid servant indistinguishable in dress and deportment. Jerry seemed to know quite a few of the ladies and threw a greeting here and there as the hall filled up. The girls sat on the chairs ranged around the hall, the boys generally stood in a bunch in the doorway, from where they assessed their chances with the girls.

A four-piece band struck up music from the stage. At first no one took the floor, then a couple (who were married, engaged, or going steady enough to sit together) moved out and started to dance. A few girls then got up and began dancing together; after that, as if by ritual, the boys moved in to claim the girls they had marked down. The knowing girls had purposely taken seats near the door or had stood around in little gossipy groups, fairly close to the boys. This saved the boys having to walk the length of the hall and be conspicuous as they invited the girls to dance. Usually, the top end of the hall was occupied by girls with their mothers, acting as chaperone, and by shy girls, who seldom got asked on to the floor.

Willy was standing behind a group of boys with his back to the wall, fascinated by the music and movement. He had no intention of trying to dance, and stood there with the blue haze of cigarette smoke making his eyes smart, and with the boys' talk of sport, work and girls, eddying around his ears. He saw Jerry in conversation with some fellows that he had met, and went over to join the group. He found that the subject was the rowing club, and he was not included, so he returned to his place by the wall and lit another cigarette.

During the evening, he saw Jerry venture on to the floor once or twice. Dancing did not seem a very involved thing to do, just walking, it seemed to him, but he had not the courage to try. There was a thing called the Charleston that was very noisy and boisterous, and he noticed with a sudden interest, how nice the girls' thighs were, as the dance waxed hot and the skirts rose even higher. Halfway through the evening an interval was announced and double doors were opened into a small room where refreshments were served. Some of the boys went outside to the pubs for a drink, but most stayed for the tea and cakes offered by the ladies committee.

"Come on Will! called Jerry, and Willy found himself being propelled towards the tea urn. "Enjoying yourself?"

"Yes, fine;' said Willy, realising that it was the conventional reply required.

"You'll soon get into it," retorted Jerry, and before Willy could make any sort of response, he suddenly turned and, looking over Willy's shoulder, said "Hello Madge, I didn't see you before."

Willy moved to one side and found that the girl Jerry had called Madge was standing beside him.

"Shall I get you a tea?" Jerry continued, "and what, a sandwich?"

"Yes please," replied the girl. "But I'll get some for my friend too."

"You get those, Will, and bring 'em over," said Jerry, moving off with two cups of tea and a couple of sandwiches in the saucers. Willy was suddenly electrified into forced action. He had, from the moment of first seeing Madge, been dazed and confused by the nearness and femininity of her so close to his side. He had felt a shock run through him, an emotion unknown till then, and was now suddenly included in Jerry's easy acceptance of the situation.

Willy collected the two teas and sandwiches, paying ninepence for them and thanking his lucky stars that he had a half crown in his pocket.

Jerry and the girl had gone to some chairs beside the stage, and Willy went to join them. The girl, referred to by Madge as "my friend", patted the chair next to her and accepted the refreshments with a "thanks luv," and then opened up the conversation with the well-tried gambit of "You been here often?"

Before Willy could think of some nonchalant rejoiner, he had blurted out the truth. "Oh my!" said the girl, "don't you dance then?"

"Well, no, not much," said Willy, wishing himself elsewhere or wishing he had had time to prepare himself for this encounter.

It was then that Jerry, prompted by Madge, did some tardy introductions. "'This is Will, my friend," he informed the girls.

"And I'm Madge, and this is my friend Hilda," said Madge to Willy who found himself getting hot, feeling awkward and confused. Hilda was saying something to him, but he didn't know what; he was looking at Madge and his throat had gone dry. Fortunately, the music started up again, and Hilda, who had been sitting out all the evening, grabbed her opportunity and taking Willy by the arm, said "Come on, its a quickstep. I'll show you how it goes!"

Willy, already nervous, was a dreadful pupil; his feet felt a yard long, seeming to have a will of their own whose sole intention was to trample Hilda into the floor. He was glad when the end of the dance brought merciful relief. So was Hilda. Worse was to come though.

The band leader announced, "Now there'll be a Paul Jones," and Jerry took Willy firmly by the arm and made him join a circle of men enclosing a ring of girls, both revolving around the room. The music stopped again, and to Willy's terror, he found himself in the firm grip of a portly matron who had joined the Paul Jones as her only hope of a dance.

Willy found himself being pulled and pushed around the room, treading on his partner, being trodden on, being barged into, knocking others; until once more the music stopped and he was again in the men's circle. His head had cleared a little, and having by then realised the purpose of the circling, he determined to escape the moment the time came to take a partner again.

The music stopped, and there before him was Madge - her dimpled face smiling up at him and her arms reaching. He took her hand and encircled her shoulder, but, with the other dancers all a-dancing, he stood there, red faced and miserable.

"I can't do it, I don't know how," he said.

"Don't worry, just walk," said Madge. "Everybody's like it at first, come on." They had shuffled half the length of the hall before the music changed again, but this time Madge took his arm and deftly extricated the two of them from the crush. "Let's sit it out," she said.

Seated, she took the initiative, "You're Jerry's best friend," stating the fact as authoritative. "He's told me about you, you're a clerk, aren't you? I'm a nanny, I love kids, don't you?" She prattled on, Willy only half listening, and bereft of speech except for a stammered "yes" or "no". The girl seemed quite capable of maintaining the conversation.

The Paul Jones went on and on; the band leader was no fool, and he knew that there were at least a score of wallflowers who depended on the mythical Paul Jones to make their evening for them. When one after another began to drop out and the ritual was brought to a close, Jerry and Hilda reappearing from the throng.

"Cor, I'm sweating streams!" Hilda informed all and sundry, announcing a fact that was very obvious to anyone within yards.

"What you two been up to?" enquired Jerry of Willy.

"We've just been talking," Madge broke in.

"Cor!" said Jerry, running his finger around his collar. "It's hot, I'm going outside for a breather." He went, as he always did, without apology, just an easy smile, as if to say, "Well, that's the end of that."

The music started up again and the three sat in silence. A bird was singing somewhere inside Willy and he didn't know what to do. He suddenly realised that both girls had been claimed and that he was alone again. He went back to the doorway, and stood there awhile. His eyes were smarting from the smoke and his throat was dry with the dust and chalk. He went outside and filled his lungs with the clean night air.

Willy did not try to renew his acquaintance with Madge. He dare not ask her to dance and there was no other reason to approach her. He wished he could do like Jerry, just sit down beside her, smile and chat easily, then get up and walk away.

"But I wouldn't walk away," thought Willy, "I would stay."

He watched Madge for the rest of the evening, heard the band leader announce "The last waltz, ladies and gentlemen - everybody on the floor." and he saw Madge dancing with a man, just a man, he didn't notice him, only Madge. Then the cymbals crashed, all stood to attention for *God Save the King* and the hall began to empty. Willy ran all the way home; he didn't know why, but he did know that something had happened to him. It was past midnight. He drank the cocoa left on the hob to keep warm, and crept up to bed.

"That you, Willy?" came from Gwen's room.

"Yes' m."

"Enjoy yourself?"

"Yes'm. Goodnight."

It was hours before he slept, hours before the strange tingling in his body ceased.

The following day, Willy was restless. His usual, relaxed behaviour at once a trial, and a comfort to Gwen, seemed to have deserted him. He fidgeted, he prowled, instead of lounging with his head in a book. He had no concentration at work, and was irritable. He got told off by the senior clerk, who was amazed when Willy showed his temper when spoken to. Gwen knew from the moment she saw him, the day after the dance. She sensed his frustration and drew her own conclusion. "Some maid!" she said to herself.

In the evening she made casual enquiries as to who was there, but got no satisfaction from his replies. As the days passed, she felt his frustration like a constant stress. She wanted, desperately, to know what had happened, but feared to ask in case her anxieties were confirmed, but she noted that Willy stayed at home more than usual, so was obviously not meeting anyone. Whoever the girl was, Gwen hated her.

Willy knew that he was in love. That night after the dance, the hours before he slept were vibrant with a fierce joy, a trembling delight, as Madge filled his whole consciousness, made alive to the allure of her femininity; the sweet perfume of her, the soft, brown wallflower eyes, the apple blossom of her breasts.

Willy had never encountered a woman in evening dress before. Even at these little "hops", the girls wore low-cut dresses, and their bare arms and shoulders had been a revelation to him. When the music for that Paul Jones changed and he found Madge before him, her arms lifted towards him, her eyes smiling; he had felt himself engulfed in such a delight of feeling that he had been bereft of speech, almost of movement. He had only regained some sort of normality when it was too late and another had claimed her. The following days were filled with bitter regrets and furious chidings, with the tantalising picture of her loveliness ever in his mind. By some chance he could not contact Jerry. The milkman told him that he was away on a job and that he'd promised to see to his rabbits and pigeons for him till he returned

So Willy fretted and waited, hoping that Jerry could tell him where Madge could be found, so that he might, at least, catch sight of her. At the weekend, Jerry returned and Willy, suddenly shy, went in a roundabout way to draw him into comment on the dance, but Jerry was full of what had happened during the week. His firm had got a contract to build houses in a town thirty miles away, and he was in lodgings there for months to come. The money was good and Jerry saw a prosperous future and talked excitedly about it. A motorbike was part of his ambitions now, and he talked on and on. Willy heard little of what he was saying, or paid heed to it.

Presently, when the cows were milked and the dairyman asked "Like to take 'em back for us?" Jerry said "C'mon Will!" and set off towards the pasture. The cows stopped at the fountain, and the boys leaned on the school railings to wait for them to move on. Willy suddenly found himself asking "Who was that girl, Madge, at the dance?"

"Oh, I dunno really. I seen 'er about, she was at a hop I went to a few weeks ago - 'ere, you did all right with 'er, didn't you, did you see 'er home?"

"No," said Willy. The idea that he might have done so - that she would have allowed him to - was a realm of imagination that he had not yet considered, even in his wildest dreams. With his head swimming with the notion of so doing, he asked "Where's she live, anyway?"

"Oh, somewhere down by the park, those big houses. She looks after some kids, I think."

"I love kids," that was what she had said to him at the dance, looking up at him, her lips compressed, yet smiling; her dimpled cheeks soft and pink; her eyes shining. There was so much kindness and tenderness in her look, that Willy felt a clutch in his throat at the remembrance.

"Are y'comin'?" said Jerry, already moving towards the fountain.

Willy realised that the cows were strung out along the road to the fields and Jerry was waiting.

"You fancy her," said Jerry, grinning, stating it as a fact, not a question. Willy flushed furiously. "She's all right," he said.

"Well, are you coming?"

"No, I'm going home," said Willy turning towards the cottages. Jerry ran to catch up the cows. "She goes to church Sunday mornings - Sunday school with the kids," he called back.

Next day, Sunday, Willy dressed with unusual care and made his way to church. Gwen was at the Big House as usual until after she had cooked lunch, so there was no one to question him. He did not intend to go into the church, what little acquaintance he had with church going had been with the little church on the Green. The Parish Church was unknown ground to him. He was content to picket the approaches, and had arrived with half an hour to spare, to perfect his campaign. Which way would she come? Straight from the park was his guess, that meant he would see her from when she entered the lower end of the street, two hundred yards away. But she might cross the park and come up through the town, in which case she could well enter by one of the side doors. Where could he observe both? A quick check showed that he could not. Twenty-five minutes to go - say twenty. Willy trotted off through the churchyard and into the town square. Here he had a good view of three approach roads. There was a Sunday morning hush on the town with few people about. He spent five minutes in the square, then, checking that nobody with any resemblance to Madge was in sight, he dashed down one of the roads, turned the corner, and was able to see across the park and along the approach road to the church. Just one or two people, easily disregarded, and no one accompanied by children. Willy did some calculating and decided that he had at least five minutes grace from that vantage point, so immediately hurried back to the square, swiftly appraising everyone in sight and saying to himself, "Not her - not her - not her."

The clock in the tower chimed the three quarters. Willy began to feel that the fates were against him - perhaps it was some other church that she went to. In a panic he set off for the lychgate entrance again, wondering if she had somehow slipped in unseen. He was fairly trembling with anxiety and frustration. No one that could be mistaken for her was in sight, but groups of children were arriving, most very prim and proper in their Sunday best, others romping around the gravestones, heedless of the tut-tutting of the few adults marshalling their well-drilled charges.

There was a shoemaker's shop on the corner opposite the lych gate. Being Sunday, the yellow Holland blinds were drawn, so that no wordly interest should distract the Sunday strollers. Just the sign, written in a half circle "J. Grimes - Boot and Shoe Maker." Then across the base - "Hand Sewing a Speciality."

Willy sat down on the window sill. He decided he would wait until the hour struck, but by now he had decided that Madge would not come. Twice he raced around for a look at the path to the side door, then back to his seat and the long view down the road. Five minutes to go, and still no sign of her. He knew then, common sense told him, that she wouldn't be any later, not with children, perhaps small children, who would walk slowly. He moved to the other side of the road because a car had arrived at the lych gate and was blocking his view. No go. "That's it.'" he told himself miserably, "she's not coming now."

The car moved away, and the miracle happened. 'There was Madge, busy with four small children. Willy had not considered any means of arrival except on foot. She turned towards him and he immediately spun around to gaze in the shop window, a tailor's shop, with the usual "out of business hours" blinds drawn. The blinds acted like a mirror and Willy saw the four children arranged, the two biggest hand-in-hand in front, the smaller pair each holding hands with Madge. The car turned, came back, and just as the little group entered the gateway, the driver leaned out and called "Nurse! I'll pick you up on the corner afterwards, not here."

Madge acknowledged with a little nod and walked on. Just as she entered the church porch she looked back, and for a moment, Willy thought she was looking at him. Then she was gone.

Madge had seen Willy as she was driven up to the church. "Oh! There's that boy!" she thought, and she looked at his thin, worried face and wondered what he was doing sitting on that window sill. "I like him," she told herself. "He's nice." Then they got out and the car moved away to turn. She had lost sight of him for a moment, then saw he was on the opposite side of the road. She saw his sudden recognition, saw him flush and turn away. A quiet little giggle was somewhere in her breast and a loving smile crept around her lips. "He's come to see me," she told herself with certainty. She looked back before entering the church, but all she saw was his back. "I bet he's scared to death," she thought delightedly, "and I bet he'll be outside afterwards." She couldn't keep the grin off her face all during Sunday School. She sat a little away from the children with other nannies, parents and press-ganged older children, and thought to herself, "He's nice, he's funny, I like him!"

Willy's heart was thumping and his body tingled with excitement. "I'll pick you up on the corner" - that meant a two-hundred-yard walk for Madge and her charges. Dare he? Could he? Willy didn't know how he would do it, but he knew he would. He would somehow talk to Madge after Sunday School. Somehow arrange to meet her again.

He went into the churchyard and sat on a low table-like tomb. It's a

71

lovely morning, he told himself. The sun shone, a blackbird was fluting from a pinnacle over the church wall. A great mass of golden laburnum blossom hung like happy laughter, over the ancient graves. Lilac grew on gravestone near him and his poetic soul swelled with delight with the sun, the birdsong and the blossom.

"These old graves are yesterday, today is beautiful and tomorrow is just beginning." He quested in his mind for words worthy of the occasion, and sat there in the sunshine, daydreaming of a wonderful world, just as his father had done over his saddlery. A world of happiness and delight with no dark clouds coming unobserved to cover the sun.

Thus he sat, hunched on the tomb, his chin on his knees, his long, thin arms wrapped around his long, thin legs. In spite of his excitement, the scent of the lilac and laburnum, the warm sun and the lulling music of the birds made him heedless of time; even though each quarter was chimed above his head. It was the sudden eruption from the church of the unruly element of the Sunday School, that brought him back to reality.

He positioned himself amongst some gravestones where he could see without being too obvious, and waited. Soon Madge appeared with her charges. She looked casually in the direction of the road and, had Willy known, was disappointed not to see him. Willy followed at a distance as she passed under the gate and into the road. He then made a flanking movement that would enable him to make a casual approach, as though overtaking, and then to greet her in surprise at seeing her again.

Madge was all woman; she saw him coming long before he screwed up enough courage to draw level. In fact, he left it so late that they were nearing the corner all too soon. Madge found it necessary to gain time by stopping to wipe some noses. This meant that Willy had to overtake, and when he did so Madge was bent forward and the opportunity of surprised recognition was lost. A dreadful dismay filled Willy as he blundered on, but some benign force came to his aid. His gangling legs somehow managed to twist their feet into knots and Willy found himself stumbling wildly into the gutter where he cut his hand on gravel, trying to save himself from falling full length. This brought all the heads of the group up, eyes round in astonishment, all gazing at him.

"Oh dear! I'm so sorry," said Madge. I didn't realise there was anyone behind me."

"Oh! That's all right, you didn't do it, I wasn't looking where I was going." His voice trailed off as he looked at Madge, his cheeks blushed red. "I met you at the dance, remember?" he said.

"Oh yes," said Madge. "I remember, we sat out a bit didn't we."

The car drew up just then and Madge was occupied with the children. Willy stood back, holding his bleeding hand. The fourth child was lifted in and Madge turned.

"Sorry about your hand - perhaps I'll see you Friday?" She was in. The door slammed and the car moved off. Willy didn't even manage a smile as a farewell, but Madge smiled to herself. "Clumsy great oaf! But he's nice, "I'll go on Friday," were her thoughts.

Willy went home by way of Well Street and called in at the dairyman's yard on the way, thinking that Jerry might be there. He was not; only a small boy who was feeding Jerry's rabbits and pigeons.

"Where's Jerry?"

"Dunno. Won't be 'ere today. I'm doing 'is feeding for 'im, and while 'es away all week."

Willy heard this news with surprise, and felt a bit annoyed. He wondered why Jerry hadn't asked him to do it - he often had, and felt this imp of a boy was an intrusion into their partnership. He realised then that he had not enquired how Jerry was managing while working away, and felt more annoyed still. The boy went on, a note of pride in his voice." "He's my friend!"

"Oh. How's that then?"

"He helped me when I was getting the roast - some boys tried to get it off me, and he clipped 'em round the ear 'ole. My mum told me to say thank you, and I did, and he showed me his rabbits and stuff."

Willy immediately saw the whole scene. It was the practice of many cottagers, who were without adequate cooking facilities, to send the weekend joint, surrounded by sliced potatoes, all nestling in a baking tin wrapped in a clean cloth, to the baker. He, for a small charge, would slide the dinners into the bread oven once the bread was done, then around about noon, these roasts, all sizzling in their fat, would be drawn out on his long-handled shovel, wrapped in their respective cloths, and delivered to fleet-footed youngsters, who raced for home with them before they cooled.

Willy had never had to perform this service because his mother cooked their meal at the Big House, and the mistress, out of kindness to Gwen, that extended back all her widowed years, still allowed Willy to have his main meal of the day with Gwen in the kitchen. Many the time though, that he had seen these couriers from the area and elsewhere, harrassed by the street toughs when taking a short cut home, the metal burning their fingers through the cloth, and the hot fat an imminent threat should the dish be tilted, and the coming week's staple diet in terrible jeopardy. It was only a brutal form of teasing really, but the children suffered agonies of fright. Often a whole family would go to act as a convoy, but this did lead to trouble as the family fought a rearguard action while the roast was hurried home. Willy saw it all. How many times had Jerry fought his battles for him, till at last he was recognised in the street as Jerry's mate, and allowed to pass in peace. Now, a grown man, he could still feel a kinship with this small boy, and his annoyance faded. He felt a warming towards the absent Jerry. "Just like him," he thought.

"He's my friend too," he told the boy, and began to talk about the pigeons sitting on the roof of the cow shed, telling the boy the history of each.

"Hey! What you done to your 'and?"

Willy suddenly remembered the small cut and graze and decided he had better clean it up before his mother began fussing over it, so he walked up the street, around the school (hoping his mother did not see him from the Big House), past the fountain and the little shop, and into the cottage. He washed his hand. There was only a tiny cut, hardly enough, he thought to have bled so much. Then he changed from his best suit to his workday one, and carefully brushed the best one before hanging it behind a curtain in his bedroom. "Till Friday," he said, as he did so.

The distraction of the Well Street interlude had in no way diverted his thoughts from Madge. It had merely calmed him down enough to think coherently of his next move. His object in trying to see Jerry was to find out if he was intending to go to the next Friday-night dance. Willy was too unsophisticated to think of going alone, though from the last experience, he would have little support from Jerry once they were there. But now he knew that Jerry would not be home again until the next Saturday, so he must decide what to do by himself. There was no doubt about the decision - he would definitely go to the dance, but once there, how could he approach Madge. He couldn't ask her to dance, because he had no idea of how to do so. The few tentative steps he had taken in the Paul Jones had been a disaster. Madge's friend had shown obvious relief to be freed of him, and both she and the stout lady who followed, had suffered much from his size ten feet that seemed suddenly bereft of all cohesion with his legs. Only Madge had been understanding, and she, as he remembered with increasing dismay, had suggested that they sat out her turn. Not out of wanting his company, just so as not to be trodden on! But he couldn't just walk up to her and say, "May I sit this dance out with you?" He couldn't ask her to dance, and he couldn't just sit beside her and talk. Jerry could. Lucky devil. He would just throw himself down on a vacant chair, smile charmingly, and make some remark that would have everyone laughing. But Willy couldn't. He knew that.

At one o'clock, prompt, Willy sat down in the kitchen of the Big House with his mother and Amy, the "daily", to have the meal that Gwen had prepared. Gwen saw that he was more his old self. In fact, he was feeling an excitement that brought colour to his face and brightness to his eyes. They were having soup - Gwen was great on soup. Amy was happily slurping hers without thought of manners. Gwen and Willy took theirs from the end of the spoon, quietly, as gentry did. Gwen had noted all the niceties of behaviour during her years of service, had copied them and brought Willy up to observe them too. Amy finished her bowl and belched contentedly. Gwen was only halfway through hers, and Amy would have to wait for the next course until Gwen gave her permission to serve it.

Willy, on some quite spontaneous impulse, said "Amy, do you ever go to dances?"

"No," replied Amy, "I used to before I was married, not now." Gwen waited, sipping her soup in unison with Willy. What was coming next? she wondered.

Willy, emboldened by his mother's silence, said "Can you dance?'

"Yes, I suppose so - if you call it dancing. Not this 'ere Charleston, mind you. I used to Waltz and that."

"Could you show me?"

Amy let out a shriek of laughter. "Oh ho! You going to dances?" How long's that been going on then, Gwen? 'e's growing up aint 'e. I bet e's got a maid - aah, look at 'is face! Willy's got a maid!" An unseemly scream of laughter finished the witticism.

Willy's face was scarlet, so was Gwen's. "That'll do," she snapped, "fetch the meat." Amy, still shaking with gleeful laughter, went over to the oven. Gwen glowered across the table at Willy, her mouth hard, her eyes condemning. Willy realised that he had said something both ridiculous, and for some reason, wrong. "I just thought I'd like to be able to dance, that's all," he said. "Not much good going to dances if you don't dance, is there?"

"Well," said Amy, "you can always sit 'em out - amongst the gravestones or somewhere." The raucous laugh that followed was loaded with lewd suggestion. Gwen banged the table.

"I'll have none of this talk," she said furiously, "Willy put a decent question, and I'll not have you making your nasty jokes about it."

"All right, all right, no need to get upset about it," replied Amy, putting the mutton on the table before Gwen, then looking over Gwen's head towards Willy and winking wickedly. "Young Willy's too young for girls yet, isn't he?"

Willy, red and squirming, decided to keep quiet and the meal continued in silence, broken only by Amy's noisy eating. Afterwards Willy helped with the washing up. He, and a succession of "dailys" had done that for years.

When it was finished, Gwen was completed for the day and, on Sundays, Willy's help enabled her to go home a little earlier. The operation took about an hour as there was the family's crockery and utensils as well a those of the kitchen staff, and all the cutlery to wash, dry and polish; the range to be cleaned up; coal to be fetched; and the kitchen and dining room tidied.

Gwen usually left Amy and Willy together at the sink, but today she took no chances. She hovered near all the time, and sent Amy to clean the dining room. Willy's bright day was clouded. His mother looked worried and cross, and Amy, who smelt of sweat and dirty feet, kept smirking at him in a repulsive manner. He thought of Madge in her crisp blue, cotton uniform, her round, blue hat pushing her dark hair around her cheeks, and felt that she was being sullied somehow by what was being said. He suddenly felt that he was no longer a part of the life he had always known. This kitchen in somebody else's house. The weekly ritual of washing up, his mother's unspoken censorship. A new world was opening, and he wanted to go into it. Most of all he wanted Madge.

That afternoon he walked down to the park, mooching unhappily around the lake, stopping to watch some people playing tennis, then sitting on a seat by the stream, all the time looking and looking. Perhaps she took the children for a Sunday afternoon walk. There were many families doing just that and there seemed every chance that she would, especially as Jerry had said that she lived in one of the houses flanking the park. The afternoon wore on. He decided that he would not see her again that day, so he returned home, sitting moodily at table for the special tea that Gwen always made on a Sunday.

His mother desperately wanted to talk to Willy, to find out what was behind the secretive, sullen silence, especially after the bright and happy start to their midday meal. She looked at Willy and thought, "I'll kill that Amy! I'll tell the Missus to get rid of her, she's a slut, not fit for Willy to be with, her with her nasty talk."

Gwen had grown up completely ignorant of obscene behaviour and lewd talk. After her orphanage days she had been under the dominance of a good and decent woman who was cook at the Big House. She had never suffered the attentions of lecherous suitors, and when Dave had come into her life, their courtship had been happy and innocent just as was their love for each other, and when they married Gwen had given

Dave all that he could have wanted to satisfy his bodily needs. That was their private life, not to be spoken of, even to each other, not even to be cherished much, until it was too late. Gwen had learned, though without seeking to, and without interest in it, that there was another mode of conduct, one that had women talking behind their hands, squawking with rude laughter, and suddenly falling into a tittering silence when someone approached. Gwen ignored it all, as she did the sight of drunkards, and kept herself to herself while the world went by. A world that was changing so fast that she had little knowledge of its way of life.

The shock of knowing that her Willy was grown up, almost a man, was profound; and the added realisation that he was in love, was a torture. There was a feeling of resentment against fate too. Ever since Dave had been killed, she had led a very secluded life. How secluded came home to her now. She had never been to a dance, she had no idea of what a modern dance was. Like the many thousands of young war widows, women who had lost their generation of prospective husbands, she was resigned to a lonely life, filling it as best she could, with work and caring for her son. There were certain highlights during the year such as the Regatta Fair, to break the monotony. That, Christmas and Willy's birthday, all called for dressing in her best, and making an occasion of the day, but otherwise she led an empty existence. She had always told herself when Willy was a big boy, how they would do things together. She had even looked further ahead to when he was a man and she might have grandchildren to entertain her, but now , when, so suddenly it seemed, that became a possibility, all the empty years cried in bitterness for she knew that Willy would go from her to some other woman.

He would never know how much she had wanted his love and companionship. She was proud of his gentlemanly appearance and behaviour, of his good speech, and of his literary prowess as shown by his reading. She knew that she hardly knew her son - a son so silent, so lost in thoughts never shared, that she constantly failed to find a common ground for understanding. She thought miserably that it was years since they had had a real conversation, and now, when she wanted so much to know who the girl was, and to know about her, she was incapable of even opening up a friendly enquiry and, thanks to the wretched Amy's intervention, it seemed that Willy was not likely to take her into his confidence. Seventeen, she thought, seventeen, going eighteen. He couldn't possibly marry for years yet. Calf-love, it would pass; but supposing some hussy had got her eye on him, some scheming wretch who might trap him into marriage. He couldn't know the dangers - how could he? He'd never had anything to do with girls and those girls that went to dances, she'd seen pictures of them, half naked some were, with dresses up their thighs. What did he know of them? They even rode astride the pillion of motor cycles, with their tight skirts indecently high - what company for a decent boy!

Her own circumscribed girlhood, from the orphanage to service, had given her no inkling of the joyous exuberance of the post-war youngsters, hardly less moral than she but uninhibited in their play. She didn't know, and she knew that she didn't know, and feared for her son with a lonely, angry fear that boded ill for any woman whom he might love. She was jealous of a life opening up for Willy that might have echoed her own had the tragedy of the war not intervened.

Willy sensed the vague hostility in his mother. Not that they saw much of each other, as Gwen left the house before he was up and he usually spent his evenings at school, or roaming the countryside, or reading in his room. He was quite unaware of his poor mother's distress.

On the following Friday, Willy removed his best trousers from under the mattress where they had been pressed, and carefully brushed out the spring marks, then, having shaved the slight down from his upper lip and chin, put on the clean, white shirt that Gwen had hung over his chair - he was glad she had. Then he chose the best of his two neckties and pulled on his jacket; this was rather large for him, but it had been bought with the idea of him filling out before the suit was worn out.

He tried his best to see himself in the little swing mirror that stood on his chest of drawers and decided that he had done his best, and went downstairs.

"Thanks for doing my shirt mum," he called.

Gwen's resentment melted at once. She came to the kitchen door.

"My! You do look smart. I hope she'll appreciate it!"

"Oh mum.' Don't start again, I don't really know her. I just like her, she's pretty. All this said with his head down while he fastened his laces and Gwen unable to see his red cheeks. Gwen felt so pleased. At least he was talking.

"Well enjoy yourself, I'll leave your cocoa." was all she could think of saying.

When Willy reached the church hall, there was a quarter of an hour to go before the time set for the start of the function. There were some ladies there, evidently part of the organisation, but few others. Even the band had not arrived. He decided he would walk down to the town for a while and time his return so that he would not be conspicuous. He spent a long half hour loitering along the shops, almost to the harbour. Strolling back, he met some youths whom he recognised as the group that Jerry had been with. "Seen Jerry?" they enquired. "Well, if you do, tell 'im we'll see 'im at the club house," they said.

Jerry understood this to mean the rowing club and suddenly realised that there were a lot of young men going in that direction. "Must be a do on, or something," he told himself.

When he got back to the hall, he could hear the band playing, so he paid his one shilling and threepence in the porch and went in. To his dismay there were no more than a score of people there, and most were girls. The boys who had herded themselves around the door last time were conspicuous by their absence. One couple, and three lots of girls in pairs were on the floor and the seats around the hall were almost empty. He looked around and realised that he was being noticed by the few seated girls and, in the same moment, he became aware that he had been appraised and rejected by the sophisticates nearest him.

"Oh Lord!" he thought. "Everyone'll see me." He wandered out again. "Not going, are you sonny?" enquired the man who issued the entrance tickets, "We'll want all the men we can get tonight, with the rowing club dance on. Here, let me mark your ticket so You can come in again it'll soon buck up, so come on back."

"I will," said Willy, "I just want to get some fags." He walked around the churchyard for another half hour, keeping a look out all the time for Madge, then decided as it was nine o'clock, he had better return as Madge must have arrived by now. It suddenly occurred to him that she might have been in the cloakroom when he first went in. He lit a cigarette and tried to appear nonchalant as he entered the hall again. It was still poorly attended, and a quick look around told him that Madge was not there. He had taken it for granted that she would be, and he felt suddenly desolate as the hopes that had buoyed him up all the week, evaporated. Then he saw Hilda, the girl who had been with Madge at the previous dance. Hilda had seen him, before he had seen her, and had quickly decided that anyone was better than no one. She bore down on him with pretended surprise.

"Hello Will," she said brightly, "got a fag to spare?" Willy produced ten Wills' in their golden packet and offered her one, giving her his half smoked cigarette to light it from.

"Are you expecting Madge?"

"Oh no, not really. Well, yes, perhaps," he stammered.

Hilda inhaled deeply, shaking back her bobbed hair and blowing the smoke out between her teeth. (Just like a man, thought Willy, in disgust).

"She's not coming. She was, I mean she meant to, but the kids got a rash, measles I expect, so she had to stay with them."

Willy's heart sank. The evening was suddenly a bore, and he wanted to go home.

Hilda had weighed him up. "Come on," she said, taking his arm. "Let's sit, I've been on my feet since half past six this morning, and they're killing me."

Willy found himself being led to the top of the hall to where they had sat previously. "Madge and me generally sit here," she volunteered. Willy was no conversationalist, and Hilda might have been excused if she had given up, and found another partner forthwith, but she was well aware that the men were outnumbered ten to one, and she was determined to hang on to Willy until ten o'clock, anyway. Then, after the pubs shut, there might be a few more men drift in to see if there was a chance of picking up a girl to walk home, and, with luck, have a quick fumble with in some doorway on the way.

Hilda was not averse to this manoeuvre, as long as the man was reasonably sober, and would take "no" for an answer to the ultimate question. There was a short drive, lined with shrubs at the house where she and Madge worked, and she had known more than one passionate encounter among them. Not that she even contemplated Willy as such a one. She was wise for her years and recognised in Willy the greenest of green novices at the oldest game of all, but he would do for the moment, and might be prevailed upon to provide a cup of tea at refreshments time.

Tiring of talking to an unresponsive Willy, she suddenly asked him why he hadn't invited her to dance.

"I can't dance," said Willy, miserably. "I don't know how."

"Come on," she said, "it's easy." And pulling him to his feet, she seized him, and by sheer strength got him circling the room. "One long, two short, now turn." Willy found himself being pulled and pushed along, stumbling and awkward at first, but after a time beginning to shuffle in step with Hilda.

"That's fine," she told him. "Just. keep doing that and by the end of the evening you'll be as good as anybody. Willy persevered and found himself warming to this girl who was giving him so much attention. He realised that with her he was mastering the art of dancing sufficiently to be able to think of asking Madge to dance, when next she came.

When the refreshment interval came along he was feeling almost happy, and bought two teas and chocolate biscuits for himself and Hilda. Hilda noted the improvement in his demeanour and was pleased. "You'll make a good dancer," she told him. "You and Madge will go fine together." Willy flushed at the mention of Madge and a little bird inside him seemed to be beating its wings at the thought of dancing with her.

"You're sweet on her, aren't you?"

The shock of this statement made Willy catch his breath.

"I don't know her really," he said, feeling confused and embarrassed at having his emotions diagnosed so bluntly.

"Course you are, anybody can see that, and you needn't be ashamed to admit it. Madge is a nice girl, she's good, not like me - I'm a bit of a one, I am. Still, she's a good friend to me and I like her."

Willy was listening, yet not, as wild fancies leapt and cavorted in his mind.

"Do you know her well? I mean, where do you see her, and that?"

"I work at the same place - I'm the parlour maid - housemaid in the mornings, mind you, but black dress and cap and apron, afternoons. Madge is the children's nurse; not just a nanny, she's got certificates!" Hilda looked up at Willy as she handed him her cup and saucer to return to the serving lady.

"She likes you, she told me so!"

Willy stared at Hilda, unbelievably dazed, then the blood rushed to his face and his hands shook so that he nearly lost the crockery. There was nothing he could say, speech seemed anchored somewhere in his chest. Hilda saw his agony and a sudden compassion made her turn him about and point him towards the refreshment lady. When he returned he was a little more composed and took Hilda on to the floor again. By shuffling, and walking rather bandy-legged, he managed to get around the room without treading on her feet too often - but his mind was flying wildly in all directions, and he took little heed of poor Hilda's words. When the music stopped and they returned to their seats, Hilda looked at him quite affectionately.

"Didn't you know she was gone on you?"

"No," said Willy, suddenly feeling that he could speak to Hilda in confidence. "I've only seen her twice."

"Well, don't tell her I told you, but she is - and she gets Wednesday off, two to five and eight to eleven, Friday nights seven to eleven. Only if the kids have got measles, she won't be out."

Willy smiled his thanks. "Where do you work," he asked.

"Sycamore Lodge, Parkside," she told him. Then looking up she said "There's a chap I know, just come in. I want to see him - be good!" And she hurried down the hall to greet a man who was propping up the doorway and surveying "the field" through eyes narrowed, peering through the haze of cigarette smoke.

83

Willy sat awhile, with every kind of emotion racing through his head and body. Hilda's words had been so unexpected that he was almost bereft of reason. Then the band stood up and played "The King" and Willy found himself outside in the clean night air. Madge liked him! "She's gone on you". The incredible words went round and round till they suddenly made sense, and delight sent him hurrying home to his little room, where he could sit on the bed and really start to believe it. He felt like laughing, shouting, singing - it couldn't be. Why should she - but she did! It was an hour before he composed himself enough to undress and get into bed, then it was long before he slept.

The next Sunday, as the week before, he positioned himself at the church gate to wait for Madge to arrive with the children. This time he was content to wait, seated on the shop window sill, and concentrated on looking for the blue Essex car that had brought the party to church on the previous week. He told himself that if the children had measles there was little hope of her coming, and though disappointed, he was not in despair when the service commenced and she had not arrived. He crossed the road and ran down a flight of steps opposite. Then on through the maze of cottages that backed Well Street. Boys were playing there, and he passed through them, a tall, gangling youth who could grin to himself at the memory of the terror those narrow streets had held for him just a few years before. All the time he felt he wanted to laugh, and tried in vain to keep his mouth from grinning.

The small boy was feeding Jerry's stock, as he had been on the previous week, and Willy sat on a bundle of hay and discussed the behaviour of the rabbits and pigeons for a while. But presently he fell silent, looking up into the roof of the barn, seeing pictures amongst the cobwebs; happy laughing pictures that sent his mind reeling through a litany of praise and delight. "Madge!" he kept saying, "Madge!"

He went back up Well Street, past the island at the top of Church Street and then down the hill to his home. It was a long way round, but he did not want to risk his mother seeing him wearing his best suit, and having to make up a plausible story to account for it.

Gwen had not seen Willy since the previous evening and as soon as he appeared in the kitchen of the Big House for Sunday dinner, she noticed the brightness in his eyes and his happy expression. She greeted him as usual with "Hello m'dear. Ready for dinner?"

"Cor.' Yes Mum.'"

"Won't be long. Amy's just taken it in. Lay the table, there's a dear. I've got treacle pudding for afters."

Amy appeared and an appetising dish made from the bits and pieces of the meals served in the dining room, was dished up, followed by the boiled duff, all sweet and tacky with golden syrup. There was no conversation while the meal was eaten, apart from "more gravy?" and "few more potatoes?" Meals in the kitchen were strictly functional, not social occasions. Gwen had had words with Amy before Willy arrived, and she made no attempt to tease him. When the meal was done and the clearing up was under way, Amy was sent to clear in the dining room and, in contrast to the week before, Willy started on the washing up without ado, and started whistling *Carolina Moon* as he did so.

Gwen smiled at him. "You seem happy today - enjoy yourself last night?" She watched him as he answered, and saw how alive his face had become, how the corners of his mouth kept twitching, as though a smile or a laugh was on its way. "He's in love," she told herself, "or he thinks he is!"

"Yes," said -Willy, "it's quite good - I'm learning to dance."

"How's that then? Who's showing you?" Desperate curiosity made the words hard to form.

"Oh, some girl, she was on her own and offered to - there's not much to it, just walking and sort of skipping."

Gwen's spirit groaned. "Some girl" - what girl? Who was she; was she after Willy? Gwen saw the inner laughter had gone from his face, and he was frowning at some secret thought.

"I don't like her much, she sweats, but she's good for teaching me." Then, with the hidden grin creeping back, "Next time I go, I'll be able to dance like the others."

"Good," said Gwen, "That'll be nice!'

She wondered what was responsible for his obvious joy - not the girl who sweated, certainly; his face had been solemn with some subtle judgement, but how the delight had come back when he said "Next time I go".

"Well," she thought, "I'll just have to wait and see."

On the next two Fridays, Willy attended the church hall dance. Hilda was always there, but she could only tell him that Madge was fully occupied with the children who all developed measles in succession, so Willy tried to hide his disappointment, and used the time to improve his dancing. By the third week he had got so much confidence that he abandoned Hilda and tried his luck on other long-suffering partners.

Jerry was still away and Willy missed his company. He went often to the dairy yard and even took the cows back to pasture, but he felt restless and frustrated.

His work in the solicitor's office interested him. He was intrigued by the titles of the properties being conveyed, and liked to imagine the forebears of the vendors, and the town as it was in their day. His typing had improved so that he was given most of the correspondence, and many draft deeds, wills and other documents to prepare.

Sometimes he took things to clients' homes, for their signature. This had been an eye-opener to him as he saw the style other people lived in. His own humble home seemed terribly impoverished in comparison and, for the first time, he realised that Gwen and he were poor. Because of Gwen's insistence on good manners and cleanliness, he had always imagined himself to be a cut above the general crowd, but now he discovered that a hard working, artisan family could be affluent by his standards.

The gentry were another thing altogether. He was used to observing their way of life at the Big House, but it was so beyond the bounds of imagination that he might ever live so, and it hardly entered his dreams that he could. He discovered too, that "his" gentry at the Big House, were small beer indeed to some of the real big "nobs", who lived in the mansions overlooking the bay.

He still attended night school, and could loose himself in the literature that was studied. The master invited him to his home on some Sunday afternoons, and he spent happy hours reading and listening to the poets being explained by his mentor. This was Willy's stuff. His mind soared away on the golden beauty of words, and clung to the grief and glory, the simple happiness and the consuming love that minds long dead offered him. There was no public library in the town, but the master had a house that seemed to be built of books, and Willy was given free use of them.

Gwen despaired sometimes at the silence that filled the cottage, while Willy curled his long body on the old sofa and read. Mostly he didn't hear her when she spoke, so she got used to the lonely evenings and almost gave up trying to find some way of reaching companionship with the boy.

It was on a sunny morning, some four weeks after Willy's introduction to social life, that he left the office to buy his elevenses at the cake shop across the road. As always, he ran down the first half of the stairs, then leaning forward on the bannisters, took the lower half in one leap, finishing up by the greengrocer and florist's shop door that was set within the side passage of the building. There he landed with a resounding thump and a full stop, learned after many collisions and near misses with the florist's customers.

"Cor! 'That boy! I'll do 'ee one day!" was the florist's daily threat.

On this occasion, someone had dropped a small spring onion as they left the shop. Willy, all legs and arms, managed to plant his big foot on it, and the next moment was staggering wildly to keep his balance. He groped for the shop door to save himself from falling, and found himself grasping, not the doorpost, but a lady shopper. It was sheer good fortune that the lady had instinctively leaned back to avoid him, or they might both have finished up amongst the display of vegetables arranged on a bench beside the window. Willy's apologies died in his throat as he realised that he was holding Madge in his arms. For a moment he held her, then, panic stricken, he started to say "Sorry - I didn't mean - I slipped I'm very sorry." Madge laughed, looking up from her five foot three inches to his gangling height.

When Madge laughed, her whole face took part, even the short curls hiding her ears seemed to ring little bells of delight. "Do you always fall down?"

Willy gazed at Madge and the gates of heaven opened to him. Madge looked at his red-faced embarrassment and into his eyes, and saw that he loved her. They had to move to allow other shoppers to enter, so found themselves on the pavement. Madge, with a woman's sense, did not leave Willy to grope for words. "I missed going out on Friday," she said, "the children have measles, and I can't leave them - I'm glad to be out shopping to get a bit of fresh air." Willy's tongue was still paralysed, so Madge continued. "The Doctor said that I must have at least an hour's fresh air and exercise while I'm nursing the kids, so I'm doing the shopping." She gave a little sway towards him, and an impish smile, "and I'm glad I met you.'"

Willy found himself swimming in a sense of warm pleasure. He knew that they both realised that they were in love. Suddenly shyness left him and he looked at her with worship in his eyes. "I missed you, I missed you ever so. When will you be able to have time off again?"

"Not for a couple of weeks at least." She paused, glanced away, and with a little sideways turn of her head, said "I'm supposed to go for walks each day." Another pause. "I thought I'd go over to Cockington, perhaps, it's lovely there; I thought perhaps next Saturday 'cos I could have all the afternoon if I asked." She finished this little speech looking straight up into Willy's face.

"Can I come? What time?"

"Two o'clock."

"Where?". A pause for reflection. "Better be by the park gates."

"Yes, I'll be there."

"I've got to go Willy - I've got lots to do, see you Saturday." She walked away, neat in her blue uniform. She didn't walk with a willowy sway, or with the grace of some ethereal being. She was short and broad, and put her feet down firmly in her black brogues. Willy watched her go, and whole stanzas of poems poured through his head. He hurried up the office stairs to scribble down some of the words before the golden moment faded.

"Where the heck you been? And where's me bun?" Demanded the senior clerk. Willy raced back down the stairs, and returned to reality, but every bird ever born was pouring out a chorus of joy in his heart.

Madge walked down through the town, finishing her shopping, then crossed the park to the big villa where she worked. As she went she smiled to herself and at everyone she met. She had been surprised by the intensity of her emotions when she was with Willy. From the moment of her introduction she had found herself attracted to him, in a protective sort of way, but not much more than to the children in her care. She had an outgoing nature, always ready to give affection, but this morning she had found some far deeper feeling doing quite unexpected things to her emotions, and when she had looked at Willy and seen the dumb adoration in his face, she had known instantly that she loved him too, and her soft eyes had brightened and had told Willy so.

Hilda was busy cleaning silver in the kitchen when Madge entered by the back door. She looked up to make some grumble about her work, but when she saw Madge's wide smile and heightened colour, she put down the cloth she was using and asked with eager interest: "Aye, aye, what you been up to then? You got a look like the cat got when its been at the cream!"

Madge put the shopping bag on the table and removed its contents. She couldn't keep a smile from her lips.

"Come on, what's up?"

Madge did not answer her directly, instead, "'Would you stand in for me, in the nursery, on Saturday afternoon if the Missus will let me have the time off?"

"Saturday! - You got a hope, it's my evening off!"

"I'd be back in time, really I would. 'The kids are better, they only to be kept amused so's not to make a row. Please Hilda, I'll do as much for you sometime!"

"What you up to Madge? Come on, you're goin' out with some chap, I can see that in your face! - saw it the moment you come in.'"

"Yes, well, I met Willy Churchward, and he asked me to go for a walk on Saturday afternoon. Be a sport, Hilda, I've been shut up in this house for weeks."

The last part of her plea was lost on Hilda, who was cackling with delight. "Going to take you walking? Innocent little, Willy! Where you going, Shorton Woods?"

Madge flushed with annoyance at the lewd merriment in Hilda's voice, but she let it pass, and waited for Hilda to get over her amusement. "All right then, I'll do it, but not later than six, mind."

"Oh Hilda, thanks ever so much, I do so want to go."

Hilda looked at her and grinned. "Well, make sure 'e be'aves. 'ee looks like a saucy one to me."

"Oh no, he isn't Hilda," said Madge with distress in her voice. "He's quiet and kind, I'm sure he's nice."

"Yes, so'm I. 'ees still wet be'ind the ears if you ask me. Watch out you don't get run in for baby snatching."

Madge grimaced and left the kitchen. Hilda looked thoughtfully after her. Somehow, she thought, it was nice, nice and romantic to see Madge, her high colour and bright eyes, getting so worked up about that silly boy with the big feet, and the terrified look of a cornered cat, when confronted by a woman. "Oh well, good luck to them," she told herself, "they'll soon find out!" Hilda had found out all about life and love as a youngster, barely into her teens, and it all seemed suddenly tawdry and as unromantic as the beer-laden breath of so many groping oafs behind some bush or other.

Madge chose her time carefully and asked the mistress if she could change her Friday evening for the Saturday afternoon.

"I'd like to get some fresh air, Ma'am," she excused herself, "and Hilda will keep an eye on the children, and I would be back by six."

"Very well, Nurse, but only this once, mind. I can't do with my routines being upset."

Saturday was so long in coming. For Madge it was a joy to look forward to. To Willy it was an agony of waiting. Each evening he crossed the park and loitered awhile around the villa that housed his beloved, but he caught no sight of her. Long after he went upstairs to his bedroom, he stood at the window doing things that would have seemed stupid to anyone not in love - like picking out stars and willing them to shine down on Madge so that she would see their twinkling light too, just as he did, at the same time - so forming a bond between them. Or he would tell himself that she would be in bed and asleep after a long, tiring day caring for the children. He thought of her sleeping, but did not dare to think too much, it didn't seem right. Willy's imagination had elevated Madge to the stature of a goddess and his mind built a shrine wherein he worshipped. He was a very unsophisticated boy, who had just awakened to the emotions stimulated by his developing body.

But Saturday did come. Willy dashed home at midday. He lit the gas oven to heat the shepherds pie Gwen had left him, and hurried to change his clothes, putting his office suit on a hanger behind the curtain that made a wardrobe of an alcove in the bedroom wall. He put on grey flannel trousers, grey flannel shirt, a cable-stitched pullover, made for him by Gwen, and a Donegal tweed sportscoat, made for him by the tailor by the church. His pie had hardly started to warm by the time he had washed and dressed, but he wolfed it down, cold and congealed as it was, and was away and down by the park gates by a quarter to two. He did not know which way she would come, so for ten minutes he hovered around the gate in desperate anticipation. Then he saw her, the goddess herself, short and square in an apple green costume, hatless and beaming. She was there, she was his!

Madge was a practical little soul, and she gave Willy no chance to become tongue-tied or abashed, her broad grin dimpling one cheek and welcoming. "Hello Willy - got your walking shoes on, I hope. Where shall we go? You know the place better than I do, or you should do, you've always lived her I believe."

"I thought you said Cockington?"

"Oh, did I? Well, OK if you like, but I don't mind where, so long as it's nice."

Willy had anticipated a ride on the tram, then walking through Cockington to the forge, and around the village; but now, given the choice, he thought of more favourite haunts, nearer home, where he and Jerry had roamed and adventured for years. "Well," he said, "we could go along the cliffs to Broadsands or (here an enthusiastic note crept in) we could go to Shorton Woods."

Madge remembered Hilda's vulgar reference to Shorton Woods and looked keenly at Willy's excited face. There was no guile there, so replied, "Wherever you say, but I must be back by half past five, latest."

"Right," said Willy, "this way then."

Shorton in those days, was unspoiled. The woods clothed a valley that ran from the village of Marldon down to the sea. It was privately owned, but was the haunt of small boys, adventure bent callow youths, with air guns, always optimistic that they might bag a wood pigeon or rook. It was also the haunt of courting couples who sighed sway the long summer evenings before the gentle dusk brought out the owls and gave some privacy to their love. Willy, in all innocence, remembered stalking rabbits, crouching long, midge-tormented vigils in hopes of seeing badger cubs, or spying where a blackcap lurked in the depths of a bramble thicket, while it poured its song into the summer sun. It was the first time that he had ever been in the company of a girl alone and he had no thoughts on how to spend the afternoon beyond the sheer bliss of being with her.

There were two quiet roads that had to be walked before the fields and hedgerows met the town - a mere couple of hundred yards beyond the Big House, where Willy's mother worked. Willy carefully avoided the road that led past the house and took another that looped around behind it.

Once in the lanes, the small-talk laboriously stimulated by Madge, died away, and for a little while only the country sounds kept up a conversation. Then Willy pulled a stalk of sorrel and, stripping the leaves, put them in his mouth. "You can eat these," he said, "they're called Zour Zabs."

From then on, Madge found Willy an articulate guide to the countryside, naming flowers and plants, identifying birds, full of talk of bygone adventures. They were not hurrying, the lane was steep and rutted, and every gateway presented an opportunity to pause awhile and look down on the town and bay, the view becoming ever more wide as they gained height. They came to a sharp turn in the lane where the hazel trees met in an arch above them, and formed a tunnel some two hundred yards long. Madge stood and looked along its length, "It's almost like being under water," she said. The sun, where it pierced the leaves, sprinkled little discs of light on the ground. "It's like the bottom of a pond," she murmured.

"And you, like some lovely water maiden," said Willy, suddenly brave in the pleasure of her nearness to him. "'That was nice, Willy. That was a very nice thing to say."

"It's true, Madge, you look beautiful with the sun sparkling on your hair." Then, suddenly intense, he stood, a good head taller than she, looking down at her upturned face, and in a voice quiet and full of emotion "There is apple blossom in your cheeks, wallflowers in your eyes and soft, sweet rose petals in your lips." As he spoke he stooped towards her slightly, and Madge, her cheeks flushed, moved away. Willy checked and felt the blood rush to his face. "Oh gosh! I'm sorry, I was thinking aloud, please don't be cross!"

"I'm not cross, I'm flattered. I'm just surprised, 'cos I'm not beautiful, though its nice of you to say so."

Willy thought to himself "Heavens, I didn't mean to say that, it wasn't half good enough."

Madge thought, "If I hadn't moved I believe he'd have kissed me."

Kissing, in respectable circles such as those Willy and Madge lived in, was a serious thing to do, almost like plighting a troth. If the girl was good and the fellow was a rascal, it was almost like rape, and if the boy was honest and the girl naughty, it spelt the beginning of a decline in the young man's standards. If both were kissing lightly, then, they were "not nice to know", and unwelcome to the generally strict conventions of the artisan fraternity. Madge had no doubts as to Willy. She had recognised from their first meeting that he was an unsophisticated, inexperienced boy, desperately in love with her and talking from his heart. She was by no means wordly-wise herself, but had been brought up to decency, honesty and cleanliness as a natural way of life.

Madge moved to the gateway and Willy followed her. The meadow rough grazing, thistles and docks grew in abundance. The grass was cropped by sheep and rabbits. Beside the hedge was a well-trodden path that led to the woods that bordered the far end of the field. The gate was padlocked.

"Come on," said Willy, "the woods are over here." Showing off, at the same time, by mounting the middle bar of the gate, leaning over the top, grasping the middle bar on the other side and cartwheeling over.

"I hope you don't expect me to do that!"

Willy laughed in sheer amusement. He laughed aloud - something he seldom did, but everything was joyous then. "Climb up, I'll help you over." Madge sat on the top rail and swung her sturdy legs over. Willy reached for her and she put her hands on his shoulders and jumped. Willy, totally unprepared for Madge's healthy eight stone, failed to brace himself, and the next moment was on his back. Madge, whom he had clutched in reflexed need, fell on top of him. She scrambled to her knees, then burst into laughter.

"Willy Churchward! Do you always fall down?" They both laughed delightedly, then Willy became apologetic.

"Oh gosh! I'm sorry, I was trying to help you down." The ground was dry and the day warm. Madge looked down at him then took his arms and half lifted him to a sitting position where he faced her.

"You're not hurt?"

"No, no." Then suddenly concerned, "You're not, are you?"

Madge shook her head. "I think we've come far enough, it's a good way back and I'd rather be here in the sun, than in the woods, they look spooky!"

"All right," said Willy, leaping up. Let's just go up on the bank by the gorse bushes. You can hear the seed pods popping in the heat, we'll sit down there for a bit, then we can go back another way I know."

He offered Madge his hand and helped her to her feet. Her hand was firm, but warm, and the touch thrilled him. Except for the time that he had danced with her, he had never touched her intentionally. Apart from knocking her down twice, or almost, this was his first physical contact with her, and he loved the moment. They moved a few yards to some rising ground and reached a little arbor amongst the gorse. The sweet coconut scent of the blossom was heavy on the air and, as Willy had predicted, the snap of exploding seed pods was all around. They seated themselves side by side, and Willy took off his jacket and placed it for Madge to lean on.

"It is hot, isn't it!" she said, I'll take off my coat for a while." So saying she wriggled out of the apple green jacket, and Willy was fascinated to see the thrust and vibration of her breasts against the thin white blouse enclosing them. "Oh Madge! You darling, you beautiful darling!" were the words whispering behind his eyes. He said nothing but Madge had seen the sudden look of surprised wonder on his face, and with a gentle, natural movement, she placed one arm across her bosom as if to straighten her collar, then let it stay there. She lay, reclining, on the bank. Willy sat, knees to chin, long arms enclosing them.

There were grasshoppers and bumble bees loud against the myriad sounds of insect life so busy in the gorse; bird song and cattle noise, muted by distance, and on the warm grass were Madge and Willy, three feet apart, both looking down the valley but wholly conscious of each other

Then Willy said "Keep quite still, there's a slow-worm by your leg." Madge looked and drew her legs up in alarm.

"It's a snake."

"No it isn't, it's quite harmless, look." Reaching out Willy lifted the beautiful yellow-brown creature by its middle between his finger and thumb. "It's a lizard really, only it's not got any legs. You have to be careful or it will drop off its tail."

"I don't like it, it looks like a snake to me!" said Madge.

Willy leaned over and let the animal go under the bushes. "Me and Jerry caught five once. Jerry took them to school in a box and they got out. Cor! You should have seen Miss Blake, the teacher, and the girls, they were standing on the benches and screaming. When Jerry caught them again, one dropped its tail and some boy put it in a girl's inkwell, still wriggling!" Willy related the incident with such glee that Madge could visualise the naughty boy of years ago, and loved him for it.

"I bet you and Jerry were a couple of rascals," she said. "Tell me about yourself."

Willy's story was told in a few sentences, but Madge wanted more. "You mean there's just you and your mum?"

"Yes," replied Willy.

"I think your mum must be ever so lonely."

"Oh no," said Willy, even though the thought had never occurred to him. "She's all right!"

"But what does she do, when she's finished work in the evenings?"

Willy looked away over the hazy bay and frowned in concentration. "Well, I suppose she looks after me!"

"Doesn't she go to pictures, or whist drives?"

"No."

"Well, Willy Churchward, you ought to take her to the pictures sometimes, it sounds as if she deserves it."

"Jerry doesn't take his mum - none of the chaps do."

"Well, you ought to tell her to go anyway, it'd do her good!"

It seemed to Willy that somehow some of the magic had suddenly gone. He had been so busy hugging his love within himself, and delighting in the company of this wonderful girl, that the unexpected criticism and the introduction of his mother into his idyll, seemed to cloud the sunshine, and still the whisper of teeming, tiny things all around him. Madge felt something of his dismay and sat up, hunching her knees the same as he.

"You've got a hole in your stocking."

"Oh damn!" wailed Madge. "They're new ones, first time on; it must have been when you fell over with me."

"Willy felt another shock. Madge wasn't smiling, she looked cross.

"Oh well, it doesn't matter," she said.

As she made the remark she pulled her skirt tight across her legs just above her knees and spitting on her finger, applied moisture to the top of the run in her stocking. Willy suddenly realised that it was the first time he had really noticed a girl's legs. They were different. His bony legs had great knee-caps standing out like plates. Madge's knees were smooth and round, she didn't seem to have knee caps at all, and there was some sort of beauty about her legs that called to something in him that had only just become aware of the mysterious allure of a woman's body.

She looked at him sideways. "Sorry to nag you about your mum," she said, "and it was my fault you fell down."

"I was looking at your knees," Willy said, ignoring her apology. "I think they're beautiful."

Madge turned to him and saw the intense look on his face, his bright eyes and heightened colour. She giggled, "That's all right then."

("That's far enough today Willy, my lad," she told herself).

Somehow it seemed that the early spell was broken. Willy no longer felt shy in her company and when Madge got to her feet, he jumped up too, and brushed some broken grasses from her skirt. Madge pretended not to notice, but she was fully aware that the boy Willy, who had cartwheeled over the gate and sat beside her on the grass, had got to his feet a man.

"Come on, let's go," she said.

Willy led the way down to the woods in the lower part of the valley, where there was a proper path following the stream. They walked along quite happily, Madge drawing him to speak of himself and of his adventures with Jerry. "You must miss him," she said.

"Oh, I don't know. I don't think I will so much, not now I've met you!"

They were walking along the narrow path in single file, with Madge in front, so he couldn't see how she took this information. There was no reply, so with new-found confidence he continued. "You will go dancing with me on Fridays, won't you? - please, or (here he took a plunge into barely-considered opportunism) perhaps we could go to pictures?"

"So we could, with your mum."

"Oh, Madge! You don't mean it do you? - I mean, I want to go with you, just you." The path had widened and he could walk beside her. "Madge, I want you to go out with me. Will you please?"

They stopped and faced each other. Willy's pleading face looking down into her soft brown eyes, and flushed, dimpled cheek.

"I'll see you at the dance next week and perhaps I'll go out with you again - it depends!"

She knew it didn't "depend" at all. She knew she would go wherever he wanted to take her, but she was a sensible little thing, and she had found that the transformation of Willy from an attractive, awkward boy, to the blushing, but ardent, young man, was a little disturbing. She didn't want to commit herself too far. Once again, as he stood above her, Willy felt the tremendous desire to draw her to him, feel her warm body in his arms and kiss her sweet mouth. He did not try to do so, it was one thing to yearn, quite another to take such a liberty.

Madge didn't slip away so quickly this time. She, too, felt the strange magnetism of sex. She felt a happiness that came from love, and would have liked to have ruffled his hair and snuggled against him, but he was too tall for the action to come easily, and the moment passed.

"Can I say you are my girl?"

"No, Willy, you can't. I haven't said so, have I? You must wait and see."

They resumed walking. "Well, as far as I'm concerned, you've been my girl ever since that dance, but I won't tell anyone till you say so."

Almost at the end of the valley, before the town was reached, there was a little zoo called locally The Jungle.

"Let's go in, it's early yet!"

Willy paid the two sixpences and they passed around a sprawling farmhouse and found themselves in a small meadow with swings and a seesaw, several tethered goats, a donkey and a clutch of peafowl.

"The monkeys are around here," said Willy, moving towards a wire-fronted barn, where half a dozen sad looking monkeys swung down at their approach, obviously looking for food.

"Oh, what a shame," said Madge, I could have brought something for them if I'd known."

The zoo didn't take long to explore. A large bird of prey sat alone in a narrow cage. A grubby looking badger was curled into the corner of another and a flock of noisy geese and a solitary peacock completed the exhibits. There were a few children playing on the swings and a little family were being given seesaws by their parents.

"I don't like it much," said Madge. "Those poor monkeys, and that eagle (brown buzzard, Willy mentally corrected her) they all look so sad ought to be free."

"Yes," said Willy, "especially the badger!"

They had circled the farm buildings and now came to the front of the farmhouse. Here there were tables and folding chairs and a sign saying "Refreshments - Cream Teas 1/6d".

"Hey," said Willy, "I could do with something to eat! - Shall we?"

"Yes, let's."

A bell pealed somewhere at the rear of the house when Willy pulled the bell handle, and a hubbub of barking broke out, soon stopped by a commanding female voice. Then a large lady appeared; she had flour up to her elbows and did not seem too pleased to see them.

"Yes?" she enquired.

"Two teas, please, with jam and cream," said Willy, as if it was an everyday occurrence for him to order a meal, instead of the very first time, "and can I have lots?"

"You can 'ave a double helping if you want, but it'll cost you twice."

"That's all right," said Willy.

"I'll be ten minutes, I got no 'elp today and kettle's off the boil."

"All right, we can wait."

They unfolded a couple of chairs and sat beside a table under a lichen covered apple tree. There did not seem much to talk about, and Willy sat with his elbows on the table, moving his bony bottom now and again as the slatted seats bit. Madge seemed to have no such problem. She produced a tiny mirror and a comb, and began to tidy her hair. Willy watched, fascinated. All those little movements, the turn and tilt of her head, the supple movement of her arms and the delightful little quiverings that went on in the part just below her throat.

"You'll know me again!" said Madge, acknowledging that she was aware of his scrutiny.

"I'd know you if there were a million people all around you, and I'd know you were there, even if I was blindfolded."

Madge smiled into the mirror and busied herself with a little piece of hair beside one ear. ("Oh Willy, Willy," she said to herself. "I don't know if I can handle you - you're lovely and I love you, but when you talk like that, I'm afraid. I'm just an ordinary, plump - no, be honest, - fat girl. I've got good eyes, but that's all. It's no use making out I'm a goddess, because I'm not.")

Willy, now quite at ease and unabashed, continued to watch her, grinning with the pleasure of her close company. The large lady appeared with a tray. On it were cups saucers, plates, knives, a huge plate of baps, a jar of jam and a bowl of cream.

"I'll have to come again with the tea," she said. "There wasn't room with two lots of all." She came back with a large enamel teapot and a matching milk jug. "'That's four and six," she said, "bring the tray back when you go."

Willy paid her. ("Four and six - gosh," he thought) and she retired.

"I've counted them, there's twelve scones - you're not going to eat that lot surely?" queried Madge.

"You watch!" said Willy, well knowing the vast amounts of fodder that his skinny frame could absorb without effort or any visible effect. The jam was new, home-made raspberry, and the cream was a great thick lump with a golden blanket on top of it, quite an inch thick. Once they started, Madge as well as Willy realised how hungry they were, and once she had taken a bite of the new-baked bap, with real fruit jam and thick scalded cream, she decided to forget that whatever she ate made her put on weight, and ate with gusto. When there were six baps left she decided that was enough and sat back while Willy piled jam and cream on another and another. The jam gave out with two baps to go, so Madge said "Save the last two for the monkeys."

Willy grinned, scraping out the cream bowl on to a piece broken from the two left on the plate. "One more cup of tea first," he said. While they were drinking this, Madge said "How long will it take for me to get back home?"

"Oh, half an hour."

"Well, it's gone half past four, and I truly mustn't be late."

"Righto, but there's tons of time."

Madge stacked the tray and Willy set off to return it. Madge meanwhile went to a little door marked Ladies. When she reappeared, she found Willy anxiously scouting around for her. "Oh! That's where you were!"

"Yes, and if I'd known what it was like I'd have waited," she said.

They left the zoo and came to the last of the lane before the town. Willy came to a sudden decision and spoke before he knew it. "Please can I take your arm?"

"Yes, if you want."

"I've wanted to, only I thought you might not like me to."

While making this admission, he had slipped his arm through hers, and a great joyous delight sent tremors to all parts of him. He didn't understand them but they were wonderful. After a moment, Madge said "Here, you're too tall, I'll take your arm." That was even better, and Willy shortened his lumbering stride to match her short step more nearly.

It was all too soon, for Willy, when they reached the park. They had time in hand and dawdled through it. Children were feeding ducks on the pond and they stood and watched a while.

"You've still got ten minutes," said Willy, "let's sit down till it's time. When will I see you again?"

"Oh! I expect I'll be back to normal next week, but you work on Wednesday afternoons don't you, so I expect I'll go to the church dance on Friday."

A whole week seemed ages to Willy. "Can't you get even an hour off some evening? I'd meet you at your gate and we could come and sit here or somewhere. I (here inspiration flashed) could bring some chips and we could have them together!"

Madge laughed. "I don't know about chips, but perhaps I could get away some time - I'll have to see. I'll let you know somehow. Can I telephone you at work?"

"Yes, but make it sound important, nobody has ever rung me before, and they might not like it."

"Right then, now I'll have to go. Thanks for a lovely afternoon and the tea."

They walked to the road and Madge squeezed his arm. "Thanks again," she said and was gone behind the high "Tradesmen's Entrance" door before Willy could answer. So, waiting until her footsteps ceased, he set off home. Gwen was not yet in, so he made himself a pot of tea and cut a big slice of bread pudding from Gwen's favourite standby that was usually available in the cupboard. Gwen always made full use of the bits of 'overs' at the Big House, and bread pudding was a good way of filling the apparently bottomless pit of Willy's stomach. Willy munched the heavy stuff, sweet with sultanas and custard, and. remembered they never fed the monkeys after all.

101

He felt despondent somehow, after the excitement of the early afternoon. Some little cloud had seemed to come between them, and Madge had seemed less responsive than at first. Willy felt a new feeling for her he was no longer singing songs to her in his heart. He was seeing her as sweet, desirable womanhood, and he trembled at the warmth and sweetness of her body, even though he had done no more than hold her arm through his, and held her hand when helping her to her feet. It was all new and, until then, unthought of. He lived again the brief moment when he had brushed the grass from her skirt. He had not thought to touch her, but the roundness of her bottom that he felt quiver, ever so briefly, under his hand, did things to his own body that had embarrassed him. Now he liked to remember it.

Madge went up to the attic room she shared with Hilda, changed into her uniform and went down to the nursery. Hilda was glad to see her.

"Cor! I don't know how you put up with 'em. Had a nice time? Been good I 'ope! Where you been?"

"It was nice, I enjoyed it." Then in a mischievous moment, added "We went to Shorton Woods."

Hilda did not respond with the vulgar guffaw Madge expected.

"I bet it was nice up there today, I'd 'ave liked to 'ave gone too."

"Willy took me to tea at the Jungle."

"Oh, did he then, quite the gent, eh! Well, I'm off, glad you had a good time." Hilda thumped up the back stairs to the attic. A moment later she was back again, peering around the nursery door, then holding Madge's stocking out with her finger through the hole. "And how did this 'appen then?" she enquired, with a wicked grin, "and there's mud on your skirt. Don't tell me Willy got you on the ground!"

"Willy's not like that, I fell off a gate!"

"Oh aye, a likely story - but I won't tell!" Madge made to grab the stocking, but Hilda retreated giggling.

Later, when the children were in bed, Madge sat at the nursery window. It was twilight and the blackbirds were having their neurotic pre-roost clamour. She thought there must be a cat disturbing them and peered all ways to see. There was no cat, but wandering through the park was Willy, unable to rest or stay far from her. She saw him idly kicking at some bit of litter on the path. He did not see her and soon passed out of sight.

"Oh lor!" thought Madge, "what am I going to do with him. He's so good, and I do love him, but I'm not dotty about him, like he is on me. I'll have to tell him, I suppose, but I needn't yet, but he loves me so and I want him too, but I can't hurt him."

Madge sighed. She was lonely. She had no friends because she had no opportunity to make any. Hilda was all right, but not her sort, and now Willy had suddenly appeared and everything was complicated.

She was happy in her job as children's nurse. She loved the children. She was well fed and comfortably housed. The pay was small, but it was enough for her modest needs and she had no wish to change her mode of life for some time yet. The eldest of her charges was seven, the youngest of the four was just gone two, and there was another on the way. Her mistress was aloof, but kind, and there seemed no reason why she should want to be rid of Madge for several years to come, should she want to stay.

Madge decided to find out more about Willy, then weigh up the possibilities, before making any decisions. "The trouble is," she told herself, "he's so lovely, and I'll never be able to give him up if I once let him really love me - I'll have to be ever so sensible."

Darkness had crept up from the grass, the bushes had become dim shapes, trees still stood out on the skyline but lovers were already moving out of the little pools of light around the few park lights, and establishing themselves on the shadowy benches. Madge moved away from the window and put on the light. Immediately, the outside dimness was utter darkness against the window pane. She pulled the blind down and shut out Willy, who was just in time to glimpse her as he made another circuit of the park.

Gwen was worried about Willy. He had come home well after dark, and gone upstairs at once. Gwen called to him that there was tea in the pot if he wanted it; this reminded Willy that it was some time since he had stuffed himself with cream baps at the Jungle and bread pudding later, and that he was hungry once again. He clattered down the stairs, his large shoes resounding on the oilcloth. "I could eat something, mum."

"I thought you must have had tea somewhere!"

"I did, up at the Jungle, but I'm hungry again."

"You been up the Jungle? Who with?" This last query was out before Gwen could stop from asking.

"I went for a walk up Shorton with my girl, and we had tea there."

"I didn't know you had a girl! You never mentioned her before."

"Well, I've only just got to know her really, and she isn't really my girl, only I think she is, but she says she's not - not yet anyway."

Gwen listened with a sense of stupefaction. It was so unexpected to be almost unreal - her Willy, talking about "his girl". Willy, who had never given any indication that he was involved with anyone. True, she had noticed his restlessness and irritability, and there had been that talk of dancing, but never any reason to think that he had actually got a girl. As the truth sank in, her defences rose. Who was this woman? And what was she doing to Willy?

Gwen had used the pause in the conversation to go to the cupboard and bring out a thick chunk of fruit cake, salvaged from the Big House. She put it on the table and turned to pour the tea.

"What's she called then?"

Willy had his mouth full, but when he could speak he surprised Gwen by becoming suddenly animated, his face flushed and he looked eager and happy.

"She's called Madge and she's a children's nurse, down by the park." Another bite and steady chewing, then - "She's beautiful! She was sitting beside a gorse bush this afternoon, with all the golden blossom shimmering around her as if she was an angel caught by some painter and put in a golden frame! I love her!"

Gwen didn't know what to say - she knew that her son was given to daydreams and she had occasionally glanced through the exercise books that he filled with words and expressions that she hardly understood. Mr Fox had told her years before "Your boy's a poet - don't fetter his mind with menial, mundane work, let him grow in spirit so that he may perhaps see his promised land, even though he may not reach it". "Like Moses," Miss Blake had interjected, thereby throwing Mr Fox into some confusion, and the realisation that he was talking way above Gwen's head. "Yes, like Moses," he had said. Gwen had always remembered the gist of this instruction. "That's bible," she had told herself.

At the time she had looked on Willy as some sort of embryonic prophet but as he grew up she just thought of him as being educated beyond her range of vocabulary, so conversation diminished between them. In a gorse bush, in a golden frame! Her mind, still shocked, stammered towards understanding.

"Well, why don't you bring her home? I'll make a nice tea!" Willy suddenly felt a rush of gratitude and affection towards his mother.

"I'd like to Mum, but she doesn't get much time off. Usually it's Wednesday afternoons, and I'm working, and Friday evenings; only today she had the afternoon instead because the kids have got measles. I'll ask her though."

"Well, be sure to give me warning, I want the place to be looking nice."

"It always does and I don't expect she's fussy."

"Well, you let me know, don't bring her unexpectedly will you. I can't do with that!"

"All right, I won't. Anything else to eat?"

Well, Gwen thought, love hasn't affected his appetite, and to look at him you'd think I starved him! "What's she like?" (Apart from being an angel in a gorse bush she thought to herself.).

Willy munched on while he considered the question. "She's got brown hair, and lovely brown eyes, and she's got a dimple in this cheek." He put a finger to his own cheek to show where.

"Is she tall, like you?"

"No, she's not. She's short really, she just comes up to my chin."

Up~to his chin, thought Gwen, seeing in her mind's eye a dark eyed, angelic creature, reaching up to Willy, the top of her dark head nestled under his chin. Oh! What can I do against that, she thought in despair not yet having considered that this creature was in any way desirable, but rather what she could do to protect the boy from her wiles.

"I'm going to see her one evening. She's going to telephone me."

"Right, well you mind what you're doing son, don't forget you're only seventeen, that's young yet, and you've got to get on in your job, and there's lots of time yet." Gwen's desperate attempts to put her fears into words, trailed off, her worried face carrying on the warning with a pleading that even Willy could not fail to notice.

"Mum, I'm growing up, I'm a man. I know what I'm doing. I love her, and I'm not being foolish, so don't worry - just wish me luck and be nice to Madge when you meet her." Quite to Gwen's surprise, Willy took her by the shoulders and kissed her, then ran off upstairs to his sanctuary. Gwen sat down. "Well'." she thought. "Well!"

On the following Wednesday afternoon, there was a letter addressed to 'W. Churchward, Esq.' among the firm's third delivery post. It had been hand delivered and was marked 'Personal'. Willy knew at once that it was from Madge, and slipped it into his pocket before taking the afternoon's post into the boss's office.

Back at his desk, he opened the envelope with great excitement "Dear Will" she had written. "I will be able to pop out for ten minutes this evening, about eight. Can you be by the back entrance?" The note concluded "Love Madge".

"Love Madge!" "Love Madge!" The two words rang in Willy's head like a peal of bells. He read and re-read the note, seeing in his mind's eye Madge's hand writing each word, and concluding with the wonderful word that he took to be a literal admission of her love. "She loves me, she says so, she loves me!"

Willy must have been in a sort of trance for a while, for he suddenly became aware that the senior clerk was standing beside him and had asked him something; what, he did not know. "Oh sorry!" (hastily putting the note in his pocket). "I didn't hear you, what was it?"

The older man surveyed Willy's embarrassed face. "I've been asking you for the Primley Abstract, for the last five minutes (thirty seconds would have been nearer the truth), and I've had to come out myself to get it! What the dickens happened to you? You look as if you've been moonstruck! For goodness sake, shake yourself, and get on with your work!" Willy did his best, but his heart was not in it that afternoon. He got through it somehow, most of the time with a far-away look, and a secret smile on his face, then he raced home and in the sanctuary of his room he held, read and re-read Madge's note, exulting at the words, and doing all the simple, silly things that lovers have done for aeons.

By half past seven, he was walking with apparent nonchalance, past the parkside villa, then a brief pause at the end of the road and back again. It seemed hours before Madge opened the gate and stood waiting for him. He ran to her and without ado, took her in his arms and kissed her on her lips. Madge was surprised. She hadn't expected Willy to be so bold, but when he held her away for a moment, laughing in pure joy, then kissed her again, she returned the kiss, and all her intentions of being firm and sensible melted in the sweetness of her happiness.

"Oh Will!" was all she could say, and neither had need to speak for long moments. Then, from close against his chest, she said "Will, dear Will. I've got to talk to you, there's things I must tell you, but there's no time now, I can't stay. I might be wanted inside. I'll have to go, I really must." The moments ticked away and still they held close, Madge's words muffled as he held her, her head little higher than the crook of his shoulder and her face upturned.

"What must you tell me? Is it important? Nothing matters except that I love you, and you love me."

"Yes it does Will, we can love, but I may not be here much longer, I might have to go abroad, then what will we do?"

"Go abroad! Go away!" The words seemed frozen in the air between them. "Why, where, when?" The queries were like sobs of anguish. "You can't. You mustn't!" Madge pulled herself away and her face showed pitiful distress as she looked at Willy standing, white-faced and aghast. The wonderful moments were so swiftly fled that she burst into tears. Willy hugged her again, but she struggled free and, in near panic, said that she must go, she was afraid of what might be happening to the children. "It won't be yet, Will, but I had to tell you. Meet me here on Saturday night and I'll explain it all." With that she was gone, and Willy stood, still stunned by the news, then slowly and miserably, he made his way home.

It was late when he arrived there, for he had wandered down to the harbour, then along the cliffs and over the meadows to the golf course, then back to the main road and towards home again. He still could not believe that Madge had come into his life, that he had had those few moments of bliss, only to know that she was not for him. She must be! She had to be! It was gone eleven before he crept into the house and wearily mounted the stairs.

" 'night dear! Had a nice time?" came his mother's voice from her room. "Yes'm. Good night," he replied.

Willy had told Gwen that he was meeting Madge this evening, and Gwen had worried over him as the night drew on, wondering where he was, eventually comforting herself with the conclusion that he had taken Madge to the pictures, then had some chips to eat on the way home. That meant he wouldn't be back before eleven, she told herself, and now he was in, and she could sleep.

Sleep did not come to Willy though. He lay on his bed without removing his clothes. He felt soaked in misery. The only crumb of comfort he had was her last words to him "It won't be yet". He felt weary of thinking, his brain seemed to go around and around like a caged creature seeking escape and finding none. Eventually he undressed and got into bed. He pulled the bedclothes over his head, a little boy again, and held the only little bit of Madge that he possessed, her note that he had received that morning. He held it to his face and wept, and weeping, slept.

Next morning, he was late waking. Gwen called him twice before she left for the Big House. He had no time for breakfast and was almost late for work. He scooped the early morning post from the letter box and took it upstairs to the office. It was expected of him that he would place the letters on the boss's desk, neatly piled, big envelopes at the bottom, small on top, all the right way up. As he shuffled the letters he came to a thick, unstamped one, addressed to "W. Churchward Esq." It was in his pocket with him hardly knowing how it happened. He could feel his heart thumping like a drum.

Swiftly, he went through his chores, emptying the wastepaper basket, putting clean blotting paper in the blotter, straightening the pink tied files on the table, emptying the ashtray and flapping a duster around the most obvious places. Then he went into the outer office and stood, looking white and woebegone before the senior clerk.

"I'm sorry, I don't feel well, I think I'll have to go home," he said making the request in the way of a statement. "I must have eaten something!"

"Well, if you've just got the runs, you can go here, no need to go home," said the man.

"No, it's not that, I feel ill, I keep getting dizzy."' In truth the terror Willy felt, because of the news he feared he had in his pocket, made his wan cheeks an effective plaintiff for his request. The senior clerk had a liking for Willy. He did his work well and neatly, and caused no trouble though given to daydreaming at times, especially lately the man had noticed.

"Have you done inside?"

"Yes."

"Oh well, shove off then, take some Andrews' and lay down a bit. Come back after lunch - you'll be' all right by then!"

"Oh thanks, I'll try to," said Willy gratefully, hardly hearing the parting advice given him as he hurried away.

Back in his room, he took the letter from his pocket, staring at the writing, then as lovers will, he kissed the words, and pushing his thumb under the flap, he ripped the envelope open and took the letter out. It was a long letter, but for long moments he looked no further than the opening words "My dearest Will."

His pounding heart steadied itself, "She loves me," he told himself, "it must be all right." Then he lay on the bed and read on.

She had written:

My dearest, dearest Will,

It is nearly eleven, and I can"t go to sleep until I've explained things to you. I've had to wait for Hilda to go to sleep before I could come down here to the nursery to write. I've only got a candle, so I hope you can read it.

I do love you Will, truly I do, and I know that you love me. You have ever since that dance, I could tell, and I loved you then too, but I pretended to myself that I didn't, and last Saturday when we went for that walk, I was loving you all the time, only I couldn't let myself. Then, this evening, I only meant to talk to you and say I'd meet you again on Saturday, but you kissed me, and I couldn't help it. I do love you so.

Will, my dearest, you don't know anything about me, you've never asked, and I haven't told you, so I've got to tell you now. My dad and mum live in Bristol. When I was at school I told them that I wanted to be a nurse when I left but I had to wait till I was sixteen and then they wouldn't take me because I hadn't taken my Junior Oxford Examination. I had been at home helping mum till then. I've got three sisters and two brothers, so there was plenty to do and they didn't make me take a job anywhere because mum didn't want me to go into service, and dad said the factory girls were common. They were upset when the hospital wouldn't take me, and then mum said that I could go to work as a nanny. I wanted to, because I love kids and often take our neighbours' and I've always helped with our own.

Dad said if I was going to be a nanny, I would do it properly and take a training course so that I could get a situation as a proper child's nurse, so he sent me to a convent for a year and the nuns taught me everything. There were six of us there and we worked in the orphanage the nuns ran. Dad had to pay for me and find my uniform and things, and it was hard on him and mum to do it because he only got three pounds a week, and there's the five and mum at home without me to pay for.

Anyway, I passed an exam and they gave me a certificate signed Mother Superior, and a doctor, to say I was proficient. Then mum saw an advertisement in the evening paper for a child's nurse, competent to take charge of small children and be responsible for them when the parents were away. I went to see the lady and when she saw my certificate, she said I could have a month's trial. Then she said I was satisfactory and could stay, only I had to agree to stay for three years and to go anywhere they went to live, and to go abroad with them if they went.

The master is a Major in the army. They have been in Egypt and now he is at Plymouth, but the mistress doesn't want to live there, so he comes home weekends. Anyway, Will, that's what I wanted to tell you before we really became lovers, but you kissed me and I couldn't. They may not go abroad again, but they may move to Yorkshire and the mistress says she expects they'll go abroad, so I don't know what will happen. I was happy with the four kids I look after and I didn't expect to fall in love. Still, we're both seventeen and three years will go by and they may stay here. Meet me here on Friday at 6 o'clock, my dearest, and we'll go for a walk instead of the dance and I'll try and explain better.

Love Madge x x x

P.S. I'm going to get up early and put this in your letter box.

The misery lifted from Willy's spirit. She loved him, so what else mattered. He'd forget the going away, perhaps they never would. Anyway, they'd get around it somehow. He read the letter again and again, matching the loving and the kisses, till he felt confident and happy once again. He went downstairs and cooked the egg Gwen had left him, then with the rest of the morning free he went down Well Street to the dairyman and, finding him there, helped him to swill out the milk churns and shovel out the milking shed. Just occasionally, the shock he had had sent a nervous quiver through his stomach, but the world seemed bright again, and he'd see his lovely again on Friday. In the afternoon, he went back to work.

That evening, he wrote a long letter to Madge. It was full of hope and minimised the threat of parting. It was loving too, Willy used all his literary skill in eulogising her attractions. He had long been writing for the pleasure of so doing, and now found delight in being able to give his thoughts free rein in a beautifully worded paean of praise of his beloved.

That done, he took it to the house where she lived, and dropped it into the letterbox. He waited awhile in hope of glimpsing her at the window where she had appeared before, but she did not come and eventually he left.

Hilda found the letter and took it to Madge. "Good job the Missus didn't see it first," she said. "She'd have wanted to know who it was from, and you'd have got a lecture about keeping away from men."

Madge had had a miserable day. She had been long getting to sleep after writing to Willy. She had been up early to deliver the letter and the unhappy day had seemed endless. She had looked so tired and unwell that even her mistress had noticed and asked if she was ill. "I do hope you are not sickening for something," she had said, thinking at once of the children.

"Oh no, Ma'am, it's just the usual," Madge had said, so allaying the woman's fears that her bridge parties would be threatened.

Willy's letter gave her the first happy moment of the day, though she dreaded to read what it contained. She pocketed the envelope and continued ironing the children's clothes, as she had been doing when Hilda brought her the letter.

"Aren't you going to read it then?" Hilda asked. "You been looking like death warmed up all day - what's up? 'ave you and the innocent Willy had a row?"

Madge said "No, we haven't quarrelled, but things are a bit difficult, it's nothing much, I'll read it later."

Hilda decided there was no point in waiting to hear if there was any excitement to be got from the missive, so said "Well, I'm done, see you later," and left the children's day nursery where she had found Madge. Hilda, as house-cum-parlour maid, was free after eight. Madge was obliged to stay within earshot of the children except on her Friday evening off. Once Hilda had gone, the ironing was abandoned, and Madge opened Willy's letter. She read it disbelievingly. Her knowledge of literature was scant, being confined to an occasional novel, and the perusal of her employer's periodicals. When she was at home she had read the serials in a weekly magazine that her mother took. These were of love unrequited, rags to riches romances, and such-like fantasies, none of which she had ever identified with, and she found Willy's letter so loving, so filled with tender concern and so rich in delightful praise of herself, that she held it to her breast and hugged it as she might have nursed Willy's head on that warm haven, had he been there.

She knew, from the last two meetings, that Willy had, what seemed to her, an unusual manner of speech, and very nice it was too, like that once in the lane when he had spoken of apple blossom and wall flowers and roses; that had made her want to giggle, but this letter was beautiful, and as she nursed it against her, she felt excitement and warmth and longing. She knew then that she could never part from him again, they were for each other, come what may. On Friday, she decided, they must make plans.

Friday came at last, and Madge was free of the children. Willy was waiting for her at the gate, but this time there was no enthusiastic hugging. Both felt some apprehension. "Hello," they both said to each other. Then Madge slipped her arm through his and smiled up at him. "Let's sit over by the pond," she said, "and have a talk."

At that time of day the children had all gone home to tea and bed. The old people had drifted away too, and it was too early for courting couples to stake their claims to the pond-side seats, so they had the place to themselves and chose a seat set in a little hedge of veronicas, where the painted ladies and red admirals trod the blooms. Only the ducks noticed them, and they soon paddled away when no paper bags appeared to indicate a meal.

They sat awhile, somewhat ill at ease, then Willy put his arm around her shoulders, turned her face to him and kissed her, gently, on her mouth. She looked into his eyes, so close to hers, and had no need to speak.

"You do love me, don't you?" whispered Willy. She nodded and offered her lips again.

"That was a lovely letter you wrote me. I'll keep it always and always, whatever happens," she said. They were quiet again for quite a while, holding each other close, and lost in loving. The chaffinches 'pink pinked' around their feet as they searched for crumbs. Mallards quacked their raucous way around the pond, two blackbirds chased by with hysterical chatter, but the lovers heard only the soft breath flowing between them and the steady murmur of their hearts.

"Darling," said Madge at last. ("Darling!" thought Willy, rejoicing). "We've got to make plans. I've thought and thought, and I can't think what to do really. I can't leave this job, 'cos my dad and mum would be mad, and they've done so much for me, they'd think I was throwing it all away, I know they would. I promised when I got the job, to stay, and I thought in three years we would only be twenty, and wherever I went I'd always love you and come back to you, and anyway we could save up meanwhile. I could easy save ten shillings most weeks.

Madge dared not say "We couldn't afford to get married for ages," because Willy had not asked her to marry him, that was his prerogative, and in any case they could be "unofficially engaged" for years. Willy wouldn't get a man's wage for ages yet.

Neither of them had looked so far ahead as when they might marry. Madge knew it must be years away; Willy had given it no thought at all. To him it was an inevitable future, sometime, after an inescapable waiting for maturity, and the means to provide a home and living, but meanwhile, an idyllic loving - that was all he desired.

The frustrations to come had not been thought of. Content for the moment that she should be in his arms, he made no effort to extend the suggestions that Madge had made, but after a while she insisted on talking, "Would you wait for me?"

"All my life, if I have to - but I won't, because I'll find a way, I'm sure I will."

Still nothing definite. Madge, with her face buried in his jacket, her muffled voice disguising the determination in it, asked "Will, when we can, will you want to marry me?"

"Of course I will. Will you?"

"Will I what?"

"Will you marry me?"

At this she turned her face up to his again. Her cheeks were red, maybe partly from pressure against his chest, but proclaiming the joy that shone in her eyes. "Oh Will, my lovely Will, I'll love you for ever and ever." Then their words were smothered in kisses and no more was said for a long time.

During that time of holding close and caressing, Willy had thought "I'm engaged! I've said that I will marry her. How can I? When will I earn enough? Where will we live? What will mum say?" It was not that he regretted promising her, or that he hadn't assumed that they would marry eventually, but the step had been taken so suddenly, as to leave him aghast at such an impetuous decision.

Madge was happy, she cuddled close contentedly. Will had asked her to wed him; the problems to come could all be met, if he was prepared to wait. She would be a good wife, she'd fix things, they'd manage.

They had sat there by the pond for quite an hour, when they realised that a few dog walkers and elderly, lonely men, were circling the pond and eyeing them with curiosity and disfavour. One lady, walking a pekinese on a lead, tut-tutted at them and a nasty old man stationed himself on the opposite side of the pond, hoping to see what he hoped to see.

"Let's go somewhere," Willy suggested. "How about second house?"

"It's too early, it's only seven."

"Well, how about coming home with me and meeting my mum - she told me I could bring you."

"Oh lor! I don't know, I won't know what to say! What have you told her about me?"

"I said I loved you and you were beautiful."

"Oh Will, I'm not, what will she think?"

"Come on home with me and find out."

Gwen had got home soon after six that evening. She was tired and felt depressed. The cottage was dark after the sunny kitchen at the Big House, and smelt stuffy after being closed all day. It was particularly dark at the back where the quarry face rose straight up, close to the windows. There was always a smell of mould about the place. She opened the front door to let some air circulate. The goldfinch sensed the change of atmosphere and started its restless hopping from perch to perch and back again. "Sweet, swe-e-e-t," said Gwen to the bird, but got no response. The place was tidy, except for some dirty dishes and scattered crumbs in the kitchen, showing her that Willy had eaten the meals she had left him. She supposed he would be out late as he had been the last few Fridays.

"Out with that girl!" she thought. "Well, it had to happen I suppose! At least he told me." She washed up and cleared away a litter of papers Willy had left, then sat in the old armchair by the front window and put her tired legs up on the edge of the high fender. She started to knit. The window was behind her, and just too high for her to see out when seated, so only her ears told her that Will's big feet were on the front steps, and she heard his voice saying something to someone outside. He was saying "Wait a minute till I see if mum's in." for he had just remembered Gwen's admonishment not to bring his girl home without warning her.

The door opened and Willy's head was poked in. "Mum, I've brought Madge to meet you."

Dismay, then panic, then anger swept through Gwen. She'd got her work clothes on, and her comfortable slippers with holes in the toes, and she hadn't done her hair and there was nothing in the larder to offer. "Oh lord! What a thing to do," her spirit wailed.

"Sorry I didn't warn you, mum, but I didn't know I was going to bring her." Then, brightly, and with no condescension intended, "You look all right, and she wouldn't mind."

"Well, you can't leave her on the step," said Gwen, angrily. Bring her in." Oh, what must I look like? What'll she think? thought Gwen, trying to straighten herself up, patting her hair and hooking up the top of her corset through her dress.

"Mum, this is Madge. Madge, this is me mum." Then in a flood of contrition - "The best mum in the world."

Gwen heard the introduction, and, if she had not been so preoccupied in sizing up the girl, she would have wanted to weep. Willy had never been one to pay her compliments, but all her attention was on Madge, and a wave of relief and something akin to pleasure, heartened

116

her enormously. From Willy's description, she had imagined some dark-eyed nymph, a child, hardly come to womanhood, proud in her beauty and clever in her entrancement of Willy, Gwen's little boy!

She saw instead, a young girl, obviously nervous, as nervous as Gwen was herself. Dark-eyed, yes, and pretty, with healthy colouring and a warm smile dimpling her cheek, but of the nymph there was little trace, for she saw at once that Madge was, well, plump'. She had a bust line as big as her own, the long slim legs she had imagined, were sturdy and round. Altogether, Gwen thought, moving to greet Madge, a nice girl.

"Hello," said Gwen, holding out her hand. "Hello," said Madge, taking it. "I'm sorry you didn't know I was coming. Will just asked me, my mum would've been mad if my brother brought a girl home like that."

"Well, you're welcome," said Gwen, hardly believing her ears as she said so, but Madge was welcome. Gwen suddenly realised how good it would be to have a nice girl like this calling.

"Have you had your tea?" enquired Gwen, hoping the answer would be yes".

"Oh, don't fuss mum, we're going to second house, and I thought there'd be time to bring Madge here first."

"Yes, well, sit down dear. Willy tells me you are a nurse, that's nice. Do you like it? Are the people good to you?"

Gwen flustered on, but soon found that Madge was easy to talk to, and for half an hour Madge chattered about "her children" and her work and training. Then about her family in Bristol and then, bravely, about the possibility that she might have to go abroad with the family.

"But surely," said Gwen. "If there is another baby (fancy me talking about that in front of Willy," she thought) they won't be going until it's born?"

"No," said Madge, but it depends where he goes. If it's a bad climate she will stay here with the children, only then, if she does, she will go to live near her parents in Yorkshire. She told me that."

Willy had been silent till then, standing, bending forward with his elbows on the window sill, letting the women chat on. Now he turned, and going to stand beside Madge, he said to Gwen "When Madge goes away, we'll wait for each other, and when her time's up, she'll come back to me. We've promised that."

"Yes," said Gwen, "of course you will, and you're both very young yet, and lots of things can happen." Gwen's mind was busy thinking of what those things might be, and she found herself hoping that whatever did happen, this nice girl would come back to her son.

"Come on then," said Willy, "we'd better be going, there'll be a queue tonight."

"What are you going to see?" asked Gwen.

"Oh, it's a wild west and a travelogue, and there's the heavyweight match on the Pathe." Gwen thought: much he cares for what's on, as long as he's got his girl beside him! Then she thought, I suppose it's the first time he's ever taken a girl!

Gwen was right. In the warmth and darkness of the cinema, Willy paid scant attention to the screen. Madge was warm beside him, her hand in his and the fragrance that seemed to exude from her ("like a flower at evening," thought Willy), filled his doting senses. Afterwards they walked through the park again, found a secluded spot and stayed there till the church clock struck eleven, and Madge had to hurry in. "I'll look out for you at Sunday school tomorrow" promised Willy

That he did next morning. He saw her and her little charges arrive by car. Madge looked around, her cheeks flushed when she saw him propped on the shoemaker's window, then she smiled and waved a little, rather furtive wave, and vanished into the church porch.

Willy noted her employer, a tall, dark man, with a heavy moustache. He looked like a soldier, Willy decided, and not likely to take kindly to 'followers'. During the service, Willy lay on the flat top of a tomb in the churchyard. There was a huge lime tree between him and the sun, so that hundreds of little, twinkling sunbeams filtered through. There was a clear sky, and he could look straight up into the vault, high, very high, where soaring gulls constantly circled.

It was warm, the lichen covered slate irked his bony frame, but he felt nothing but happiness. The swifts, screaming around the church, were no more exultant than he. It was only four weeks ago, h thought, that he had waited here to glimpse her, hardly daring to hope that she would recognise him, and now they were 'walking out' and were promised to each other.

When the service ended, he assumed a nonchalant stance near the porch. The car was waiting across the road so Willy decided to stay within the churchyard. Madge came out with the children clustered around her. She looked happy to see him, and he decided that in her neat, blue uniform, she looked pretty, and a picture of glowing health. For an instant he thought 'Lor', I can't match up to her.

Madge delayed their departure by wiping the children's noses, saying, as she bent to do so, "You should have come in, you could've sat by me."

Willy said "I've been waiting outside, thinking of you - I'll come in next week." Madge moved off and was gone.

Willy went to midday dinner at the Big House, as usual on Sunday, and Gwen was pleased to see him looking so happy. When the meal was served, Amy remarked archly "A little bird told me that somebody I know was queuing at the pictures last night with a girl on his arm."

Gwen flushed with annoyance, "If you mean Willy, I know he was, and a very nice girl she is too." Willy hadn't had chance to reply himself and he glanced at his mother with relief and pride. They exchanged looks and a bond of affection seemed to join them. They smiled knowingly at each other and Gwen thought, isn't it lovely.

Willy thought: Good old mum - I didn't think she'd understand!

Now that they were officially "keeping company" it was hard on both of them to have just one evening a week together. Willy suggested that Madge got her Wednesday afternoon changed to Saturday, but Madge explained that her mistress rested each afternoon and played bridge in the evening. She spent a lot of time with her children, sometimes taking them for walks and playing with them in the nursery, but Madge always had to be there, or on call, because madam could not be tied; that was why she employed Madge. "It's my job," she told Willy. "I agreed when I took it."

So Willy wrote Madge letters and sent her some of his favourite books to read. "It's good of you Will, but I just don't get the time!"

"No time to read!" It's an appalling thing, said Willy. "You miss so much.'"

"If you had my job, you'd understand, but I love your letters - I read them in bed." The thought of her reading his letters in the cosy privacy of her bed, gave Willy all sorts of thoughts, and there were some letters that he wrote that he did not dare to send.

During the week, Willy's days were spent as they had been before the arrival of Madge. Jerry was still working away and did not come home at weekends even. Willy was surprised when he called in on the dairyman one day, to see Jerry's rabbits gone.

"He' s gived' em away," said the dairyman. "I'm giving up here, me rheumatics is too bad, and they've sold me fields for building; cows be going to market week after next." The little tragedy, so curtly expressed, did not disturb Willy, who in the unconscious arrogance of his youth, had no inkling of the loneliness and despair of the dairyman, bereft of his sons, of his livestock, of his living.

"What about his pigeons?" Willy asked.

"Oh, they'm breeding wild anyway, nobody ab'em bin feeding 'em and they'm looking arter themsels."

In years to come, the pigeons and their progeny, were to populate the whole area. The town was creeping out into the country as the new post-war world blossomed. There were still many horse-drawn vehicles, but cars and lorries were commonplace, and the country village style of living was only preserved in little enclaves within the town. Colley End, the Green, Well Street and the church area was one of these, but within that area, people were changing. Women seldom appeared in their "service" aprons or men's caps. The younger generation would have none of the old ways. Well Street was more prosperous, better dressed and better behaved the homes were more comfortably furnished and gas lighting was installed in the better end. Effie Wilkins still flaunted her sins to the disgust, or envy, of whoever saw her red head (still flaming after all those years, but doubtless with the assistance of potions now available at all the chemists) being proudly carried along the terraces. Boys were no longer dressed in father's cut-downs, nor had their heads shaved. A way of life had gone; only in the old were the echoes to be heard.

Although the standard of living had improved, life was still hard. The post-war boom in employment had fizzled out even before the rest of the country felt the pinch. The union battles and the General Strike had made little impression on the town, but by the end of the twenties there was little chance of employment for anyone coming new, or growing up in the area. Willy, safely ensconced in his job at the solicitors, was very aware that he was fortunate. Many businessmen argued politics and commerce within his hearing, and he had acquired a knowledgeable opinion on most current affairs. In that way he was very mature. He continued his studies at night school and still found great pleasure in the English literature class. The school had closed for the summer months, but Willy kept up his friendship with the English master and called on him each week, borrowing books, discussing them, and of late listening with fascination to the literary programmes broadcast on the master's wireless.

Gwen often wondered what Willy spent so much time doing up in his bedroom, and was bemused by the sheaves of paper, all written in Willy's hand, that were usually clipped in neat piles on his table. Sometimes she read them, wondering at their meaning, or smiling to herself at some amusing phrase. It keeps him happy, she thought.

Some of these essays and poems Willy took to the master and shyly asked his opinion, then the two of them would go through the writing, word by word, correcting, substituting, paragraphing, until the article was concise and correct.

Willy's poems were a special pleasure to the master, who taught him how to compose in classical form. These were happy hours for Willy and the master, and it was the master who decided that it was time that Willy turned his literary ability to good account. Without telling Willy, he began submitting essays to various magazines in hope of publication.

The summer took its course. Holidaymakers swelled the town's population. Swindon week came and went - the same GWR families staying at the same little guesthouses that they came to every year.

Willy and Madge spent her evening off together, sometimes in the lanes and countryside, sometimes at the cinema. These were cherished hours of rapture, that were so long in coming and so quickly past. On Sunday mornings, Willy used to wait for Madge to take the children to church, then slip in after her. The children were given their scripture lessons in a chantry chapel at the side of the nave. Parents and others who brought them, sat in the nave, within sight of the children but not with them.

After giving Madge time enough to deliver her charges, get them settled, and then go to a seat, Willy would enter the same seat, prop his behind on it, lean forward on his arm, count twenty, then sit up in a casual manner, pulling up the knees of his trousers, blowing his nose, and generally trying to disguise the fact that he was edging nearer to Madge. There were never more than half a dozen adults present, so he didn't have to be very clever. Madge used to wriggle her nice bottom along the seat too, so that in no time they were close together and could hold hands. Madge was given to the giggles at Willy's antics, but managed to appear quite conventionally pious. It was terrible not being able to kiss, but it all made the week shorter for them.

There was one week in August when they had Madge's Wednesday afternoon together. It was the town regatta, when the shops and offices closed at midday. They spent the afternoon at the fair that accompanied the annual regattas along the coast; it was the townsfolk's annual holiday and everyone was there.

Willy dug deep into his savings and spent more than two pounds, taking Madge on the swings, roundabouts, cake walk and helterskelter. He tried to show off at the coconut shies, but his aim was woefully bad, so he took her instead to the hall of mirrors where they laughed themselves silly.

Everyone was happy, and all the girls and boys were arm in arm or waisting each other. Willy and Madge took advantage of the lack of conventions and were exhilarated with the noise, music and carnival atmosphere. They had both moved into another world, a world of their own, but one that coloured every little happening of the day, and this day was very special for them.

The year faded, the baby was born, and there was no word of the family moving. Willy tended to forget the threat, just hoping that it wouldn't happen. Sometimes, on a Wednesday, Madge called on Gwen. At first it was always a short visit, because Madge had to return by five, and Gwen could hardly get home by then, but she had taken a great liking to the girl, and one day had a bright idea, suggesting to Madge that she came to the Big House instead. So Madge did, and Gwen bustled about in the big kitchen, chatting away and getting them tea and a piece of cake before Madge had to leave. They both enjoyed these visits and Gwen was disappointed if Madge did not show up. She used to think to herself - Dave and me was married when I was her age.

Of course, Dave was seven years her senior, not a seventeen year old, like Willy She told herself that Willy would be a lucky boy if Madge stayed with him. The thought that Madge expected to leave the town for a long period worried her. I hope she waits for 'im, was her unspoken thought each time they met; sometimes followed by - and to think I used to worry that he'd meet some girl, and what he'd do.

As the winter approached and the days got shorter, the longer evenings meant that willy and Madge were able to enfold themselves on a sheltered park seat almost from the time that Madge was free to leave the house. There was a healthy honesty about their loving, Madge allowed Willy to delight in the warmth and softness of her body, hugged close to him. But when his longings were betrayed by fingers that undid buttons or hands that probed too nearly, she gently but firmly, dissuaded him. "No, my love, we mustn't!" Then she would kiss his mouth and caress his head, pulling him down to her and whispering consolation.

Once, when she sat across his knees, holding his hands to stop them exploring, she put them on her knees, then pulled her skirt tight across her thighs about three inches above them, and told him "There, you can go so far, but that's the limit!"

Willy laughed and kissed her round knees "All right then, I love your knees! They're nice knees! Too nice for my peace of mind though!" Madge hugged him. She was sorely tempted to relax her new made regulations right away - more out of love for him than for her own desires, for she was a healthy girl and wanted to be petted, but she had been brought up with a strong moral code, and would have felt that she had soiled, not just herself, but Willy too, if she had allowed him such privileges so soon in their courtship. She used to lie in bed after those blissful evenings and relive the happy moments, remember his loving words, and all his longings so easily shown, and she would say to herself "Ah Will, my darling, I'll make up for it, my love. When we're married. I'll give you so much love you'll wonder where I find it all!"

Thereafter, as the nights grew colder and they did their loving either in the darkness of the cinema, or wrapped in each other's overcoats in some nook in the park or down by the sea, Willy would caress the soft curves and crevices, warm and so close, but so far under her clothes, and wheedle her "Still limits?" And she would nod reluctant agreement, and he seldom made it difficult for her. He had the feeling that it would be indecent to spoil her cherished privacy.

He, too, used to lie abed afterwards and think, almost despairingly, of what might have been, then he looked forward to what would be, when they were wed. In this he gave his imagination full rein. It was imagination, for he had little more than shamefaced glimpses of reproductions of classical pictures to guide him, them and the parts of Madge that wobbled when he handled them. He determined to get Jerry to tell him things when he saw him again. Jerry would be sure to know Till then a woman's body was a wonderful mystery to him. There was a lot he knew, but, he decided, there was a lot that puzzled him. Madge wasn't quite as innocent as Willy. She had been warned to be careful of men by her mother when she was about to leave home, but the poor woman was inarticulate and confused, and confined herself to saying "Well, be careful and don't let anyone try to maul you about!"

Madge had learned the clinical processes of reproduction on her nursing course, but, since meeting Willy and having her sensitivities aroused, she had looked at the immature genitals of her little charges during bath times and wondered. It was only when she had unintentionally placed her hand on Willy, when moving in his arms, and feeling an unexpected hardness that she had thought with satisfaction "So that's how it happens."

Chapter 9

Willy had enrolled for another winter session at the night school and looked forward to a series of university extension lectures that the literature class was to attend en bloc, and to another evening each week with a debating society, being organised by the master, Mr Watts.

The only times that he felt happier and more fulfilled than at school, was when he was writing long letters to Madge, or held her in his arms. One evening, when the class had settled down and Mr Watts had opened up a discussion on Galsworthy's *Forsyte Saga*, he took a copy of the weekly called *Answers* from his desk. He carried it folded in his hand as he wandered between the desks, and reaching Willy, he paused until Willy had finished a criticism he was making of a classmate's opinion of Fleur and Wilfred's association. Then he placed the periodical in front of him, and said "Have a look at page 10, column 4."

He stood beside Willy and put in a word here and there to keep the discussion flowing, while Willy opened the paper, expecting to find some advertisement for books or something similar. What he found was a half column, headed "From my office window" and under it an edited version of an essay he had written months before. Below it was the name W. Churchward. It was quite incredible. His name, printed under an essay, in a national magazine. He looked up at his tutor, who grinned down on him.

"How did they get it?"

"Ah! That's what I want to tell you - wait for me afterwards. In the meantime read this." He gave Willy an envelope bearing his name but the master's address. He opened it. Inside was a letterhead with the name of an amalgamated paper group and a stereotype letter:

Dear Contributor,
I am pleased to tell you that your contribution 'From my Office

Window" (this had been written in, in a space left for a title) *has been accepted, and will be published in* Answers (again written in) *for week December 4th.*

I enclose a cheque for half a quinea (written in) *and suggest that you forward further contributions of a similar nature for my consideration.*

Yours faithfully.

The master had returned to his high desk, and when Willy looked up from the letter, he beamed delightedly down on him, and gave him a thumbs-up sign.

Willy was really astounded. He read and re-read the little article, wondering at seeing his name under it, hardly believing it could be true. But it was. There was the article, there was the letter, there was the cheque. After a few moments, the shock wore off and delight took its place. "Hey everybody! I've had an essay published and I've got half a guinea for it!" Galsworthy was forgotten. All the class crowded around him. The master joined in too, even more delighted than Willy.

The paper was passed from hand to hand, congratulations and ribald comment were called to him. There was only one spoilsport who sought to diminish Willy's triumph by saying *"Answers!* Good God! who on earth reads rubbish like that? If I had something published I'd want it to be in 'T.P.'s' at least."

"Only place you'd get anything you wrote published, would be on the wall of some bog," replied one of his class-mates amiably, and joined in the general hubbub of talk.

After a while the class was called to attention. Willy was handed back the paper, and *The White Monkey* returned for discussion.

Willy was so pleased, he didn't bother to join in, and Mr Watts, understanding, did not call upon him. After class Willy plied the master with questions, but the man just said that he'd put it in for Willy, and suggested that they went to his home to talk for a while. This they did. Mrs Watts was all smiles. She knew her husband was happy, and was pleased with Willy for making him so. She had a tray with fruit cake and teacups on it waiting, and went off to boil up the kettle. Then the master told Willy how he had been sending off his work for months. "I did it from this address because I didn't want you to get discouraged when they were rejected. That chap Jenkins said Answers is not exactly a high class publication, but it is a start, and half a guinea is better than a kick up the backside. Lots of authors have to write pot boilers to keep the wolf from the door. You've got writing ability Will, it's something you can work on. Find out what different papers publish, and write for the readers they cater for. I'll not be surprised if you do well, once you've had a few articles accepted."

Over the tea and cake, Mr Watts broached the subject of Willy's future. "Are you content to stay where you are? What'll you earn when you're twenty-one - two pounds and ten shillings? What's fifty shillings - not exactly riches! Supposing you want to marry (his face was lowered to drink from his cup as he said this), I imagine you'll want to one day." He looked up then, and Willy blushed scarlet proclaiming at once his interest in the question.

"Oh ho, you've got a girl eh! Well, good for you. Adam must have his Eve, but having a girl, and getting married, are two different things. What are you now? Seventeen, going eighteen - well, you can't marry for years yet, can you. Have a hundred pounds in the bank and three quid a week coming in, that's my advice. Now! Why not really try to write for a living - try journalism, freelancing at first to see how you get on. There's lots to be learned in it, it's a trade, or rather an art, but I believe you can do it."

Here his wife interrupted from the head of the stairs - "Do you know it's gone eleven?"

"Oh dear, the voice of authority," grumbled her husband. "Well, young man, think of what I've said and come and see me on Sunday afternoon and we'll talk some more."

Willy left, having his thanks brushed aside with the excuse that he was no more pleased than the man himself. It was past midnight before Willy got into bed. The hot water bottle that his mother put between the sheets on winter nights, had been there for hours, and was nearly cold. Willy pulled his feet up to try and catch a little warmth from his body and lay there, knees to chin, shivering, as the cold bed sucked the warmth from him, but he did not notice it. That's how it always was on cold nights, and that night was not a night to bother about such trivial things. He was wide awake. The excitement of seeing his name in print had subsided to a cosy satisfaction, but that was not what was keeping him wide-eyed and sleepless. It was the idea of breaking away from his ordered life and making a way for himself and a livelihood with his pen. He had no idea how he should start, but dismissed that with the intention of seeking the advice of Mr Watts on the following Sunday.

What kept him wide awake was the master's advice on marriage. Willy had not had anyone to talk to about Madge except his mother, and he had lacked a father figure to go to for help. Mr Watt's calm acceptance of his intention to marry, and the man to man simplicity of his approach made him feel strangely content. "Adam must have his Eve", struck a chord in his mind, and had suddenly made the somewhat abstract idea that he would marry Madge a reality, and he hugged the idea to himself with a sort of glory. All he had to do now was to write and write, and make a steady income, then he would marry Madge.

Sleep approached, and with it warmth. As he drowsed, he said to himself "My Eve" and fell to thinking how Madge would look clad only in a fig leaf. He lingered over this delicious thought a while, then went on to wondering how she would look without it! Strange, he thought, that all those pictures and statues never showed anything down there, and that was silly, there must be something there, there had to be! He fell asleep determining to ask Jerry when he came home again.

Gwen was up, and had got Willy's porridge cooked and in the porringer, and was over at the Big House by half past seven. Willy, whose job commenced at nine, usually lay in bed till gone half past eight, then got up, had a perfunctory wash under the cold tap in the kitchen, bolted his porridge and a mug of milk and just made it to the office in time. This day; however, he woke early, in spite of his late night, and having gone through his morning ritual, was finished with half an hour to spare, and surprised Gwen by appearing in her kitchen at the Big House, when she was at her busiest, cooking eggs and bacon for the family.

"Hello Mum."

"What ever brings you here?"

"Thought you might like to read this."

"Willy! How can I stop to read now, I'm busy. They'll be ringing in a moment."

"Well, just look at it." Willy had the page folded back and put his finger on the half column.

"Look who it's written by."

"I can't, I really can't, not now, and you'll be late for work - why is it important anyway?"

"Because it's written by W. Churchward. W. Churchward, that's me, Mum. It's an essay I wrote and it's been printed and they've paid me half a guinea!"

"Oh Willy! How grand, that's lovely! Oh Lor! They're ringing. Willy, tell me tonight, but I'm so pleased." She was too. Fancy her Willy having his name in Answers. She wondered what it was he had written, and could hardly wait for the evening to find out.

Willy went through his work light of heart. The sudden broadening of his horizon seemed to make the day full of promise, but most of all it was the realisation that marriage was possible that was exciting him. Till Mr Watts had accepted it as a practical eventuality, the idea had not had substance. Now it was settled, and he just had to get to work to bring it about.

The essay that had been printed was one of many that he had amused himself by writing, months before he had met Madge, and were cameos created around imaginary happenings as seen from the office window. He had followed this inspiration for some time, and had a dozen or more filed away along with several that he had left with the master.

He showed the article to the senior clerk, who read it, and looked at Willy with a new respect, then said "Right then, we'll have your from the window if that's what, you're doing."

Willy laughed, for he was on good terms with the older man, and asked him to cash the cheque in the petty cash. Later the senior clerk spoke to the solicitor. "Young Churchward has had an article printed in *Answers* and got a half guinea for it."

"Has he indeed, well keep him busy, at his age he should keep his nose to the grindstone." When the boss went to lunch he bought a copy of *Answers* and put it in his pocket. He could hardly be seen reading a rag like that - not until he got home.

Willy bought himself a couple of spare copies of the periodical and spent his lunch hour writing to Madge, telling her about it, then he cut it out and enclosed it with the letter, ready to deliver it in the evening.

When Gwen came home he gave her a copy and was pleased by her praise. "Well Mum, it's not much really, but it's a start and I'm going to try lots of ideas, and if I can get them published I'll be able to save for when we get married." This last he said with such certainty that he surprised himself. It was as if he had planned it for months, instead of within the last few hours. He did wonder if he was being over-optimistic, but consoled himself with the thought that Mr Watts would advise him.

On the Friday following, when Willy and his mother were having their evening meal, Gwen said "I suppose you're going out tonight?"

"Yes."

"I just thought, as it's so cold and wet, you could bring Madge here, if you wanted to, there's a whist drive at the school, and Mrs Hammicott asked me to go, it's for the Scouts."

"You never go to whist drives Mum, can you play?"

"Yes, well - not very well, but she says it doesn't matter, and it's more like a social really - with refreshments and that."

Willy thought a moment or two, He had intended to go to the pictures with Madge but, with so much to talk about, a cosy evening by the fire with Madge on his knee, was very attractive. He was surprised at his mother suggesting it, and suddenly realised that she was doing it for him.

"Thanks Mum, very much, it would be nice. I'll ask Madge if she'll come."

"She'll come all right!" thought Gwen, but only said "Well, it's about time I had an evening out sometimes, and it's only opposite, so I won't get drenched on the way." She looked at Willy, seeing how animated he looked, and how bright of eye. It might have been Dave standing there, with the look on his face that he had when he came courting her. She put a hand on his shoulder "I can trust you, can't I?"

"Oh Mum! Of course, I wouldn't, I..." His protestations trailed off as Gwen smiled, and said "I know I can. Anyway, bring her here, I'll be back by half past ten."

She thought to herself - I've brought him up as decent as I could, and he's a good boy, but there's many a maid I'd not leave him with for all that, but this one's all right, I'd bet my life on that.

While Gwen was across the road, sorting her cards with painful care, and driving occasional expert partners near mad with her inept play, Willy and Madge were squeezed into the old armchair before the fire. The oil lamp was on the table, throwing its pool of light well behind them, so that the flaming coals threw flickering light on to their faces as they cuddled close. It was the most intimate situation that they had been in yet. Madge had given Willy her congratulations on the way to the cottage and had told him how pleased and proud she was, then as they whispered together in the firelight, Willy told of how he planned to make himself a real writer, who could provide her with home and comforts, far beyond any he had thought of. Madge listened and encouraged him in his optimism, crooning softly with her face tucked under his chin, and her lips ever ready to reach for his. She was no light weight, and, squeezed into the armchair she caused Willy great discomfort, his bony legs had little resilience to the chair frame against which her well-cushioned thighs pressed them. After a while he said "My legs have gone to sleep! Let's put the cushions on the rug and sit on the floor,"

This they did, rearranging themselves, and somehow Madge was lying on her back and Willy was lying across her. He was supporting himself on his elbows, kissing and nuzzling her face and throat, in a rising passion. She had never seemed more desirable and his yearnings became so great they became difficult to control. Madge knew, and said "Let's sit up against the chair, it'll be more comfortable." So they sat, warmed by the fire and loved each other. Twice she took his hands and held them, but gently, and he did not object.

"When we're married Will, you'll be able to love me when ever you want to, and I'll be the best wife you ever could have." It was the first time she had been so explicit and the picture her words conjured up, made his throat contract strangely.

"I can't help wanting to hold you," he told her. "You're so warm and soft, and. it's awfully hard not to feel you."

"I know, my love, and I'm glad you do, it's natural, so you needn't mind, it would spoil things for us afterwards if you did now. I want to wait until we're married, then I'll want you to love me all the time."

She caressed his head as it lay on her breast and, stooping to kiss his ear, she whispered "And I'll want your babies, oh I do want my own babies. I love kids, I'll want a football team!"

Willy sat up, and held her close again, revelling in the prospect. "Do you really want a lot of children?" Madge nodded.

"All you can give me," she said.

Willy had a moment to realise how he had seemed to mature from a youth to a man so quickly. "Well, if it's going to be a football team, I'll have to start writing in earnest!"

They laughed together. "I hope it's a soccer team, not rugby," he told her. "How long do you think we'll have to wait?"

"Till we're twenty, perhaps twenty-one."

"We'll manage somehow by then."

"Three to four years. Gosh! It's a long time."

"Yes, but then it will be for ever."

Gwen made a great to-do, shaking out her umbrella and wiping her feet in the passage before she opened the door. When she did, Madge,was squatting on the hassock by the fire and Willy was sprawled in the chair.

"Win anything?" he asked his mother.

"'fraid not," she said. "Shall I make you two a cup of cocoa?"

Chapter 10

When Jerry left home to go to work in Plymouth, he did so with some relief. At nineteen, going twenty, he found it embarrassing to be living with his mother, knowing full well how she made a living.

Effie always made a point of pretending to be a respectable working woman. She never considered herself to be a tart, not like the two hoydens up the road, who proclaimed their calling by their make-up and style of dress when they loitered around the pubs and along the sea front in the summer. Effie had nothing but contempt for them, and always dressed well and as elegantly as she could, never flamboyantly, never over made-up or perfumed. She was a handsome woman with a statuesque figure, and she made the most of it. She kept her little house well furnished, warm and spotlessly clean. Situated where it was, conveniently central to the town, secluded and approachable from three different directions, she provided a haven for her clients that was comfortable, with an element of refinement. They felt relaxed and cossetted in a secret world that was a pleasure in itself, apart from the delights that her bedroom offered.

To bolster her respectability, she found employment in the town, seeking out morning work that left her free for more lucrative pursuits later in the day. There were several good hotels in the town, and she took work in one or other of them as a chambermaid. This had the added benefit of allowing her contacts with commercial travellers, whom she just happened to meet in the course of her duties, and with one professional glance, was able to form an alliance. Thereafter, several became "regulars" at her little home.

Never, no matter what the sum offered, would she oblige at the hotel. She could never forget the humiliation of the past. The publican's wife's disgust was such as she never intended to invite again. Men she could manage, they were all vulnerable, but a righteous woman's scorn, when earned, was unendurable.

Jerry used to enter the house by the back door, and keep himself as inconspicuous as he could. so as to avoid other traffic on the stairs. This behaviour had developed over the last few years, since acquiring his knowledge of carnal matters.

The chance of work away gave him the opportunity of making the break from Effie that for a long time he had been trying to find an excuse to do. He made no moral censor of Effie's "goings on". He accepted them as part of her, and he was truly devoted to her. He was also very proud of this handsome, vibrant woman, a veritable goddess when dressed for her evening court. All the other women in the road were mean and dowdy in comparison, and not a man who saw her but quickened his step and brightened his eye. But Jerry hated some of her callers. He could not avoid seeing them at times, and it infuriated him to think that beery, pot-bellied letchers should be allowed to have her. (Had he ever told her so, she would have told him that she felt the same, but allowed for her revulsion in the price she charged).

When he told Effie that he was going, she allowed herself a rare expression of affection by giving him a hug, saying "I'll miss you, boy. I like to know you are about, and I'm proud of the way you've got on." Then she got to more practical things, and hid a real sense of loss by questioning him about his needs. Finally, she said Your room will always be here for you, and you can walk in any time, day or night, that you want to."

So Jerry left home, and when he left, having taken the plunge, he knew that he would never return. Willy, and the dairyman, were the only other people that he had enough affection for to be able to regret leaving, otherwise he looked forward to moving, and always his ambitious spirit quested forward for new worlds to conquer.

The firm that employed Jerry was engaged in building houses for the local authority on land just outside Plymouth, and near a village that had existed from time immemorial in a tree-sheltered river valley. It was no more than a church, a public house, a cluster of cottages, a mill, long-disused, by the river, a scattering of farms and farm cottages and the ruins of a manor house set in a tangle of woods and scrublands. The council estate was being built on what had once been the parkland of this property, lying behind the church and reaching away from the river. New roads had been made and the terraces of identical houses were going up apace, each with its strip of garden enclosed by link fencing supported by concrete posts, and barren of trees and protecting walls.

Compared with the ancient dwellings in the village, it was an eyesore, and an affront to the gentle mellowness of the old park. But, as Jerry's workmate pointed out, the houses were light and dry, and easy to live in, not like the dark, often damp, little thatched hovels, so picturesque, but "sich buggers to live in" as the old man said.

Jerry was very fortunate to be working with this man, nearly seventy years of age and a master of his trade. He could make a staircase, a window frame or a coffin, with a precision that seemed effortless, but came from handling and appreciating good timber since his father had set him sweeping up shavings back in the 1860s.

Jerry had joined a small firm with a working boss, four joiners and an apprentice. When he was taken on as a second apprentice, the main work was making window frames, doors and staircases for speculative builders who, during the building boom of the post war years, were buying up land and extending the town on all sides. Jerry soon showed an aptitude for timber work that was noted by the old man, who told the boss - "'ers a gude boy, you let me 'ave' un, 'ers too gude to waste running arrants."

And so Jerry became the old man's slave, never being allowed to get away with anything less than perfection, subject to the old man's curses, ribald criticism, and repetitious trials, that gradually developed his natural ability with his hands, and an affinity with timber and his tools, that at times were rewarded by a grunt from his tutor, and the acceptance of the article, instead of the more usual "Now cut' un orf, and start again".

When Jerry was in his third year, his boss got the contract to build a section of the council estate, and most of the firm moved there, taking on additional joiners from the city. They set up a workshop in a hut near their scene of operations, and there the old man and Jerry laboured to make the frames, doors and stairways as the houses were built.

The village may have been resentful of the new development, but it brought new life and prosperity to the community, so depleted by the war, and post war slump, that hardly a working man continued to live there. The boss had found lodgings with a farmer nearby, and had managed to get the old man and Jerry a room and meals with the lady who ran the village shop and post office.

This was simply her front-room, and until the arrival of the builders, and then new families from the city, she had counted her weekly turnover in shillings. Now she had two lodgers who paid her a pound a week each, and the flow of money into the drawer under the counter, exceeded more in a day than she had taken in a week.

Jerry liked his lodgings. They were in a cottage facing the church. There was a long narrow garden leading from the road to the shop door. The path was right in the middle of the garden, that had current bushes, runner beans and rhubarb on one side and gooseberry bushes and cabbages on the other. There was a narrow border of flowers on each side of the path. He had never lived in a house with a garden before and found it a pleasure to behold. The only snag was that he had to share a room with the old man. They got on well together, but working with him all day, was more than enough of his company. Jerry missed his own room and his comfortable bed. He had to make do with an ancient truckle bed that had probably seen service in the manor house generations before, and the old man snored abominably. He was also having to pay out a pound a week for his board, when his mother would never take more than ten shillings. Jerry considered these things, and decided they were worth enduring for a time if they brought his plans for the future nearer. After a while the old man, no more anxious for Jerry's company than Jerry was for his, got lodgings in one of the completed houses, and Jerry had the room to himself.

Mrs Cooper, his landlady, was not loath to see the old man go for he smoked a reeking pipe that offended her, after twenty years of smokeless widowhood, and splashed the nicotine and saliva from the pipe stem into the fire with scant regard for its surroundings. She found pleasure in mothering Jerry who responded with his usual charm, giving the old lady comfort in his company.

On Saturday afternoons, Jerry caught a bus for the short journey into the city. There had been a time when the village must have been remote from the city, but over the years the city had crept out, engulfing hamlets and farms as it spread, and since the war there. had been a surge of building that consumed the countryside with disastrous speed.

The bus ride took only a quarter of an hour to reach the city centre, where the narrow streets were clogged with traffic and noisy with the whine and squeal of trams. The busy shops intrigued him for he had never been into a departmental store, and the bustle of the market far surpassed that of the one at Totnes. If the weather was fine, he usually found his way to the shore, where he watched the clay-boats loading, and timber and coal being swung ashore. Further along he would find a vantage point and sit and watch the ships coming and going through the sound.

Sometimes a great Atlantic liner would sweep inside the breakwater and a tender would go out to disembark passengers, before the ship steamed on to France. There was always something to be seen, from the sailing barges carrying sand, cement or clay, to the majestic men-of-war that passed in and out of the naval docks.

These ships, big or small, had a fascination for Jerry. He was reminded of his life in the orphanage, from where he had seen navy ships going about their daily business. The only pictures in the home were of men-of-war, Jack Cornwall, the boy V.C., and the king in naval uniform. Most of the boys joined either the Royal Navy or the Merchant Marine when they left the home, and the orphanage was run on navy discipline. He had hated his time there so much that even now, at nearly twenty, he shivered at the memory, yet something seemed to call to him when the great ships steamed by.

One lucky day he saw a great fleet enter the sound. They came in, in line ahead, the mighty battleships with their sixteen-inch guns, the great cruisers and the sleek, low destroyers. He felt a thrilling excitement as he watched them swing into positions and, at some synchronised moment, let their anchor chains roar out. "I wonder what my dad did on one of those?" he thought.

Effie had never even known what ship he was on when he died, and had merely told Jerry, when he had asked, "Well, I used to get an allowance from 'O.S. Wilkins' - with a number."

"Ordinary Seaman," Jerry had thought. But he only joined for the war - else he'd have been a killick or an A.B. at least. He talked to the old man about the navy, and he had suggested that perhaps Jerry could join when his apprenticeship was done.

"Join as a tradesman, there's always work for a chippy aboard, an' you'd see a bit of the world - must be jam these days just goin' around showin' the flag," he had said, then adding "Not that I'd want to, but for a young chap it's all right."

It was an idea that intrigued Jerry, but he did not give serious thought of taking it further. He had other plans and was impatient for his time to be finished so that he could get on with them. After six months working in the workshop, he persuaded his boss to let him go on to the houses themselves to do actual construction work on the floors, roofs and partitions. The work was not nearly as meticulous as the making of fitments and he enjoyed the freer conditions. All the time he stored up knowledge and took advantage of any opportunity to extend his skills.

Being a small firm, seldom employing more than a dozen men, and not involved with union restrictions, it was often possible for Jerry to spend time bricklaying and even tiling. As an apprentice, he was welcome at times to lend a hand wherever one was needed, laying sewers, for instance, and digging and filling footings with the necessary plan reading and level finding, so that over the months he was getting experience in building construction that was necessary for his future plans.

For want of any other confidante, he divulged these to his landlady. She was a kindly soul who had fallen victim to Jerry's charms, and was beginning to look on him as a grandson.

One evening Jerry had come in after work and had helped her to chop up some firewood. There remained, afterwards, a thick, mishapen branch and he decided to saw it up into logs. When he came to do so he found the scaley bark and hard wood unusual. He sniffed the sawn wood, trying to identify it by its scent, but was unsuccessful, and the peculiar twisted shape defeated him too. When he carried the logs in, he asked Mrs Cooper if she knew what wood it was and she proceeded to tease him.

"You're a woodworker, you ought to know, but I bet you can't tell me go on, have a try."

Jerry held a log in his hands, smelled it again, picked at the crocodile skin bark, and shook his head. "I've worked on all British timbers, and foreign hardwoods, but I've got to give up on this; though whatever it is, it must have grown around here or it wouldn't be in its natural state I give up! Do you know?"

"Yes, I know. The tree's still growing not far from here, and it is English. Sit down, boy, and I'll tell you a story."

Jerry put the log on the fire, then took it off again as a small swarm of woodlice crawled out from under the bark. He shook them off into the wood box and replaced it.

Mrs Cooper was sitting at the kitchen table, peeling brussel sprouts, for tomorrow's dinner, and Jerry took her armchair and said "Well, let's hear it - is it a magic wood or something?"

"No, not magic. It's a branch of a medlar tree, that's an old fashioned fruit tree, you don't see many about now, but all old gardens had one, and quinces, and mulberries and things like that. That-branch came from a tree in the garden of the manor. It's at the end of the kitchen garden behind the house. I've heard tell that they're going to build there next, so it won't be there much longer.

"My husband was a gardener at the manor and I was cook. The house was falling down then, but one wing was still used and the grounds were kept up. A Major Fawcett lived there. He bred horses, mostly for the army. The stables are still there, I expect you've seen them. They're in better repair than the house.

"Well, we was both young, and Henry - that's my ex-husband (only we wasn't married then); he fancied me, and I took to him. He was a big chap and knew his job. He used to bring in the vegetables or fruit for the family and he'd say - 'Yer they be me'andsom, and none of 'em finer than you!' Or he'd bring in the cut flowers for the missus and say

'Yer',s the flowers, and the purtiest one is the one I'm giving 'em too,' and daft things like that. Anyway, one day the missus said she wanted some medlars for some lady to try making jelly with - (that's what you do with them, make jelly, but to my, mind it's tasteless stuff and a waste of good sugar), and would I tell Henry to bring some in.

"Well, I went down to the garden to the greenhouses looking for Henry, and of course, there he was, and it was nice and warm in there, and he makes some daft remarks and tries to get me cornered amongst the chrysanths."

Jerry sat still. He was interested in these reminiscences, and he could see that Mrs Cooper was enjoying recounting the years long lost.

"So I says - 'The missus wants some medlars', but he says - 'Oh! I'm a good meddler,' he says and I picked up a trowel and I says - 'And I'm good at beating carpets,' I says, 'and I could put some practice in on your thick head,' I says.

So then he says - 'All right girl, come along 'o me, and us'll get the missus what 'er wants, tho' it don't look like I'm gonner get what I want,' he says.

"So us goes down the garden and at the bottom there's this tree. The leaves had mostly fallen and the branches were mostly covered in hundreds of little brown fruit, funny looking things, and the ground was covered in them too. When you picked them up they were soft and mushy, like rotten apples. Well, Henry has a garden rake with him, and he shaked a branch with it and the medlars come down like hailstones. Then we picks 'em up and fills a basket. I was careful to keep an eye on Henry, but he manages to get around over my behind side and the next I know he's pinched my bottom. I goes to swing a slap at him but he ketches me hold by both arms and holds me tight. He was a strong man then, was Henry. Then he says 'Liz', he says, 'Will you marry me?' Well, I'd been mazed about him for months and I says 'Yes!' right away, and I could see he was surprised, as if he didn't think I would, and I wondered if he were only teasing, but he wasn't, and all at once he changed, like another man somehow, only lots nicer, and he said some lovely things to me. Then he says 'And it's all because of this here old medlar! Do you know girl', he says, 'This old tree's been 'ere for at least a 'undred years,' he says. 'Look at the bark, he says, 'and the shape of the branches - first they turns under and goes back along again. Do you know girl,' he says, 'my old man, who worked here afore me, told me when I was a nipper that a medlar tree was like people's lives - they starts off one way and then, all of a sudden, all unexpected, they goes off in another, and sometimes doubles back they way they come. Then they shoots out forward again,and when they get old the bark goes all wrinkled and sometimes a branch splits open and soon it dies or someone cuts it off.'

"Then he says 'That's our branch, look - the straight, smooth one, growing from where an old branch had been cut back. That's us - soon it'll turn sideways and start off in another way. That's us girl, when we're wed.'"

"Us got married, and both of us stayed on at the manor, that was in '75. We had three children, two girls and a boy. The two maids be still hereabouts, but the boy went to New Zealand just after the turn of the century. I never reckoned us'd see him again, but us did. He came over with the Anzacs in the war. He come down here on leave and us ad'un for a week. Us never saw un agin. 'e got killed just afore the war ended, so that was a branch on our medlar that got pruned.

"It was a bit mazed really, but that old medlar got a hold on us, and what come as a bit of a joke when us got engaged, come to be a proper thing with us, and everytime something happened, I'd say to 'enry ' 'ave 'ee looked at the old tree lately, to see what's happening to us?'"

"When the boy left 'ome for New Zealand, Henry swore that the branch had turned downwards. Then 'ee reckoned that there 'ad been side branches for each of the kids, and when the maids give us grandchildren, there was side shoots. When the boy was took, one of the side branches never come into leaf, and 'enry pruned it off. I dunno if it was true, but 'enry got really superstitious about it, and if it didn't behave like we did, 'e'd find a branch that did.

"Well, our branch had got old and rough. I used to go and look at it sometimes for old time's sake, and when the family left the manor and it all went to rack and ruin, 'enry grafted a bit of it on to a hawthorn and it's out back now, in behind the shed. Then one day, three years ago, a chap come to say 'enry had passed out down on the line, where 'e 'ad a job with the railway, mending track. They took 'im to hospital, but he was dead. About a year later, that's best part of two years ago, I was thinking about packing up here and going to one of my daughters, and I couldn't make up my mind. Then I thought, well 'enry would 'ave looked at our old tree, so silly like, I went up the old garden. It was all gone wild, but the tree was in bloom - it 'as flowers, a bit like a wild rose - all except our branch and that was dead. I must admit I cried my eyes out.

When I come 'ome I got out the saw, wheelbarrow and stepladder and went back and cut the branch off. It made me sweat, I can tell you - never thought I'd get through it, but I did and I wheeled it home. I dunno what I thought I was going to do with it, but I put it in the lean-to, and thought to myself: now I got it yer, me and it'll stay put, till my time comes to pass on.

"Still, you've cut it up now, and just as well, t'was all imagination anyway, and you're a good boy to help an old woman out."

Jerry, from listening with tolerant patience to Mrs Cooper's rigmarole, finished feeling guilty and embarrassed for bringing the old lady's mysticism to an untimely end. Afterwards, he confided in her his plans to buy land and set up as a speculative builder as soon as his apprenticeship was over, musing: "Perhaps it's just as well that I haven't a medlar tree to consult!"

"Son," she replied, "we've all got one, only we don't know what direction it's going to next. It's only afterwards we know, and then it's past doing anything about."

The estate was half built when Jerry arrived there, and as soon as the houses were finished, families moved in, so that the little village, with its native rustics, was soon almost submerged by newcomers from the city, and the post office business grew so much that Mrs Cooper was unable to handle it single handed, with the general store and her household work as well. So, through the head post office, a young woman with post office experience arrived, as an assistant. She was one of the new council tenants on the estate, who had moved out from the city with her parents. She was a Midlander who had come south, as a child, when her parents came to the city after the war. She was a brash, breezy, young soul, aged 23, and married to a merchant sailor, who was on the P&O run to the Far East. Jerry heard about her from his landlady, who, giving her credit for being quick with money, and efficient in handling all the forms required to be dealt with, nonetheless, was not very approving of her as a person.

"'ers a bold one," she said. While to her neighbour, and whist drive confidant, she added rather more. "'Too fond of tight blouses and short skirts. None too particular, I shouldn't wonder, and her man out to Hong Kong or somewhere. I'll 'ave to keep an eye on 'er I reckon! Jerry didn't meet her until the Saturday following her arrival. During the week their hours of work prevented it, but on the Saturday, midday, when he came home, the girl was in the kitchen eating her meal.

"Hello beautiful! You're Jerry, I suppose. Mrs 'C' told me you lodged here, but I was beginning to think you must be a ghost! I'm Dorothy, only my friends call me Dot, so you can if you like. Hey! - you're a bit of all right, aren't you? I can do with.a few like you around - this dump is dead!"

(Jerry had been weighing the girl up while she chattered. "Not bad! Plenty of it, beautiful bottom," was what he thought).

"Hello," he said, "I've heard about you from Gran. Dinner smells good. I'm starving!"

"Hey! 'tisn't only the dinner that smells good is it? What about me? Give us a kiss then," she said; proffering her face. Jerry gave her a dutiful peck and sidled past her into the shop.

"I'm in Gran!" (He had taken to calling Mrs Cooper 'Gran', as a convenient and informal mode of address that secretly pleased the old lady). "I'll just change me boots."

When he returned, Dot was reading one of the weekly magazines sold in the shop. She looked up. "Hiyah, big boy," she said. "Hey! D'you like dancing? There's a big do Saturdays at the Plaza. There 's a bus in, but it's a walk back if you stay to the end - unless you take a taxi!"

"Oh no," said Jerry, "I'm meeting someone this afternoon and I won't be back till late."

"Oh ay! Got a girl then?"

"I might have," said Jerry, who until that moment had not considered what he would do with his half day, but was not prepared to allow this girl, even if she did have a smashing bust, to arrange the day for him. She was married too, and that, to Jerry, was an automatic bar.

Mrs Cooper came in and took Jerry's dinner from the oven. "There you are get yourself outside of that." Jerry saw that she was red in the face and was glowering at the girl. He grinned and winked at the old lady who looked relieved to see he was well aware of Dot's advances. "Cor! Just the job, Gran," he said, starting in with knife and fork.

Mrs Cooper, standing between him and Dot, pursed her lips and, inclining her head toward the girl, gave it a cautionary shake, that said "Don'ee do it, boy!" Jerry winked again, and the old lady raised her eyebrows in acknowledgement.

"S'funny," said Dot, with well-acted innocence. "I never met a Jerry before - 'cept the one under the bed!" She shrieked with laughter at her joke, and was quite unabashed when Mrs Cooper rounded on her.

"That'll do my girl! Us don't want none of that talk 'ere. You leave the boy alone and think of your man out foreign!"

"Yeah, think! That's all I have to do, and it don't do me much good!" With that the girl heaved herself up from the chair, and walked past Jerry, slowly, pouting her lips and giving him the full benefit of her sensuous hips as she went.

"Oh! She's a bold hussey, that one. I'll not keep her, if she starts any of that nonsense 'ere," worried Mrs Cooper.

"Oh, let her be," Jerry laughed. "She's just a joke really, and I expect she's lonely without her bloke. Anyway, she doesn't bother me!" There was the sound of the noisy flush from the lavatory in the yard, and the girl came wriggling back, walking her fingers up Jerry's back to the top of his head as she passed.

Mrs Cooper bridled anew. "Go on," she said, "you got the stamps to do before the counter opens, and there's some registered post to see to when the van comes."

"Not two O'clock yet," Dot replied, draping herself, hipshot, against the mantleshelf, "and I want to chat to Jerry!"

"Chat on," Jerry said. "I'm easy." ('So is she,' said some dark, near unplumbed depth in Mrs Cooper's mind. "I'll have her out of it, soon's as I can!").

Mrs Cooper went to work on the Head Postmaster, but she was not able to get Dot exchanged for some weeks, in fact, if it hadn't been for the postman collecting the post, passing the word at the various sub-post offices on his round, that there was a ripe plum waiting to be picked at Avonford, and a Sub-Postmaster, who had no joy with his conjugal rights, who suddenly found a vacancy behind his counter at Millsteps, on the other side of the estate, Dot would have remained where she was. She evidently found the proposed move to her liking, and a recently widowed lady who had some post office experience, took her place.

Dot still lived on the estate, but to Mrs Cooper, out of sight was out of mind. Not so, to Jerry. Before she left, she had a last meal with the boy, and afterwards, going to stand beside him, she put her arm around his shoulders, pulling his head against her ample bosom and said "See you, big ears! You know where I live."

Jerry made some facetious reply, but his body stirred, and he thought to himself "I bet she's all right." He thought no more than that then, but on occasions when his masculinity disturbed him, it was the curves and bulges of Dot, that teased him.

He was not a promiscuous boy. In fact, at that time, he had never touched a girl. He liked to have easy relationships, with a little banter and saucy talk, but ones that could be taken up and dropped, as he wished. His experience of living with his mother, fully aware of her profession, had given him a fear of involvement, and distaste for crude sexuality, that had always caused him to shy away from girls' blatant advances. But now that he was living away, and had reached maturity, the primeval male urges had suddenly become more insistent, and Dot's ripe sensuality had awakened desires till then almost dormant.

Mrs Cooper was relieved to see her go, feeling some responsibility towards the boy, and telling herself "Us don' want none of that there 'ere." But Jerry found himself going the long way round to work on the off chance of seeing Dot running for the bus of a morning. He saw her on a couple of occasions, and they had exchanged waves, while Jerry had noted the heaving of her bosom as she ran "Like a couple of pups fighting in a bag," he told himself with pleasure.

The months passed. The building contract was nearing completion, and Jerry's sunny nature continued to find pleasure in his work and in the countryside around him. When the boss's lorry was transporting goods from his home works, he had managed to get his old bicycle brought to him from the back yard of Effie's house, and on his weekends and summer evenings he had explored the villages, lanes and riverside for miles around.

He was much nearer the moor than he had been at home and he delighted in the high, heather covered hills and wooded valleys. He often thought to himself, "I wish old Will was here, we could camp out, and stalk the wildlife at night, and at dawn, before it takes fright." He wrote to Willy occasionally, and received letters back, but, as the time passed, they seemed to have drifted apart, and Willy had little to~write about, except Madge, and Jerry was amazed to learn that they were unofficially engaged. Jerry's reaction was slight dismay. He felt he had lost his best friend or at least, would be a second best in Willy's regard. "Wants his head seeing to," was his comment.

He had written to Willy telling him the story of the medlar tree, and that had produced a long letter in reply. It had really caught Willy's imagination, and he wrote, saying that he had looked up all he could find about medlars, and gave Jerry the information gleaned. He also told of Mr Watts' interest in the tale and how he had told Willy of the several references in Shakespeare to the tree.

"There's a rather naughty one in Romeo and Juliet," he wrote. "It suggests that saucy ladies refer to the fruit as part of the male genitals".

"I suppose he means 'balls' thought Jerry. "Old Will gets more like a blooming lawyer every time he writes."

It was sheer chance that he met Dot one Saturday. He had been out to a farm on the edge of the moor. He had met the farmer's son one day when the son was carting away timbers and doors from the manor, where a demolition firm was clearing the ground for more building. Jerry, in the happy way he had, struck up an acquaintance with the lad, and later visited the farm when harvesting was in progress. On this occasion he had been pigeon shooting. He had enjoyed the experience until, with a borrowed gun, he had actually brought down a bird. It wasn't killed, and Jerry felt some revulsion when the farmer's son broke its neck with his finger and thumb and gave the body to Jerry. It was no more than a pitiful bundle of feathers, but the firm, oily feeling of the flights told of the tireless winging, and Jerry hated himself for destroying a beautiful bird, that could rise on clapping wings, like some spirit of the woods.

"It's a shame really," he said.

"Geddout! The buggers eat 'alf the seed we puts in. You don't need to worry about they!" was the other's comment.

On the way home, Jerry was free-wheeling through the narrow street of Millsteps when Dot emerged from the post office. It was after six; and the shop had just closed. Dot saw him first, and ran into the road with arm upraised and blouse ajump.

"Hey.' Jerry.' Give me a lift - I got half an hour to wait for the bus."

Jerry stopped and sat astraddle the bike, arms on the handlebars. "Now how can I give you a lift?"

"Course you can, I'll ride on the step." Jerry suddenly found that something somewhere, inside him, or in his brain he didn't try to think what, had taken over his emotions. He laughed and there was a strange excitement about him.

"All right then, hop up."

Dot put one foot on the hub bar and knelt on the bracket with the other leg. Jerry pushed off and, after an initial wobble, they set a steady course down the village. Only one person seemed interested to see them go, and his beady eyes glowered jealously from inside the shop door, before he pulled down the blind with the inscription 'closed' on it, and retired to the back room, where he sighed his wicked frustration, and savoured the sight of his wife's inaccessible hips, well rounded, as she stooped to fill the coal bucket. 'Gawd!' he thought, "if I was only even ten years younger!"

It wasn't long before Dot's shin began to suffer the painful bruising that had punished Willy's, years before, on the memorable trip to the market. She had Jerry in a tight embrace from the rear, her bosom making itself very obvious to his shoulder blades. "Ow!" she wailed, "I can't stand this any more, my leg's bruised to hell, you'll have~to stop." She stepped off, and bent to massage her shin. "Look," she said. "It's all red and my stocking's laddered." She proffered her leg for Jerry's inspection, then hoisted her skirt, undid the suspender clip and rolled her stocking down. Her leg was shapely and the thigh milk white. A turmoil in Jerry's consciousness said, "Golly, she's got the lot!"

"Well, how are we going to get you home?" he enquired. "It's a good two miles; you'll have to walk - unless you ride the bike, and I'll walk."

"I can't ride a bike," she said, "and I don't fancy walking. Why can't I sit on the cross bar?" Jerry's body suddenly seemed to have developed a completely new nervous system that threatened to act quite independently of his will.

"Let's try then," he said. Dot groped up her skirt and found the suspender. She snapped it into the top of her stocking and dropped the skirt again. Jerry watched the operation with a sort of throbbing glee. Moments later she was seated within his arms, her arms tight about him and her body tantalisingly close. There was a perfume about her that near drugged him. His throat seemed contracted and his mouth dry. He had sufficient reasoning power left to think, "So this is what it's like! No wonder they do it." (His mind flitting momentarily to the callers at his mother's house.). Dot turned her round face up to his with a mischievous grin. "Enjoying it, big boy?"

Jerry glanced down at the cheeky, upturned face, and without any intention of doing so, kissed her, on her full, soft lips. Dot squealed. "Hey, watch out, you'll have us both off in a minute - I'll have to hold you tighter!" And she did.

It was the shortest two miles Jerry ever remembered. "What about meeting tonight?" asked Dot, when they arrived at the estate.

"Oh, I don't know - what could we do?" asked Jerry with naive incaution.

"Oh! I can think of lots of things," she said, "only where could we do 'em?"

The answer had already sprung to Jerry's mind, "See you by the ford, about half past seven," he said. Dot looked at him, serious for a moment, as if weighing him up, then evidently reaching some conclusion of her own, said "O.K. big boy, don't keep me waiting!"

Jerry ate his tea in silence, the tingling excitement that suffused him, made him almost oblivious of his landlady's comments. When he did answer, it was in a vague fashion that was quite unlike him. He finished as quickly as he could and went up to his room.

"That boy's up to something," thought the old lady, "some maid, I'll be bound!"

Jerry sat on his bed and made a fearful appraisal of his behaviour. He knew that he was going to "try his luck", as men say, with this girl. He was, at the moment, besotted with her sensuality. He didn't really want to, not he, Jerry Wilkins, didn't, but that other he, the primeval Adam was in charge and would not be subdued. He hunched himself, elbows on knees, head in hands. "I'm mad!" he told himself. "I don't know what she'll make of it, she could make me a lot of trouble, and she's married suppose her husband finds out? What then?

He felt torn apart with conscience, fear and plain commonsense battling with desire for her warm body. "I'll not let her make a monkey out of me," he decided, and went to meet her.

He was there with time to spare. The ford still existed, but a bridge had been built upstream of it to carry traffic. Now the ford was only used by carters to swell their wagon wheels in dry, hot weather, and by the few village children to play the water games played by children from time immemorial. It was almost dark, and very still. An occasional bat, out for an early breakfast, fluttered its convoluted flight above the water. Jerry stood, in shade, under the trees at the end of the bridge. He thought again "I must be mad!"

His few previous assignations with girls had always been open and above board, with an affable greeting, and a platonically friendly evening at a dance or at the cinema, then a walk home, a paper of chips shared on the way, and a cheery 'Goodnight then, see you again, bye bye', and home to an untroubled bed.

This was different. It was wrong, and he knew it. Almost, he decided to make a run for it before the girl appeared, but the awful gnawing excitement held him to the spot. Then she was there. She had crossed the river by the higher bridge and come down the road. She had spotted the light patch of his shirt in the dusk, and seeing him, turned the other way, crept up on him from the rear, poking her finger into his back and saying "Reach for the sky!"

Then laughing at his surprise, she put her arms around his neck, pulled his head down and kissed him on the mouth. Really kissed him, not a conventional peck, but a languorous kiss of lips that were offered invitingly apart. Jerry Wilkins, the sensible young builder with his future planned and all to work for was brushed, tremulous, aside and wicked old Adam leaped gleefully into her arms.

After a moment she said "Where are we going? I came the other way so as not to let people know! I've got to be careful you know."

Jerry said "I gotta place," and turned into the wooded lane leading to the remains of the manor. Thinking of it afterwards, it seemed almost pre-ordained that he had somewhere to take her.

Weeks before he had wandered around the ruins of the manor and had come upon a small building at the end of the partly demolished stables. It still had a roof, window and door, and was half filled with straw. At the time, Jerry had just thought it funny that it had not been stripped like the stables, and had never given it another thought, not until a couple of hours ago, when Dot had asked if he would meet her, and where they could go. Her invitation was so blatant that only his aroused senses prevented him from being shocked. Instead, the instant remembrance of the abandoned storeroom had contracted his throat with excitement, and now he was walking her towards it.

It wasn't all that successful. Dot seemed satisfied after some long while in the straw. Apparently her own voluptuousness and his hungry mouth and busy fingers had given her ease, but before then she was furious at his refusals.

"No, Dot", he repeated again and again. "You're married, and I'm not going to."

He went almost all the way though, and, hours later, when he walked her to within cautious reach of her parents' home, she was mollified, and kissed him goodbye quite kindly, saying "You're a peach out of reach, that's what you are.

"Sorry," said Jerry, "but it's the way I am, I suppose."

"O.K. big boy, but I'll see you again won't I?" The exertions and frustrations of the evening had exhausted Jerry and the old Adam was grumblingly subdued. So he replied "If you want to - I'll see you sometime." And she slipped away in the dark. It was Jerry's first experience, and he went to bed not at all pleased with it. "If only I could have forgotten she had a husband!" he thought, "it would have been heaven on earth!"

The following day when Jerry came down to breakfast, Mrs Cooper eyed him with disapproval. "You were out late, wasn't you?" (Late to her was after 11 p.m., when only owls and poachers were abroad). There could have been a dozen reasons, all innocent, and until that morning, he would have met the censure with a cheeky reply, but today the telltale red suffused his stick-out ears, and he did not meet her eye.

"Oh, I was with me mates," was all he could say.

"The boy's lying! What's he been up to? He's been with some maid, I wonder who?"

The old lady felt a genuine concern for the boy for whom she had developed a protective affection, and she worried away with the problem all day. Jerry felt better as the day wore on. Remembrance of the previous night stirred him again and again. Last night he had told himself that he would not see her again, but now, a naughty, gnawing niggle kept nudging his eroded will.

"Go on! Why not?" whispered through his senses. He had gone with her last night, thinking that he could refuse the ultimate, because he had not had the opportunity to provide a precaution, but she had anticipated this, and provided her own. So he knew that any time he went with her again, he'd have to be very sure of himself.

"She's a devil, that's what she is," he thought, but the craving within him stayed.

The village, in spite of the growing estate, was a tiny community, and hardly a breath was drawn but all were aware. In the circumstances, it could hardly be imagined that Dot's journey from Millsteps to Avonford, with her plump bottom on the cross bar of Jerry's bike, would have gone unnoticed. Hardly had the shop and post office opened on the Monday, before an early customer drew Mrs Cooper out of earshot of her assistant, and confided in her "That hussey you had 'ere, the one married to a seaman, and 'im out foreign - 'er was on the cross bar of your young lodger's bike, arms around him, bold as brass. Come all the way from 'steps, looks like it, and 'er skirt right up over 'er knees. Disgustin'. 'er orter be ashamed."

Mrs Cooper was really distressed. She stood up for Jerry, not liking neighbours to bring her unpleasant news that confirmed her suspicion that Jerry had been up to something.

"Well," she told the woman. 'I expect he didn't mean nothing, he's only a lad."

But Mrs Cooper felt quite depressed. She felt she ought to warn Jerry, but then the boy knew all about the wretched girl and, after all, they might only have been into the city to pictures, or something! But she remembered these flaming ears and worried the more. Dot was a phenomenon to her. She had grown up in the structured culture of village and big house service. She had never encountered a woman as free as Dot. There had been some gypsies on the outskirts of the village, when she was young, and there had been sinister hints of dreadful doings in the hedgerows, when any ploughman, cider mazed, and with sixpence to spend, fell into their clutches. But those were things never spoken of outright, and the poor woman felt quite unable to imagine the full enormity of the girl's possible effect on Jerry. She decided that she would wait and see.

The following Saturday was a torment to Jerry. He told himself that it was sheer folly to waylay Dot again. He knew that any involvement

153

with her invited fearful consequences, but as the day wore on, some force seemed to be compelling him to do just that. After his midday meal he went into the shop and, all innocent smiles, said "Not much left on the woodpile Gran. Like me to go up the manor and bring a bit back? I can put it across me handle bars."

"That's a good lad," replied the old lady with real pleasure and relief. "But don't go getting too much, you don't want to damage your bike."

"No, I won't. I'll just bring a couple of good branches." Butter would not have melted in his mouth as he said it, but he was careful to keep from directly under her eye. He told himself that he would do just that - go up to the ruined garden, collect some branches from the apple trees, lately cut down, bring them back, saw them up, and fill in the rest of the afternoon pottering about in the garden.

He sensed that Mrs Cooper was suspicious and worried, and thought that by being helpful he would make amends. He really intended to do that, but all the time he was trying to suppress his real intentions. He began to feel that no matter what he did, some sort of fate was dictating his actions, and again the tingling, mouth-drying excitement, swept through him. Nonetheless, he did wheel his bike up the lane and into what had been the manor house garden, past the ruined greenhouses, their panes removed and the stovepipes rusted, and into the fruit garden. Here he looked around for some suitable wood to take back.

The trees had been felled and the stumps torn up. A huge circle of grey ash showed where the timber had been piled and burned. There was little left worth taking. "Fate again," he thought, kidding himself that he was a pawn in some game. "If there's none here, I can't take any," then bowing to what seemed the inevitable, he walked over to the storeroom. He had the observant eye of a born naturalist, and immediately noted wheel marks and odd whisps of straw on the ground. Suddenly he became alarmed and ran the last few yards to the building. It was empty. After a week of telling himself that he was not going to repeat last Saturday's foolishness, making strong resolutions to be firm with himself and to resist temptation, he knew a crushing disappointment at the first hint that he might be compelled to renounce his naughtiness. He looked around. The floor was muddy and damp, the deep straw had disguised the fact that it had been used as a hen house. It was impossible to think of bringing Dot there again. He rode back to his lodging. "It's all gone, Gran, they've burned it all."

"Well, never mind, thanks for trying."

Jerry had lost interest in the garden, and instead rode across the estate to the next village of Millsteps. Dot was serving a customer with stamps when he entered the shop. He stood awaiting his turn. Dot had not looked up, and he watched her yearningly. Her arms were round, her bosom invitingly full, her round face smooth as a child's. The woman in front of him was posing some question concerning money orders. She gabbled on and on. Jerry stood looking at the girl, living again the illicit delights of the previous Saturday, feeling the desperate need of her soft warmth. The woman finished at last.

"One sixpenny postal order," Jerry said.

"Hello! Fancy you! Sevenpence please. What makes you come over here? Mrs C. run out of sixpennies?"

"I'll be outside at six."

"OK, but I'll go by bus. Tell you then." This with a jerk of her head towards the sub-postmaster who was standing behind the sweet counter.

Jerry had not taken any notice of him, but realising that trouble might be brewing, and very conscious of the dangerous role he was playing, he walked casually towards the door, then paused and asked "Quarter of Allsorts please?" While being served he noticed how the man glowered at him, and thought "What's he got against me, I wonder?" (Any idea of a man as old as that, coveting a girl like Dot, seemed impossible).

Jerry spent the rest of the afternoon by the river, watching the pond-skaters, and trying to still the clamour inside him. He had an hour to wait, and with a quarter of an hour to go, the rain started. It had been overcast all day, but he had been too preoccupied to notice how the sky had darkened in the south west, and now the rain came down in a steady deluge that dimpled the river, and soaked his shoulders before he could find any shelter. "Blast the rain," he thought. "She'll not come on the bike in this." He got on his bike, stopping in the village street and taking cover in a doorway next to the post office. Promptly at six Dot appeared, she wore a shiny red mac and put up a matching umbrella.

"Look," she said, without any other greeting. "I'm in trouble at home. Somebody, and I reckon it was that old creep in there (nodding at the shop she had just left), told my mum that I rode to Avonford on your cross bar last week. She's been playing hell since. Reckons she'll tell my Chris if I do it again, and she won't have me in the house if I'm letting Chris down and, cor! She just went mad! I can't see you again big boy, my Chris'd murder me if she told him!"

Jerry heard this outburst with dismay, tinged with relief. It seemed the fates had suddenly done an about-turn. "Surely it's nothing terrible to have a lift on a chap's bike, is it?"

"Ah yes, but then I lay in on Sunday morning, and she came in with a cup of tea, and there was all bits of straw on the floor, from my clothes, (here she gave a wicked giggle) and she put two-and-two together."

Jerry felt his ears burn and a spasm of fear shook him, damping down the ardour that her nearness produced. He had nothing to say for a moment and his face gave him away. "Well, nothing to worry about big boy, you didn't take it when you had the chance, did you! Mind you, I was cross then, but I admired you afterwards when I'd cooled down, and I'd not like to think I was your first, and you were ashamed of it." She looked up at him quite fondly, "You're a peach though, it's a pity! That old creep! He's been trying to get his hands on me ever since I been here, never misses a chance to press up against me behind the counter, dirty old devil!"

"Is Chris your husband?"

"Yes, you might say so. When we married he worked down the docks. We had rooms and it was OK, then he takes a job on a P&O! Steward! More money he says, big tips, stick it for half a dozen trips, and make enough to put down for a house. But what about me? Stuck out here with me mum, and we never did get on, that's one reason why I married Chris, to get away. Now I see him 'praps two weeks at a time, once in three months. All right for him, I bet he don't go short, but I'm supposed to be a bloody nun! Anyway, thanks big boy, it was fun while it lasted."

The bus arrived and went and she was gone. Jerry watched it go. He half raised a hand in salute, but the rain obscured the windows, and he lost sight of her. She had gone so abruptly that he had not even said goodbye. Withdrawing into the doorway for shelter, he suddenly felt a wave of relief, he felt purged of desire. Fate had stepped in and solved his problem. 'It was fun while it lasted', she had said. That was all it had meant to her - fun.
"Yes, and by gosh, it was," he said to himself, grinning. "She was just yummy!" He was already thinking in the past and now his thoughts were clear. He knew a lot that he had not known before, and he assumed that there would be plenty more cuddly lovelies, if he wanted one. Life was a surprise all right, but next time, he'd find one without complications. "I'll have to get myself a medlar tree," he thought happily as he rode off, head down into the rain.

He was soaked to the skin when he arrived at his lodgings. "Got caught in the rain Gran, I'll change for me tea first."
He went on to his room and stripped off his wet clothes. He felt extraordinarily lighthearted. He had had every intention of having some fun with Dot that evening, but his basically honest nature was in revolt against the guilt of playing with another man's wife, and he was glad to feel the unease go. All the same, he could not still the tremors that shook him, as they had done all the week, at the remembrance of the incredible allure of Dot's soft, warm flesh. The idea that the same allure was to be found in a middle-aged woman seemed rather disgusting to him, but he found himself thinking often of the men who slipped quietly into his mother's house, and some of the anger that he had always felt against them was mollified. He understood their need now. He tried not to think of his mother's part, he felt he dared not know, for he knew that if he did he would never want to see her again. He began to marvel at the ignorance that had allowed him to stay in the

house until he was a grown man, wondering how he had managed to shut his mind to the situation. He thought, too, of the several girls that he had escorted to cinema and dances, in all innocence, without a base thought, or any attempt to titillate them. Now, he wondered, were they willing too? Had they even been hopeful? His thoughts turned to Madge. "I wonder if Will and she have done it?" he thought. Then reflected, "I doubt it, old Will's such an innocent - but once he's taken up, you never know, look at me, I wouldn't have believed it!" He realised that he had matured to real manhood that last week. It was exciting, but he didn't know whether his new knowledge was a blessing or not, it seemed to make life more complicated.

The rain had stopped by the time he had finished his meal, but the evening seemed too short to make any revised plans. "Can I listen to the wireless Gran?"

"Course you can dear, I want to hear 'In 'Town Tonight' if I can finish writing my orders by then." ("He's not seeing' 'er tonight, anyway. Perhaps it was just that he gave her a lift, after all. He never seemed very interested when she was 'ere anyway, so I expect I've been worrying over nothing," she thought happily. "Young 'ussey! Wish she'd never come 'ere all the same!"

Mrs Cooper's worries were not over though, for on the Wednesday half closing, she was surprised to receive a call from Dot. "Can I come in, Mrs Cooper, she called from the back door."

"Well my, what are you here for?"

"Oh! Just social. I didn't know where to go, there isn't anywhere really, is there, and mum's up the pole about me again, so I thought I'd get out of it for a while. How's Jerry?"

Mrs Cooper's fears reawakened. "That's what she's come for," she thought "Chasing up that boy again." Aloud, ignoring Dot's question, she said "Your hubby still out foreign then?"

"Yes. should be home in three weeks. I'm hoping we'll go up to his people in Birmingham, see a bit of life again, and if I have my way, I'll stop up there till he gets a shore job again."

"Yes, and good riddance too!" thought the old lady, saying "Well, that'll suit you better I don't doubt, it's a bit quiet for you in these parts."

"Quiet! It's dead, I got to keep pinching myself to make sure I'm still alive too!" Dot, who was not a very sensitive girl, had hoped that Mrs Cooper would have welcomed her for a chat and a cup of tea, but neither seemed forthcoming, so she enquired again, "How's Jerry?"

This time an answer could not be avoided. "I thought you'd know, I heard you was riding on his bike last week."

"Oh! The gossip mongers been busy have they! Well, what's the harm, he only gave me a lift from Millsteps 'cause I missed the bus. He's not likely to get the chance again I can tell you, it was no fun, riding four miles on his cross bar, with his gear change stuck up my arse!"

She hardly noticed Mrs Cooper's shocked recoil at this vulgarity. She was thinking how nice it had been bumping along snuggled up to Jerry's chest. The gear change handle was fiction, her plump bottom had suffered not on the journey. "Is he all right then?"

Mrs Cooper's forbearance was exhausted. "He's all right, just as long as you leave 'un alone. You got no business, you a married woman, teasing a boy like that, you be on your way, I don't want to see no more of you, so you can go!"

Poor Dot had called out of boredom and a happy social wish to chat a while, and her simple amoral nature was quite untroubled when finding pleasure where she could. It was the reaction of other people that upset her. Mrs Cooper felt a slight twinge of remorse when she saw Dot's lips quiver and thought the girl would burst into tears. She didn't though, she just tossed her head and flounced out of the house. Mrs Cooper watched her go. "Maid's lonely, I suppose! Never ought to 'ave married a sailor if her wadden prepared to wait for 'un though," was her thought.

Out of Mrs Cooper's sight Dot did have a little weep. "Old cat, you'd think I was going to eat Jerry - he's old enough to look after himself,' Why in hell does everyone pick on me!"

The bad weather continued and the building of the estate fell behind. Jerry was able to work under cover with the old craftsman, but the building could only proceed in fits and starts, so when Saturdays were fine the men worked overtime to catch up. So it happened that Jerry saw no more of Dot. Perhaps her husband came home and they departed to 'the smoke', or she went back on her own to the city. Anyway, she was seen no more.

Mrs Cooper did not know this, so all her worries flooded back, some two weeks later, when a man presented himself at the post office and enquired, "Does Jeremy George Wilkins reside here?" He had a small leather pouch in his hand which he opened to extract a legal document, giving Mrs Cooper the impression that he was on very official business. Her thoughts flew in all directions. Was the boy in trouble? If so, how? What about Dot? Was there trouble there?

"Yes, he lodges 'ere," she replied. But 'es out to work and wont be back till dark."

"Where is he working?"

"I don't rightly know," lied the old lady in distress. You'll 'ave to come back again this evening."

"I can't do that, I'm afraid. I've come from Bristol and must get back.

Here, the lady assistant, trying to be helpful, broke in - "I know where he is," she said. "You go up the estate and right at the top there's a hut with a builder's name on it, they'll tell you where he is." The man thanked her and departed, driving off as directed.

Mrs Cooper turned on her assistant. "There was no call for you to tell 'im that," she said.

"Why ever not?"

"Well, there was no need," was all Mrs Cooper could think of saying. "He was a policeman, that I'm sure," she told herself.

When Jerry came in, he put on an expression of studied indifference, though bursting to tell his news. He'd eke out the announcement to make the climax the more exciting.

"Did the man find you?"

"Yes." No further explanation. Mrs Cooper's concern could not be held in any longer. "Was it about that Dot? Are you in for trouble there? What've you been up to?"

Jerry was taken aback by the suggestion. It was a month or more since their short lived affair.

The old lady's worry was appeased when she saw the grin on his face. "There's no trouble, Gran! But come to think of it, Dot done me a good turn all the same! I wanted to talk to her up at Millsteps where she works, so I went in and bought a postal order, just as an excuse. It was raining, so she went home by bus and I've not seen her since, but I used the postal order for a competition I saw in a paper and (here huge delight lit up his face) I won!" That man come to tell me, I've won a brand new Norton motorbike, and I got to go into Plymouth next Saturday afternoon to get it! Me! I won! Cor! I can't believe it. A Norton, like they ride in the TT in the Isle of Man. Oh gosh! It can do 100mph, I can go anywhere on it!

"Well now, I'm glad to hear it. I thought it was a policeman, and I was worried, and I'm sorry for being suspicious about that maid, but 'er did come 'ere one day, backalong, askin' after you.1'

Jerry was too excited to resent the inference and fell to quoting mechanical data from a handbook that had been given him. It was completely unintelligible to her but, happy in his delight, she let him prattle on, admiring the illustrations and clucking with pretended astonishment at the details, then said "Won't it be expensive to keep? I mean petrol and that, and you got to pay tax and insurance in case you kill somebody. (Her opinion of motor bikes was akin to her fears of any lethal weapon). You're going to find it hard to afford, I reckon."

"Yes, I'd thought of that, but it will be taxed and insured for a year, so I can see how I go by then."

"Can you ride a motor bike?"

"Not yet, but they reckon it's easy - I'll soon get the hang of it."

Mrs Cooper pursed her lips and shook her head with foreboding. "You mind you don't kill yourself first.'"

On the following Saturday, Jerry went to Plymouth, and had to appear on the stage of the Palace Theatre during the interval. The motor bike was on the stage and Jerry was introduced by the manager of a city garage as the lucky young man who had answered a questionnaire correctly and had completed a caption that the judges considered was the most original reason for owning a Norton motor cycle. The caption was 'I would choose to own a Norton motor cycle because...'.

Jerry had given the caption even less thought than he had given to arranging a list of attributes in the most popular order, and had simply written '...I would be king of the road'. What devious method had selected this unimaginative effort as the winner he did not bother to ponder, sufficient it was that the bike was his.

After a little applause from the audience, a representative of the motor oil company sponsoring the competition came on the stage, in company with the comedian who was top of the bill that week, and between them they had a few jokes that helped to further the interest and advertise both the bike and the oil. Then the comedian sat on the bike and kick-started it with a roar that filled the theatre. Finally, Jerry was given a key and some documents and the curtain came down.

Once off the stage, the cycle dealer asked if Jerry could ride, and on learning that he could not, suggested that he allowed him to take the cycle back to his showroom until the following Saturday, when Jerry should come in early and get some tuition before riding the machine home. Jerry was disappointed at not riding away then and there, but commonsense prevailed, and he agreed to do so. The next Saturday he got some half hour's practice around the garage yard, then drove the powerful thing back to Avonford without great difficulty. During the evenings that followed, he became more and more proficient, and by the next weekend he felt capable of riding anywhere. So on the Sunday morning he set off for Paignton, anticipating all the way the surprise and envy of his friends when he roared in.

Chapter 11

It was Mr Watts who instigated the next move in Willy's career. Having shaken Willy from his acceptance of the hum-drum work of a clerk, by getting an article accepted for *Answers*, and firing his ambition with the prospect of more money and the consequent practicability of marriage, it pleased the old man to try and forward Willy's interests further. On his advice, Willy revised many essays made previously and converted them into interesting and provocative articles, that were atuned to current events. Willy had no immediate successes, but he persevered, spurred on by Mr Watts, and at the same time developed no less than ten cameos of life as 'Seen from my Office Window'. These were sent off to *Answers* . Mr Watts had meanwhile taken some of the other articles to a literary friend of his, and they had discussed the insight of life that Willy showed, together with some good objective reporting, and it was this latter that appealed to the friend.

"That boy should take up journalism," was his advice. "Get him on some local paper as a part-time reporter, if that is possible, or as a junior if there is a vacancy."

Mr Watts hummed a little to himself, then said "You know a few strings that could be pulled, don't you? How about mentioning him first, so as to give him some advantage, eh!"

No more was said, but the man took a short article, written about the appearance of Welsh miners in the town, under a government sponsored scheme to relieve the terrible unemployment in the coalfields. These men were tunnelling a new sewerage system through the hills to the outflow miles away. Willy had written a humorous, yet compassionate description of these strangers squatting on the doorsteps of their lodgings, in clothes stained bright red by the Devon soil, and had wondered at their apparent dejection in this alien country, then had felt humbled when he heard three or four, or more, get up, place their arms around each other's shoulders, and burst into song that swelled and softened in natural harmony, like captive bird, singing of the life they had known.

About a week later, Willy received a phone call at his place of work. It was Mr Watts who told him that he should go and see the editor of the local paper, who wanted to talk to him. Willy rang the paper's office during his usual morning calls up and down the town with the hand-delivered correspondence, and made an appointment for the next evening immediately after leaving work.

He found that the editorial offices comprised two rather seedy rooms over a shoe shop, and that the entire staff consisted of the editor and typist. The paper was owned and printed by a local printing firm and was published once a week. Willy was already familiar with it for Gwen had taken it for years, though her interest seldom extended beyond the 'hatched, matched and despatched' column; she then glanced through its pages and sometimes delved 'into the exciting lists of local whist-drive winners, and the hospital matron's weekly acknowledgement of gifts. Her employees appeared there regularly as donors of magazines (back numbers, carefully saved) and, when fruit picking time came, the beneficent bestowers of windfalls and surplus rhubarb.

Willy knew the paper's editor, for he had called on Willy's employer on various occasions since Willy had been there. He was small and rotund, and when Willy was called into his office, he was seated behind a large desk that was littered with papers, and clips of cuttings, folders and books. An over-flowing ashtray spread ash amongst this disarray, and the air, stuffy with smoke and dust, did nothing to instil in Willy the feeling of the mighty power of the press that the little man's opening remarks suggested that it should.

"So you want to be a journalist! Well, sit down boy. Now! Have you ever thought of what the world would be like without newspapers? Without leaders to stimulate thought and formulate opinion? Have you thought of the heavy responsibility that the press carries in keeping the populace informed of the truth? How many lies are nailed, how many evil doings are exposed by the great free press of England? Hey! Have you ever thought of those things boy?"

Willy had been a solicitor's clerk for over three years, and had grown quite sophisticated in thought, both in local and national politics when, as an unnoticed junior clerk, he had overheard discussions between his employer and his clients, many of whom were the local professional men and traders, who comprised the Chamber of Trade, as well as some gentlemen of independent means, who lorded it in the big villas or who managed to live precariously on tiny incomes or pensions, but who scorned 'trade'. So he was not impressed, in fact, he felt he wanted to laugh, having visions of the paper's columns of names of persons attending funerals, reports of local social engagements, police court proceedings and the like. Not yet having been given a reason for the interview, he managed to look interested and replied "Oh yes! I've always found the press interesting, I take the *Express* and I see the *Financial Times* and *Telegraph* every day."

He managed to say this with such an inflection of voice, that seemed to infer that, with the experience so gained, he was well able to appreciate the little man's ragbag of gossip in all its vast power.

"Ha! You do, do you! Well, I like people who appreciate the national press, not that I'd be proud to be associated with some of them: muckrakers and instigators of anarchy - that's what they are. I tell you boy..."

What he was going to tell Willy was interrupted by the entrance of the typist, who asked if there was anything else, because it was gone six.

"No, no, you can go, I've got hours of work here yet, and an important meeting to cover tonight. I'll leave the copy on your table, I'll want it by about eleven, I've got to cover a ceremony at the 'Palace' first thing." (This was the presentation of a wrist watch to an ageing usherette who was retiring, her arthritis making the constant climb up and down the stairs of the 'Bug House' (as the picture palace was known), no longer possible.

Having thus established the fact that the great wide world was being monitored for the benefit of his readers, the editor picked up what Willy instantly recognised as his essay. He pursed his lips and wrinkled his brow, and read the article slowly to himself.

"I hear you've got an eye for the unusual, a different slant on the news," he said. "I like that, shows individuality - um, I might be able to use that, must be good mind, and accurate. The *Echo* prides itself on its journalism! How do you say? Two hundred words, in by Tuesday each week, five shillings a time?"

"I thought half a guinea," said Willy.

The little man looked at him in surprise. "My dear boy, this is just an offer to give you experience, I thought a few shillings would encourage you, but I hardly think I could offer you a professional fee - most people, when they send me letters and reports and things, are only too pleased to see them in print - you're not exactly an established literary figure you know! Still I'll stand by my offer of five shillings."

Willy looked very thoughtful for a moment or two, then said. "I'll give you six articles, two to three hundred words each, and if you want them, I'll have more when the six have been printed, so as to make a regular feature, would that do?"

"Well done boy! You're a businessman, let me have them and, if they're up to this standard I'll print. Five bob a time."

"Half a guinea," said Willy, doggedly. "After all, I didn't send you that, you asked me to call, so you must like it!"

The editor was genuinely taken aback. "Well, you know your own mind I must say, and I suppose that's good in a youngster. Tell you what, send me six, and if I print, you'll have your half guinea."

On his way home Willy exalted. "Madge, Madge, I'm going to make it, I'll have the money, and we'll have each other!"

At home, he told his mother of the interview, and was as pleased at her pride and pleasure, as she was with him. After his meal, he wrote to Madge, telling her of the day's news, and then went on to woo her love with all the charm and loving that his literary talent allowed. He always did this. He wrote to her daily and popped the letters into her employer's letterbox on nearly every night that they had not met. They had arranged a time for him to do this, so that Madge could collect the envelope before her mistress could do so. This night, excited by his prospects, he went further with his love fantasies than he had dared to do before. He told her of his desire gently and honestly in such a way that Madge found his excitement stirring her too. She pressed his words to her cheeks, and found herself longing for Willy himself. She was still sitting in the nursery, flushed and tremulous, when Hilda popped her head around the door to say that she was off out.

"Oh ey! lover boy, in the letter box again? Hey, what's up. You look moonstruck!"

Madge sighed, "Oh Hil, I don't know what to do. Will wants me so much do you think he'll wait for me? If he feels like he says, how can he do without me when I go away?"

"Oh, make up your mind girl, if you want him, give the Misses the sack and make the boy happy to wait till you can marry - you can't yet, can you! You're too young!"

"I can't just tell the misses I'm not going to stay - I promised!"

"Well then love, you'll have to do the obvious - they won't want you if you're expecting, and he'll have to marry you, so you win both ways!"

Madge flushed scarlet. "I couldn't! Will isn't like that, we're not going to do anything wrong, it would spoil everything." Madge was genuinely shocked and hurt. She knew that if she allowed Willy to possess her once, it would sully their love, and if it became anything less than ecstasy, then their love would die - her's would anyway, for the shame and guilt would be unbearable. She sat looking at Hilda, the happiness gone from her face, her eyes now bright with tears.

"All right girl, I know you won't, but it's what I'd do, only I've never found a bloke yet who's worth it - cheer up, I'm off, see you later."

When they met again, Madge made much of Willy's success. She really did feel proud of his ability to put into words so much that was usually unspoken. After a little discussion of the new opportunities opening, they succumbed to their loving and it was then that Willy, his cheek on the top of her head, her face close against his chest, mentioned the letter. "I hope you weren't shocked or disgusted?" he asked, "but sometimes I have to think of you like that, and I was a bit excited about the *Echo* and got carried away a bit."

"No Will, I loved the letter, and I understand, but we couldn't, could we! If I did, you wouldn't love me any more, and I couldn't bear that. We must wait - when we're married, everything will be all right, I promise you that, I know it's hard for you, but it is for me too." Willy put his hand under her chin and lifted her face to his. There was no more said for a while.

A fortnight later, Willy received a letter enclosing five guineas for his contributions to *Answers*. This seemed to confirm his new status as a free lance journalist. The *Echo* had printed his first article, and the editor had accepted the six more that Willy had promised. The editor was a good journalist, with years of experience on a Yorkshire paper. He had come to the *Echo* some ten years previously, and had settled down to the production of a local paper in order to enable an ailing wife to benefit from the better climate. He had got used to confining his talents to the parochial chit-chat of the town, but even so, was conscientious about providing good English. He spent some time evaluating Willy's offerings, and gave him sound advice on presentation. Journalism was a craft, he kept impressing on Willy, it needed to be learned, and was not easy to accomplish. He encouraged Willy to continue and agreed to look at anything that he might come up with.

Mr Watts was delighted. He felt that he shaped Willy's success and did all he could to stimulate his ambitions. They met once a week at the master's house and worked on Willy's articles, but Mr Watts was intent on improving Willy's chances and suggested that Willy took up journalism properly. "Try your hand at reporting actual events," he suggested. "Pretend that you are representing some paper, and write reports of happenings, then we'll get them criticised and edited, so that you'll learn how reporting is done."

Willy found this very hard. It was one thing to conjure words to play upon things imagined, but to make a factual report interesting, was difficult. First thing was to find something to report!

He was hurrying to work one morning, when a car passed him and a little further on suddenly lost a wheel. The wheel peeled off, then, wobbling like a child's over-sized hoop, fell into a shop doorway, slightly injuring a man who was cleaning the shop window.

Willy immediately got busy. He had written a good descriptive piece by the time the senior clerk arrived, and when on his morning delivery round of correspondence, dropped the 'copy' into the *Echo*.

After work he called on the editor to see what he had done with it. The man told him he'd put it in the wastepaper basket!

"Now I'll show you what I've made of it," he said, giving Willy a typewritten page. On it was a bare account of the accident, with, as the editor pointed out, the news value added. "The name of the injured man. I had to go and get that," he told Willy. "Nobody is very interested in a car wheel falling off, but they all want to know about Joe Bloggs who got hit in the backside - that's the news! There you are. Statement of fact, actual occurrence, result - human interest. Thirty six words instead of your one hundred and fifty. But I'll give you credit for trying!"

In the following months, Willy made many contributions to the *Echo* and worked on others for periodicals. He found that he was earning a substantial addition to his salary. He was thrifty and was gradually building up savings in the post office savings bank. Madge's threatened departure had not yet come about and Willy was a happy boy. They had been going out for more than a year. Once they had managed to get a day off together, and go on a day-excursion by rail to Bristol, where Willy met Madge's parents.

He was impressed by their comfortable, bright home, so different to the dark little cottage that was his own, and was even more struck by the family atmosphere, and Madge's parents' obvious affection for her, and their pleasure at seeing her again. He found himself rather an outsider while all the family gossip flowed back and forth, but he was included as much as was possible, Madge's mother ignoring his shyness and making him feel at home.

Her father seemed to be a quiet, kindly man, very concerned for Madge's happiness and not slow to voice it. "You've been seeing a lot of my girl, so I'm told. Well, if you make her happy, I'm glad, but never doubt boy, if you harm her in any way, you'll have me to deal with, and you won't find me easy!"

He said this, looking Willy straight in the eyes, his voice quiet, but very determined. Willy flushed, more out of indignation than embarrassment, but answered equally firmly, "You'll never have to worry about her happiness with me, I'm going to marry her as soon as I can."

Madge's father had held Willy's eyes with his, and when Willy made his reply he relaxed and smiled. "Well said, youngster, I'll trust you, but I don't know about betting married, that's a long way off yet, I reckon. Mother, this lad reckons he's going to marry our Madge! What do you think of that?"

His wife smiled fondly at Willy, she had already decided about him in her mind. "Well," she said, "that'll be nice. If they're both of a mind when the time comes, I'll be pleased." Then both parents were kissed by Madge, and her brother and sisters grinned and made faces at them.

On the long, slow journey back, they were lucky to have a compartment to themselves for part of the way and were able to exchange opinions of the day's happenings.

"Weren't you sad to have to leave home? Didn't you feel lonely in your job - I mean, your mum and dad and all - they seem so comfy somehow, it must have been hard?"

"Yes," said Madge,."it was, I used to cry a lot at first, especially when the kids were in bed and there was no one to talk to; still, I found you, didn't I, and then it was all right."

"No," said Willy, "I found you!"

"Well, that's what I mean," said Madge, snuggling close, "we found each other!"

The happy family home was much in Willy's mind as the journey continued. It had been a day full of new experiences, for he had never been more than ten miles outside of Paignton so all was fresh to him, but mostly it was the insight into family life that had surprised him. Willy's life had been very solitary. He could not remember his father and had no other relatives that he knew of. His friend, Jerry Wilkins, had stepped into the void, and he was the nearest that he knew to a brother, and in his younger days, a father too; a comforting source of strength and protection. During the two years that Jerry had been away, and since that coincided with his courting of Madge, he had not missed him as much as he might have done, but now, with the revelation of what family meant, he looked back on his years (so few, but seemingly so long) with a new appreciation, and he realised with sudden clarity how much he owed to Jerry. "Cor!" he thought to himself. "It would've been pretty rotten if I hadn't known him'."

It was in the middle of the summer of 1931, early July. Willy was waiting for Madge at the back gate by the park. It was a Friday, and her evening off. When she appeared, Willy sensed that something was amiss.

"You all right?"

"Yes."

"Sure? You don't look too good."

"I'm all right, let's go."

"It's going to rain," said Willy. "Shall we go to the pictures? Mum's not going out tonight."

"I suppose so."

Willy took her arm and looked sideways at her pale face with some concern; then he remembered some information that he had obtained from *Home Chat* (a womens' magazine to which he had submitted some poems, so far without recognition) and thought that perhaps Madge was having her 'difficult days', so much mentioned, in mysterious language, by the paper's nurse-somebody, and cheered up, squeezing her arm and saying no more.

There was the usual long queue for the picture house, and a half hour of their precious evening was spent in silence as they gained ground, foot by foot, to the folding glass doors of the foyer. Willy still felt some unease for Madge was unusually quiet and seldom looked up at him, but when eventually they gained admission and were seated, she put her hand in his and leaned towards him so that he could put his arm around her.

They had arrived in the middle of the secondary film (as the performances were continuous) and then there was an interval when the lights went up, and bodies straightened. Still Madge had little to say, and when the advertisement slides were over, and the house darkened again, they resumed their rather uncomfortable, close posture, the seat arm between them chaffing Willy's bony frame. He felt an increasing foreboding of some misfortune as the Pathe News was followed by a cartoon, and then by the main picture. Half way through that he felt a tremor shaking Madge, and was aghast to realise that she was weeping.

"What is it? What's the matter?" he whispered. This seemed to open the floodgates of her tears, and he could only hold her close while she stifled her sobs against his chest.

"Let's go," she managed to say at last, and they stumbled their way over knees and feet to the gangway, and to the red exit light. They took the shortest route into the park, just opposite. It was not yet dark, but the lights had been lit and the bats were out already. They walked in silence as far as the pond with its circle of embrasured seats, and there Willy sat her down, put his arms around her and asked "Now what's the matter my lovey, what's wrong?"

"I'm going Will! They're taking me to Malta!" Her tears came afresh and Willy sat in shocked silence. He hadn't given a thought to Madge's always threatened move from the town. It had been so long coming that he had almost persuaded himself that it would never happen, and had put Madge's distress down to some trouble at work or some other domestic bother.

"Malta!" was all he could say, vaguely thinking the name as 'foreign'. Then with a heartstopping clarity came the realisation of what was to happen. He still couldn't find words, just held her tight, while his mind raced with shocked apprehension.

"When? How soon? When did they tell you?"

"This morning. 'They're going in about a month. He's going first, next week, then she's going afterwards."

Having unburdened herself of the dread news, Madge's sobbing degenerated into miserable little sniffs that Willy, being completely inexperienced in such circumstances, was at a loss to soothe, but suddenly they both found words and Madge told him, that the Missus had told her, that the family would follow the master in about a month or so, and she was to have a few days off to go home to see her mum, and to get thin clothes for the hot country, and all that.

The Missus would pay for two uniforms, and she would have to get her other things herself. The Missus had told her that she had been to Malta before and they would be sure to have a nice house and good servants, and she had said that Madge would enjoy it. It was a chance to see the world as they might go on to Egypt from Malta, or Palestine, because the master was an important officer who was on the staff (whatever that was) and had to go on important jobs.

"She called them missions," said Madge, "but I don't think that he's anything to do with missions - you know, to the heathens - he's army." All this came in a lot of disjointed statements that beat upon Willy's stunned mind like so many cudgels. 'Egypt - Palestine', the words stood out from what Madge was saying.

"How long will you be away?" he demanded, almost shaking Madge in an effort to bring reality out of the rigmarole. "It sounds like years. You can't go, can you?"

"She says about two years, but she can't be sure, he'll be out there longer, but they'll have to see to the kids' school, but she doesn't know."

"Two years!" The time stretched away from them like a century. "We'll be twenty-two by then," said Willy, as though middle age would have already been reached, "but we could get married then." A new hope lightened his voice. Madge looked up at him, seeing that he had already leaped the years and was regaining optimism. "I'll be earning lots by then. I'll buy a house and you'll never have to leave me again."

"Oh Will!" was all Madge could say, but a little later came the doubts. "Will, you will wait for me?" For another half hour the queries and protestations were pleaded and promised, back and forth, till when it was time for Madge to go back to her charges, both had found some solace in their sorrows.

When Willy reached home, Gwen was just about to go to bed. "Your cocoa's by the hob," she said. "Good night boy."

She moved to exchange the 'near miss' kiss that was their usual mode of greeting. She smelled Madge's perfume on his coat and, as they lightly brushed cheeks, she noticed how pale he looked. "Feeling all right?" she echoed his words to Madge earlier. "You don't look too good!"

Willy stooped to pick up the mug of cocoa from the hearth. "Madge's going away, her boss is off to Malta and she's got to go."

Gwen knew at once how this affected Willy, but felt none of the misery. "Well," she said, "I dare say she'll enjoy it and it'll be exciting!"

"Mum! She's going for two years, or more!"

"Well then, you'll be able to save up, and be in a better position when she comes back. It may be just as well really, you'll be a full grown man by then, and then, if you're both of the same mind still, you can marry."

Her words rang a bell that tolled in her own mind, tolling for the day when she'd be left alone, with her boy gone from her. Willy heard the words, "If you're of the same mind," like a physical hurt.

"Oh, mum!" was all he could say, but she didn't know what he meant.

Madge, lying sleepless in her room across the town was recalling, word by word, all the promises Willy had made. The despair of the day had lifted and she was beginning to see the future in a more cheerful light. When she came back, Willy would be a prosperous writer, as he had promised, and they'd have their own little house, and they'd marry, and she'd have lots and lots of kids, her very own kids, her's and Willy's! But, dreadful nagging doubt, would Willy wait for her? She first scolded herself for doubting him, then reasoned with herself that Willy would need her so much, and without her, there were so many girls on the look-out for a boy, and lots could give him more than she could. "After all," she told herself, miserably. "I'm no great catch! I'm not pretty, and I've got no figure - or I've got too much, I'm fat! But Willy likes me that way and I've been strict with him, I know he's always wanted to pet me, and it wouldn't have mattered really. Hilda says everybody does, perhaps I should have - supposing he goes out with some girl, just 'cos he's lonely, and she lets him - what happens then? He might give me up - think I'm a prude."

Then she turned on herself for thinking such things of Willy, but the doubts remained. She had no hold on him, nothing that she could claim gave her a right to him.

Willy, staring at the starfilled rectangle of his bedroom window, thought "I wonder if she'll find someone else out there - all those soldiers! I'll write to her every day so that she can't forget me, and I'll write and write and be ready to marry her as soon as she comes back."

In the turbulence of his mind, Willy turned to fantasy, calling Madge his Juliet and staring at the trembling stars caught in his window frame, told himself "We're star crossed lovers." The elevation of his problem to literary grandeur pleased him, and he slept.

Neither of them thought of avoiding the separation by the simple expedient of Madge refusing to go. She had accepted the position of nurse to the family children on the understanding that she would do so, and it would have seemed quite dishonest to have backed out. Originally, it had been an added inducement to take the job. Madge's parents had thought her fortunate to have the opportunity, though they little knew the circumspection and the loneliness involved, only thinking of the imaginary glamour to be found in foreign places. So they had urged her to take the job.

Her stay in Paignton had been intended to last a few months at most, and Madge had looked forward to travelling. Then Hilda persuaded her to go with her to the little dances in the church hall, and after a week or two Willy had appeared, then quite soon, Madge had no wish to go anywhere except with him.

On the next Sunday morning, Willy did as he had done for months past, and took a seat at the back of the church before Sunday School, ready to move up and sit beside Madge as soon as she had delivered the children to the Sunday School teacher. Children arrived and took their places in the chantry chapel where the school was held. Those who brought them then went to sit in the nave. At each little commotion at the church door, Willy's hopes rose. He delighted in the sight of Madge in her neat, blue uniform, her dark hair, bobbed in the fashion, framing the lovely apple blossom of her cheeks. His heart went out to her, and she, busy shepherding her charges, would spare a quick glance to make sure he was there, and to give him that cheeky dimpled grin that he loved. That day he saw the children first, then, looking for Madge, he was dismayed to see that it was Hilda who had brought them, and what was more, Hilda stayed out of sight up by the side chapel, so it was a tormented hour that he spent before he could close up behind her before she reached the door.

"Where's Madge?"

Hilda turned in surprise to see Willy. She thought to herself, "Well, well, the crafty devil, that's what she's been doing."

"Where's Madge?" repeated Willy.

"Gone out with that other bloke, I reckon," said Hilda, wickedly. Then giggled to see Willy's anxious face. "No, she's got to see to the baby, the Missus is off somewhere with the boss. I've had to walk this lot over. Cook's going mad, with me away, but they won't be back till dinner. Hey! you can walk me back home if you like!" She saw her invitation was not going to be accepted, so added, "I'll tell 'er old faithful was 'anging around. Bye-bye."

"Tell her I'll be by the back gate this afternoon if she can pop out, will you?"

"OK, I'll tell her."

After Sunday dinner, still, after all those years, taken in the kitchen of the Big House, and the ritual of washing up, Willy went to the telephone box outside the post office and phoned Mr Watts. He excused himself for not going there to tea and books as usual. He was honest about it. "I've got a chance to see my girl, Sir, hope you don't mind."

"That's all right, come next week, we'll have to get those articles sorted out, you've not too much time."

"Young Will's seeing his girl," he told his wife. As he looked towards her, the years fell away and for a moment he remembered long gone Sunday afternoons. "Lucky young beggar!" he thought.

Willy went down to the park and took up a position where he could see the villa's back gate and the nursery window He always waited there, and usually Madge would come to the window, wave when she saw him, and then come to the gate. That day, Willy waited without sight of her, though Madge had seen him, but had kept well back in the room so that he should not see her. She was trying to think of a way of nipping out, but the children could not be left unattended, and there was no hope of enlisting Hilda's help, as the cook had her on the run downstairs. Then on some errand to the bedrooms (Hilda was housemaid, parlourmaid and kitchenmaid as the occasion demanded), Hilda poked her head into the nursery.

"Your bloke's outside, did you know?"

"Yes, but I can't get out."

"Go on, be a devil, bring him in - you could have a quick cuddle in the airing cupboard!" Hilda's advice was given with her usual wicked grin and a rolling of eyes that spoke volumes.

"Don't be daft, I couldn't, they'd be mad if they found out."

"Please yourself Snow White, but I only wish I had the chance," said Hilda, making a 'grrrr-ing' noise as she flexed her hips, indicating exactly what she would hope to happen in the airing cupboard.

The Major and his wife were expected back by six, and the children's tea and baths and everything had to be got by then, so Madge went to the window, and when Willy saw her and waved, she blew him a kiss. It was all she could offer, but she felt life was difficult enough just then without complicating it further. Cook would tell on her if she knew, and it was hard enough to keep her emotions in check without Willy's presence to break her control. Willy understood, pretended to catch the kiss and hold it to his heart, then he waved again and, as Madge disappeared, he mooched dejectedly away. He wished he had not told Mr Watts that he would not be going to see him. It was hardly four o'clock and there were six or seven hours to fill before bedtime.

He walked home past the church, down Well Street, around the playground of the school to the fountain on the green. He was skirting the school railings to go up the hill to his cottage when someone, vaguely noticed, who was sitting astride a motor bike on the higher side of the fountain, suddenly kick-started the machine, circled the fountain and roared alongside of him. The rider was wearing an overcoat, in spite of the July heat; he had a woollen scarf wrapped around his neck, a cap on his head with the peak turned to the back and goggles. It was an effective disguise but, at second glance the stick-out ears identified Jerry even before he pushed his goggles up on top of his cap.

"Jerry!"

"Hey, Will, how goes it?"

Willy looked at the Norton with astonishment. "Is it yours?"

"Yes - come for a ride?"

"Well, I - "

"Come on, hop up - better than the old bone shaker, eh?" Willy straddled the pillion. "Now then, put your feet on the brackets, put your arms around my waist, and lean tight up against me - right?"

"Right!"

With an acceleration that betrayed his inexperience, Jerry had the bike roaring up Barns hill, past the Smithy, down Winner Street and away out towards the country almost before Willy could find enough balance to stay on the pillion. The wind in his face made it impossible to keep his eyes open till he adopted a posture that buried his face in the back of Jerry's muffled neck. Something akin to terror kept him limpet-like against Jerry's body, and he was only dimly aware of pedestrians on their leisured Sunday strolls (always taken in the middle of almost traffic-free roads), running to safety. Snatches of shouting reached him but their onward rush left all behind. In no time at all it seemed, they were crossing the river into Totnes from where they had herded sheep when they were boys.

Jerry roared up the ancient narrow street with its shuttered shops and Sunday somnolence. The buildings echoed their passing, drowning the mellow chime of the church clock and rousing the people who dozed behind the aspidistras in the rooms over the shops.

"Noisy varmints," muttered they, as the sound receded into the distance, but not for long. Jerry circled the empty market and shook the high street once again as he descended to the river. He pulled up there and stopped the inferno that lived beneath his crouching body. He pushed up his goggles, pulled off the muffler and, consulting his watch said, "Not bad, eh? Seven miles in just under ten minutes!"

Willy, his eyes streaming, and his body twitching from the release of tension, said "Cor, Jerry! What a speed!"

"Did you enjoy it then? I bet you had the wind up, didn't you - it's quite safe though, you just got to go with the bike - like you do on a push bike, but this one takes you, all you got to do is step on the gas."

"How long have you had it?"

"Last week - you know how I got it? - I won it - straight! I learned to ride around the garage yard, then in the evenings last week - isn't she a beaut'. Just like the T.T. racers have!"

Willy was recovering meanwhile, and except for some grit in one eye, was beginning to feel the exhilaration of experience and to enjoy the ride. "Shall we go then? Tell you what - remember when we drove those sheep? We'll go that way - took us all afternoon then, reckon we'll do it under ten minutes now."

The Sunday peace was shattered again as the motor came to life, and they were away, over the bridge and up the endless Bridgetown Hill on the other side, but this time it seemed to flow like water under their wheels, and the turnpike cottage raced towards them and was past. Willy tried to identify the roads but, peering through slitted eyelids, his face turned into the shelter of Jerry's back, all he saw was a blur of hedgerows. The drowsing lanes were mercifully free of farm carts, cattle and other traffic. When once the main road was reached again, Jerry let the bike go beyond his capability of control. Fortune favoured him though, and within minutes he was roaring around the fountain, showing off for all to see. There weren't many to see him. The Gurney tribe stood and stared, one or two passers-by screwed up their faces and protested at the noise, and when Jerry shut off the motor, and Willy's ears began to function again, he heard the shopkeeper from opposite the fountain say, "Never ought to be allowed, he'll kill hisself, you mark my words."

"Come on home and have some tea," invited Willy, and a few moments later he shattered poor Gwen's Sunday afternoon peace by coming in with "Mum! Here's Jerry, he's got a motor bike, we've just been to Totnes and back in under half an hour!" Gwen was aghast. "Oh.' How could you, you might have been killed going at that rate! Was that you I heard rushing up and down the street?"

"That was me Mrs Churchward, with Willy up behind. You needn't worry, I can ride all right - I've been riding every night for a week and I've come up from Plymouth this morning."

Gwen's anxiety deepened. "I don't think those things should be allowed, there's always accidents in the paper, and I don't like Willy going with you."

Willy laughed, "Don't worry Mum! I enjoyed it - what's the chance of some tea?"

"You'll have to make do with what I got - I wasn't expecting you in, much less Jerry, so it's bread and jam and a bit of slab cake, that's all."

"That'll do Missus, that and your fair company," grinned Jerry.

"Oh! Get on with you!" said Gwen, secretly pleased by the flattery. "Much you care for my company. What you been doing with yourself all this time?"

Jerry kept the talk flowing, telling of his work, and the village and his landlady. Willy reminded him of the story of the medlar tree, and that led to superstitions, and so an hour or more passed, before Jerry enquired, "How's you and Madge?"

This brought Willy back to realities, and he realized that he had not given Madge a thought since being introduced to Jerry's bike a couple of hours before. Some of the excitement faded at once.

"She's going to Malta soon, probably for a couple of years."

"Go on! Cor! Lucky her," was Jerry's comment.

"Even Jerry! thought Willy, "nobody seems to understand! Why do they all think it's such a good thing."

"Do you both good," continued Jerry. "Plenty more pebbles!"

"We're engaged," said Willy, angrily, "we'll get married when she comes back."

"OK, if you still want to, what I mean is, it gives you a chance to make your mind up, don't it."

"My mind is made up," said Willy, indignantly. Jerry grinned and shrugged. "Good!" he said, "then you'll have to wait!"

Gwen listened to this exchange, and though thinking that Jerry was right, she felt for Willy; so she changed the conversation by referring to Willy's contributions to the *Echo* and his other pieces in *Answers*, and so the next hour went. Willy did not feel very happy. He was hurt by Jerry's unfeeling attitude towards himself and Madge, his eye was smarting from the grit that still seemed to be in it. He had to sniff constantly and mop his eye from time to time. Gwen made him sit with his head over the back of a chair, while she poured water under his eyelid, but he still felt the scratching under the lid and depression settled on him. Jerry departed with a roar of exhaust, after saying that he might run up again soon.

Willy went up to his room and wrote a long letter to Madge, protesting undying fidelity, and indulging himself in all his longings for her. He took it down to the house at the recognised time, and slipped it into the letter box, then he took up his sentry go in the park, till Madge came to the window again, held up the letter and blew him a goodnight kiss.

The next week was desolate for Willy, On the Wednesday, Madge went home to Bristol for a week to get her outfits and say goodbye to her family, so Willy was denied all sight of her. He wrote to her at her home, and she wrote to him. His letter was the usual outpouring of his feelings, done with a literary skill that made each endearment a whisper for her ear alone. Her's to him was a brief little note saying that she had arrived safely, was busy being measured for her uniform, and how her mum was making things and so on, but she finished with, 'I love you dearly, and sleep with your letters under my cheek. I'm always and always yours.' This was followed by a childish string of kisses and a P.S. to say she had kissed each X. When she came back she was so busy helping to get the children packed and ready that she had to forego her time off and Willy was able to see her for but a few minutes at a time.

In the last week, before the family sailed, Madge was allowed the Sunday afternoon free, to 'say goodbye to my friends' as she had asked. It was a hot day, the sort of July day that so often seems to precede an August Bank Holiday that turns cold and wet. Madge was wearing a light coat, in spite of the heat, but her body seemed supple and free when Willy hugged her."

"Will, do you know what I want to do today?" I've been hoping it would be fine, so we could go up to Shorton, like we did the first time we went out together. I want to go up, and sit by the gorse bushes, and look down on the woods just like that time, shall we?"

Willy had thought of a long cuddle in the little sitting room of the cottage - till his mother came home from work - but he readily fell in with her suggestion. He had not gone to the Big House for the midday meal as was usual, but had waited for Madge to come out, grudging any moment wasted. They had sat close together in the cool of the church while the children were at Sunday School and afterwards he had walked back to the house, with Madge and the children. There still seemed a sense of unreality to him that this was really the last day.

They were soon in the lanes and climbing the long, steep hill to the head of the valley. They did not hurry, arms entwined and speaking little, they were so close to the final, desperate break, that only feelings cried to each other for some denial. There were no words that mattered. They came to the gate where Madge and he had tumbled, and this time he took care to lift her carefully, and set her down. Doing so he sensed again the suppleness of her body, and its movement. His body tingled with a reaction that exalted in her. They climbed the bank. The gorse, that lover's flower, was full of bloom, and the ripened pods kept popping in the heat. They were both hot from their climb and threw themselves on the close cropped grass. Little beads of perspiration were on Madge's face, a face flushed with heat, and, had Willy known it, nervous apprehension.

"Why don't you take your coat off? You can't possibly need it now!" said Willy. He had offered to carry it for her a couple of times before, on the climb up, but Madge had excused herself. There seemed to be no possible reason for her not to take it off now. She knelt facing him, sitting on her heels, her rounded knees together, and her thighs pressed tight. She leaned a little forward, he put his hands on her shoulders and she pressed her forehead on his chest.

"Will, my darling, will you promise not to think me wicked, and you won't be ashamed of me, if I - if I - tell you something?"

Willy held her away from him, and putting his hand under her chin, turned her face up to him. He looked at her, she blushed, her skin, that was her greatest beauty, (it always reminded him of alabaster, so clear and smooth was it) was dark flushed, her eyes, warm and tender, seemed huge, the pupils lustrous with love. Her lips were tremulous, she looked so vulnerable, that Willy felt a surge of pity that brought a constriction to his throat.

"What is it, my love?"

"Promise?"

"Of course I promise, how could you ever be wicked?"

She sank her head on his chest again, her short, wavy hair hid her blushes. Willy caressed the bowed head, winding a tendril of brown hair around his finger and gently rubbing her ear.

"Tell me."

"Will, I wanted to give you something to remember me by, for you to think of while I'm away and for you to be able to look forward to when I come back." Here she started to wriggle herself out of her coat and he helped her, letting it drop around her heels as she knelt. Then with his hands around her shoulders he realised that the thin, white dress was all that she wore. He held her away from him again and she, holding him with her shining eyes, unbuttoned the front, and shrugged the dress away to let it fall around her hips. She was smiling, yet looked near to tears.

"Oh-h-h." Willy allowed the long sigh of wonder to breathe itself against the beauty of her naked body. "Oh Madge!" was all that he could say, then his head was pressed against her lovely breasts and his lips did what primeval instincts said was right. They were long moments embraced, then they drew apart so that he could look, and look again, and that he might fondle and hold in an amazed delight.

"I've been a prude all this time, Hilda says so anyway, but I didn't want to spoil it for when we're married, and I thought if I let you before, I'd have nothing to give then, but I knew you wanted to, and I wanted you to, too, and I thought, if you couldn't think of me properly - like you say in your letters, only they were your imagination, then you might not be able to wait till I came back."

This stumbling little speech, blurted out in bursts of words, pleading for understanding, came to Willy as the sweetest song ever sung. He took her in his arms and devoured her, laughing in sheer happiness and telling her of his delight and thankfulness. Madge relaxed in his joy and returned kiss for kiss, endearment for endearment, then it was time for him to feast his eyes again. She knelt, pressed back on her heels, her dress around her thighs. Willy fondled her smooth skin, kissing where it was irresistible, then let his hands drop to her hips, pressed her dress down, till full plump thighs made junction with her tummy.

There was a tiny line of dark curls at the apex of the join and he made to move further, but Madge held his hands. "No more, my darling, I'm all yours, for ever, but remember me like this - not with shame, please." Willy protested, but she was firm. Loving and gentle, but firm. "You'd wish you hadn't, afterwards," she said. "I know I would - when we're' married it'll be all right. I'm not teasing you, really I'm not, I just wanted you to be able to think of me - please?" With that she scooped up her dress, wriggled her arms into it and, with a sudden shameless display, showed Willy her bosom before. she fastened the front. Then they cuddled and cooed awhile till she suddenly shivered, and they realised that the sun had gone and a wind was bending the tree tops below them.

She pulled the coat on, smiling at Willy's devouring gaze as her plump breasts swayed and quivered with the movement. Willy was in torment. The thin clothes served merely as a drape that concealed, yet accentuated the languorous curves, and he could not let the magic moments fade. When he held her close again, and found his way between the buttons, she let him. She was glad, and it was long moments before they drew apart.

Time was running dangerously short, it was nearly gone. In no time at all, it seemed, they were back at the house, and this time it was the final farewell. Madge later remembered it only as having pushed Willy away, to force herself to leave him and running into the house in tears. Hilda greeted her. "'Thank gawd your back, those blasted kids! - Hey, what's up? - never mind love, he'll wait, he's that sort!"

Madge changed into her uniform. As she did so she looked at her bare body in the wardrobe mirror. "I'm glad I showed him," she thought, "and I'm not too bad really! I'm not as marvellous as he said I am, but at least there's plenty of me!" She hurried into the nursery and went to the window. Willy was still there. He saw her and waved.

His vivid imagination told him that he was making the longest wave that he would ever make, a wave that was to follow his beloved away and away, by train and by ship, ever following, ever calling her back. He hurried home to write pages of eulogy of her wondrous delights. He wrote on and on, spending his frustrated desires, his love and his misery at their parting, in a turmoil of words.

He decided that he'd take it to the house right away, so that she could read it that very night. He sealed the envelope and thumped down the stairs. His mother called him. "I've got some cold ham and salad that I've brought home, if you're hungry."

"Oh yes Mum!" Willy suddenly realised that he'd had nothing since breakfast, and once he'd demolished the meal, began to feel a little more cheerful. He thought of Madge reading the letter. She'd cry, he supposed, and feel more miserable than ever. He retrieved a small new potato that had rolled off the dish; put it in his mouth and rolled it around with his tongue. Gwen watched him furtively. He was frowning, looking sad "Poor Kid," she said to herself.."He must be very unhappy, it's a shame!"

She comforted herself with the thought that he was very young yet, and, anyway, his appetite didn't seem affected. Willy came to a decision. He returned to his room and tore the letter up, then he wrote another, a cheerful one this time, praising her beauty and full of warmth and love for her, telling her he would keep all the promises he'd made to her, and that he would be with her all the time, everywhere she went. He finished with the endearments that he always used, endearments that had become a code, only understood by the two of them, meaning moments of love that they had known. It was pathetically child-like, but meant much to both of them.

Chapter 12

During the week following Madge's departure, Willy gradually accustomed himself to her absence. He was in constant trouble at work for being forgetful and careless. The senior clerk was well aware of the cause, and being a man of course nature, made constant allusions to what he imagined Willy was enduring, lewdly attributing to the boy the longings his mainly sterile marriage prompted in himself, lascivious longings, that bit deep into his body when he strained against marital restrictions. Willy flushed, not with embarrassment at home truths finding their mark, but at distress that anyone could think of Madge in that way. He endured the teasing, and wished the day away until he could escape to his room, and continue to write in an orgy of sentiment. It was work that would be destroyed almost a soon as written, but it gave an outlet to his emotions. Among these was a little composition that spoke of the coconut scent of gorse blossom warmed by the sun, the drowsing of bee hum, the skylark's trilling above the shimmering heat and the laughter of the yaffle, as it crossed from wood to wood - sensuous perfume, sounds and warmth, spelling satisfaction, until the cynical laughter told of its transience. That one he saved, pushing it into a folder with others. "I'll do that again," he told himself. "I'll ask old Watts what he thinks of it; perhaps *Home Chat* would take it." The satisfaction of writing something that pleased him bucked up his spirits and the weight of depression that had enervated him, lifted.

A few days later, there was a letter lying on the doormat when he came down in the morning. He swooped on it, hoping it was from Madge, but recognised the handwriting as Jerry's. He fried the bread and egg put out for him, and opened the letter to read while he ate.

"Dear Willy," he read. "As you can see I'm in hospital. I had an accident on the way home after I took you out the week before last. I must have taken a bend too wide, anyway I hit a bank and came off, the bike shot across the road and hit a wall I hope it will be O.K. with the insurance. I was lucky. I finished up in a bed of nettles, but somehow I broke my leg. It's in plaster and I'll be here for several weeks, they say. They told my mum and she's been down and she's seeing to the bike. I don't know where it is, but somebody's looking after it. My landlady comes in quite often. She nags me to death about driving too fast. Still, it's a good job you weren't on the back. I hope they'll get the bike repaired. Good job I didn't hit anyone else. The police say it's nothing to do with them, so I'm all right there. They've got my leg in a metal thing with sand bags on the end. I can't move much, and I've got a sore ass, but they all say I'm lucky."

Willy had a vivid recollection of the tearing wind, the road flashing by under them, the badly turned bends that had terrified: "Gosh! I might have been killed!"

The letter continued - "Be a sport Will, and ask my mum what's happened to the bike - you'd better drop her a note and say when you're calling in case it's not convenient."

That evening Willy told Gwen about Jerry's accident. Her face paled at the news. "Oh my dear days! It could have happened with you on the back - you could both of you been killed or crippled for life!"

"Yes," said Willy. "I've thought of that, he should have had more practice."

"More practice! He shouldn't never have been riding the thing, much less taking you. They ought to be banned, they're too dangerous, there's no safety to anybody with things like that roaring around."

"Well anyway he says the bike's smashed up, and he doesn't know where it is, but his mum does, and he wants me to go and see her, and find out what's happening to it."

"You're not going to that house," Gwen flared with anger. "You can't be seen going there!"

"Why not?" asked Willy in surprise.

"Willy! You can't, she's - she's not nice. You can't go there! - Surely you must know how she lives - didn't Jerry ever drop any hints?"

"No. I know he'd never let me call for him, and I couldn't go inside. He never said why, I thought she didn't want me to, or something."

Gwen looked at him in despair. How could she tell him things that were beyond her vocabulary, almost beyond her knowledge, for she had never been one to join the nudge and wink gossipers. "Well you can't go! And that's flat! Willy, you're a man now, but you've never mixed with bad people, except that Jerry - and I've never been happy about him, though to give him his dues, he's always seemed decent, but he's one of the Well Street lot, and he's his mother's son. She's a bad lot, a real bad lot and I'll not have you knowing her!"

"How do you mean, she's bad?"

"She's a tart!" cried Gwen in desperation. She'd have said "prostitute" if she'd been sure of the word, but her reading and conversations had never embraced the subject, and "tart" was a word that Ada, the daily at the Big House, had used on occasion when pouring scorn on some poor, raddled, old soul, who had attended bridge evenings there. Willy was not so innocent that he was unaware of the things called "carnal knowledge" in the legal parlance of his work, but he had never really considered professional prostitutes. His appreciation of the pleasures of the flesh had not stretched that far. Sometimes the senior clerk made remarks about women that might have enlightened him, but as he had not understood them, he had not questioned their meaning, and the older man, who would have been happy to oblige, found himself rebuffed by Willy's disinterest.

"Jerry says I'd better drop her a note so as she'll know I'm coming."

"You're not to go, do you hear me? I'll not have it!"

"Oh Mum! She can't be that bad! Jerry always says she's been a good to him - It's only that she's got men friends, and she's a widow after all!"

"That's it - men friends! Men who pay her - she's a harlot! Like the bible says - no decent folk would have anything to do with her!" (Harlot - that was the word she'd wanted, only she couldn't think of it before).

There was a troubled silence, then Willy said, "I'll write to her and ask her to phone me at work, they won't mind if I explain that my friend's in hospital."

"Well, you post the letter. Don't you go near that house, and don't let her get you involved - you remember your Madge when you're talking to her".

"I will. I'm remembering her all the time - how far do you think they've got now? As far as Gibralter?"

"I'm sure I don't know," said Gwen, relieved to have changed the subject. "I don't rightly know where Malta is!"

Effie Wilkins telephoned Willy in reply to his letter. She'd got a friend, she told him, who was in the motor business, and he knew what to do about the bike, but Willy need not bother himself because she was going to see Jerry again in a few days, and would tell him what was going on. She called Willy "luv" and thanked him for enquiring.

"She sounds nice," thought Willy. "Still, just as well I'm not going to have to do anything about the bike."

He wrote to Jerry commiserating with him, and asking about his leg, and what he would do when he came out of hospital. He then rambled on about local news, and Madge's departure and so on. A week later he got another letter from Jerry. It was full of excitement and optimism. His mother had been to see him and had told him that she had got a friend, who was "in the know", to buy the bike for eighty pounds, plus a second hand car.

"I was mad at first," wrote Jerry, "but she said she'd never have a good night's sleep as long as I was riding a motor bike, and four wheels were safer, and would get me around much more comfortable."

Evidently Jerry with his leg in a Thomas Splint, anchored by a hefty sandbag, had been no match for his formidable mother. Anyway, the job was done. Jerry then went on to tell his further news. "Hey! What do you think! Mum's setting me up in business, like I'd planned, only I was going to do it on my own. She's turned up trumps all right. Some chap she knows is going to back me to start with. He's got some land, up Shorton way, and we can build thirty houses on it. Mum reckons he says I'll be able to pay him out, and have enough to buy land and go ahead on my own, as soon as the houses are sold."

Willy told his mother the gist of the letter, and when Gwen flushed and said, "I'm sorry you ever got to know that boy, he'll be using tainted money, and I'd rather you stayed clear of him," he made no comment, understanding her repugnance, but not wishing to say anything against Jerry. He had felt the excitement the prospect had caused him, and was glad for him. His first thought had been "Good! He'll be coming home and it'll be like old times."

Since Gwen's first outburst against Jerry's mother, Willy had confided in his friend, Mr Watts, who had given him kindly advice, and some information about what was just underneath the facade of conventional life. It made Willy aware of the way some people lived, without tittilating the knowledge with lewdness. Mr Watts had placed his arm on Willy's shoulders and said, "It goes on all the time, son, everywhere, all over the world, and always has done, but people like you and me, and millions of others, needn't know. It's human nature and there's some who can't help it. You just stick to your girl, and let them that wants to, find their own pleasures."

Willy was so obsessed by Madge that he felt no curiosity about people like Effie, and could dismiss them from his mind, but he could not forget Jerry, nor their friendship, and was looking forward to resuming their old comradeship. When Gwen said she hoped he'd stay clear of Jerry, he allowed a moment to pass, then said "Jerry's all right, Mum, he's always been my friend, I'll be glad when he's back here again - there's nothing wrong with Jerry, and I know, from work, all the builders have to have somebody to back them at first, till they get established, then they go to building societies. I think I'll go down to Plymouth on Saturday afternoon and see him.

"Well, you do what you think best, but I'll not have anything to do with that woman, and neither will you if you've got any sense!"

"I'm not going to," replied Willy, beginning to feel annoyed. "I never have, have I? I've never even spoken to her - it's just that Jerry's my friend." Then, suddenly voicing feelings that had been lying dormant for years. "After all, I never had any brothers or sisters, and he looked after me when I was a kid - I never had a dad to show me anything."

"No dear," said Gwen, a sudden misery in her voice, "you didn't, it was the war, and I didn't have anyone either - only you.

"Well you've still got me Mum, and I won't let you down!"

Uneasy at the rare display of emotion between them, Willy hurriedly ran up to his room. Gwen sat down by the window, looking out at the dusty valerian crowning the wall opposite, and tried to close the dreadful door of her memory, kept long shut by her devotion to Willy, but now suddenly prised open. "Now he'll be going, soon as that maid comes back, then what'll I have to live for?" she asked herself.

Chapter 13

Willy went to Plymouth on the following Saturday afternoon. He had never been to the city before, and the journey was something of an occasion for him. He could well afford the five shillings return fare on the Devon General bus, for he was doing quite well financially, what with his job, that was paying him two pounds, his articles for the *Echo*, and various contributions to papers and magazines that were being accepted more frequently. For the time, when unemployment was universal, and wages arbitrarily cut to the bone, he was quite an affluent young man, able to afford his twenty fags a day and many other little extravagancies that had only been a dream a few months previously. He was wearing a new suit that he had paid three pounds ten shillings for at the new Montague Burton shop, lately opened in the town. He was quite a man about town that afternoon.

The narrow city streets were jammed with Saturday traffic. There seemed to be a million shoppers on the pavements and overflowing on to the road, where constant snarls of cars and wagons were seemingly prised apart by tram cars, clanging their warning as they ground their way forward. The August heat, hung with dust, was like a blanket laying over all. Willy had no idea where the Prince of Wales hospital was, and spent a weary hour finding it, by which time he was wishing that he was wearing flannels and open-necked shirt instead of the suit.

Jerry, propped up by a pile of pillows, was delighted to see him. All the other patients seemed to have their families around them and Jerry had been feeling bored.

"Hi! Will!" he called, when he saw him come into the ward and stand, searching the rows of beds for him. "Hey! Down here."

He was in the bottom bed, next to the window, and waved and beckoned. "Fancy you coming all down here! That's awfully good of you, old man!" (This last in the affected voice of what he thought was "wireless English").

They had a few words about Jerry's leg and what they were doing for it. Jerry waxed eloquent about the nurses, one of whom was "a bit of all right" but was, unfortunately, off duty that afternoon.

"Cor! She's a smasher Will. I could do her a bit of good, anytime at all. There's one on night duty, as well - she's only a probationer, about seventeen, she's got a pair on her I can't take my eyes off. I was hoping she'd give me a blanket bath, but it was one of the sisters - I told them I could wait till Nurse Rowlands could do it, but she told me not to be cheeky or she'd complain to Matron - she's all right, though, I get on with all of them."

I bet he does, thought Willy. He gets on with everyone. Willy asked about the plans for building and Jerry told him all about it. Then he became very serious, and looking askance at Willy, asked "You know about my Mum, I suppose? Well, I've been embarrassed for years. I was glad to leave home. She's always been good to me though, I had it much easier than most kids, and she told me that when she heard of my smash up, she realised I was the only family she had, and wanted to do something for me." (Effie had always had little Jerry's stay in the hated orphanage on her conscience, and had suddenly seen a way to assuage the guilt).

"I've always been fond of her, Will - proud of her too, in a way." (He shied at admitting that he loved her - though Willy was the one person who would have understood). "She's so... so elegant. I mean, she walked in here as if the place belonged to her! All the blokes in the beds watched her walk down to me. One of 'em said, afterwards, that she looked like a duchess! My little nurse said she was an 'eye-opener' and she liked her dress. Anyhow, she's seen the Almoner and paid for me, and got everything fixed up, and she's got some chap to go into partnership, so I can get a start. Oh Will! It's what I've wanted! I'm out of my time this month, and I can make a do of it, I know I can." Then after a pause, Jerry said - "So this bike smash up worked out all right for me. My landlady's coming in tomorrow, bless her - she's a good old duck - seem's to have taken a shine to me. I'll ask her to look at that young medlar tree her old man planted out the back, and see if there's a good strong bend in any of the branches that wasn't there a'fore."

"You and your medlars!" said Willy. "Still, I'm glad, you'll be a rich man before I will! Though I'm not doing too bad."

It was Willy's turn then to voice his hopes and ambitions, and he was a bit taken aback when Jerry, his mind on much more earthy things than good journalism, butted in on one of Willy's repetitious "when Madge comes back".

"Look, Will, you've got shot of the old ball and chain; now she's gone you want to break out a bit - take a bit of skirt out, and have some fun! You're not married yet you know - there's a hell of a lot of it about you know, waiting to be picked! You wait till I'm back! We'll have some fun! I've been finding out things; as long as you're careful, they're as keen as we are!"

"I'm not interested," said Willy, resentful of Jerry's assumption that fidelity was unimportant. "With Madge and me, it's different."

"Go on! You want to find out what goes on, Will. Cor! It's marvellous!

The bell announcing end of visiting, cut short Jerry's remark, and saved Willy from further embarrassment. "I'll be off," he said. "Let me know how you go on. If you're still here in a week or two, I might come down again."

"Thanks, I'd like you to, and thanks for coming now - cheerio!" Willy left, and, as he went he met two nurses, fresh faced and wholesome in their crisp uniforms, wheeling in the tea trolley. Willy found himself looking at them, not as nurses, as he had done on arrival, but as buxom young women, and thought to himself, "Oh Lor! Jerry can't half spoil things!" The thought persisted during his journey home. "He's changed, he's got different somehow," he thought. But I suppose we were only kids when he went away - still, he never talked of girls like that, he never seemed very interested. He must have been up to something, I reckon. Perhaps Mum was right, and he's like his mum, not to be wondered at really. I don't want that sort of thing though!

Willy was right in his surmise. Jerry had been up to something! When he left home, he not only had little interest in the company of girls, but, because of goings on in his home (to which he had deliberately closed his eyes and determinedly ignored) he had an unconscious revulsion to sexual experience and was scared of it. The voluptuous Dot had changed all that, and after her departure, Jerry had, for a time, worked with an ex-naval joiner, who had fed the boy's awakened interest with tales of shore leave adventures all over the world. It was with this man that he had gone to a place, in Stonehouse, where "Jack Ashore" was made welcome. His inexperience and nervousness had made the visit a shameful disappointment, but later in the day, after refreshment and consideration of pleasures unfulfilled had restored his energies, he had returned to the house and acquitted himself well. Since then he had made two more calls there, and had also "tried his luck" with a girl at a local dance, with success. It was this that had channelled his thoughts and talk of feminine conquest, and in the coarseness of so doing, had given poor Willy's gentle nature some disgust.

For the moment though, firmly anchored to his hospital bed, he was restricted to fantasy. The nurses were well aware of his appraising looks, but well able to parry his advances. They were used to male hospital patients falling in love with them, some with heartfelt gratitude, some with the simple pleasure of having a kind gentle woman tend their needs, and others, like Jerry, who with no enervating illness, had a virile longing for the soft flesh beneath their starched aprons. It provided a giggle and a relief from the terribly hard work demanded of them.

Chapter 14

Madge posted her first letter on the ship at Gibralter. It was a series of statements of facts. "It was very rough for two days when we started. The children were seasick and so was I. It is very hot in our cabin. There isn't a porthole and the children won't go to sleep. The Missus was sick as well, and I had it all to do. I felt like dying. We're better now and the sea is calm. We are going to stop for a day at Gibralter and I can post this letter."

So the scraps of information were jotted down. Poor Madge found it hard to find the time and energy to write even so little. "I've had it all to do", should have told him everything; of the wailing and the retching, the constant battle to keep at least some of the children quiet, while she herself was weary and wracked with nausea. A few words of love, and the line of kisses cheered him, and he was stirred anew to write more to her. He had written daily, and had posted the letters twice a week to the address in Malta that she had given him. He knew that she wouldn't get them for about two weeks after posting, but he had posted one on the day she had sailed, and hoped that it might even be waiting for her when she arrived, if it went by a faster ship. He had discovered that mail went by different routes, some by fast liners that dropped the post in Egypt for forwarding to Malta, and some that went direct to the island. He dreamed of his letter being actually on the ship with Madge. His letter travelling close to her all the way! He liked that thought!

It was a slow ship, calling at Algiers and Tunis before reaching Malta, and Willy's first two letters were waiting for Madge when the family arrived. It had seemed an age to the girl, and though the sickness had passed and the last week had been plain sailing, she was exhausted with the care of the children, and was homesick and lonely.

When at last it was quiet, she took Willy's letters to bed with her and read and re-read them. It seemed that he was speaking to her from another world that she had left years, not days, before. His first letter was full of the delight of that hour amongst the gorse bushes and, Madge though "I'm glad I let him, he loves me so." She stared into the dark thinking, "Three years or more, oh God! - make him wait for me!"

Madge had been gone a month when Willy's prospects took another step forward. A large estate, that lay on one side of the town, was offered for sale for speculative building. Willy's boss was appointed solicitor for the vendor, and to make economic sense, many of the builders left the mortgage arrangements to him also, and he anticipated that many of the purchasers of the houses to be built would be content to let him arrange their conveyances and mortgages also. This gave the prospect of a great deal of business, and after the solicitor and the senior clerk had examined the title they decided that it warranted a clerk to itself. In those days an "Abstract of Title" (which was a precis of the title, right back to the original purchase, perhaps hundreds of years previously, and with details of all covenants restricting its use etc.) had to be furnished to each purchaser's solicitor, and these had to be "examined" against the originals, then the paraphernalia of "Requisitions on Title" had to be gone through, and finally a hand-written deed, "engrossed" on parchment, had to be prepared.

Willy; was called into the solicitor's inner sanctum, and told that he had been given the donkey work to do. He had been "engrossing" for a good while, for he had developed a fine copper plate hand, and found pleasure in making the first word of each paragraph a small work of art in Old English. The rest of the work was routine copy typing, at which he was good. Willy's salary was raised to two pounds ten shillings, and he was relieved of most of the menial jobs that had been his ever since he had joined the firm. A new junior was to be employed.

It seemed likely that it would be some time before any of this business materialised, but Willy's wages were increased forthwith. By reckoning his weekly half guinea from the *Echo* and an additional pound a week from various magazines, he was delighted to go home and tell his mother that he now earned more than most top tradesmen or bank clerk. Gwen could hardly believe it. He had been paying her a pound a week for nearly a year and now he said he'd make it thirty shillings.

Willy decided that he would go to Plymouth again and tell Jerry the news. Meantime he confided in Mr Watts, who was as pleased for Willy as Willy was himself.

"When this gets going, they'll have to pay you more, as soon as you're of age," he said. "But as it is, you'll be able to save and get your own home." He plugged this idea in case Willy might find less profitable, or honourable, ways of using his money; reminding himself that he had never been paid four pounds a week in his life, and thinking of what a temptation it could be to a boy.

"I might get a car," said Willy. "There's plenty to be had for about ten pounds, and I could afford five shillings a week for petrol."

"You think carefully, boy, and don't be talked into anything."

"No fear of that Sir! I'm going to try again with *The Passing Show*. I've got three articles done, and I can do more. I've got the feeling of it now."

They talked on, as usual, until Mrs Watts appeared with some of her fruit cake and cups of tea. Willy's depression over Madge's absence had lifted, and his old enthusiasm returned.

"Soon's I'm twenty-one, I reckon I'll buy a house on this estate, and have it all ready for Madge when she comes home. They reckon they'll sell at six hundred to a thousand pounds, and it'll only cost a pound a week mortgage."

"Good for you, son, it'll give you something to work for."

"Oh! I've got that - only she's two thousand, five hundred miles away," replied Willy, having checked the mileage by a nautical atlas.

"Bless his heart," thought Mrs Watts. "She's a lucky girl!"

"I wonder?" thought her husband, 'he's only a kid yet, and lots of water'll go under the bridge before he sees her again."

Although Willy had been able to express his hopes and ambitions to his mother, and to Mr. Watts, it was really to Jerry that he wanted to talk. He could talk to him as man to man, without feeling that he might be over-enthusiastic and naive in his plans. Jerry, tied to his bed, and desperately anxious to be up and doing, was equally glad to have Willy to confide in. He was bored with hospital life, and even the pleasure of teasing the nurses palled. For their part, they were specially attentive to him - finding a cheerful young man, with his lusty instincts unimpaired by disease - a welcome change to the poor old "bladder daddies" who occupied most of the beds, and whose helplessness and distress was a drain on their strength and emotions. There seemed to be a happy little aura around his bed, but waiting was tedious and he envied Willy his mobility.

"My old girl (meaning his landlady) 'as been in again. She told me mum had paid up my lodging for three months, so's I can go back there till I can use my leg again - they reckon I'll be on crutches for a time. Cor! you wouldn't think, would you - just falling off a bike!"

"At seventy miles per hour," reminded -Willy.

"No, I wasn't doing that, it was that damned dog leg over the railway bridge. I reckon I didn't lay over enough - hey! the bike's hardly marked! I've let it go anyway, after what mum's done for me, I could hardly argue, and I'll have a car."

"I'm getting one too'."

"Go on! What make?"

The conversation grew animated over this new interest, and when Willy left he felt quite happy in the re-establishment of their old intimacy. Jerry had not mentioned girls and Willy had deemed it advisable to keep Madge out of the conversation. Of course, he had written to her, pages of excited hopes, and she was at the centre of them all.

Madge wrote to him every week, and her letters were eagerly read and longed over. She found little to tell him; just the heat, the narrow streets, with their shuttered windows, the noise of the teeming child population, the sand-coloured buildings and the curly-tiled roofs, the clamour of church bells. "They don't ring them like they do at home, they all seem to ring at once, all anyhow, crash-bang-wallop!" Madge did not have the ability to express her love for Willy in her letters, and she told him so again and again. "... but I do love you so my darling, and I miss you more than I can say. I don't have much time to think during the day, but at night I do. It's ever so dark at night here. The sky goes black and the stars are huge. I wonder sometimes if you are looking at the same stars as me."

"I'm on the top floor of this house," she wrote in another letter, "and there's a flat roof where they dry the washing and keep goats and chickens, like a back garden at home. Some of the servants live there. I'm in three rooms at the front with the kids. The Missus is on the floor below; it's like a block of flats really. All the stairs and floors are tiles and marble. It's very nice, but I wish I was home."

Her letters always ended by thanking Willy for his lovely letters and saying that she loved him. Willy used to try and read into her words, some clue as to her life. A little description of things seen or done, was relived by him, seeing her doing it, watching her at her work, leaning over her as she wrote.

When he came back from visiting Jerry, he sat in his stuffy little room, looking at the table with his papers, all neatly filed, just as at work, with a shelf over, on which stood a photograph of Madge. She had had it taken by the photographer, down by the station as a last minute present before she went. "Five weeks today," he thought. Such long weeks that he dared not look ahead at the procession of weeks to come. "I'll write," he told himself, "and I'll get a car, and then I'll be able to get about more, and get new ideas... and I'll take mum out sometimes."

Chapter 15

Willy's boss advertised for a Junior Clerk - "knowledge of shorthand and typewriting an advantage". He received several replies, and the applicants were interviewed. They were young boys who were learning shorthand and typewriting at nightschool, and were applying for their first real jobs. Willy felt a lordly superiority over them, sitting them at his typewriter to type their panic-stricken pieces. He had been out 'paying in' at the bank, and taking his time about it as it was a lovely morning, so he did not see the latest hopeful arrive, and the senior clerk was already putting the unfortunate to test. He heard the man take the applicant into the boss's office and close the door. Willy got on with his work, his back to the communicating door, so took little notice when they returned.

"Churchward, this is the new typist," said the senior clerk and Willy turned around to find himself facing a girl of about sixteen. His immediate impression was that she was dazzling! Her fair hair shone, her very blue eyes seemed to be alight, and the fairest of complexions glowed with warmth. She was smiling at him and holding out a hand in greeting. Willy leapt to his feet, feeling confused, and suddenly shy.

"How do you do!"

"Miss Atkinson will be starting on Monday, Churchward. I'll expect you to help her settle in."

"I'm Valerie," said the vision, "known as Val'! - what's your name?"

"Will," replied Willy, suddenly finding all his superiority evaporating. I'm known as 'Will', but they call me 'Churchward' here."

The senior clerk showed her out and watched her go tap-tapping down the stairs. "How about that, eh? The old man fell for her all right. You'd better look out young Churchward, things might be a bit different now - fancy the old man taking on a girl, he swore he wouldn't have another. They're trouble all right, but she's a smasher, don't you think?"

"She's nice," said Willy.

"Nice! Gor darn it, boy - she's a hum-dinger! - and just your size and weight - but I'll have my eye on you, never fear, and the first time I catch you, I'll chop it off!" Here he roared with laughter at his own witticism.

Willy got on with his work, but he felt disturbed. He was conscious of a faint perfume that still lingered in the room, and he was aware of a feeling that he was all hands and feet again, just like he used to be, when he first started work.

Chapter 16

Jerry was at last allowed to leave hospital and return to the post office at Avonford. He was still on crutches and far from mobile. He managed to kiss and squeeze his two favourite nurses, and invited them to visit him on their days off, and they laughed and said, "You'll be lucky!" But they weren't above giving him a kiss apiece, which, if not lingering, lasted long enough for his hands to take opportunist action on their bottoms. "Go on," they said, "if you weren't a cripple, you'd pay for that."

"I'd be glad to," was the reply, as he was eased into the taxi and left the two laughing girls waving him goodbye.

He had been in hospital for eight weeks, and found his lodgings something of an anticlimax. He missed the routine and the company. He found himself thinking, "They'll be doing the beds now," or "dinner will just be coming up," or, more fondly, "she'd be doing my pillows and getting me comfortable." He was bored and depressed. Mrs Cooper did not seem very happy with him either. He was a bit of trouble to her, always sitting around in her back parlour and getting in the way. She had asked him why his mother had not had him home, and Jerry had had to find a plausible excuse, saying that she "lived in" at the hotel were she worked, but he could see that the old lady was unconvinced. Money was another worry. His sickness benefit was only a few shillings, and he spent it all on cigarettes. Mrs Cooper was at pains to tell him how lucky he was to have a mum who paid his rent, and Jerry had to agree; even more so when a letter from her arrived, enclosing three pounds, and telling him that she had arranged lodgings for him in Paignton and suggesting that he hired a taxi to take him there, as he had better meet the man who was going to partner him in setting up a business, and get on with the necessary preparations. This bucked him up. "Good old mum!" he thought. "Soon's I can walk again properly, I'll have to do somethin~ for her."

The lodging that Effie had taken for Jerry was in a short terrace of houses that, until very recently, had been the last of the town before the open country began. Now streets of houses had smothered the buttercup golden meadows and had seemed to push the old houses back into the town. The householder was a stoker at the gasworks and his wife had known Effie of old. This person, a Mrs Godfrey, confided in Jerry, "Course I've known your mum for years, and all about her, so you needn't worry, she's all right, did me a good turn once, and nobody up around 'ere knows her."

Effie called to see him the day he moved in. Her statuesque figure, dressed in good taste, made Jerry feel proud. "Cor!" he thought, "she could be anyone - a real lady - you got to hand it to her!"

Effie was a bit ill at ease, and her high colour was not all due to careful make-up. This was an important day for her and, after she had asked after his leg, she got down to business. "Here's the eighty pounds for that dratted bike," she said, putting the wad of pound notes on the table, "and here's the address for you to collect the car, soon's you can. I've paid Mrs. Godfrey three month's board and lodging for you, to start you off, so make the money last as long, as you can. Albert - er, Mr Leonard, reckons it'll be a twelve month before you see some money coming in, but of course, he'll tell you all about that."

She stood up, smoothed out a wrinkle or two from the elegant silk coat that she was wearing, then faced Jerry and said, "So that's all fixed. I've not always been what I should to you, and I daresay you're not proud of me, but I've done my best now and the rest is up to you. If you want to, you can forget that I ever existed."

"Oh Mum!" Jerry's voice was so full of shocked reproach, that it stopped Effie in full flood. "Mum! You're the best mum ever. I love you. (It was really out), and I'm proud of you - you're wonderful, you look like a real lady, I'll never want to forget you'. How could I?"

Effie was stunned by her son's reaction. She had screwed up her courage to go and see him, and had really thought that he would be glad to wave her goodbye. Tears were filling her eyes before he had finished reproaching her, but she regained her composure. "It'd be best if we parted company," she said. "It wouldn't help you to have me around, when you're a successful builder. Some of my friends might not like it, in case they got involved." She stood looking at him. "I'm glad you said you loved me," she said. "You're the only one who's ever said that so's I could believe it."

She put her hands on his shoulders, and leaning, kissed him. She was about to draw away when Jerry held her tight to him and kissed her hard, on the mouth. "Mum," he said, "if you want, I'll not bother you, but if ever you want me, for anything, help of any kind, I'll always be there, and waiting." He was embarrassed by his own emotions, so he smacked her seat and said "Now you'd better go before you start to cry and spoil your eye black, but don't ever forget, I'm your son and you've been the best of mums to me."

When she got home, Effie stood in her little kitchen and, for a moment, saw again the naked body of her little son, with the angry marks of the rope's end across his back, and said to herself, "Poor little sod, I did that to him really." Then she did cry.

During the next few weeks, while Jerry hobbled about, regaining the use of his leg, he became acquainted with Mr Leonard, who owned a field close to Shorton and was prepared to advance capital sufficient to commence building. Jerry found him a hard bargainer, who was virtually proposing to employ him as builder, with the net profits going into his pockets. Jerry, in spite of his youth, and poor education, was no fool. While working at Avonford, he had planned his future in some detail, and although not expecting the opportunity that had been offered him, he had made a very intelligent estimate of his requirements to start on his own. His old mentor, the carpenter, had given him advice, so had the bricklayers, plasterers and tilers. He had never neglected any opportunity to glean information.

The acquisition of land was very important, that he knew, and that was where Mr Leonard came in, also acting as a guarantor, and that was all Jerry wanted. He took note of all Mr Leonard's proposals, hiding his resentment at being treated as a mere servant, and begged leave to think the matter over.

"Well, you can, of course, but I'm giving you a chance not many would get. Land is getting scarce, and I can get dozens who would jump at the chance, so don't you take too long boy; remember, I'm only offering you first chance as a favour!"

It was that last "As a favour" that raised Jerry's gore. "Oh lor, to think of my mum!" was in his mind, as he looked at the man, his great paunch, double chins, slack mouth and baggy eyes; a big man, gone to seed, overweight, florid-faced with drink, flabby from an indolent life. "As a favour" - and what favours would he get in return? Jerry felt a revulsion toward the man. "I'm not putting mum in that corner," he thought, "to hell with him." Mr Leonard must have sensed something of Jerry's feelings.

"Of course, there must be some confidences between us," he said.

"Yes," was all Jerry replied.

That evening he called on Willy. They went up to Willy's room - the "Den" they had adventured from as children. Jerry told Willy all, man to man, showing Willy the respect for his maturity.

"Sounds a swine to me," said Willy. "I can imagine how you feel!" He couldn't really, he was too innocent of life but he felt Jerry's revulsion towards the whole basis of the transaction, though he was incapable of giving an opinion on so intimate a matter. They were silent for a while, Willy sitting at his desk, Jerry sprawled on the bed, his hands behind his head, gazing at the ceiling.

"I'll tell you something, Will," he said, and he told Willy of the house at Plymouth, of the women there and the mercenary trade carried on.

"I enjoyed it, sort of, I got my money's worth, but thinking back now it was pretty rotten. You know, they weren't girls to make love with, they were just things to use - and now I think of my mum, and that big slob using her, and I can't do it! I don't believe she's like those tarts at Plymouth, but he's doing what I did, and he don't give a damn for her, or for me, so long's he gets what he wants from her and his money's worth from me. It hurts Will! I've gotta get my mum out of it It makes me sick to think of her!"

Willy was way out of his depth. "I don't know what to say," was all he could venture. Then, "I say! Why not come and see my boss? There's this estate, you might get a bank loan, and the Halifax advance money in stages as you build - come and see him. I'll tell him first, and make an appointment for you - you can but try!"

Jerry turned on his elbow and looked at his friend. "I will," he said. "You do your stuff and fix me a time soon as you can." Then crossing the room, he thumped Willy on the back. "There I always thought that great brain of yours would do for the two of us - right, let the old firm go into action again." They clattered down the stairs, Jerry jumping them on one leg.

"Mrs! You got a genius for a son," he told Gwen. "Yes," said Gwen, eyeing him warily, "I know that, and he's a good son, too!"

"You bet," said Jerry, grinning and winking at Willy, as they went.

"Oh dear!"' Gwen told herself, "I wish he hadn't come back - them Well Street lot!"

Willy's boss had never given the boy much encouragement, but he admired his literary work, and the maturity that he saw developing in his character as a result of it. Also, Willy was a good clerk, meticulous in his work and to be relied upon. So he interested himself in Jerry's ambitions, and after meeting him and questioning him carefully on his work and hopes, was impressed by the boy's sound grasp of business. After enquiries as to character, he became a trifle dubious when the information on Effie's status as a chambermaid at the Cliff House, was augmented by a knowing wink and leer. He thought about it, and decided to ignore it. So arrangements were made. Willy's boss found a client who would advance enough money to get Jerry started, and a section of ten sites were marked on the map in Jerry's name.

"Now," Jerry told Willy, "I'll tell that fat gutted bastard where he can stuff his land!"

"Better write him," advised Willy. "I'll draft you a letter, if you like."

Willy wrote a short, courteous note, regretting "that certain considerations, involving a third person, made the proposed partnership unsuitable". Jerry roared with laughter when he read it. "Cor! Will'. You've certainly got a way of saying things! I was going to tell him to get lost, and stick his land where the monkey sticks his nuts, but I reckon this'll make him a damned sight madder - I'd love to see his face."

"You've got to remember your mother Jerry, you mustn't make it hard for her, after all, she did her best'."

"Good old Will, you're right! Look, write me out a letter explaining, and I'll copy it and send it to mum."

So the years crept forward. Jerry, with a couple of labourers and contracted out specialists, built his first houses, slowly, with the perfection of workmanship that was his nature. He lived frugally, still with Mrs Godfrey, saying to himself that as soon as he had got his guarantor off his back, he'd build a house for himself, and get his mother to live with him. He had no thoughts of marriage, and reckoned he could well afford to keep Effie by then.

Madge had been away for six months when the thatched roof of Gwen's cottage, rotten for years, at last gave way to the moss, ferns and valerian that had ravaged it. The landlord saw no prospect of recouping the cost of a new roof from the tiny rent Gwen was paying, so when the local authority condemned the property, Gwen and Willy were given the tenancy of one of the new Council houses, built on the meadows where the old dairyman's cows used to graze. They were still close to the green, but overlooking it The circular fountain, little used now, was the centre of the triangle below them; the abandoned cottage clearly to be seen on the hill climbing up to the smithy and the town. After the dark, damp cottage, her new house entranced Gwen, though the climb up from the Big House, was a trial, when her tired legs reached the end of the day.

This time was no vacuum for Willy who had been able to concentrate his energies on his journalism. In this he was helped a lot by the editor of the *Echo*, who found pride and pleasure in refining Willy's amateurish efforts into good reporting. He nearly broke the boy's heart by reducing pages of flamboyant prose into a couple of paragraphs that gave all the information without any of the painstaking descriptive eloquence.

Mr Watts was rough with Willy. "Keep your talents for descriptive writing for appropriate occasions, and thank God you've got a man who can make a journalist of you" was his advice. "You've got it in you to go places, so make the most of the training that you're getting!" Jerry had acquired a Morris Cowley car as part of the deal for his motor cycle, that his mother had engineered while he was in hospital. It was six years old and well used, but still very roadworthy, and Effie had battled well on his behalf, insisting on new tyres and repairs to the canvas hood. As soon as Jerry went into business he sold the Morris to Willy for twenty pounds and got himself a small lorry, being quite content to use it as work-horse and social vehicle. "Just the job for taking a girl out!" he told Willy, with a grin and nod of the head that indicated the roomy body.

Willy got a garage mechanic to take him out for an hour's driving instruction before taking it home. When he did, he insisted upon taking Gwen out on an exhibition run. Poor Gwen felt that events were moving at such a rate she was forever one step behind Willy's affluence - the new house, the car. It was almost too much for her to get used too. Her first drive nearly made her foreswear another. When they started off, it was with gigantic kangaroo hops that had Willy hanging on to the wheel for dear life and Gwen bucking up and down as if she was on the 'cake walk' at the fair. It finished with the inevitable stall, and Gwen was for getting out, but Willy overcame her fears and managed to get away in some fashion and do a perilous trip down to the sea front and back. After that it was child's play.

Willy had got over Valerie's appearance in the office. At first he found her a great distraction. She was a delightfully happy soul, well aware of her attractions, and very amused at Willy's confusion when she turned them on, but she soon saw that he was not to be beguiled, and decided that he was "nice".

The boss was nice too, and he enjoyed having her around. The senior clerk was a bit of a lad, she reckoned, only ancient! Nonetheless, to be kept at arm's length, especially on the stairs. When they had become acquainted, Willy told her about Madge.

"Malta'." said Val incredulously. "Malta - that's in the Med. My uncle was there in the navy - when's she coming back? Fancy being engaged, and her all out there - don't you get fed up without her?"

"Yes, I do, and she's only been gone six months yet - it seems ages!"

"Well, when I get a steady boy friend, I'm not hopping off to the other side of the world and leave him here for some other girl to find."

"I'm not looking for any other girl, thank you," said Willy, primly,

"Ah! Yes! But supposing some other girl finds you, eh! What then?" As she said this, half in earnest, half in fun, she leaned forward across the desk that they were sharing, and wagged a finger at Willy. Willy did not notice the finger, he saw the momentary glimpse of petal-soft bosoms and his body stirred to his discomfort.

"Oh Madge! Why did you go?" This thought recurred over and over again. He was lonely. His placid boyhood life had been so disrupted; first by Madge; then by his writing and the relative wealth that it brought him; then by losing Madge; changing homes; finding himself a car owner, and mostly by stepping into a belated manhood. He found himself desperately frustrated without Madge to confide in and to share his successes.

Jerry took a simple view. "You must have been mazed, the two of you, she needn't have gone!"

"Yes, but she'd promised!"

"Oh! Bugger that! What'll they care about her, so long's they get a day's work out of her. By the time she's come back, ten to one she'll have got some bloke out there - blimey! there's half the navy and God knows how many soldiers there! You want to get yourself a bit home here, an' make hay while the sun shines!"

They had their first real quarrel then. Willy poured scorn on Jerry's promiscuous way of life, speaking self-righteously of fidelity and decency. Jerry heard him out, then with a shrug and a patronising tone, said "Well, Will! You and me's different. You got the one idea of marrying a girl and settling down. Me - I'm not looking for a wife, least ways, not yet awhile. I'll love 'em and leave 'em, long's I can, and if I don't get caught, that'll be a long time. Gor blimey! You're only young once and what's the harm?"

They parted, Jerry without rancour, but Willy riding his high horse in anger and distress. "See you!" said Jerry. "I doubt it," replied Willy, "I don't want to hear any more talk from you." The quarrel left him more alone than ever. Gwen worried over him.

"Willy, you ought to go out more, it don't do you no good to be all the time sitting up there writing, you don't get enough fresh air - and you'll ruin your eyes."

"I'm all right Mum, I enjoy writing, and I'm going to make my living at it, you'll see! Anyway, till Madge comes back, there's not much to do."

Gwen sighed. She was out of touch with Willy - she had been for years, she knew that, never able even to guess at where his spirit played, when he stared unseeingly into space, and a secret smile creased his lips. "Just like his Dad," she'd tell herself for the thousandth time.

Willy had a poem published in the *Strand* magazine. It was written during a desperately cold spell that followed Christmas. He gave one verse to the frozen land and the population crouching by their firesides. Then in two more leapt to warmth down south, with the migratory birds awaiting the northern spring, and the soft, warm winds building up and ready to come rolling in with summer in their train. Mr Watts was full of congratulations, and when Willy told him that he had quite a lot of verse written, he told him to bring it to him. The teacher was surprised at the quality and variety of the poems, and decided that they should be offered somewhere for publication. He got together with Mr Manning of the *Echo* who was able to give valuable advice about literary agents and publishers. Meantime, Mr Watts pressed Willy into many hours of revision and correction.

He was a stickler for metric perfection, not caring much for blank verse, though he conceded that some of Willy's spontaneous lines held an insight and beauty, that got a little diminished when constricted to a classical form.

Willy still wrote to Madge every day, posting off a thick wad of pages once a week. Madge yearned over them, loving them, but more and more despairing at their contents. She wrote back every week, short letters, with little news. At first she wrote much of the pleasure that his letters gave her, but after a while she began to protest that Willy was building her into a goddess that she could not be, and was laying up disappointment for himself when she came home.

"I'm not like that Will! I never was, you know I wasn't. It's dear of you to say these things, but you'll come down with an awful bump when you see me again."

But Willy would have none of it. He eulogised all their short months of courtship and built up a future that was sublime.

"Oh dear God!" thought Madge. "He'll have to have me as I am - and how can I ever live up to him now? Surely he'll want someone better educated than me - and more attractive."

Madge worried a lot over Willy. She was terribly lonely. There were no English girls with whom she could make friends. She never went out, except with the children. Her mistress moved in a small group of senior officers' wives, playing interminable bridge. No one ever came to the apartment who had a friendly word for her. The servants were Maltese and made no effort to be other than mute and retiring when she was about, though living in a babble of sound with their swarming families, where Madge would have loved to have been invited. Over and over again she echoed Willy's words - "Why did I come?"

Chapter 17

By the spring of the year, Jerry had built and sold his first pair of houses and had more in various stages of completion. There was an insatiable demand for homes in the early 'thirties, and he had all his houses spoken for. He worked with a dedication and energy that left some of his contemporaries appaled. He had a goal, that was to clear the loan and leave himself completely independent. When that was done, he promised himself a period of consolidation, then expansion.

"Give me three years, then watch me go!" was what he told himself as he laboured late in the barn that he had converted into a workshop. He still prized perfection in workmanship and was a hard taskmaster, but when timber merchants started making doors and window frames that he could buy and use, at a lot less than he could make them, he used them gratefully, though lamenting their tendency to warp. Many a one he returned in disgust. He seldom saw Willy. He had to make an occasional call at the solicitor's office, and they greeted each other casually, but their old comradeship seemed lost. Willy tended to look down his nose at Jerry, especially as Jerry always found occasion to chat up the typist, and Val seemed quite pleased with the attentions he paid her.

"He looks like good fun to me," she told Willy. "I'd go out with him, if he asked me." Then, looking at Willy quizzically, "When he first came here to see the boss, you told me he was your best friend, so what's happened? You had a row about a girl, I bet!"

Willy made as if he were engrossed in the document that he was checking - "We had a difference of opinion, that's all."

"Well, I think Mr Wilkins is a lot more fun than you are, you're getting to be a real pompous old man. What you want is to give yourself a treat and enjoy yourself! Here, there's a dance at the Spa on Friday night, with a big band and competitions! Why don't you go? You could take me, if you like!" Willy looked at Val, all golden hair and sparkling eyes.

"You wouldn't want to go with me, I'd be a wet blanket!"

"You needn't be, you'd enjoy it, and you could give me a lift home and (with a delicious smile) I'd be safe with you."

Willy dealt sternly with the Old Adam within him that always stirred when Val made any direct remark to him, especially when she put on that provocative look.

"All you want is transport home, I jolly well know that," he said. The thought would not go away though, and it occurred to him that he might find material for an article if he went - after all, he'd never been to the Spa ballroom, the most prodigious ballroom in the locality, and it would be a new experience. Next day, Val was rattling away on her typewriter, and Willy was tracing an estate plan. Without looking up, he said, "If, you would like me to take you to the Spa, I will, only I can't dance much; I mean, I'm not good at it, and I haven't been to many."

"Oo! Goody! Not half I don't." Val's effervescence was at full strength, and she clapped her hands in delight.

"Don't worry about your dancing, there's lots to do beside," she answered him. Willy reminded himself sternly that this was business, and a perfectly respectable occasion. When a nagging little voice spoke within him asking, "What would Madge think?" he did what he'd never done before, and told it to "shut up"!

At the first opportunity, Val, smiling ravishingly, told the senior clerk, "Mr Churchward's taking me to the Spa, Friday."

The man looked at her, seeing all her bouncing, golden beauty, and said "Lucky him - don't you go leading him astray now!" Later, when the girl was out, he dug Willy in the ribs, grinning hugely, and said "Taking the beauteous Val dancing then, eh! I thought she'd get you! Lucky dog! Cor - what I could do with her! You make the most of your chance boy. Cor! - to be in the back of the old Morris with a seventeen year old blonde like that -. I daren't think of it - you rotten, lucky kid!"

"It's nothing like that, it's business. She's just going with me as a partner."

"Business, my foot! If you don't have a good time with that girl, you'll want your head examining - something else! You watch out for her old man though - he's a local preacher, did you know that? Came to see the boss when he took her on, wanted to see if she was in decent company.

"She is except for you."

"Now, now, no sauce from you, young man! Here'. I wonder he lets her go dancing. I expect her mum's on her side - yes, you'll have to square it with her old lady."

"There's nothing to square, I'm simply going as a reporter."

"Yes, well, when you get to my age, you'll think of all the memories you could have had if you hadn't been so stupid as not to take your chances! Boy! I envy you! Twenty years old and fancy free! I dunno!" With this last remark he returned to his office with the melancholy thought that he had been pressured into promising to paint out the back lavatory over the week end. "If you could only live your life backwards," he thought savagely.

On Friday night, Willy told his mother that he would be home late, "About half past two - I'm doing a report on a ball at the Spa." Gwen accepted this. He did go out sometimes to report for the *Echo*. Willy felt some unease. "Why didn't you say you were going with Val?" whispered his conscience, but he gave it no reply. He called for Val at her home. Her mother opened the door to him. "She's just coming, come on in, she won't be a moment."

By the time he had taken the few steps to the sitting room, Val's mother had decided Willy was all right. Val could do worse, but with her looks she hoped she'd do better. The girl's father did not offer to shake hands. He sat by the fire blowing clouds of smoke from a reeking pipe. "I want her home right after the dance finishes, mind. I don't hold with these affairs, but the wife and daughter are against me, so I'm outnumbered. She wouldn't be going, mind, only Val tells me you don't drink. I don't hold with drink! So you see her home safe by two-thirty, for I'll not get a wink of sleep till she's in."

When Val appeared, Willy's breath was taken away, She was golden from the top of her pretty head to her golden shoes. The alluring parts were sheathed in a close fitting golden dress, her arms and shoulders were bare and Willy found himself looking at the cleavage of her bosom above the lowcut top of the dress. "There! Doesn't she look a picture?" enquired her mother. Willy's throat had gone suddenly dry, and his "Yes" came as a sort of croak, that he had to disguise by a coughing fit. Val's mother wanted to giggle. She knew what Val's appearance was doing to the boy. "Here you are, love, just put this round your shoulders," she said, giving the girl a fur wrap. "Now off you go, enjoy yourselves and be home prompt, so's your dad won't worry."

She watched them go with a wistful sigh. She had been every bit as pretty as Val, some eighteen years ago, when she had married Val's father. He was then a handsome young sailor, on leave during the first year of the war. They had felt then that tomorrow might never come, and had married with all the haste that the times urged. Her husband was shore-based at Plymouth and they had been able to have nearly a year of happiness together. He was a happy-go-lucky Jack Tar, one of the boys, and hilarious company in the off-duty life of the service, much envied by his mates for his lovely wife.

Then he was drafted to Scotland and within days was afloat in one of the mighty ships of the times. It was two years before he came home, having survived actions in distant waters, and when he did get his demob, his wife found him a strangely changed man - introverted and given to melancholy.

He was demobbed in 1919 and returned to her like someone lost. He got a job as a postman and then suddenly "got religion", as his wife described it, or "found Christ", as he preferred to say. He moved to Paignton and got promotion when the opportunity offered. After that he became much happier and they had a loving life, but the old playboy that had captured her heart was gone forever, and now she saw herself again in her lovely Val, the baby of their early love, an echo of her own effervescent joy.

Driving into Torquay Willy was acutely conscious of the girl by his side and felt a certain jubilant thrill to think that she would be his partner for the night. He was thankful that he had recently invested in one of the Montague Burton's dinner suits. He had paid the five pound odd that the suit, shirt and tie had come to with satisfaction, feeling that he was equipped to venture into any social spheres that opportunity suggested, and this was only the second time that he had worn it.

Val snuggled down in her mother's fur, wrapping it close around her head to keep out the draughts that whistled between the ill-fitting side panels of the car.

"You do look smart in your dinner jacket - it suits you! Do you like my dress?"

"You look smashing!"

"Mum made it, you know, it's the first long evening dress that I've had. I've never been to a Ball - only 'hops'."

"I expect this'll be a bit much of it - all the 'big wigs' and that."

"Well, I expect we'll find a little corner."

As they circled the harbour and climbed the hill to the Spa, they passed little groups of people, hurrying along, heads down to the wind. The girls had their long dresses hitched up under overcoats, and everyone had a paper parcel, containing their shoes, tucked under their arms. Car owners were in a distinct minority in those days, and Willy felt very pleased to be chugging up the hill in the old 'bull-nose'. Taxis were depositing people at the entrance, and Willy had to wait his turn, then dropped Val at the door. He parked the Morris at the first attempt, and, feeling this augered well for him, rejoined Val and entered the beautifully decorated foyer with its banks of potted plants. He waited there for what seemed ages, while Val deposited her coat in the cloakroom and engaged herself in the mysterious business that always precedes a woman's final appearance on the social stage. She appeared at last, and Willy felt again the sudden tremor of delight at her beauty. She took his arm and they entered the ballroom. The band was not playing and Willy felt very conspicuous as they moved up the room to find seats near the stage. They were on the side of the sunlounge converted for the occasion into a bar and buffet. The music started and couples moved on to the floor. Willy felt again the nervousness of his first dance at the church hall. All these people seemed to be so sophisticated and graceful in their movements, that he had a moment of panic at the thought of joining them.

"Do you dance much?" he asked Val.

"Well, I haven't been to many, but I manage."

"I told you I'm not much good, I'm afraid."

Val didn't look overjoyed at this information, but said "I expect you can do as good as most." Then she suddenly aware of Willy's size ten feet, so close to her own little toes in their golden sandals. "Let's see how we get on, shall we? It's a quick-step, I think, and you only have to walk, and do a sort of skip now and then."

"All right," said Willy, realising that she had described the only process of dancing that he had evolved. As they moved to the floor, they had to pass a group of tables, round which were seated superior-looking persons in full evening dress, and Willy noted that there were "reserved" notices on each table. He noticed, too, with a flush of pride, that they, or at least Val, was creating quite a lot of interest, as they passed. They walked and 'sort of skipped' their way around the room. It seemed a terribly long way, and Willy seemed to be constantly saying 'sorry' to either Val or some other person, but he gradually mastered some sort of rhythm that kept those little golden toes from under his great feet.

They were at the other end of the room when the music stopped, and had to walk all the way up to their chairs. Willy realised that Val was thoroughly enjoying holding the centre of the floor. He felt half proud, half amused.

The Ball was one of the big social occasions of the year, given by the Chamber of Commerce as a farewell to the last year's Chairman, and a welcome to the new Chairman. So the band, a twenty-piece orchestra from Plymouth, had carefully prepared a programme of dances to suit a wide range of patrons. It ranged from the occasional Valeta, to the ever-popular St Bernard's Waltz, interspersed with foxtrots, waltzes and quicksteps. There was the inevitable Paul Jones also, and even the out-of-fashion Charleston, to please the maturing matrons with giddy memories of their youth.

Willy would have been quite content to sit out, smoke, and watch the scene, but Val was of no mind to do that. For one thing, they were seated in an inconspicuous corner of the room, and for another, all the unattached boys were standing around the door. She was well aware of the furore that she caused amongst them when Willy shambled his inelegant way past. He had to submit to Val's entreaties, "Come on, it's only one, two, three, you can do it easy!" or "Just do what the one in front's doing."

"Oh all right, but it's your feet that'll suffer." At the first Paul Jones he was adamant he would not dance.

"You go! You can, it's all right to go on your own!"

Val went, and there was a sudden movement amongst the boys by the door, to join the circle. After that it seemed that there were no rules to be obeyed when the music stopped. Val was grabbed each time with the amount of graciousness usually reserved for acquiring the last seat in a game of musical chairs. She enjoyed herself hugely, collecting in the ten dances, two offers of supper at refreshment time, and three offers of an escort home. She declined these gently, with "I'm with my friend!" But her nimble little mind was busy with treacherous ideas, only every time it came back to "But what'll Dad say?" so she returned to Willy, glowing with excitement, and giving her last partner a smiling thanks that sent him away aglow with pleasure, and with a pity for the lanky youth who was stupid enough to let her off his lead.

At eleven o'clock, after a roll of drums, the senior officers of the Chamber of Commerce appeared on the stage, and the ceremony of transferring the Chairman's chain of office was carried out. Then the Chairman thanked everyone for coming and reminded them that all the profits of the evening were going towards the provision of a new ambulance for the local St John's Ambulance Brigade. After that there was a supper interval, and then a cabaret by a local dancing school. To allow for the entrance of the dancers from the room where they had assembled, the tables occupied by the "top people" were moved a little, and Willy and Val found themselves more or less sharing the table of the new Chairman and his lady. This gentleman was a long-established ironmonger, and also an alderman. With a gentle courtesy he apologised for crowding them, and his wife (who in her time had worked hard in the business and in bringing up a family, and who did not believe in "airs and graces") invited them to move forward and share their table. Val, who seemed to know how to behave with perfect naturalness whatever happened, smiled a deferential thanks and took a chair, patting the next one for Willy to accept. Almost out of nervousness, after a brief "Thank you, sir!" he said to the Chairman, "Why did you choose an ambulance sir?"

The man looked at the boy addressing him, then taking a cigar from a case and preparing it for smoking, said "I'm glad you asked me that, actually I used to belong to the Brigade and I feel it's high time they were better equipped."

Willy suddenly found spontaneous talk. "I'm on the *Paignton Echo* Sir. I will be reporting this event. I would like, if I may, to quote you on an appeal for more support for St John's Ambulance Brigade. May I?"

"Yes, of course. *Echo*, eh? I don't see it often. Very parochial, isn't it?"

"Well, I do hope to extend its scope a bit - go further afield, you know."

"Good idea, but of course, it needs more than that. The three towns in the Bay should get together, speak with one voice, so's they can make themselves heard at Exeter. Amalgamation, that's what it needs!"

Willy's pencil had been flying all this while. He felt a growing excitement. He was getting a "scoop". The Chairman continued with what was evidently his hobby horse, while Val sat with twitching toes, watching the dancers wheeling by.

The Chairman's wife could see the girl's impatience. "Are you this young man's fiance?" she enquired.

"Oh no, I'm just (inspiration) a business acquaintance."

"Well, I think it's a shame for you to sit here wasting your time while these men talk politics - they're all the same, my dear, but he's no business to abandon you like this. I tell you what, I've got a nephew in that crowd over there, who's without a partner. He's a nice boy; come along, I'll introduce you."

A moment later they joined several tables, all pushed together, and surrounded by a dozen or so young men and women. "George, dear, your uncle has got this young lady's partner trapped over there, and he can't get away, be a dear and look after her for a little while."

"George dear" moved with alacrity, like a cat being offered a canary. The other boys smiled a delighted welcome while the girls tried to hide their consternation. Next moment, Val was lost somewhere on the floor, and "George dear" had decided that there must be a God in heaven after all.

Mrs Chairman returned to her table where she found that another man had joined her husband, and the two of them were having an impromptu debate, for Willy's benefit, over the amalgamation issue. Willy had warmed to the subject, interjecting an enquiry, or a deferential opinion whenever the spate of words slowed down. He was really enjoying himself. Eventually the other man was claimed by his wife and the Chairman declared the interview closed. Willy then remembered Val. She was in the middle of a wild melee on the floor, busily popping hundreds of balloons that had been released from a net in the roof.

"Gosh! She is pretty'. he thought.

"If you want the company of your companion, you'll have to fetch her," the Chairman's lady told him. "I knew you would be tied up for ages as soon as I heard the word 'amalgamation', so I introduced her to some young people that I know. You know, young man, I think she is quite beautiful, I've been trying to think what I can compare her with, and I think she could be described as a 'Rose of Sharon'. If there is no romantic attachment between you, I can't.understand why not!"

Willy smiled down on the motherly little lady. "She's a nice girl, and she's pretty, but it's only that I work with her in the same office, that's all."

"That's all! thought the lady. "Dear God! What is the silly boy looking for!"

Willy wandered towards the young people's table and propped himself against a pillar. The balloons were soon demolished and the Master of Ceremonies announced that there would be a 'Falais Glide'. Val, a little conscience stricken, ran over to him, grabbed his arm and pulled him into a line across the floor. "George dear", just happened to squeeze himself next to her at the last moment and another hard tryer got on the other side, both encircling her vibrant young body with their arms. Willy found himself in a similar embrace with other girls. Though the bar had closed, spirits were still high, and the "Glide" was repeated several times before the band called a halt.

Val took Willy's arm and walked him back to her new friends. "This is Will Churchward," she announced. "Gossip writer and poet!"

Willy had a protest on his lips, but he saw from the expressions on the faces around him, that his status had increased. He took a chair beside a tall, dark girl with an intense looking face. "Are you a poet?"

"Well, yes, I suppose so, but only spare time."

"Have you had anything published?"

"Yes, *Strand* magazine."

"How interesting! And what about the gossip writer bit?"

"I do a column in the *Echo* and odd bits in periodicals."

"Well, I think that's very interesting - have you studied anyone in particular - Belloc Perhaps, or Chesterton?" From there on the wallflower bloomed in Willy's company, and the "Rose of Sharon" glowed more beautifully as the night wore on. On the stroke of two, the cymbals clashed and the drums rolled. Movement and noise subsided, while the national anthem was played. The ex-servicemen, in particular, stood like ram-rods until the music died. Val was surrounded at once by eager young men, invitations flying from all sides, but she declined them all, saying that her friend was seeing her home, whereupon "George dear" fell upon his knees and implored her with mock alarm, "Put not your trust in poets fair maid."

But with banter and laughs, the group gradually broke up and when Val had reclaimed her wrap and Willy had fetched his car, they all saw them off with cheers, and roars of laughter, when Willy squeezed the bulb horn with its well-known corncrake croak. The lights were out and the streets deserted. Val snuggled lower into the fur against the bitter cold wind, sweeping into the car from all sides.

"Enjoyed yourself?" asked Willy.

"Oh yes! It was the loveliest night ever! You're not cross, are you, that I didn't stop with you?"

"'course not. I'm glad you had a good time, you see, I'm not very good at socialising."

"Didn't you enjoy it then?"

"Oh yes! I got a smashing article lined up for the *Echo*, and I had a most interesting conversation with that dark girl on modern literature. She's at college and it's a subject of hers."

Val, still elated with the evening, stuffed her mouth full of fur to stop Willy hearing her laughing. "Oh Will" she thought, "What's that poor girl in Malta coming home to." Then she wriggled with pleasure at the memory of all the admiration and attention she had received, sobering when she thought of how her father would greet the news that "George dear" wanted to take her out for a run on Dartmoor on Sunday. "On Sunday," she thought. "Gosh! He'll have a fit. I'll have to ask Mum." She didn't know yet that "George dear" was in his father's business as a wine and spirit merchant. They reached her home with five minutes to spare. Willy did not switch the motor off in case, as sometimes happened, it was temperamental at re-starting. "Well, off to bed with you," he said. "I was proud to be with you. Do you know what the Chairman's wife called you? A 'Rose of Sharon'."

"What's that?"

"It's a beautiful golden flower. It was a great compliment, but it hardly did you justice!"

"Ooh! Will Churchward. Are you paying me compliments?"

"No! I'm speaking the truth! Off you go now, we've got to be at work in seven hours."

"Good night Will, and thanks, you've been very sweet." With this, Val planted a swift kiss on Willy's cheek and scampered up the path. He saw her inside then drove home. Undressing, he realised that he had not written to Madge. "I must do it tomorrow. I'd like to tell her about Val. I wonder if she would worry. She's nothing to me, or me to her." He was soon asleep, but his "goodnight" thought had not been about a vision amid the golden gorse blooms that usually cradled his sleep, but about a gloriously golden girl, popping balloons in a riot of laughter, a girl so aptly dubbed a "Rose of Sharon".

Next evening, Willy got to work on his article about amalgamation. He popped it into the *Echo* on his way to work on the Monday, then called around to see Mr Manning when he left work.

He waited while his article was read. "You're coming on young man, that's a good article, too long by half, but good. I've been thinking about it. Of course, old Gannicott's had this amalgamation idea for years, always trotting it out. 'course Torquay would like it - they'd get our sands, and a deep-water port, but what would we get - higher rates for certain and nothing much else. No! Paignton wouldn't stand for it, not on your life, nor Brixham. Still, it's an idea that hasn't been aired for a year or two, and it might stir up some interest, get people talking. I could invite opinions in the correspondence column, I might even get the *Torquay Times* to print something. I doubt if the *Evening Herald* would take it up again, they tried something once before, but didn't think it worthwhile. That's where it ought to go though, so all three towns get arguing!

He mused a while over Willy's page then said, "Yes!' I'll run it, try and get a real discussion going - won't come to anything, but it will stimulate sales."

He put the copy into a folder to take home with him, then said "Good lad Will! That was a good bit of reporting!"

Val had looked a bit wan that morning. "The Rose of Sharon looks a bit faded today," said Willy.

"I don't know if I'm here even," said Val.

"Never mind, you've got the weekend to catch up your sleep."

"Yes, meantime, if I seem to be unconscious, throw something at me before I fall down."

"Was your dad all right?"

"Yes, but he says next time I've got to be in by twelve, and only if he knows who I'm going with - he means good, but it's a bit difficult!"

The following Thursday, when the *Echo* came out, it had a two column headline in the centre of the front page, saying "Amalgamation. Is the Time Right? Alderman Gannicott returns to the fray. An exclusive interview given to our roving reporter on the occasion of Alderman Gannicott's introduction as the new Chairman of the Abbeyfield Chamber of Commerce." Then followed the interview and debate recorded by Willy. The Editor had managed to emphasise certain points to stimulate discussion. In particular, the suggestion that Paignton's excellent and abundant water supply, from a relatively new reservoir on Dartmoor, would be used to augment the Torquay supply, already dangerously short of demand. This was a very sensitive point with the Paignton Urban District Council, and they were loyally backed by the townsfolk.

The next evening, there appeared two letters in the *Evening Herald* lambasting the idea, and another strongly supporting it. A letter appeared in the *Torquay Times* too, suggesting that Alderman Gannicott should be encouraged to organise a lobby to unify the three towns, thus bringing great benefits to the whole area. Mr. Manning grinned knowingly when Willy commented on them. "I've got friends," he said.

It was Willy's good fortune that at the time the humble *Echo* had raised the question of amalgamation, there should be a dearth of news in the locality. Both the evening paper and the *Torquay Times* were hard put to find anything of interest to report; also Alderman Gannicott was anxious to increase his notoriety with the townsfolk. So when the *Times* asked him if he had any plans for pursuing the scheme, he replied that he was already submitting a draft proposal to the appropriate authority. The Alderman managed also to leak this information to the Evening Herald, so that suddenly both papers broke into print on the subject. It happened too, that the monthly meeting of the Paignton Urban District Council was held on the very next day and a noisy debate, or rather protest, developed, with councillor after councillor condemning the suggestion and vying with each other to find words to describe the devious schemes of Torquay Town Council and Alderman Gannicott in particular. Brixham went as far as sailing a trawler into Torquay harbour with a banner stretched between its masts proclaiming "Hands off Brixham".

The *Echo* was delighted. Mr. Manning fanned the flames for all his worth, and on the following publication day commenced his leading article with the words Paignton has been alerted to the danger of an unobtrusive take-over by Torquay Town Council by the *Echo*. What has become the talking point of the three towns might have gone unnoticed but for diligence on the part of our reporting staff.

Willy enjoyed all this with a feeling of excitement. He marvelled at the development of his report to the Editor.

"Didn't I tell you, boy, the first time you called here, of the power of the press! Just think, magnify it a million times and realise what the national press can do if they wish! Think how many men have been exalted, how many broken, by a careful campaign or a careless word, picked up and splashed on front pages all over the land - across the world, come to that! Just think of this as a bit of harmless fun - we all know that nothing will come of it, but it gives a lot of people the chance to emulate Shakespeare and posture on the stage of our little world. It gives old Gannicott some good publicity for next year, when he's due for Mayor, and we've printed an extra ten quires this week. I give you credit for grasping the opportunity, but it would have died if we hadn't all pulled together - not of course that there was any collusion between us!"

The subject did not die all that quickly, though it wandered on through correspondence columns, council meetings and bar and club arguments. Then Willy was given the means of stirring it all up again. On a Sunday morning, he was mooching along the sea front, making his way to the breakwater, where he sometimes leaned on a rail, with the picturesque harbour before him, and worked out in his mind some idea that slowly came to words, or in a flash of inspiration, came ready made, a verse or couplet. The harbour was in a mess, the tide was out and, in spite of it being Sunday, a gang of men were working frantically to connect up giant concrete pipes in a trench scooped from the sand. It was, he knew, a storm water sewer being laid to relieve the new sewerage scheme, now nearing completion. Two gentlemen came and stood a few yards away and watched the work. Willy, through his job, knew most of the influential local men by sight, and idly recognised the two as a local councillor and the man who had been talking to Gannicott at the Spa. What electrified Willy was to hear the councillor say, "If the amalgamation did come to anything, Torquay could connect up with us, switch all their sewerage to our outfall right out in the channel, beyond Brixham and leave the bay totally clean. The whole of the loan could then be spread over the three towns, and your council would be saved building a new outfall, because that's what they must have soon, with all the development they're allowing. Of course, there'd be hard bargaining on our part - we'd want tit for tat!"

The two men moved away then, and Willy went to a telephone kiosk nearby and rang the Editor. Half an hour later he was closeted with him in his dingy office. Willy had jotted down a report, as near verbatim as made no matter, of the words he had heard, and Mr. Manning read them with pursed lips and dubious expression.

We can't use this, you've no proof it was ever said, and he'd have me for libel - it's dynamite though! Boy! You've got a knack of being in the right place at the right time!"

"Why not just say that a little bird told you, and name no names?"

"Look, write it up again and let me have it, and I'll think on it but not a word mind! You could be in real trouble if either of them got wind of it!"

By the time the next edition of the *Echo* was printed, Mr. Manning had managed to have a casual meeting with one of the local councillors, who was most vociferous in his opposition to the amalgamation proposal, and had asked him what, in the event of such a thing taking place, Paignton could demand in exchange for her three famous stretches of sands, her water and (this in a most innocent manner) access to her new sewerage system. The councillor, "pooh~poohing" the whole idea until then, fairly leapt into the air. "The sewer! They don't intend to take that, do they?"

"Oh! My dear sir, I'm only asking a question, but one has to look for reasons why Torquay are so keen on joining us all up."

"Joining us up! Taking us over, you mean! Here, do you know something? Why do you suggest the sewer?"

"Well, I was looking up some notes I have, and I found a piece from a couple of months ago, just that Torquay could not go ahead with development in the Old Town Road area until a considerable improvement had been made in the sewerage system. The Borough Engineer had reported that it would require either a pumping station or tunnelling, and at that a councillor had remarked that it was a pity that

227

they had not carried through a mains sewer towards Paignton that could have connected with the new scheme now under way. It was just a chance remark, thrown out at random, and no discussion was reported."

The Councillor's face was grim.

"That's it, that's it, depend on it! Right! Now we'll see what's what! That's typical, that is, devious as monkeys the lot of them! Well, I'm glad I happened to run into you, you may have done the town a service here - but then it was you who spotted the scheming blighters in the first place, wasn't it? But they won't get away with it! I'll demand a special full council meeting, and a public meeting, if necessary."

Nothing ever did come of it. But for a week or two, Mr Manning enjoyed himself more than he had done since leaving his beloved Yorkshire for the somnolent Devon coast. Willy got no mention in the *Echo* apart from the first article, but Mr. Manning was proud of his protege, and wished that he could afford to employ him full-time. Willy's boss looked kindly on him, and in a rare moment of personal talk, remarked, "You stirred up something there didn't you! But I bet it was all a mare's nest concocted by old Manning!" The Paignton councillor had his moment of glory at the council meeting, and the potential Judas kept his fingers crossed and thanked God when the furore died down. Alderman Gannicott laughed, knowing that the project was not to be for years yet, and told his wife, "That was that lanky young chap with the pretty girl, at the Spa, started it all. He must be a go-ahead boy. He could do better than the *Echo* - that's about as exciting as a parish magazine usually!"

Willy told Madge all about it. He thought it a comedy, and wrote it as such. He enclosed all the cuttings from all the papers, and Madge began to think that she had a lover who was more of a genius than even she had thought. She worried a bit about the several references to Val, but felt relieved when one of the letters said, "You remember I said I took the office girl (Willy was naughty there - he said "office girl" instead of "typist" so that Madge would think of her as a juvenile) to the Spa, on the night this all started? Well, she got off with some chap, and he took her on the moors in his car the next Sunday. Did I tell you her father is very strict Chapel? He is, anyway, and she has to get her mum to persuade him to let her go out anywhere, so when he brought her home, he was dragged inside, and quizzed by the old man, and it turned out he was a brewer's son and in the business with his father. I gather that he was blasted from the house, by father, emulating some prophet of old, and now the poor girl is more or less chained to the table leg. Shame really! She's potty on the bloke."

Nothing could detract completely from the beauty of the young girl, Val, just in that enviable state, so transient, of the adolescent bud unfolding into the perfect bloom of womanhood. But the Val who turned up for work in jumper and skirt, with hair raked through in haste and make-up nonexistent, all betraying the last-minute scramble from bed, with breakfast taken during a brief hover over the table, before the flying dash down the road, was a very different girl from the "Rose of Sharon". Furthermore, she was depressed and petulant, not at all the bubbling bundle of giggles that had enlivened the office for the past months. Willy was sorry for her, for he knew the cause, but he did not waste too much sympathy on her, thinking to himself, "Well, there's plenty more chaps around, she'll get over it," and got cross when Val's depression settled over the whole office. He got crosser still when the senior clerk asked him in malevolent tones, "What you been doing to that maid?" Then one afternoon, when, for some reason, they were behind with the work, and the day's letters had not been made ready for post by the time they should have shut up shop, Willy snapped at her, "For goodness sake! Pull your socks up girl, forget your miseries for five minutes and do some work for a change!" Val replied by bursting into tears and dashing down the passageway and locking herself in the toilet.

"Oh lor!" thought Willy. "Poor kid, I know how she feels," and he set about finishing up himself. When he had done, an unhappy Val reappeared, red-eyed and sniffing. She glared at Willy, mutely daring him to comment. "Come on!" he said. "It's all done, I'll give you a lift home, O.K.?".

Val nodded and gathered up her things. They drove up to the post office, then on to Val's home. Outside the house, when the girl, who hadn't said a word all the way, went to get out of the car, Willy, on impulse, said, "Look here, there's a dance at Deller's next Wednesday. If you like, I'll ask your old man if I can take you - if you'd like to go?"

"He won't let me."

"Well, I could ask."

"It's no good, but thanks all the same."

Again he stopped her from leaving. "Look! I'll come down after tea. Don't say anything to them, I'll just ask if you can partner me on a reporting job, like last time. What do you say?"

"All right, but it won't be any good!"

After he had had his tea, Willy set off to do as he had promised. He had become so self-assured this last year that the coming interview gave him no qualms. He hadn't bothered to ask himself why he was doing it, which was just as well, for if he had, the unwelcome voice of conscience might have undermined his determination. Val's mother opened the door. She greeted him kindly with an unspoken question in her eyes.

"I wanted a word with you and your husband, if I may. Is he in?"

"Yes, of course, come in."

They went into the sitting room where Val's father was seated at the table. Notepaper was before him and an open Bible by his side.

"I'm afraid we're disturbing you, Harry, but Mr. Churchward has called to see us."

Willy thought, " He's writing a sermon I suppose." Then he said, "I do apologise for butting in, I write a lot, and I know how annoying it can be when someone breaks your concentration."

The man was pleased with Willy's appreciation of the situation, and said, "It's all right, it can wait. I'm not very good at it - sermons, you know. I've got two, and I've been working on a third for some time - can't preach the same one twice to the same people. They may seem to be asleep, but they remember, and they don't mind telling you!"

"Where do you preach, if I may ask?"

"All around the circuit, about fifteen chapels. 'course I only get the evening services, but once a month soon takes you around, and I'm nearing my second circuit, so a new one is imperative."

"I have to write to certain dates - I do a bit of freelance journalism so I know the problem, and the nearer it gets the harder it becomes, don't you think?" Val's mother had seated herself and taken up some knitting.

"A really nice boy," she thought, "but I wish he'd come to the point, it must be about Val. Still he's smart, he's getting Harry into a good mood."

"I mustn't take up too much of your time, Sir, I came to ask you and your wife's permission to take Val with me to an event that I'm reporting at Deller's on Wednesday."

Mr. Atkinson froze, pursing his lips and looking down at the table. Mrs. Atkinson dropped several stitches and held her breath. Mr. Atkinson drummed with his fingers on the table, then looked up at Willy.

"I daresay that the girl's told you that I disapproved of the young man she became acquainted with at the last place you took her to. I know she's unhappy about it, but it's my duty as her father to protect her from the evils of modern society, and that I will do, regardless of any who think me hard . . . "

"There wouldn't be any evils at Dellers, I'm sure of that. After all, the old man Lambshead is a circuit steward of the Wesleyan Church. He never has any alcohol on the premises, and Mr. Craze, the Manager, is always there, and he wouldn't allow anything untoward to happen - and it's for charity - it's the Hospital Extension Committee running it. There's a whist drive till ten, then a buffet and dancing till two. I'd take her and bring her back, she'd come to no harm'!"

"Whist, my boy, is a form of gambling, minor, no doubt, but who knows how many get their first taste for cards at a simple whist drive? And think of the untold misery caused by the gambler losing all his possessions, often his family, and certainly his self-respect, in the gambling lairs of the world. I said 'evil', and you disputed it, but you're young, and you haven't seen what drink, gambling and other degradations can do to a man."

"We wouldn't go till ten, just for the dance, and I'd bring her straight home afterwards, Mr Atkinson. Val's a good girl and sensible, if there was anything wrong there she wouldn't have anything to do with it, nor would any of the people that she might be introduced to."

Mr. Atkinson sat back in his chair and looked at Willy's honest face. He folded his arms and for a moment sank his chin on his chest. "Winifred," he said, ("Oh Lor! It's Winifred, not Winn," thought his wife, "that means trouble.") "Winifred, will you please find something to do elsewhere and leave this young man and I alone. I have something to say to him, and I'll be obliged if you'll see that we're not disturbed."

Val's mother flushed red with annoyance. She stood up and seemed about to protest, when her husband added, gently, "Please Winn!" At the change of tone, his wife gathered up her knitting and left the room to join Val in her bedroom. The two women looked at each other, both understanding the other's distress.

"What 's happening?" asked Val.

"I don't know, he asked me to leave them alone, but that young Churchward's a trier, and he's not afraid of your dad, that's certain."

"It's no business of his anyway, I didn't ask him to come - what's it got to do with him, anyway?"

"Don't you know, dear?"

Val flushed. "No, it isn't that, Mum, he doesn't think anything of me, he's all wrapped up in that girl in Malta!"

"Well, he's doing his best for you, anyway, and I don't think he'd trouble if he didn't care at all."

"If he did, it would be too bad. He's a self-opinionated bore, and he behaves like some old man of forty - and I hope to meet someone different to that - like George." Her lips trembled and tears were in her eyes. "Mum! Surely he doesn't think that I can't be trusted? Or does he just want to do me out of being happy - just because he likes to be miserable? Mum, why don't you stand up to him? What sort of a life do you have?"

"It's a long story, dear, and in his way he's a good man. I think I'll go down and make some cakes to fill in time."

When his wife left the room, Val's father rested his elbow on the table and put his chin in his hand. He looked at Willy, but blankly, as if his thoughts were elsewhere. "I'd like to tell you something, I don't know why, but I feel you'd understand. These are hard days, a terrible war behind us, unemployment and starvation with us. The poor turn to anarchy to redress their wrongs, the rich exploit the workers, look at the papers and see the degradation that stinks like a midden all over the land, the people sunk in squalor and vice, as the only hope of surviving their misery." (Willy listened, he enjoyed the phrasing and was interested, as always, in another slant on human nature. "This must be one of his sermons," he thought.) "And so few, so few, are given the grace to follow Christ and in Him find hope and peace." ("I bet this is his new sermon," thought Willy.)

Mr Atkinson paused, put both elbows on the table, folded his hands, and placed them under his chin. "I'm going to try and explain, if you find it not to your liking, say so, and go. I won't be hurt, I'm used to it by now, but I have the wish to take you into my confidence more than I have done with anyone." A long pause. (Willy thought, "He's ordering his sequences - good for him, it must be awful to have to listen to sermons badly prepared.") His next words came as a surprise. "I joined the navy as a boy. I grew up in it. It was my life. I enjoyed it and lived life to the full. When I got shore leave I was one of the boys, drinking and fornicating with the rest. I was strong and healthy and happy as you please.

"I was twenty-six when the war broke out, ashore at Devonport. The fleets had been ordered to sea days before, and I was fed up at not going too, but it just happened that way. I didn't know why. Life was hectic. None of us knew where the fleet was, all sorts of tales circulated. Anyway, it was 'eat, drink and be merry, for tomorrow you die' as the saying goes, and it was at a dance in Plymouth that I met my wife. I was on a weekend pass, and had had enough drink to make me merry and we had a rare old time. She was like Val, golden hair, just the same, and I fell for her, really fell. Till then, girls had just been girls, Jack Ashore's comfort. Then I realised that she was the one. I stayed at the Sailor's Rest and saw her next day, and the next. We went up on the Hoe and lay on the grass in the sun. It was late August by then. I asked her to marry me and she said she would. I was twenty-six, so the navy couldn't stop me, and we got married within a month.

"Then rumours started about a new ship being mustered and I was given a two-week leave. We went and stayed at a pub at Newton Ferrers and, looking back now, I suppose it was what I thought then to be a perfect honeymoon. We spent the day fooling around on the river, drinking a lot in the evening - laughing, singing, bawdy stories, then I'd pick my missus up and carry her upstairs to bed, and all the people in the bar laughed and shouted rude advice. Then I got sent up to Scotland and joined my ship, she was a brand new cruiser, just commissioned. I joined as a leading handstoker. She was coal-fired, of course, four boilers and the heat of hell when she wanted steam.

I left my wife with her family in Plymouth, and did not see her again for nearly four years. Val was born, and was a little girl with pigtails before I saw her. I'm not going to tell you much about the war. It's all gone now anyway, but my ship was sent to the Indian Ocean and right down to the Antartic and around the Horn into the Pacific. It was just like peacetime manoeuvres to us. We joked about it. Of course we didn't know what we were there for, we just assumed that someone at the Admiralty did, and we hoped that we'd be left where we were. Anyway, it seemed there was a plan somewhere, because we found ourselves in action in what was later called the Battle of the Falkland Islands. You've heard of it? No? Well, it didn't affect the war much as far as I know. But there we were, shovelling coal like demons in hell, when we were struck." As he spoke, Willy saw his hands were trembling, and he was talking with his teeth clenched on the stem of his pipe, that he had started to fill then abandoned.

"I saw such dreadful things then, through scalding steam and cremated flesh, that I could not believe. The ship survived. They got it under control, patched it up and fought on. It was only my boiler that had gone. I didn't know what was happening. I can't remember. I know I was pushed about, the Chief hit me on the jaw once and knocked me down, but I didn't do anything. There was a terrible ringing in my head, and wherever I looked I saw an open furnace, and I knew it was hell. After a while I was told to report sick. I can't remember much. I know I kept on crying and I got shouted at and pushed around, then I had to go before the Surgeon Commander, and there was another man who had had a burn on the arm. We were both told to report for duty, but I didn't hear what was said because of the bells I could hear all the time. The other man was all of a shake and when the P.O. marched us out, and we came on to the open deck, he suddenly jumped overboard. They turned the ship and steamed a full circle but he wasn't found. I didn't know that then. I was told later by a shipmate. We put into South Africa for repairs and I was sent to a hospital, but they sent me back again.

"Gradually I got better. I could hear again and I stopped crying, but I was always in trouble, and lost my seniority. Then we went on convoy work and finally got back to Portsmouth. We had leave, but I was afraid to go to my wife, I was ashamed of myself, so I went to a navy hostel, and never let on to the wife. I got a shore posting after that, in Ireland, and then back to sea on an old destroyer. All that time I was like a dead man and I can't remember what happened. It was just stoking and in the last ship it was all manual and very hard. All the time I kept on thinking I was looking into the fires of hell. I thought that I was singled out as a scapegoat for the evils of war, and the terrible pain and suffering.

The wife never knew, she used to write to me through the P.O. box and I hardly ever answered. My time had expired during the war, so I got an early demob. and went home. I could see my wife was frightened by the change in me, and I couldn't talk about it. Her father got me a job on the post office, and I just worked, went home (we were living with her parents), ate and slept (when I could) and went to work again. After a bit the flames of hell seemed to get closer, sometimes I felt I was being sucked into them, and I found, when I had finished my rounds, that I had to go on walking so that I wouldn't fall in. Her father and mother used to try and find out what was wrong, and kept on urging me to see a doctor. I began to realise that they thought I was mad. Little Val didn't know me and always ran away when I came near. Then I thought I could hear bells again and I thought that they were right - I was mad.

One day I had done my round, but I couldn't go home, because the fires seemed to beckon me. I went up on the Hoe, and sat in a shelter. I thought I might be out of sight there Presently, a woman came and sat at the other end of the seat. I hardly noticed her but then she came and sat beside me. She had a cigarette in her mouth, and the first thing I noticed was the flare of a match close beside my face as she went to light it. "Feeling lonely, postman?" she said. Then I did go mad. I knocked the flame away and went to grab her around the throat, but she ducked away and ran down the path. I still had her scarf in my hands and I tried to tear it up, but it was strong and wouldn't tear, so I screwed it up and threw it on the ground. It must have been silk, for it opened up and floated gently away. I stamped on it, as if I was killing it, and then took it and twisted it as if I was strangling the woman. Then I sort of 'came to' and I looked around, expecting to find a dead body, and for a moment, I was puzzled, thinking that I had killed her. Then the horror of it came. I knew that I might have been standing there a murderer. I was a murderer, in all but the act.

"I thought that this was the end, I couldn't go on any longer, I'd kill myself. Then the miracle happened, and it was a miracle. I turned to pick up my postman's bag and saw a little handbill that someone had stuck on the wall of the shelter. It was torn and faded and scribbled over, but some words were there. It said "God so loved . . . he gave his ... son.' In that moment I heard the voice of a padre who had talked to me one time when I'd been picked up - not drink, just exhausted - up somewhere in the Firth of Forth. I hadn't taken much notice then, he was just a sky pilot talking a lot of platitudes, but I heard him then again as plain as if he were standing beside me. 'Don't try to carry all the agony yourself, Jesus carried it for you. You need not suffer like this, just turn to him, and he will take the load from you.' "

Having come so far in his story, Mr. Atkinson seemed almost too tired to continue. He sat in silence, the room had grown dark and his face was almost obscured. Then he said, "I hardly dare say it, though I do, again and again, when I try to bring Jesus into people's lives, but I feel that I was a little like Saul, on the Damascus Road, for I felt a great lifting of the spirit and an exaltation filled me as I knew, perfectly surely, that I had been called out of the valley of the damned, to praise and preach the Lord to all who were sore tried and weary of the world."

There was a silence again. Willy, who had been completely absorbed by the terrible tale of suffering, waited for him to continue. "So now you know why I want to protect my daughter from evil, and bring her to the knowledge of God."

Willy said quietly, "You must have had a terrible breakdown, and, as you say, a miraculous cure, but how did you get on with your family?"

"I went home. As usual, my wife had gone to bed. She was lying on her side, as far from me as she could get. In my joy I wanted to tell her of what had happened, but I did not. I stayed thanking God until I fell asleep. I had to be at work at 5 a.m., and before I left I walked around the bed and kissed her forehead. I could hear her crying as I left the room. We hadn't kissed since my train ran out of Plymouth in 1914."

Willy said, "All that you've told me, I'll treat in strictest confidence, but why did you tell me?"

Mr. Atkinson sighed. "I don't know. You just seemed the sort of person to tell. I suppose you have a receptive nature. It's been so many years that I've had that dreadful secret of the intended murder on my mind, and all the time I was in England and Ireland during the war without letting my wife know. Nobody has ever known until today. God knows what you think of me. You're only a young chap, you don't know what life's about yet."

"I'm glad you found you could talk to me, and it's safe with me, you know." Willy paused. "I've been thinking, what about Mrs. Atkinson and Val? Do they have to be part of your crusade? They, especially Mrs. Atkinson, suffered too, and she must love you, or she wouldn't have stayed with you, would she?"

"You're right, she did suffer, and the girl to some degree, that's why I feel I must take them with me, as I follow Christ."

It was now almost dark. "Shall I turn on the light?"

In the sudden brightness, the spectres of the past seemed banished, and normality returned.

"Well, said Willy, "can I ask you to think of giving Val some pleasure by letting her come with me to the dance? And, if I may be so bold to suggest, why don't you come too, and bring your good lady? It will all be quite decorous, and they'll love you for it."

"I'll think about it, yes, I will. Now I've kept you too long and I must say I'm grateful to you for letting me unload my guilty secrets on you - I feel all the better for it."

"I admire you, Sir. I appreciate your confidence in me. Say my goodbyes to your wife and Val."

The man still sat at the table. He looked at Willy and appeared to be going to speak, then thought better of it, just nodding a farewell as he busied himself with the filling of his pipe.

Next day, when Val arrived for work (late as usual, and, also as usual, making a dash for the toilet where she did things to her hair and face that she had not found time to do at home) Willy waited to see if she had any comment to make on the previous evening's happenings, but all she said was, "What on earth were you and Dad talking about last night? You were at it for ages!"

"We had a bit of a discussion about me taking you to Dellers but he wouldn't say 'yes' or ' no'."

"I haven't seen him since," said Val. "I went to bed, and he'd gone to work when I got up this morning. Did he get nasty with you?"

"Not at all. In fact, we parted quite friendly, I was hoping you'd say that it was all right for you to go!"

"Some hope," grumbled Val, noisily ramming paper into her typewriter and banging away on it to relieve her feelings.

Willy had found the revelations of Val's father of absorbing interest. In particular, the horrors of his tortured mind. He hardly felt sympathy, for it was beyond his understanding, but he was intrigued by the years of guilt that had been locked in the man's mind, and the sudden spate of words that had opened the dam and allowed festered secrets to be spoken. He knew that it must have been spontaneous, and wondered if Mr. Atkinson now regretted telling him, and whether, having done so, he would be careful to avoid meeting him again.

All the time there was something at the back of Willy's brain, a germ of an idea, and he felt a new stature. Before going to bed that night, Willy kept his tryst with Madge, standing at the window at exactly ten o'clock, he looked up at the tiny North Star, and wished her goodnight.

Madge, he knew, would be doing the same (allowing for the time difference). It was a romantic idea that Madge had suggested, and Willy had embellished by adding the Pole Star as a recipient of their thoughts. Madge always kept the tryst, and Willy, no matter where he was, usually managed to send his mind's voice away into space to seek their rendezvous. That night, as he gazed into the night sky he said, "I'm going to be a novelist. I'll be a famous bestseller, I'll write and write, and I'll dedicate it all to you!"

In the morning, as soon as Val came in, she looked at Willy in her old happy, cheeky way.

"Will! You old miracle worker! What on earth did you do to my dad? He says I can go to Dellers and he's taking Mum as well!"

Willy laughed with pleasure at seeing her happiness. "I suggested that he did."

"Yes, but - well, Dad going to a dance! Mum's on top of the world, she's never been out for donkey's years! She says she wants to see you, and Dad does, and will you come in tonight, after work?"

"O.K.," said Will, "but I'm going to a gardeners' meeting at eight for the *Echo* so I won't be able to stay long."

Val was her old self that day, bubbling with life, and just a joy to behold; so much so that the senior clerk had envious thoughts as to who was the damned lucky swine, who had caused the lovely flower to bloom again.

There was no urgency in their work that day. Val had told her parents, when she had gone home at lunchtime, that Willy would be bringing her back, and had seemed just a little less effervescent than in the morning. She was licking envelopes and sticking them down. "Lucky envelopes," thought the older clerk, as he came in with a further bunch. "What'ed I give to have her little tongue doing that to me!"

She looked over the one she was moistening, and said, "Will! You're not gone on me, are you?"

Willy met her blue-eyed gaze and his colour deepened, but he smiled, quietly confident in himself. "No Val, I'm not. But if I wasn't already in love and engaged, I expect I would be; you're beautiful and you're nice to know, but I've got Madge."

"That's good," said Val, in a relieved voice. "My mum seems to think you must be after me, and I told her you weren't, but she said you must be daft! Sorry! I didn't mean that really, but I like you Will and you've been kind to me, but I don't feel like that - you know."

'I know," said Willy. "Not like you do about George, eh?"

Val smiled ruefully. "Actually, I've gone off George a bit. After all, he can't be much of a man to let Dad boot him out and never even try to see me again, can he? I mean, Dad couldn't eat him, could he? And even you had the nerve to tackle Dad, didn't you?"

Willy smiled to himself over the 'even you'. He felt no rancour, only a certain gratitude, to the man who had instigated the strange excitement that kept filling his mind.

"I dare say there'll be other Georges," he told her. Then he thought awhile, and after checking that the Senior Clerk was in conclave with the boss, consulted the telephone directory and dialed a number. "Is Mrs. Gannicott there? May I speak to her? Churchward of the *Paignton Echo.*" He turned to Val, and winked knowingly. "Oh, Mrs. Gannicott, you may not remember me, but we met at the Chamber Ball at the Spa." A pause while he listened to the reply. "Oh good! Well I wonder if you would care to do a little thing to help our Hospital Extension Fund? I remember that you introduced my companion and myself to a group of young people, and it occurred to me that I might ask you to mention to them, if you have the opportunity, that the Extension Committee are holding a dance at Dellers next Wednesday, and we're looking for all the support that we can get. I know you do a lot for your own hospital, but this'll be a very enjoyable event if they cared to come along." Another extended silence, then - "Thank you so much, I do hope you don't mind me asking you, I'm sure the Committee will be most grateful."

Willy hung the receiver up and grinned at Val. "There," he said, "now you'll find out if George is a man, or not, won't you."

"Oh lor, Will, I don't know - with Dad there he might make a scene! You shouldn't have done that!"

Willy looked a bit taken aback. He'd forgotten about her father.

"Well, I dare say George won't come anyway."

Val didn't look too pleased at that either. She went on entering up the post book, then - "I didn't know you were on the Hospital Committee."

"I'm not!"

"Yes, but you said - well it sounded as if you were."

Willy laughed. "Ah, but I never said I was, did I?"

"Mr. Churchward," said Val, primly, "you're a bit of a devil, on the quiet."

Willy laughed. "Well, don't let on to your old man," he said.

When work was done, the two of them got into Willy's Morris Cowley, that had been parked all day outside the office. There were practically no traffic regulations, and the traffic, though chaotic at times, was allowed to flow or stop, as it would. Policemen on 'point duty' regulated it at busy crossroads, but in small towns like Paignton it was the 'Devil take the hindermost' and 'Pedestrians jump for your lives' mode of driving.

Willy drove to Val's house and was given a warm welcome by her mother.

"Do come in, Will, Dad would like a word with you." Then, speaking to Val, "Your tea's all ready dear. Be a love and have it in the kitchen." This with a knowing look, that Val interpreted correctly, moving off down the passage, as Willy was ushered into the living room.

Mr. Atkinson had just finished his meal, and rose from the table, at the same time motioning Willy to take the chair by the fireside, opposite his own. "I've wondered, since we met last, what you must have thought of me - unloading my troubles on you like that. After all, you're almost a stranger, and hardly old enough to have had experience sufficient to understand them, but you seemed to convey a sympathy to me, and it seemed right to tell you. As I told you, I had been moved before to accept consolation in time of trouble without knowing why and although, thank God in his great mercy, I was saved then, I still had the terrible weight of guilt on my conscience for having practically abandoned my wife and child in those dreadful days. After I had admitted so much to you, I felt a great lightening of spirit, and afterwards I thought a great deal about the words you spoke. You may not remember, but you said to me, 'Your wife must have loved you, or she wouldn't have stayed with you.' Here he motioned to his wife, who had been sitting at the table, to come near, and when she did, he drew her down on to the arm of his chair, and continued. "When we retired that night, I told her all that I had told you about the years that I had been at home without letting her know, and to my astonishment, she told me that she had known. She had asked the navy, and had been told that I was in home waters. Yet, when I was demobbed, she never told me, and all during the time that I was having a breakdown, she gave me kindness and care, that I now humbly recognise as a manifestation of love that must have almost transcended reason."

His wife made a sort of derogatory noise and placed her arm around his shoulder. "I couldn't ever forget the man I fell in love with," she said, "and I knew that when he got better, it would be all right." "Ah! But it wasn't," he continued, "for I forswore all my old self, and insisted on carrying you and Val along in what I recognised as a sincere following of Christ - and that, I realise now, was unfair, because you, my dear, without the benefit of any call to Christian witness, have all these years set me an example of fidelity, honesty and love that make my striving to find an antidote to the wickedness of the world no more than a sounding brass and a clashing cymbal."

Willy listened, yet did not hear the words. His mind was leaping into the tangled emotions of the man, and words sprang into his mind to describe them. When the biblical quotation came, he heard the lovely sound of it, and relished it for its own sake, thinking to himself, "That's a bit he puts into his sermons, I bet!"

The man was continuing: "A feeling of calm had come upon me, and, on returning home this evening, and anticipating this conversation with you, I went to the Good Book to find some inspiration for words that would adequately describe the great debt that I owe to my dear wife."

He picked up the Bible that lay open on the table, "And I turned to Wisdom, seeking just that, and immediately my eye was caught by some verses in chapter 7: 'I prayed and understanding was given me. I entreated and the Spirit of Wisdom came to me. I esteemed her more than sceptres and thrones; compared with her I held riches as nothing. I reckoned no priceless stone to be her peer, for, compared with her all gold is as a pinch of sand, and beside her silver ranks as mud. I loved her more than health or beauty, preferred her to the light, since her radiance never sleeps. In her company all good things come to me, at her hands riches cannot be numbered.' "

He put the Bible down and Willy saw that he was unsteady with emotion. There was a moment's silence, then he smiled at his wife, "I think that it was more than coincidence that I opened the Book at that place, and the verses shamed my arrogance, so I have decided that from now on, I will no longer dictate a life style to my wife and daughter, but will try and care for them lovingly, protecting them by example, rather than force. My own Christian life will, I hope, be improved rather than diminished, and joy, not unhappiness, motivate me. As a start, I intend to try and enter into the pleasures, innocent pleasures of course, of the social life that surrounds us, so I thank you for your invitation, given to my daughter, and I have decided to take her, with my wife, as a beginning."

"Oh good!" said Willy. "Well I'm glad that things are working out - see you there then!" Mrs. Atkinson suddenly realised that she hadn't even offered Willy a cup of tea, but Willy pleaded his spare time reporting and left, calling "Cheerio Val!" as he went.

On the way home, he thought, "There's more and more to human nature, it's more extraordinary than anything you can imagine. What ever can it be like, living with him? If he doesn't think he's God, he certainly seems to claim divine rights over his wife and Val." Then he thought, with a sudden realisation, "That poor kid! How the heck can she be so cheerful and full of life, coming from that household? I hope to goodness he doesn't cramp her style at Dellers, it'll ruin it for her! I wonder if he'll believe that you're not going to hell if you're being happy and showing it?"

When the night came, Willy called for Val, and found the three of them ready and waiting. To go out for the evening at ten o'clock, when they would normally be thinking of going to bed, seemed an ill-advised time for re-introducing Val's parents to the social whirl. Val was in her gold dress, the only evening dress that she had. Her mother was well wrapped in her fur coat but Willy noticed that she had a long dress under it. "She's been all week making it," Val confided. Mr. Atkinson had an overcoat over his sober Sunday best. The parents got into the back of the Morris, and off they chugged.

Willy parked close to Dellers in the street between the station and the sea, and ushered the three into the restaurant. The break for refreshments, between the whist drive and the dance, was still proceeding. All the alcoved tables seemed to be occupied, and a cheerful buzz of talk and laughter filled the room. Having disposed of their outer garments, Willy directed them up the wide stairway, with its carved walnut bannister rails, to the upper floor and the ballroom. There were a few people there already, and a five-piece band was getting itself organised at the top end of the room. There was no dais, so their 'claim', as it were, was staked out with potted palms and music stands, one side impregnably protected by an upright piano, the other flank guarded by the drums. In the middle was the brass, the fiddle and the saxophone.

"Let's go over on the other side," suggested Willy. "I've been here before, to meetings, and it gets very hot, what with the smoke and all, and if it's too bad, we can open the door on to the balcony."

It was, in fact, a very low-ceilinged room and was already hot and hazy with cigarette smoke from the whist drive. Val nudged Willy, "How d'you think mum looks?" she whispered.

"Fine!"

"Well, find an opportunity to tell her so, she's as nervous as a cat!"

Willy looked at Val's mother. He had not noticed her much until prodded by Val, and he was surprised how young and pretty she looked. She obviously had a flair for dressmaking, and after turning out Val in her eye-popping gold, she had done something for herself, "in black, with bits of gold and red", was Willy's appreciation of her dress. When she had put it on at home, and said, "Look dear, how do you like it?" her husband had been quite taken aback at the vision she made.

"Don't you like it?" she asked anxiously.

"Yes, yes, I like it, but it's a bit, well - a bit, you know ... but it's all right," he hastened to add, seeing the disappointment on his wife's face.

"Yes, it's very nice, very nice indeed."

"She saw that he meant it, and was pleased. She was pleased too, to see that his attention seemed to be riveted on the well-displayed cleavage of her bosoms. She glanced down, tucking her chin into her throat, and was well satisfied with the fullness below. "Not too low is it, I mean, you don't mind?"

"No," said her husband, "I don't mind, I think you're beautiful and I feel proud of you!" He made a movement towards her, but she backed away. "Oh! Not now. I've spent ages doing my hair and getting ready - when we come back," she promised him archly. They smiled knowingly together, both happier than they'd been for a very long time. "Come on," he said, "young Churchward's here. Get your coat." As she bent to lift it from the settee where it lay, he gave her round bottom a pat, and thought with some surprise, and no little thrill, "She can't have got anything on under that dress - well only her knickers, I suppose!"

He had a thought, that he was experiencing the first fruits of the seduction of the flesh, that this excursion into the world of gaiety was offering him, and a trite quotation from the Bible admonished his conscience, but he had felt his body stir, and he had seen his wife almost reborn into the buxom darling of his youth, a youth that had suddenly aroused itself and beckoned. "I owe it to them," he told himself, "I can't back out now!"

The ballroom soon filled, the seats were all taken, and groups of young men and women were standing around, calling greetings and marking down partners, or hopefuls. The band struck up and couples circled the floor. Willy and his three remained seated, Mr. and Mrs. Atkinson too unused to the scene to venture out, Val glancing hopefully for someone to claim her and Willy staying put, having no intention of taking the floor unless dragged there. "Aren't you going to dance?" asked Mrs. Atkinson.

"Oh! Plenty of time yet," said Willy. Val looked at her mother, and raised her eyes to the ceiling, turning up her pretty nose to convey to her mother the inadequacies of her escort.

The band stopped, the floor cleared, and as it did so a group of people moved into the room from the anteroom. Leading the group was

'George darling'. Willy looked at Val and marvelled at the joy shown in her face. There were four fellows and three girls. The boys looked the room over, as the predatory male always does, and all spotted the golden Val at once. Two waved, "George dear" held her eyes a moment, then continued to study the "form" around the room. He had made no sign of recognition.

Willy looked at Val. Her face was flushed a deep red and she looked unseeingly at her hands in her lap. "Oh lor! Hope she doesn't start to cry!" thought Willy.

The band played again. "Come on, Will, for goodness sake! We can't sit here all night!" She stood up and Will had perforce to join her. He did his usual inelegant shuffle around the room. They said not a word. As they passed the Torquay group, two of the boys called out "What ho! Val!" and "Hello Val", but George was drifting out of the room again.

When the dance finished, they returned to their seats in silence. Val's parents still sat there, just watching the passing show. Willy felt embarrassed and wished he hadn't come. Then the cymbals clashed and the drummer announced, "Now, to get you all to know each other, here's the 'Paul Jones'." "Here we come gathering nuts in May," sang the music, and the lines of dancers circled each other. Val evidently had no intention of joining in, but Willy, scared now of upsetting her parents, took her hand and pulled her on to the floor, where she soon vanished into the throng. Willy struggled valiantly with the dance. He could just about manage to do something resembling a quick step, but the band alternated dances and Willy had no idea what he was supposed to do when they played a waltz or foxtrot, and left more than one lady determined to avoid him at all costs during the rest of the evening. Paul Jones died eventually, much to Willy's relief, and he returned to his seat, expecting Val to appear as the dancers thinned on the floor, but she was not there. "Oh Lor!" he thought, "if she's gone off with some bloke, her old man'll do his nut!" The next moment came another thought. "She might be in the 'ladies' having a good old howl. Crumbs!"

When the music started again and Val still did not appear, her parents had a word together, and her mother then asked Willy, "Was Val all right? She wasn't feeling faint or anything, was she?" "Well, she was upset, that chap - you know, the one that her dad didn't like - he sort of cut her, if you know what I mean!"

"Oh poor Val, I'll see if I can find her." With that she edged her way around the floor en route to the 'ladies'.

Mr. Atkinson said, "What's going on?"

Willy said, "Val's mum thinks Val's gone faint or something."

"I wouldn't wonder, in this fug, you can hardly see across the room."

"I'd better go and make a list of the people running this dance and what not, to write it up. They'll all want to see their names in the *Echo*." So saying, Willy moved away, glad of the chance to do so.

He left the ballroom and went to the hallway leading to the anteroom. Here he could see all who came and went.

Mrs. Atkinson came upstairs a few moments later. "She's not down there," she said, looking at Willy, worry sitting heavily on her face.

"Did you see who she was with?"

"No, I lost sight of her."

"Oh dear! She is naughty, she might have said something."

Willy knew that she was worrying about how her husband would behave and tried to cheer her up by saying, "I expect she's sitting out with someone. Let's look in here."

They entered the semi-circular anteroom, that sat like a miniature dome of St. Paul's over the colonnaded entrance below.

Willy saw the Torquay Gang (as he called them to himself). "Hello. Seen Val at all, anyone?" One of the boys who had waved to Val across the room answered. "Yes, but not in time, some fiend snatched her away from under me nose before I could even start to exert my charm!"

"Where'd they go?"

"Search me! But the back seat of his car might be a good place to start looking, I'd think!"

Willy hesitated, then said, "This is Val's mother, and she wondered where she'd got to." The boy hadn't seen Mrs. Atkinson standing by till then and began to make embarrassed excuses. "I was only joking, she's all right, she's with a friend of mine, I expect they're in the refreshments downstairs."

"Is she with George?"

"No, George shoved off, almost as soon as he came. I expect he missed being able to have a drink."

"Let's just have a look, to set your mind at rest," suggested Willy. They went downstairs to the restaurant and looked through the glass door. A long table with crockery and plates of sandwiches was being presided over by a lady who stood behind a gleaming tea urn. Business was slack, but at a table set in one of the alcoves, that made Dellers such a popular rendezvous, was a young man in evening dress, and seated opposite him, with her back to the watchers, was the golden girl herself. As they watched, the two of them threw up their hands and heads in simultaneous laughter, then the two heads bent forward to each other across the table in conversation.

"She's all right," said Willy.

"Yes," said her mother, "she's all right."

They went upstairs again. As they reached the ballroom, the band leader began an announcement. There was a crush at the ballroom door, mostly of unattached boys, and they had to wait a few moments before squeezing in.

"Now, ladies and gentlemen," said the band leader, "we'll have the popular dance of the moment, to the tune of 'He played his ukulele as the ship went down', so everybody on the floor for the polka!"

The couples rushed the floor for the craze of the moment, and Willy and Mrs. Atkinson threaded their way across the room. "Val's having supper downstairs," she said to her husband. He started to query that, but she quietened him with, "No dear, it's someone Willy knows. He looks very nice." Then she said, "How about us having a go? It's only one, two, three, hop!"

"Oh no, please, I'd rather just watch, but you go, you do it with Will!" "Yes, come on Will."

Willy had perforce to do the gallant, and to his surprise, found the steps quite easy, though, like most of the couples, it tended to get a bit wild. After a while, he remembered Val's suggestion and said, "I say, your dress is very nice, you must be very clever at dressmaking."

"I am, I've been doing it for years. I'm glad you like it, it makes me feel elegant."

"You don't need a dress to do that," said Willy, unconsciously speaking the lines he might have written for some character to speak. "You are beautiful, you and Val are the most beautiful women here."

"Oh-h-h! What a compliment! That's the nicest thing I've had said to me for a long time." ("No it isn't," her mind told her. "Harry said the wonderful things I'd wanted to hear, only a week ago, but it's the nicest thing anyone else has said for years and years.")

With the effort of making his speech, Willy lost the rhythm of the dance, and was going hop when he should have been going either one, two or three, so they dropped out at the end of the room to catch their breath and for Willy to sort his feet out. When the music stopped, the dancers, red-faced and panting, shouted, "More, more."

"All right, all right, let's have it as a lady's choice," said the band leader, and the band started again, the drummer singing 'All the crew were in despair, some rushed here and the others rushed there, but the Captain sat in the Captain's chair, and he played his ukulele as the ship went down."

Willy turned to Mrs. Atkinson to resume the dance and saw her with an amazed look on her face, and following her gaze, saw that Mr Atkinson was standing vigorously protesting something to a large lady, all teeth, bust and bottom, who was virtually man-handling him on to the floor and propelling him into a galloping romp down the room. The lady giving vent to loud 'yoo-hoos', they came up to the band at such speed that in a desperately late turn, they took a music stand with them, to the shrieked delight of the lady. Val's mother was doubled up with laughter. "Oh, poor Harry! Whatever will he make of it?"

They watched the wild stampede go down the room and start to cross the end to come back up again. The lady, with bosoms heaving, legs kicking and teeth at the gnash, was clearing a way through the dancers like someone scything corn. At some point Mr. Atkinson must have mastered the simple rhythm and, amazingly, took charge.

"That's it, you've got it, yoo-ho!" shrieked the woman. They bore down on the band again, this time in some sort of control. The drummer, in mock alarm, picked up the big drum and held it out of harm's way. Mrs Atkinson caught her husband's eye as he careered past and was surprised to get a quick nod and smile. "Good God!" she said aloud, "he's enjoying it!" By that time, most of the dancers had drawn to the sides of the floor and roars of laughter greeted each wild gyration of the lady, and when the music stopped everyone clapped. The lady left Mr. Atkinson where the music had left them. "Cor!" she observed to him, and anyone else listening, "I'm in a sweat, I ought never to ha' worn me corsets for a lark like that!"

The three resumed their seats, and Val's father, mopping his brow, said, "Who on earth was that? She wouldn't take no for an answer. Still it was harmless fun, wasn't it? I didn't make too much of a fool of myself, did I?"

His wife was so pleased, she could have kissed him, then and there. "Of course not, dear, you really woke the party up!"

The band was playing again, and she said, "It's a waltz, you remember that, don't you?"

He stood up and took her in his arms and joined the dancers. "Must be nearly nineteen years," she thought. "Pray God he's come back at last."

Val appeared shortly afterwards. Her face was alight with joy. "This is Harry Michelmore," she said to her parents. "We've just had supper together." The young man, big, dark and completely at ease, greeted Val's parents, shaking them by the hand and making a courteous apology for monopolising Val, then swung her off into the dance.

Willy sought out various persons and found out that the Polka lady was a farmer's daughter, reputed to be able to hoist a two-hundred-weight sack of grain unaided, and that Val's escort was the unattached and much sought after son of the leading fuel merchants in the county.

By one o'clock, the Atkinsons, unused to late hours, and weary from dancing together for most of the last two hours, would have gladly gone home, but Val was so alive and positively gleaming, that they could not find it in their hearts to take her away.

Willy had composed a little report in his head, giving a humorous account of the dance, headlined 'Polka dancers get standing ovation'.

He laughed to himself, "What a change in a man, it's really done wonders, and for his wife. I couldn't ridicule them in the *Echo*, but I could work it into something another time." He was watching them from across the room, and saw their stifled yawns. "I bet they're itching to go. This smoke is enough to put you to sleep, anyway!" Going over to them, he said, "If you'd like to go, I'll run you home and come back for Val."

"Oh, would you! You are a kind boy, we're both tired - so long past our bedtime."

"Right, I'd better tell Val."

Willy nipped into the dancing couples and ranging alongside Val, said, "I'm taking your folks home now, I'll be back again for you." He returned to the couple. "Okay, I've told her."

They collected their outdoor clothes and went on to the steps to wait for Willy to fetch his car from down the road. The fresh air fairly sawed into their lungs after the fug of tobacco smoke in the ballroom. "Ah-h! Fresh air," said Mr. Atkinson. "Enjoyed yourself?"

"Yes! Oh yes! It's been wonderful!"

Willy pulled up then, and as they were about to get in, Val's new friend appeared, and asked if, in the circumstances, they would mind if he brought Val home. "That's my car, across there," he indicated a massive Bentley.

"Can I trust you, young man?" asked Val's father, showing that the night's thaw had not gone deep.

"You can, Sir, I do assure you. I'm well known, and as far as I know, respected."

"All right, not later than half past two."

"On the dot! Depend on it!"

Willy drove the couple to their home. On the way Mrs. Atkinson said, "You shouldn't have been quite so abrupt with that young man - I'm sure he looked decent enough."

"Looks aren't everything. If he's on the level, he'll appreciate my concern for my daughter. If he isn't, he knows I won't stand any hanky-panky."

"Well, Will knows him, don't you, Will?"

"Actually, no I don't," said Willy, cautiously avoiding any blame, should things go wrong. "I only know that he is one of a gang of Torquay chaps, who seem to go about together. His father is the boss of Mitchelmore's the fuel merchants, of Exeter, and this one runs the Torquay branch. He must be very well off - did you see his car?"

Mrs. Atkinson's imagination was already seeing Val as a rich man's wife, and the excitement showed. "Gosh! What an opportunity! Oh Dad! I do hope you'll take to him, it could mean so much to Val."

"My dear, money by itself never brought happiness to anyone; ease and comfort, yes, but contentment - never! All I want for our girl is happiness, and if she finds it with a man, rich or poor, I'll be satisfied, but it can't be bought, though most people think it can, and I'd want to know a lot about any chap who thought he could give it to her."

"Yes dear, you're right of course, and (sighing) there may not be anything in it. Poor Val, I don't want to see her hurt again!"

"Again? Well yes, I get what you mean, but I can't drop all my convictions when I know that if I did I'd be putting the girl at risk. She's too young to judge for herself yet - she's only a baby!"

"Yes, the same age as I was when I married you, dear, and I knew what I was doing."

"Sorry! I won't say any more, and I'll certainly not preach any sermons to you tonight. It's been a lovely night, hasn't it?"

"Lovely!"

The noisy car prevented Willy from being aware of the conversation going on in the back of the car. "Here we are then," he said, as they reached the house, you'd better try for some beauty sleep before your beautiful daughter arrives in that huge car."

"Beauty sleep! Some hopes, I've got to be on duty at half past four - hardly worthwhile getting into bed." As he said it, he knew that he was lying in his teeth. The warmth and softness of his wife cuddled up close to him in the car had inspired marvellous ideas of how the night might yet be used before they slept.

When Val came into the office next morning, she dumped her handbag on the desk and collapsed on to her chair.

"Oh gosh! I feel as if I hadn't slept for a month," she said, sinking her head into her hands.

"How did it go? Did you have a good time?"

"Um, um! Pretty good! He's all right, terribly, terribly good mannered, and awfully well educated, Blundells and Oxford, you know!" She said all that in an affected voice, aping the upper classes.

"Well, he seemed struck on you enough to ask your old man to let him see you home. Didn't you like him much?"

Val looked up to the ceiling and smiled a dreamy smile. "Yes, he's rather sweet, and he wants to see me again."

"Oh yes. What about George?"

"George can take a running jump, the rotten blighter. It wasn't my fault that dad threw him out. If he was a man he'd have tried again, at least once more. I don't want to see him again!"

The wanness of her early morning make-upless face had changed to a bright pink with the indignation she was feeling, and Willy thought, for the thousandth time, "Gosh! She's beautiful! I'll get her into my novel somewhere." Aloud, he said, "How about your dad, will he let him take you out?

"He thinks my dad's a very responsible person. Seems he was warned of trying anything on with me."

"Yes, I know," said Willy, wickedly. "He told him to keep his hands to himself."

"He didn't! He couldn't!" Val cried in alarm.

"Well, not in so many words."

Val relaxed. "He must have a good job to have a car like that."

"He sells coal - goes around with a horse and cart, with a leather thing on his back, shouting, 'Coalman!'."

Val looked at Willy, not knowing if he was teasing or not, but Willy's face was all innocence. "His hands didn't look as if he was a coalman - you're making that up!"

"Would you care?"

"I dunnow, he'd come home very dirty!"

Willy had to give up pretending. "Come on," he said. "You've got that abstract to copy before old Collins comes in at eleven, so stop your daydreaming and get on with it."

"Oh lor! I've got to tidy up first, be a lamb and get it sorted out for me. He isn't really a coalman, is he?"

"In a way he is, only he doesn't deliver it, he's just stinking rich!"

Val's eyes opened wide. "Honest?"

"Honest! Probably picks up a couple of thousand a year!"

"Phew! Val Atkinson, watch your step!"

"Never mind watching your step, go and wash your face or whatever you do to it, or you'll be having 'old nasty' chasing you!"

During the day, while he did his work mechanically, Willy's mind was flitting about with successions of scenes, weaving a web of events that began to form a story. Val was there and her parents. He had already visualised a plot concerning Mr. Atkinson and his terrible illness and his preaching, and the repression under which his wife and daughter lived. Now it had all broken out, and begun to form a kaleidoscope of events that was ever changing, but beginning to take a definite form. "I'll get it soon," he told himself. "It's coming, it's going to be good." Then, with a bit of a smirk, he told himself, "Will Churchward, you're a clever lad! One day you'll be a bestseller."

At the weekend, he confided his ambition to Mr. Watts. The man was as excited as Willy, but he advised caution. "You will do it, I'm sure of that, if you have enough dedication to give up your leisure time. You'll find it hard work and at the end you must be prepared for disappointments when you try to get someone to publish it - it is a crowded profession, so it won't be easy."

"Every author has to find a publisher for his first book - if it's worth publishing, I'll stand as good a chance as anyone else."

"Every bit, in fact a bit better than some, because you've already been in print, in a small way, and that should help."

He also cautioned Willy to use the Atkinson work with extreme care, only making use of the inspiration, not the occurrences. No publisher would touch material that was biographical without deep investigation into its origins, he advised, "There are laws of libel, as you well know."

Willy was not discouraged. He had already realised all those things. "It's just as if a window had opened in my mind," he said, "and I'm seeing all sorts of facets of life that I'd never thought of before!" As he walked home, he wished that he could tell his mother of his great decision, and that she would see it as he did, an exciting project, a glittering future, but he knew that all she was likely to say was "That'll be nice, dear, but mind your eyes, with all that writing, you don't want to strain them, so be careful!"

He was now the main contributor to the household exchequer, but Gwen continued with her domestic work at the Big House. Willy had suggested that she cut down on it, but she had sensibly reminded him that he would be getting married and finding a place of his own soon, so she would have to be self-supporting.

"But Mum, you come home so tired! I've seen you dragging up the hill, looking worn out!"

"I feel it sometimes, Willy, but if I gave it up, where would I find another job? I've been there nearly twenty-five years - it's almost my home! I get my meals there, and it's warm in the winter, so I don't need much money, except for the rent and some clothes sometimes."

"When you were young, there were three of you to do the work, then it was two, now it's only you, you can't call that fair."

"I'm glad they keep me on, they're not as well off as they were, they're always saying how their shares have dropped and all that. Anyway, I'm content to stay where I am."

"No use telling Mum," he thought. Then he felt again the desire to go to Jerry and talk as they used to do. "I wonder if I could make him understand, it's not his line, he's so practical, he'd want to see the whole thing in bricks and mortar." The thought persisted, and after a while he decided to look Jerry up. "After all, it was a silly quarrel, he didn't mean it - or not the way I did, he's' got a different attitude to life, that's all." Then another thought. "I ought to know more about how he thinks, I've got to understand all sides of life."

As it happened, Jerry called at the office a few days later to instigate a further phase of business. He came thumping up the stairs, all muddy boots and overalls stained red with soil, a dilapidated cap set askew on his head. "Hello gorgeous!" was his greeting to Val. "Will the big white chief see me for a minute or two?" Then, turning his attention to Willy, who was seated at his desk at the back of the room, "What'o Will, how yer 'acking?"

Willy grinned back. "All right, I suppose. You starting on the next lot?"

"Sss", said Jerry, indicating the word by the Devonian method of drawing in his breath over the lower teeth, with a sibilant hiss. "I'm ready, they're all sold, and I got three options on the next."

Willy leaned back, balancing his chair on its two back legs, and looked at Jerry. "Told you you'd be a rich man before I was, didn't I? Are you pleased the way things have gone?"

"You bet! Mind you, I've worked bloody hard and I've not had much for myself, but I'm in the clear now, and what I make will be my own." When Jerry went into the inner office to transact his business, Val said, "He's nice, I like him!"

"Yes, everyone does, he's got charm or something. You just think! When other chaps, like Bellamy or Windsor or the two Shutes, come in, they wear suits and bowler hats, old Windsor always sports plus fours, and shoes with floppy tongues, but Jerry comes in just as he is for work, doesn't give a tinker's cuss for appearances. If the others did it, people would think they were hard up or something, but Jerry manages to make a virtue of it and nobody thinks any the worse of him."

When Jerry reappeared, Willy said, "I'd like to come up and see your buildings, they look good on the plans."

"I wish you would," said Jerry, with evident pleasure. "Come up Saturday afternoon, I'll be there in the office, till about four."

"Right, I will," said Willy, suddenly feeling happy that he had made an opportunity for re-establishing their old friendship.

Willy found Jerry in his office, which was a partitioned-off corner of the old barn that Jerry used as workshop and store. There was a trestle table littered with invoices, delivery notes, catalogues and plans, mostly marked with rings where tea mugs had kept them from blowing away when the door was opened. An oil stove and an overflowing carton of rubbish were all the other furnishings.

"Come on," said Jerry, "have a look at the last two, they're empty yet." He took Willy over the pair of semi-detached houses with pride. "See here," he kept pointing out, at some refinement that he had made to the building or finishing, then, "It costs money, but it's worth it - folks come over, after looking at that lot on the other side, and they always say that these are worth more than the extra hundred pounds I charge, and the building societies like it too." They stood in the front bedroom of the last house, looking out at the partly completed estate. "Seems a shame really," said Jerry. "This was beautiful country. They used to grow oats or wheat in this field - remember?"

"Yes, we came in after the rabbits one year, didn't we. Was it this field? It's difficult to visualise it now - perhaps it was further up? I always remember hitting one with my stick, and it cried! That was the first thing I ever killed."

"You didn't anyway, I finished it off, and you were sick in the hedge!"

"Yes, I remember. Of course, you would remember that I was sick!" Willy replied, laughing. "We had some good days as kids, didn't we?"

Jerry said, "We ought to get about a bit together again. I can go a bit easier now. I've hardly been anywhere or done anything but work till now. I could do with a bit of a change, and you must get fed up with being shut up in that old office all the time! Mind you" he said, with his old roguish grin, "you got a bit of compensation there in that little blonde skirt."

Willy ignored the inference and said, "Well, my job is really only sort of bread and butter now I'm doing quite well with articles and things in papers. Here, look," he said, picking up a stained copy of the *Echo* that had been spread on the floor to keep it clean. "Here's my bit." He picked up one sheet after another till he found it - a column headed, 'Seen and Heard,' and passed it to Jerry. It was a series of paragraphs, giving comments on local happenings. "That was a bit of a lark," he told Jerry, pointing out a section that read, 'Hospital extensioners had another successful night at Dellers and welcomed the support of a number of folk from Torquay. During the dance that followed the whist drive, a certain stalwart lady caused considerable interest by her interpretation of the polka. When the music faded away, she and her partner received an appreciative round of applause.'

"Oh-umm," said Jerry, not very impressed, "but what's your future?"

"I'm going to be a novelist. I shall write for my living."

"Cor! Risky, isn't it?"

"No, it isn't, I know I can do it, and I know I will do it, I'm certain of it! In the meantime, I can make quite a bit with stuff like that and articles and (he shied at saying 'poems') things."

"Well, I hope you do - and I reckon you will, if you think you can yourself, but I'd rather do something that I can see." Neither spoke for a while, smoking and gazing out at the unmade road and the shambles of builders' materials and machinery littering the land not yet developed. Then Jerry said, "You ever go on holiday?"

"Good lord! No!" said Willy. The concept of actually going on a holiday had hardly occurred to him. He had his annual two weeks, but he had always filled them up with things to do at home.

"I haven't either," said Jerry, "but people come here on holiday every summer - look at the Swindon people, every year they come! Look! I can take a week before I start the next lot here. How about us going camping for a week. Needn't be too far away. We can hire a tent and take the van. What d'you say?"

Willy found the idea exciting. Camping, sleeping in a tent, out in the country somewhere, up on the moors perhaps!

"Yes, rather! I'd like that, but my holiday isn't till August."

"Oh! Well, look, we'll plan to go, eh? And we'll fix the time later!"

A month later, when Willy returned home after work, he found Jerry's van parked outside his house. "I've fixed up a place for us to camp," Jerry told him. "It's on a farm down near Salcombe where I was working. We can camp in a field by the estuary, there's a stream for water and the farm is only about a mile up the lane, and there's a ferry 'bout half a mile up the river, so we can get into Salcombe. I thought we could go August Bank Holiday week. What d'you think?"

"Sounds all right, how about kit?"

"I'll see to that, we can hire most of it, all you'll need is your own gear."

"Right'o! Coming in?"

"Nope, I got things to do. See you again sometime!"

Gwen was in. "What did that Jerry want?" she asked Willy.

"He was telling me that he had fixed up somewhere for us to camp when I'm on holiday."

"Camp? You going camping with him?"

"Yes Mum. I didn't say anything to you, because it was just a suggestion, and I hardly thought we'd be going, but he evidently meant it, and he's been fixing it up - somewhere down at Salcombe. Ought to be great, especially if the weather's good."

"Well, I don't know! You never know what that boy might be up to - look at that bike, for instance!"

"Oh Mum! I'm not daft! We're just going to have a holiday - I've never had one - and we'll just laze about, and do some bird watching, and have a restful time. Jerry's been working flat out for years, and he's going on to a new lot of building soon, and now I've thought of it, I'd like to forget all my work for a week, it'll be a change."

"And how'll you live? Who's going to do the cooking, I'd like to know?"

"Oh! We'll manage, we'll do easy stuff, and we'll hardly starve to death in a week anyway, will we?"

"I'm glad you're going, it'll do you good, but I wish it wasn't with that Jerry. I don't trust him, he's from bad stock, and I don't want you to get involved in any of his goings on!"

"Mum! Jerry's all right. We understand each other, you don't have to worry."

"No, well, I will all the same. Still, you're old enough to be sensible, I suppose."

"Of course I am, Mum - please don't worry."

The note of concern in Willy's voice touched Gwen's lonely heart.

"Well! I'd better think of what you'll want to take. I could make pasties, and you could take some of the plum jam I've just made. I can some cake too, that'll keep a day or two."

"Thanks Mum, that'll be fine. I expect we'll pretty well live on eggs and bacon, and there's sure to be a chip shop in Salcombe - we won't starve!"

Chapter 18

As the end of July came nearer, Willy found himself looking forward to his holiday with a happy zest. The dusty smell of the office, and a lot of the repetitive work that fell to him, made the anticipation of spending a whole week in the open air, away from all his normal interests, an alluring prospect. The last few days of July ushered in a heatwave. There was little wind, and the sun blazed from morning to night.

"Pity for you it's this week, not next," said the senior clerk to Willy. "It'll piss down all next week, you can be sure of that - always waits for the August Bank Holiday! Then goes on till the Regatta's over!"

"All right, all right," said Willy. "I know an old chap, he's a gardener, and he says the moon's full next Wednesday, and it'll stay like this till the next new moon."

The older man tittered. "You wait till you're baling out your tent!" he replied.

"You're envious, that's all!" said Willy. "Just because it rained cats and dogs when you had yours, you're just hoping I'm not going to be lucky!"

The other man retired to his little office, smirking to himself, and thinking, "I'll have young Miss Bouncy Tits to myself next week anyway, so he can roast or drown for all I care!"

Jerry arrived at Willy's house on the Friday evening. He had hired two tents and ground sheets. They had each bought sleeping bags - quilted cotton, kapok-filled things, just coming into the shops, in response to the 'hiking' craze. They each had an enamel mug and plate and 'eating irons', as Jerry called them. Willy begged the use of a black cast-iron frying pan that Gwen had brought home from a jumble sale, and Jerry provided an old saucepan and also a tin kettle and a bucket. They bought themselves khaki shorts and stockings, and Willy, when he surveyed himself dressed in them, with an open-necked, grey flannel shirt, felt fit to face the open-air life, as well as any fictional white hunter.

"How do I look?" he asked his mother.

"Fine dear, you look just like the holiday campers."

This satisfied Willy, who was a little conscious of his bony arms and legs, all knobbly about the knees and elbows. When Jerry arrived, dressed much the same, Willy wished that he had the same broad shoulders, strong legs and arms, and skin all tanned a deep brown from working shirtless on the buildings.

"You'll have to be careful not to get sunburn," warned Gwen. "Well, I'm sure to, aren't I?" he replied, thinking that the sooner he did the better, now that he could contrast his white skin to Jerry's tan.

In view of the fact that the August Bank Holiday came within the week Willy was on holiday, he had asked for the Saturday morning off, and this had been granted, so he had finished work on the Friday night, and left with Val's good wishes, and the advice, "Don't forget to do everything I wouldn't!" from the senior clerk.

Val, during the Friday, had moved her typewriter to Willy's desk, and when asked why, she had said, "If I sit here, 'old hopeful' can't get behind me. Have you ever noticed how he always tries to stand right behind me, then lean over to point out something? I know he's only trying to look down my dress. This way all he can do is drop something in front of the desk, and have a quick look up my legs when he picks it up again!"

"Oh! Go on, you imagine it," Willy had said, then remembered half-noticed actions by the older man, that had not, till then, held any significance. "Poor old devil," he'd said to himself. Some time previously, Willy had questioned Mr. Watts, who was his most respected mentor, on the behaviour of his older colleague, and Mr. Watts, who long since had treasured Willy's confidences, and had not wanted to see his knowledge of life tarnished by any obscene approach to natural behaviour, had explained to the boy that some men, many men, lived a life of sexual repression, being married to women who were unresponsive to their needs, some through habit, others boredom, many by revulsion and some by being tied to husbands married in haste after a fleeting attraction whom they grew to dislike, leaving their own desires to wilt, or to increase their antagonism, as they too became more frustrated. This at the time had shocked Willy, but, as usual, his perceptive mind had found many things now explained, and felt compassion instead of disgust on many a revelation. Thinking it over, he had wondered, "Don't people feel like I do for Madge, when they marry?" and "Could it ever happen to us?" Willy's wide-ranging choice of literature had made him well informed on human behaviour, both fictional and true, but he was, at that time, still so innocent that it was not until Mr. Watts had made him see it all happening then, all around him, that a little more of his protected boyhood fell away. Now a year or so later, when Val said, "Dirty old devil!" Willy could feel sorry for the man, knowing, as he did, the desires that demanded satisfaction.

It was a perfect day, that last day of July, when the two boys arrived at the little hamlet of Portlemouth. They called at the farm and were told where they might camp. The field was rough grazing land, sloping rather steeply towards the river. The lane leading to the sands by the estuary was narrow and rutted, so they had to leave the van at the farm and hump their gear for half a mile or so. There was a stream running beside the lane down the valley and the opposite side of the lane skirted a wooded hill. They decided to pitch camp on a level patch, hedged about by bracken, gorse and stunted blackthorn. The grass was nibbled short by rabbits whose droppings were everywhere. "We'll catch 'em - save buying meat," said Jerry.

When the tents were up they didn't seem as big as Willy had imagined. He found he could just sit up without touching the ridge cord.

"Gosh! I hope we have fine weather," he told Jerry. "I don't fancy being cooped up in here for long."

"It's set fine - you see, there'll be no need to go inside except to sleep."

They had planned to use the van as a store and a refuge in case of need, and were a bit dismayed to have to leave it half a mile away.

"Where are we going to keep the grub?" Willy enquired.

"In our tents! We'll split it up - put it up the top."

"All right for you - I can hardly stretch out, as it is my feet are almost outside when I lay down."

"Oh! Never mind, it's all part of the game. Come on, first thing, collect wood for the fire."

Half an hour later they had collected a pile of dead branches from the wood, and Jerry set about excavating a trench fireplace. They had been back to the van and collected a spade, an axe and a piece of tarpaulin. Jerry handed Willy the spade and, waving towards the bracken, gave him instructions to dig a latrine pit. Willy forced his way, gingerly, into the bracken. He was surprised to find that there were other things growing there too, especially brambles. He soon found that his bare knees were suffering from all manner of thorns and things that scratched. Twenty feet or so into the jungle, he turned to call, "This far enough?"

"Blimey! Have a heart, man - go up by that gorse bush on your left."

Willy moved on, hacking at the bracken with the blade of the spade. When he came near his goal, he suddenly found a little clearing. The bracken and gorse was waist high and it seemed an ideal spot. He drove the spade hard into the ground to make the first cut, and nearly dislocated his shoulder when the spade bounced back, without making any impression on the ground. He stabbed all about the clearing without making any progress, so called Jerry again.

"It's all solid rock over here."

"Choose a place where the bracken's tallest," Jerry shouted back.

Half an hour later, Willy, sweating profusely and tormented with flies, had managed to hack a small hole amongst the bracken roots.

"Jerry!" he called. "It's no good, I can't dig a hole anywhere!"

" 'Ang on, I'll come and see."

Jerry took the spade, and with a few vigorous thrusts had the spade driven spit deep. "There you are, that's how to do it."

"Well, you do it then, I'm not making any impression."

"All right then - you chop up some wood while I finish this!"

When Jerry returned he roared with laughter at Willy's efforts to chop up the logs. "Never mind, Will, by the end of the week you'll be a backwoodsman! How about you getting on with the cooking - I'm starving!"

As boys, the two had often built fires and cooked sausages and things, and Willy was used to cooking, or heating up, his own meals at home when his hours varied with Gwen's, so it was with relief that he set about brewing tea and heating up some tinned beans. It was a bit awkward, not having a table to work on, and some of the bread acquired a lot of ash and debris, but they both enjoyed the food. They had planned to use Gwen's pasties as their first meal, but these had been consumed on the way to the camp, when they stopped at Kingsbridge and had half a pint of cider each. The next thing to do, declared Jerry, was to explore the estuary and find out where the ferry to Salcombe was. It was about four o'clock by then, and very hot. "Bring your bathers," advised Jerry, who was definitely the leader of the two. "We might as well have a swim."

They found there was a good stretch of fine sands on their side of the river. Being fairly inaccessible, it was completely deserted. "Let's see if we can find a footprint," said Willy, "and track down a Man Friday!"

The small ferry operated from a slipway at the end of the sands, and crossed over to the town on the other side. They paid their two-pences and were ferried across, then spent an hour or so wandering around the narrow street that comprised most of the town. They bought some biscuits to take back and pork pies to eat then. "Nothing like fresh air to give you an appetite," said Jerry, ignoring the fact that he spent most of his life outdoors.

Willy discovered, to his great satisfaction, that the town boasted public toilets (though on entering, he decided that they should rather not be mentioned) and decided that a cubicle in the town was worth two holes in the bracken, so he wandered along the river wall and watched the several small boats manoeuvring in the stream. When he reappeared, Willy found Jerry 'chatting up a bit of skirt', as he would have put it. She was a girl of about eighteen, dressed in cotton 'beach pyjamas' as the fashion was - thin, floral wide-legged trousers, that flapped against her legs in the breeze that came off the water. The top part was no more substantial and as she moved to lean against the rail and face the boys, there was little left to the imagination as to what the lissom young body was like underneath. Jerry looked her over with unashamed desire, and she turned her head with a feigned interest in something further along the quay.

"You live here?" asked Jerry.

"Yes, worse luck!"

"Why? It's smashing, I think!"

"Not if you lived here. It's dead, so dead - it's mummified! Look at it, August Bank Holiday weekend and hardly a soul to be seen - look over there at Portlemouth - not a soul in sight. You might as well be in a nunnery as live here. Ten minutes after the pub shuts the last lights go out and everybody's in bed."

"Not a bad place to be - with the right company," said Jerry, saucily. The girl grimaced, raising her eyebrows, closing her eyes and puckering up her nose, pretending that she treated Jerry's comment with contempt, but as Jerry told Willy later, "I knew at once that she was game."

"Where do you work then?" he enquired.

"Kingsbridge - but that's as bad, though they've got a picture house and have a dance now and again, but there's only yobs!"

"Tell you what!" said Jerry, "have you got a friend for my mate here? Then we could make up a foursome! You get Monday off, I suppose? We could make it a weekend!"

Willy heard the suggestion with alarm. He saw at once that he might be involved in goodness knows what.

"Here, hold on!" he cried. "We've made other plans!"

Jerry laughed. "I was joking," he said, winking at the girl with the eye furthest from Willy. "We're camping over at Portlemouth for the week, and got to fill in a lot of time."

Willy felt relieved, but still apprehensive. Jerry seemed in no hurry break off the encounter, and he wondered what might happen next.

"Do you go boating?" he asked the girl.

"I have, at times, but I'm not keen - generally get my clothes mucked up. Might go swimming though, if it's still fine tomorrow."

"Right, see you then, over across, tomorrow morning!"

"I didn't say I'd go swimming with you, did I? You got ideas that don't necessarily match up with mine. Oh! There's my auntie, I was waiting for her."

Without any further ado, the girl strode off, joining an older woman and vanishing behind some boats beached on the hard. Willy thought

"Good! That's her got rid of!" But Jerry chuckled to himself, and thought, "She'll be there! Look out, Will old man, you're in for some education."

"Come on Will, let's get back and have a dip," he said.

They crossed back to Portlemouth and changed into the bathing costumes amongst the bushes that grew right down to the sands. The tide was rising, running up the estuary at a fast rate, and the two allowed themselves to be carried along with it, till Jerry suddenly discovered that he was being carried over a deeply dredged channel. He called to Willy, "Keep inshore, the current's strong out here!" He swam towards the shore and rejoined Willy, who, not being much of a swimmer, had just been mucking about in shallow water. "Cor!" he said. "You could get yourself drowned out there."

"Not you, you're one of those who always come through."

"Why?"

"Oh! Self-confidence, I suppose, you're just sort of competent. I couldn't imagine you failing in anything. Like that motor bike - anyone else would have been killed!"

They lay on the sands. Jerry chucked his packet of Players to Willy and they lit up. Jerry took the packet and held it up as he lay on his back. "Makes me think, Will, sometimes. This lifebuoy and the sailor. It's funny! I hated that orphanage, and my dad was killed in the navy, but somehow, I sometimes think that I ought to be in the navy - it's got a peculiar pull, it seems as if it would be natural, but here I am, a chippy, making a success of a small building firm, that's going to be a big one before I've finished - and no possibility of going to sea, yet all the same, the feeling's there!"

"Yes," said Willy, "your destiny calls!"

"What the heck do you mean by that?"

Willy was happy. This was the sort of mental exercise he enjoyed. His mind leaped to situations and words, ringing them with mystery and allure and excitement. "I think," he replied, "you ought to get yourself a medlar tree, like your old landlady, and find your fortune written in its branches."

"Cor! What a Shakespeare! Here! That's an idea! I could go down to

Avonford and get the old dear to let me have that tree of hers, and plant it in my garden when I've built my house, couldn't I?"

"Yes," said Willy, his mind far away, then, "Here! It's getting cold, we'd better brew up some tea." They dressed and returned to camp. The sun had set and the sky was shaded in delicate hues, from orange to pink to duck-egg green. One bright star was already showing. By the time the fire was burning, and the kettle boiled, night had already drifted out of the woods, only the hill tops showed clear against the sky. Midges, by the thousand, found their way into their hair and down their necks. The hurricane lamp that they had put between their tents was a mecca for every winged insect in the locality.

"To hell with this," said Jerry, "I'm putting on my longs!" They tucked their trousers into their socks and rolled down their sleeves and sat in the smoke of the fire to drink the tea and munch biscuits.

"What do we do now?" asked Willy.

"Dunno, we'll have to organise things better tomorrow. I vote we go over to Salcombe and have a beer till bedtime."

"Okay, but the last ferry is at ten, so we won't have long."

They stamped the fire out and stumbled through the gorse and bracken to the lane, Willy's small torch lighting up hazards just too late for him to avoid. They reached the slipway at last, but it was almost ten and no ferry waited.

"Too late to ring now," said Willy, shining his torch on the ship's bell, hanging on a frame by the slip. "Anyway, I doubt if he'd come, hardly worth it for fourpence, and he wouldn't bring us back, either, he packs it in at ten."

"We should've bought some bottled beer," said Jerry. Then, pointing down the estuary, "Look at that!"

Against the star-strewn horizon of the channel, a ship was coming up river. She was a blaze of lights and made a wonderful sight.

"Must be a private yacht," Jerry said. "Some wealthy bugger on his holidays following the regattas around the coast. Let's stop and watch her berth." Jerry spoke the occasional shipping term naturally, his unhappy childhood poking through his memory like a waking dream.

As the ship crept up the channel, she seemed larger than she was, her lights reflected in the water. She was painted white and was strung all over with lights, with all portholes and casements alight as well. There were people on deck and music was playing, hardly any smoke came from her funnel, then her anchor chain rattled out, and she ceased to move forward. A boat must have put off from the other side, to come humming around her stern to a buoy, where someone was making the ship fast.

"Like a small liner, isn't she?" said Willy. "Fancy being able to run a thing like that!"

"Not only that but a 'J' class as well," Jerry said.

"I've seen them," said Willy, "racing, I mean. I had to go over to Torquay to get something signed and they were all just coming around a buoy by the Spa, marvellous sight, they had their spinnakers set as they came in, then they took them down and fairly spun around the buoy. I forget all of them, but I know there was the Britannia, All Black, Tommy Lipton's Shamrock, The White Heather, all of them, seven, I think it was. They're huge when you see them close, must cost a fortune."

They stayed on, musing on the fortunes of life. "Well," concluded Jerry, "they didn't all inherit their money, some started from scratch, and I reckon, if all goes well, I'll be in the money myself one day. May take years, because I'm not taking chances, but I'll get there!"

"And as a popular, best-selling author, I'll meet you, and we'll reminisce our childhood around the old fountain," rejoined Willy. "Come on, I'm going to turn in."

They woke early. The sun had not yet reached into the estuary, and a thin, white mist hung like gauze on the valley. Every gorse bush and bracken stem was bedewed. Spider webs, gossamer miracles dressed in crystal, were draped over everything. Willy, first up, took dry wood from under the piece of tarpaulin, thoughtfully provided by Jerry, and started to build a fire. He had a kettle boiling before Jerry appeared, sleeping bag and all, working himself out of the tiny tent like a looper caterpillar. Willy put a generous helping of tea into the kettle and let it boil for a moment or two, then poured the brew into their mugs, with condensed milk and lots of sugar. The tannin bit into Willy's mouth and throat, but he decided it was exactly right for the occasion - there was something primitive about it, a toast to the pioneer spirit.

"Cor! Bloody hell!" exclaimed Jerry. "You haven't used the whole packet at one go, have you?"

"Drink up," said Willy, who had awakened with a determination to make the most of the day. "We're going for a dip before breakfast!"

Jerry wriggled out of his bag. He was completely naked and proceeded to do a few setting up exercises. Willy couldn't help envying him his stalwart body. "I'll take one of those body-building courses," he thought. "It's about time I filled out a bit. 'course," he consoled himself, "he's two years older than me."

They ran down the lane to the river and had their bathe. Then they fried bacon and eggs and bread, and made more tea. The sun was now well up, the mist had gone, and the sun's rays, after setting the millions of dew drops a-twinkle, had sucked up the dew and the earth began to reflect heat. It promised to be a perfect day.

"Now," said Willy, "I reckon we should have a lazy morning on the sands, then go across and buy some grub, then hire a boat and muck about on the river. Afterwards, we could have a drink and a pie at the pub. Then, in the evening, we could explore the headland, see what wildlife's about. How's that?"

"Yes, fine."

Jerry thought, "Lazy morning on the sands! Just what I was going to fiddle." His eyes were grinning, but he kept his face straight.

Jerry was a most particular camp leader that morning. He insisted on everything being clean and tidied up. The water bucket had to be replenished and a fresh supply of firewood gathered. It all took time and it was gone ten before they were ready to leave camp.

When they reached the sands, they were deserted. Jerry led the way to the far end, near the ferry, choosing a spot near a huge boulder.

"How's this then?" he said, chucking down his towel.

"Good enough," said Willy, spreading out his towel. "I'm going to get myself a bit sun-burned!"

He was wearing his bathing costume under his shirt and shorts, which he removed. He was pleased with his costume. It had cost him two pounds, a terrible extravagance, but though he felt he had been conned into buying it, he felt that it 'did' something for him. Actually, he had gone into the shop intending to buy the popular cotton version, with short legs, for about twelve and sixpence, but the assistant had immediately produced "The fashion of this year, Sir," in black bottom and white top, with a belt. Willy had seen these in use: once wet they revealed all, which was very interesting for the spectator, when a well-built lady emerged from the sea, but was not so pleasant for the wearer, who had to proceed to his or her clothes, busily engaged in picking the clinging and near transparent material from the more important protuberant body areas. Willy declined the assistant's advice and asked for "just the usual black ones" - to no avail. He was offered, with persuasive guile, "The very latest, new this season, and, of course, it's from Janson." The article was spread across the counter. "All wool, of course, non-clinging, and very comfortable, also, it has sun-bathing panels on both sides." Here, the assistant had put his hand through the cut-away parts, and wiggled his fingers, to show where the sun's health-giving rays would play upon the wearer's ribs. "You will also notice, Sir, the design of the garment is new, the lower part is cut straight across from the - ahem - crotch, giving a modern legless look, and also (here the assistant's voice became very confidential) you will see that there is an insert across the front, something like the webbing between a duck's toes; this provides a modest protection for the gentleman with (here, a coy smile) prominent features."

Willy had at once realised that to refuse the article would, at very least, put his masculinity in doubt, and had succumbed. When he put it on in his bedroom that evening, and had managed to tilt his mirror enough to observe the area in question, he was well satisfied. He did not like to be conspicuous anywhere and, frankly, was well aware that he had nothing to boast about in that region. He was pleased, too, with the figure embroidered on his hip, of a swimmer in the arched attitude of diving. It put him, he felt, a cut above the usual holiday maker.

Jerry had his swimming club costume, with the town's crest, encircled with the initials P.S.L.S.A., printed on it. Willy felt that, with his body, Jerry could afford to wear any old thing anyway, and fashionable attire would have been superfluous.

The sun was really hot, the water lapped the sands, faraway sounds of boats and people did nothing to destroy the peace of the morning. "This," thought Willy, "is just right!" His eyes were closed against the sun and his mind, in that happy realm between sleep and waking, was all agog with the plot of his novel. The characters lived, they spoke their lines without prompting, no longer puppets of his imagination, but real people. It was a difficult chapter that had been written, destroyed, then written again, still without conviction. Now in that floating half-reality, they came unbidden and made their own story. Willy, completely relaxed, let them play their parts.

He was suddenly jolted back into full wakefulness by the sound of a gramophone that blared 'Ain't she sweet? See her coming down the street. Now I ask you very confidentially, ain't she sweet!' Willy sat up in annoyance. "Oh lor!" he complained, his dreams shattered. "Who the heck's making that row?"

"Couple of girls, just come over on the ferry," Jerry told him. So saying, he got up, and with great casualness, rounded the boulder. "Hello then!" Willy heard him say. "You, is it? Well, what are you hiding away here for? Come on the sunny side with us!"

The answer he got was inaudible to Willy, but he could hear Jerry continuing to chat them up.

"There must have been some ritual refusal, then indecision ("Shall we? Do you want to? It's just as good here.") before Jerry reappeared carrying the portable gramophone, and followed by the girl in beach pyjamas and another dressed likewise.

"Come on," Jerry was saying, "my mate's an expert gramophone winder-upper, aren't you, Will?"

Willy let it pass. He was resentful of the intrusion into his peaceful rest, and furious with Jerry for encouraging the girls to join them.

"Your mate doesn't look best pleased to see us," said the first girl.

"Oh, yes he is. It's only he was fast asleep dreaming naughty dreams, and you woke him up too soon for him to know if he was going to be lucky!"

"Oh! Honestly, you are awful! Were you really asleep?" she asked, turning to Willy.

"Well, more or less," said Willy, "but it doesn't matter."

The second girl had stood a little apart while this was going on. Now she started drawing arches in the sand with her bare toes. The first girl was occupied with arranging a bag, a blanket and a paper carrier, obviously containing food and vacuum flasks, against the rock.

Willy stood up, and remained standing, holding the gramophone that Jerry had handed him. "Well, if we're making up a foursome, hadn't somebody better start introductions?" asked the second girl.

"Oh yes," said Jerry. "This is my friend, Will Shakespeare. I'm Jerry. Will, this is the Queen of Sheba, and on my left is Maid Marion, who's having a day off from all her merry men."

"I think that's rather nice," said girl two, to Willy's surprise. "We're Sheba and Marion - only forget the merry men - and you're Jerry and Will. That'll do nicely, till we decide if we want to know you!"

Willy grinned. "Good for her," he thought. "She's been dragged into this too."

They settled themselves. "Go on, Will, wind'er up!" said Jerry.

The girl called Marion moved over beside Willy. "I've only brought six records," she said. "They're so heavy with the gramophone."

She knelt beside Willy, turning over the records, then, selecting one, she leaned forward to put it on the turntable, and Willy found himself looking at the delicious roundness inside her neckline. "Oh lor!" he thought, then his sense of humour coming through, "Three cheers for the little insert." He wound up the machine, and the tinny sound of 'The Lily of Laguna' offended the serenity of the day. Jerry and Sheba had adopted reclining positions facing each other and were engaged in some sort of vocal fencing that seemed to give them pleasure.

Marion continued to kneel beside Willy. Willy found himself keeping hopeful watch for her to lean forward again. "Oh hell!" he told himself, "I'm on holiday, and what's the harm!" Next time, she caught him looking, and he smiled a little shamefacedly, but she just made a funny little pout with her mouth, then smiled back. "She's fun," he thought, "and she's pretty, too."

After a little while, Willy found himself joking and laughing with her, and finding pleasure in her happy company. "She's got lovely eyes," he thought, "big and very full, and she's put black stuff on her eye lashes." That seemed vaguely 'fast' to him, but when she opened her eyes wide and raised her brows in a questioning sort of way, he felt himself drawn to her like metal to a magnet. They lay with the sun on their backs, burrowing their toes in the fine, warm sand, in a quiet harmony. Willy found her an interesting conversationalist, with a voice that had a musing quality, as though there was endless time for talk, and for soft laughter. Presently, she said, "What's your name?"

"Will."

"Not Will Shakespeare?"

" 'course not - just Will, for William. Mind you, if it was, I'd have put you in *A Midsummer Night's Dream*. You remind me of some sort of woodland sprite - or a water sprite. Umm, perhaps you'd be a mermaid!"

"How about my tail?"

"Well, your top half would make a lovely mermaid, and (turning on his elbow and looking back at the curve of her bottom) as far as I'm concerned, the other half's all right too."

The girl giggled. "I thought you were a bit stand-offish, or shy," she said, "but I'm glad you like me, and I'm called Winnie!"

"Not the Pooh!"

"Oh you beast! Everyone says that - now I'm not going to like you after all, and you can call me Marion."

Willy suddenly found that he had moved closer to her and had placed his arm around her shoulders. Her hands were folded under her face, and she feigned a sulk. Willy felt her soft, warm flesh, her dark hair hid what little of her face was exposed. He knew she was teasing him, and, unthinkingly, he stooped and kissed the nape of her neck.

"There, little Pooh, don't cry," he said. "Little girls should never cry on sunny Sunday mornings."

"Why not?" came her muffled voice.

"Because they should spend their time dancing on the sunbeams, and sparkling on everyone else, so that they will throw away their worries, and take a sunbeam each home to warm their day."

Marion sat up and looked down on Willy, who had rolled on to his back.

"You're a bit of a case, aren't you? Do you say things like that to all the girls?"

"No - only ever to one, till now, and I was only playing."

"You mean thing, I thought you meant it! And I was just starting to like you again!"

Willy laughed happily. He felt entirely at ease with this girl. He had no other intention than enjoying her company, and no warning words of conscience reminded him of Madge. "You're not married, are you?" she asked, puzzled by his reply.

"No-o-o! Do I look married?"

"You don't look old enough, but there's something about you that's not quite ordinary."

"I'm absolutely ordinary - that's why I think you're a very delightful Pooh!"

She pretended to be going to slap him, then looked down, very intently, into his face.

"You could grow on me, you know," she said, then bent and kissed him on his mouth. There was so little between her and her soft breasts that he could feel their warmth against his skin. She kissed him again and lay across him, her head on his shoulder. "I like you, Will, you're nice, and you can call me Pooh." After a moment, she said, "It's your turn to kiss me now."

That part of Willy that had its own life and being, and would not be controlled, was sending tremulous demands to Willy, the primeval male.

"Oh lor!" he wailed inwardly, "what the hell am I doing?"

Pooh placed her hand on his ribs, gently tickling the bare skin showing in the 'sun bathing panels'. Willy sat up, giving inward thanks again for the 'insert' and said, "How about having a dip? It'll be time for grub soon."

Pooh laughed, laying languorously on the sand. "You are shy, after all, aren't you?" Then she stood up too. "Come on, you two," she said to the others. "Will wants to have a dip, and cool off. Coming?"

Jerry and Sheba were otherwise engaged and had not noticed what had been going on between Willy and Pooh. Not getting a reply, they walked down to the water. "Do you swim?" she asked. "Not too well, but enough," he answered. "Well, be careful, if you go out far, there's a current."

"I'll not go far," he said.

They played the usual games, splashing each other, Pooh squealing in mock alarm. She had rolled her pajama legs up and remained in the shallows. Willy, showing off, plunged in and did his imitation of the American crawl for about ten strokes, then felt for the bottom and stood up in about three feet of water. He was only twenty yards out.

"It's lovely, you should have brought your bathers," he called.

Pooh answered something and continued paddling. Jerry and Sheba had come to life and Jerry called out something, but Willy didn't catch what, and shouted back, "Come on in, it's warm as anything!" He then sat back on the water, spread his arms and floated on his back. The water in the shallows was so warm and sparkling in the sun, it seemed idyllic, and he paddled with his hands to keep himself from drifting. The small wash from a passing motor boat splashed over his head and blocked his ears. He heard Pooh calling, but couldn't hear what, so 'back peddled' with his arms and put his legs down to stand. In a moment of panic, he knew that the bottom had fallen away and realised that he was over the dredged channel. He threw himself forward and struck out for the shore, but at the same moment, a giant hand seemed to take his legs and he was pulled under.

The tide was dropping and the estuary was emptying like a vast bathtub. There was only a moment of conscious thought left to him. He was swallowing water and going, going. "Oh God! I'm going to drown!" was all that his stunned mind could think.

There was confused noise about him. His ears did not seem to work and his body seemed to be banged and buffeted in some inexplicable way, but it all seemed far away and the only thing that mattered was to be able to breathe. His chest was wheezing and bubbling. There was a blackness about him that came and went, but gradually he heard voices and sucked in air that made him cough and splutter. Then he was flung about and seemed to be standing on his head while something pressed and thumped his back and stomach. The blackness cleared again and blue sky appeared. The sky was blotted out and a head with stick-out ears took its place. Jerry's voice came clearly, "You stupid bugger. Soon's you can stand, I'm going to kick your arse the length of the sands!" Then people continued to thump him and he was sick. Exhaustion overwhelmed him, he had to fight for every breath. His ears sang, his nose was blocked, he coughed and vomited, but through it all came the realisation that he was alive and safe. The last horrific moment was remembered, and the relief was enormous.

He lay on the warm sands for a long time, struggling back to life. The people around him departed and quietness came. Jerry shook his shoulder. "You're O.K. now - just stay where you are and try and cough up all the water you can. You'll be all right now - I'm going to see about some grub." He raised himself on an elbow and tried to speak, but there were bands around his chest and all he could do was wheeze and gasp. "O.K. now?" Jerry asked again. Willy nodded between coughs. Then Pooh came into sight. She had been standing behind him till then. "I'll look after him," she said, dropping to her knees beside him. After a moment, she said you've got all sand in your hair," and started to ruffle his head with her fingers. Willy, in his misery, found it very comforting. He still found it hard to breathe and lay face down, resting his forehead on his arms. The other girl came to them.

"Here, I've brought your flask and sandwiches. Is he all right?"

"Yes, he's all right now."

"Cor! He gave me a fright, I thought both of them were gonners!"

"Yes, and a fat lot of help you were, running away."

"I was scared, I didn't want to see them - you know!"

It was half an hour before Willy could breathe with any comfort. When he could, he rolled over and raised himself on his arms. He discovered that he was right at the other end of the sands, quite half a mile from the rocks where they had been sitting.

"Better now?" Pooh's voice came from behind him, then she moved into his view and knelt beside him. "I've saved you a hot drink - would you like it?" she asked, and taking his assent for granted, poured tea from her flask into the flask top. "Here, try and swallow it." Willy did so with relief, his throat felt raw with retching, but the drink soothed it. He still had to cough every few moments, but his lungs seemed fairly clear.

"What happened? I got into the tide race, I know, but who saved me?"

"Your friend did. He saw you floating away, and so did I. We both shouted, then your friend dashed in. He'd nearly got to you when you got pulled under. Fortunately, there was a motor boat just coming in and they turned and pulled you both out, but your friend had to dive down to find you, and he had the dickens of a job to come up again. If the men in the boat hadn't hooked your friend with a boathook, he'd never have done it."

"I could have drowned us both. I'm sorry, I must have spoilt your day."

"Go on, it could have happened to anyone, and I was glad to help."

"Where's Jerry gone, do you know?"

"He said he was going to get some dinner. There he is, he's going over to the rocks. Do you think you could walk there now?"

Pooh's concern was genuine, and Willy, looking into her face, was moved again by her big eyes, so soft and caring. He stood up and found himself unsteady, but Pooh put an arm around him, put his arm around her shoulder, and said, "Easy does it, take your time." He felt a complete fool, not only that, but he felt himself unmanned somehow, having to be helped to walk by this girl. He went to make some remark, but was overtaken by a spasm of coughing, then looking down at the nice little face turned up to him so solicitously, he felt nothing but gratitude for her kindness. "You're a dear," he wheezed. "I'm very grateful."

"That's better," she said. "You're coming alive again!"

Jerry came to meet them. He grinned at Willy. "All right for some, eh! You two seem to be doing all right!" Pooh smiled too, she was filled with a happy relief that Willy had recovered. His near drowning had been a shock, and the desperate resuscitation had been a trauma that she was still feeling. "Not so much lip," she said to Jerry. "Give him a hand, his legs aren't working properly yet."

"What! After all that lovely massage you gave them?" said Jerry, his own voice husky, and his breath still short.

"Oh! Shut up!" said Pooh. They regained the rocks and settled themselves. Sheba wound the gramophone and put a record on. "All by yourselves in the moonlight," she announced. "There ain't no sense, sitting on a fence, all by yourself in the moonlight," sang the singer, going on to enumerate the other things that there was no sense doing alone. Then as the line "Life's a farce, sitting on the grass" was sung, Jerry joined in with "Life's a farce, sitting on your arse, all by yourself in the moonlight."

Willy realised that Jerry was trying to chase away the fright, and bring back the light-hearted banter that the day had started with. He looked at Pooh, and they both laughed, with a tolerant sort of condescension, but Willy thought "But for him, I'd be dead and my body floating out in the channel somewhere. The realisation had only hit him then. He looked across at Jerry and said, "I'll never be able to thank you adequately. I'm ashamed of myself for being so stupid. You could have been drowned too."

"Ah! But I wasn't, was I? Nor you, were you! It's all in the medlar tree. We're both of us to be hanged, I expect!"

"What's the medlar tree?" asked Pooh. "Ask Will, he can tell it better than I can."

Willy told the story of the Avonford medlar tree, and the telling brought them all back to a more cheerful mood. The sun had swung around the sky, and the sands were beginning to be in shadow. Jerry said, "How about us going up to the camp, and brewing up?" Hey! Old Will hasn't had a thing since breakfast - and he didn't keep that down long! Come on, we've got tons of grub, and it'll be warmer up there." They quickly gathered their belongings and started up the lane.

"Come on She'," said Jerry. "Leave old Will to do his merry man stuff with the fair Marion! How about you helping me with a bit 'he same?"

As they went on ahead, they were soon merged together, but who was helping whom was open to question, though it seemed it needed Jerry's hand to assist Sheba's wiggling bottom, no doubt to the content of them both.

Willy still felt very weak and short of breath and was glad to reach camp. "Sit yourself down, old mate," said Jerry. I'll get a can of soup and we'll have some toast soon's I get the fire going."

"Sorry," said Willy, regaining some of his old composure. "I must retire to the bracken. Please all admire the view, or blow the fire up, or something!"

Pooh became toastmaster, as Jerry put it, and squatted by the fire toasting thick slices of bread impaled on a long stick. Jerry fed the fire with dry wood, banking it up between each batch of toast to produce charcoal for another lot. Willy was "excused duty" and sat on the short turf with his back against an outcrop of rock. He looked at Pooh, kneeling there, the day's sun and the heat of the fire had brought a flush to her face. "She's very sweet," Willy thought. "What was that Jerry said, about her massaging my legs? I'll ask her just what happened when I get her alone. Bet old Jerry won't tell me."

They had soup and buttered toast and fried eggs. Willy felt himself again, with some food inside him, and except for a husky voice, seemed none the worse. The meal over, Pooh announced that she must go.

"Oh why?" asked Willy.

"Duty calls," she said. "I promised my mum I'd be in by seven. I'm helping her with her visitors - she's got a guest house - while I'm on holiday."

"I was hoping to see more of you," Willy found himself saying. "It's such lovely weather and the moon's full, and Jerry could have run you home in his van (it's up at the farm), so you needn't have bothered with the ferry."

"No use, I'm afraid, I promised, and if I don't turn up, Mum'll worry!"

"I'll come to the ferry with you, anyway."

"Feel well enough?"

"Yes, I'm perfectly O.K."

The other girl had been having some words with Jerry, and simply said, "Cheerio Win, see you again, be good," so Willy surmised that she was remaining for a while.

The rough going, down to the lane, and from the lane to the sands, meant that Willy had to give a mannerly hand to Pooh on a score or more occasions, and he found himself disturbed by the touch of her, the warmth and the vitality that exuded from her supple little body. He almost groaned inwardly, saying "It's no good, I want her. I want to hold her and feel her all against me." It was a plaintive call from his natural desires, and he was shocked at its intensity. He had no intention of giving way to them, but he really suffered the temptation. They said little until they reached the deserted sands. The tide was rising fast, filling the estuary and chuckling and whispering as it did so. On the level sands, Pooh put her arm around Willy's waist and gave him a little hug. "What a day it's been!""she said.

"Yes, will you tell me what happened?"

"Not now, the boat's in, we'd better hurry. Come on, let's run."

"No, hold on, he'll wait. Look, I can't just say 'Cheerio' and let you go. You helped to save me, didn't you, and besides, I want to see you again." ("Go on," his inward self chided, "get yourself more and more involved! How about Madge?)"

Pooh looked at him with steady, appraising eyes. Her face was serious. "I don't know if you should," she said, "but I'm free about six o'clock tomorrow evening, so if you like to come down here about then - or, if you think better of it, don't, I'll understand. In the meantime (she put her arms around his neck and, standing on tiptoe, kissed him on the lips), don't go trying to drown yourself again."

"Come on, if you're coming!" called the ferryman, and before Willy could clutch her to him and return her kiss, she had slipped away and was being helped into the boat by the grinning boatman. "Some blokes have all the luck!" he called to Willy, as he pushed the boat into the tide.

Willy stood on the slipway watching the boat go, crab-like, across the channel, running against the current with the ferryman straining at oars, then drifting back with the tide on the opposite side. Pooh had looked towards him all the way across, but when she landed, she turned and waved. It was only a hundred yards across the channel and Willy could see her face clearly. He thought she looked unhappy, but she walked away and did not look back again.

He sat on the wooden seat under the ferry bell, and tried to take stock of himself. "Oh God!" he thought. "I feel just like I did when I first met Madge. Whatever am I going to do? What will happen tomorrow when she comes. I'm going to meet her, I must. I just can't not do so, no matter if I should or not - I want to! What about Madge? Have I forgotten her? Am I falling for Pooh? Is it just a girl I want, or am I in love with Pooh?"

He sat in thought for a long time, and deliberately concentrated his thoughts on Madge. The Madge that he had held close and caressed so many times; Madge who loved him and was waiting, week by week, for the time to come for them to be united, and then married for ever and ever. "If only she wasn't so far away," he lamented. "Oh Lord! I'm so lonely. He began to worry about his involvement with Pooh. Suddenly it seemed stupid to allow it to develop. "But I can't not meet her again, it wouldn't be fair on her. I'll take it easy, and I'll tell her about Madge, and we can be pals, like I am with Val. After all, I was smitten by Val at first, but it didn't last. We'll just have a jolly evening together!" He sighed with weariness, the jolly evening seemed a depressing anticlimax to all that his body yearned for, and he wished that he had never gone on that holiday.

A passing boat sent waves splashing up the slipway and he was surprised to see how quickly the water had spread. Everything was afloat again, and the great white steam yacht was a hive of activity as her crew prepared to take her to sea. People in evening dress were leaning on the rails, and the sound of talk and laughter reached him. Life such as theirs was almost beyond his comprehension. He did not envy them their wealth, but he thought, "They're happy - I wish I was too!"

He started back to camp. He still had not completely recovered from the morning's accident. He felt bruised and sore. His lungs still wheezed a bit and his throat was raw. Trudging across the fine sand, his legs felt leaden, and it seemed an immense effort to drag his feet from the clutching sand, like in a nightmare where quicksands prevent any progress in some dreadful dilemma. He sat down beside the spread-eagled roots of a tree, uprooted and carried downstream in some tempest long past. Exhaustion, mental and physical, pressed down on him and he slept.

It was quite dark when he woke. He was cold and damp with dew. An immense moon shone full-faced on the water. The yacht had gone and the lights of the town were few. He peered at his watch and found it was nearly eleven o'clock. After standing up and flexing his arms and legs, he decided that he felt better, and that he was hungry, and thought, ruefully, of the scant provisions that they had brought. The moon was so bright, that he could pick his way up the lane without difficulty, and when he reached the rough ground around the camp, each patch of bracken and every gorse thicket was picked out so brightly that there were faint moon shadows behind them. Just as he went to jump the stream before climbing the hillside, his eye was caught by a small spark of light in the herbage on the bank. He looked closer, then saw more. "Glow-worms." he said to himself. He had never seen glow-worms before and picked them up and held them on his palm. The luminous bodies shone like little lamps, and he spent a good while delighting in the novelty. Then he put them back in the greenery and went on to the camp. "I wonder if Jerry's seen them?" he thought.

On reaching the camp, he rummaged in the box that was their larder for something to eat. He found bread that seemed to have gone very stale, and jam. Wasps were bogged down in the jam pot, and he couldn't find a knife. He found his torch and was looking for the knife when Jerry appeared.

"Hello, still up? How'ya feeling?"

"I'm O.K. Just looking for something to eat."

"You'll be lucky! We should've brought more, but I wasn't reckoning on those birds coming to tea. Cor! I'm knackered, what a woman! I just took her home, it's nigh on forty miles there and back, just to get to the other side of the harbour. Still, I got me money's worth'. How d'yer get on with yours?"

"She had to be in by seven, but she's coming over again tomorrow evening."

"Good lad! Well, I'm turning in, must build up me strength again for tomorrow. Cheers!"

Willy sat munching the bread and jam. It was so quiet he could hear the silence ringing in his ears. Lines and rhymes chased each other in his mind. He saw rabbits chasing each other, stopping to nibble, and sitting on their hind legs, to look and listen. Moonlight made a strange sepia world, a secret, unreal world. His mind ran on, and the morning's events came back in horrid vividness. His narrow escape made his flesh creep. He shivered and scrambled into his sleeping bag. He had not kept his rendezvous with Madge, and his imagination saw her keeping hers, and he, drowned, and dead in the estuary. "Oh lor, I'm getting morbid," he rebuked himself, then began wondering how he was going to treat Pooh on the morrow. He worried away at his problems, till he fell asleep. He did not hear the anguished cry of a rabbit, caught by a stoat in the valley, nor the cry of a hunting owl. The silver peace of the moonlight took no account of the natural savagery of the wild. The spinning wheel of life never stopped, creatures large and small rode it unawares; when their time came, the riders dropped off, and the wheel spun on. Willy slept, exhausted by the effort of clinging to the wheel. Jerry slept the deep sleep of a body completely satisfied, snug and content.

The Bank Holiday Monday started as well as the day before. A cloudless day that called the sun up from the sea, to warm the hills at once, scoop up the mist from the valleys and set every ripple on the water a-sparkle.

Jerry was up first. He had a fire going and bacon in the pan before Willy crawled from his tent. He had crept into his sleeping bag the night before, dressed, apart from his shoes, and felt scruffy and dirty. He decided that there was a lot to be said for hot water to shave with.

"You take it easy today," Jerry told him. "I'll go into Kingsbridge and buy some food. You lay around and and pick up your strength - you had a near squeak yesterday, you know."

"Yes, I do realise that. I'm only here because you saved me."

"Oh nuts! I didn't mean that. I meant you need a little while to make up for lost time, sort of."

"All right, I know you don't want to make anything of it, but from now on, I'll owe everything that happens to me to you."

"Oh balls! Don't get thinking that! Anyway, it was the bloke in the boat with a handy boathook that was the real rescuer - and your girl.

She worked like a demon to get you breathing. Lucky she's a nurse and knew how."

"Is she? I didn't know."

"Well, come on, this is the last of the grub, and it's not much - I'll bring back more this morning. Give us a quid, and that'll be enough to see us through the week. We'll fill up with fish and chips when we're over in Salcombe."

When Jerry had gone, Willy heated water and shaved, then cleared up the breakfast plates and mugs. The sun was so hot he crawled into the shade of a stunted blackthorn, lay on his back and looked up at the cloudless sky through the filter of leaves. He started to think of the novel that he had begun to write. The more he wrote, the more the characters dominated the story. He had abandoned the whole concept once and started again with a new venue and a changed story, but the old characters reappeared and others seemed to emerge, unbidden, from the wings, and threatened to bog him down in endless ramifications. He drifted into a state of semi-sleep, where his thoughts became dreamlike with a sense of reality that needed instant recording, but when he was roused to remember them, they immediately lost their sharpness and were gone. Ordinarily, he would have made notes, or if he could do so, written up what had flitted through his mind, but today he felt lazy and let the inspirations die. The sky was a pale blue. Gulls were circling over the harbour on their food patrol. There was no birdsong. The nesting was over, and only a few birds could be seen. Somewhere rooks were calling, and nearer at hand a wren scolded amongst the gorse. It was a perfect morning to be lazy, thought Willy, and he relaxed and dozed.

It was all the little creatures of the turf that roused him. The teeming life of ants and spiders, woodlice and beetles that, finding him blocking their lawful progressions, must needs climb over him or wriggle under him. There were flies too, that would not take 'No' for an answer. He decided that he would replenish the water bucket and collect wood for the fire. He was wearing just his shorts and plimsolls and meandered down the hillside to the stream. He walked up it for a way, till he came to a little waterfall, where he could fill the bucket without disturbing the mud on the stream bed. Then he carried it back up the hill to the camp. The rest of the morning he spent collecting dead wood from under trees on the opposite hillside and making a pile of it beside the stream. He didn't hurry, it was cooler in the wood, and pleasant, but he began to wish that he were not alone. His thoughts had gone to Madge, and he longed for her, and fancied themselves together, there, in the summer magic. He found himself resenting her absence, blaming her, really, for his loneliness, but then rebuking himself for doing so. He was beginning to enjoy a bit of self-pity, but facing himself honestly, he told himself, "It's what old Jerry says, I'm sexually frustrated, that's what I am! There's Jerry, he must have had all he wanted last night, and he's going for more this evening! I don't know how he can do it, but he's completely amoral, I should think. He didn't used to be, before he left home, but I suppose it's natural, now he's older, and it must be in him - his mother and that!"

He pondered his emotions and, in the way he sized up all life's circumstances as he experienced them, he thought, "To be honest, I'd like to! Not I mean to make love, real love, like I would with Madge, that'd be heaven, but just to do it, to know what it's like, and not feel all het-up, all the time. Still (he mused on), I couldn't, not really, I'd hate myself if I did, and, anyway, I'd be scared that I'd be caught if the girl had a baby - never seems to worry Jerry though!"

He put an armful of branches down and, squatting, ran his finger along the grey-green lichen growing on a log. It was beautiful when looked at closely and colourful as a flower. It was only a desultory interest, he was thinking of Pooh, and his body stirred and his blood quickened. She would meet him tonight. What would they do? They'd have three hours at least, and if she would stay, and Jerry took her back in the van, they might be together till goodness knows how late. He recognised the excitement that he felt for what it was, and groaned, partly with a wicked glee, partly with dismay. "Gawd! I'll have to be careful," he told himself, but almost immediately that other self that lives in every man continued the anticipation as if he, Willy, had never uttered the caution. "Wonder what she'll wear? Will she feel like I do? Will she ... ?" In the distance, he heard the bark of Jerry's car horn as he entered the farmyard. "Bet that old dog's laying right in the way," he thought, and gathering up a pile of branches, he hurried up the hill to start a fire going. By the time Jerry arrived, his body was quiet again and his mind was at rest.

"Good old Will!" was Jerry's greeting, when he saw the fire. "I smelled the smoke and hoped you'd have got one on the go. I've got bacon and eggs and spuds enough to last the week, and bread and what not for a day or two, but I thought to meself, "Bugger the cooking, it'll be teatime before it's done, so I brought some fish and chips. They were right out of the pan, and I've wrapped them up well in me mac, so they ought to be warm still." Both boys were starving as soon as they smelled the chips, and ate ravenously. "As you might say," said Willy, licking his fingers as the last crumb was finished, "there's nothing like going back to nature, and eating simple food cooked in the open, with the tang of woodsmoke for seasoning - especially when there's a chip shop within reach!'

"What's your programme for tonight?" Jerry asked. "Well, I'm meeting her at the ferry about six."

"Ah! Pity! I'm driving round to Salcombe. Still if you cross over, I can bring you back some time after eleven, I should think."

"Yes, O.K. If I'm over there I'll wait by the road, if I'm not there, go on back by yourself."

"My bit's got some place we can go, better than last night. These tents weren't ever made for two, must have looked a laugh! Anyone would have thought there was a scrap going on inside!"

"Good Lord!" thought Willy. "They must have been in there; good job I didn't get back early." He looked at the tiny hike tent with some disgust, he couldn't easily accept Jerry's promiscuous pleasures, but at the same time felt some envy for his lack of conscience.

Jerry said that he intended to have a bit of shut-eye, have a clean up, and then drive into Kingsbridge and have a scrounge round, then get some sort of a meal before driving down to keep his appointment at Salcombe. "You do the same, old lad, then you can pick up your girl and carry on as you please."

It seemed a sensible idea to Willy, especially the meal at Kingsbridge.

They seemed to do nothing but stoke the fire and have fry-ups in camp. The commitment to meet Pooh sent little tremors through him, making him swallow hard. They did as Jerry suggested, and arrived at Salcombe fortified by hot pasties and strong tea. Jerry went his own way, leaving Willy at the ferry. After a while, Willy decided to move back amongst some boats beached on the hard, so that he could see if Pooh arrived, and not be conspicuous if she didn't. Almost as the church clock tolled six, he saw her. She came to the top of the slipway and stood looking across the harbour. Willy came up behind her and, childishly, touched her on the shoulder furthermost from him, so that when she turned, he was, for a moment, still behind her. When she saw him, she blushed.

"I thought you'd decided not to come."

"As if I would," he replied, grinning. "I was thinking you might have given me the miss!"

"It was touch and go. I've doubts if I should've come really."

Willy did not question the reasoning behind her doubts, and felt himself happy to be with her. He explained Jerry's offer of transport, saying, "So, if you'd like to stay on this side, or whatever you like, we're not tied to time."

"First, how do you feel today?"

"Oh! Fine! Never felt better."

"Right then, you decide what we do."

Willy looked at her. She was very appealing. The other Willy was whispering, "You're a lovely little darling, and that sweater shows them off to perfection." Willy tried hard to ignore his tempter, who had somehow suddenly projected a view of the camp and his little tent into his mind. "No!" he told himself, sternly. "She's too nice."

"Let's cross, and have a wander around, till the sun goes, then we could have a camp fire, and brew up some tea."

"All right, but I don't want to be too late, it's back to work tomorrow, and I've got to get into Kingsbridge to catch the eight o'clock bus."

They went down the hard to wait for the ferry, and Willy asked her where she worked. "Jerry told me you are a nurse."

"Yes, I did my two years probation here at the Cottage Hospital, now

I'm in my first year's training at the Prince of Wales. This is my first weekend off."

"I've been there," said Willy, "not as a patient, but to visit Jerry, he was there with a broken leg."

"Yes, well, it's a small world, I must have been on another ward. You and he are close friends, aren't you?"

"I suppose so, we've been pals since we were boys. He's a good sort really. We're not alike in some ways, but he's very good hearted - always do a good turn, if he could."

"Like yesterday."

"Yes, I wanted to ask you about that. I feel so ashamed, I could easily have cost him his life."

"Yes, you'd both have drowned, if that man in the boat hadn't hooked your friend by his bathers, but he wouldn't let you go."

There was a silence, as they sat on the ferry bench, in the mellow evening sun.

"I think he must be very fond of you indeed. D'you know, the man from the boat said you were gone, and we were wasting our time trying to revive you, and your friend said, "No we're bloody not, he's going to live, if we stay pumping all night." He called you awful names, but I think that was only shock, and when he was so tired, and I took over, he hunched himself up so I couldn't see, but I know he was crying - don't ever tell him I told you! It was part shock, part exhaustion, for he nearly drowned too, but when you did draw a breath and your pulse started up, he was absolutely choked." Pooh laughed, "He was so delighted, he said he was going to kick your behind for trying to get drowned!"

Willy sat a while in silence. "So I owe a lot to you too?"

"No you don't, I just helped out, anyone would've done."

She didn't say that the boat party had given up, and Willy was very conscious of her capable little self beside him.

"There's no words," he told her, "so I won't try."

The ferry arrived then, and they crossed over. The perfect summer day continued into the evening. The sun was low enough to warm, without burning. There was little wind, but a sort of rustle of life enlivened the shore, as if everything was preparing to open arms to greet the cool of the night. They sat against the uprooted tree, where Willy had slept the night before, and gradually Willy began to talk about his writing. Pooh was interested, and listened quietly as his voice went on and on. Once started, he was away. "Had she read this? Heard that? Seen the other thing? After about an hour, Pooh thought to herself, "He's very nice, but if this is all he's going to tall about, he's a dead bore." Also, she was suffering from so much hard sitting, and she badly needed to vanish for a moment or two.

"Will," she said, "we'd just as well get moving, I'm all stiff with sitting! Anyway, you go on, and I'll catch you up." With that she made her way into the scrub lining the sands.

Willy thought, "Good Lord! I've been yapping away for an hour or more. What the heck must she think!"

He walked on till he heard her following, then turned. The evening light was almost aquatic, where he stood in the lee of the wood. There was hardly a breath of wind, and all was quiet. He watched her coming, the shapely jumper, the round hips in a tweedy skirt, bare legs, bare feet scuffling the sand. She waved her hand, holding her shoes and her laughing face was ethereal in the dimpsey.

"You needn't have gone so far," she said, as she reached him. "I thought you'd gone and left me marooned, like on a desert island."

"Not likely, but it sounds all right, if I could be with you," he heard himself say.

"Oh good," thought Pooh, "he's off the literary bit."

She put her shoes on when they came to the lane. Willy encircled her with his long arm. "Seems more than just one day, since we came up here last night!" With that, he gave her a squeeze and moved his hand higher towards the round softness of her breast. He had no more than the tiniest feeling of her, before she had moved away.

"Sorry, I wasn't trying anything."

"Yes you were, and it's no go," she said.

"Idiot! Fool!" Willy belaboured himself. "You'll ruin the evening if you don't look out." He gallantly assisted the girl in a few rough places, and by the time they came to the stream, and he took her hand to jump her over, she made no attempt to let go when he retained her hand and drew her nearer to him. The sun had gone from the valley, but the sky was still alight. There was about an hour to dark and then half an hour before they must catch the ferry. Willy lit the fire. It was half an hour before it was hot enough to rake and for them to make toast, but it was a companionable time. She was a cheerful little soul, and chattered away lightheartedly. Willy was happy that she was near him, in the intimate little world of the camp, all hemmed in with bracken. Pooh had taken full cognisance of the privacy of the spot, and had considered Willy carefully, as he knelt, bottom up, blowing on the smouldering wood, and had set a poser for herself. She thought she knew the answer, but had doubts if she could make it, if the time came to do so. It was so quiet, and they were so alone and she admitted to herself that Willy was very attractive. "He's nice," she repeated to herself, and that meant that he was basically a gentleman, kind and sensitive, and she was safe with him, but all the same he'd have to watch him, and she wished she didn't have to. "He would be hitched up already," she grumbled to herself.

The toast was scorched and smoky, but with butter melting into it, it was delicious.

"Carbon is very good for you," Pooh assured Willy in her professional manner.

Afterwards, they sat by the embers, leaning against the boulder. Willy put his arm around her in a masterful way, pulled her close and said, "I'm happier than I've been for ages. I've been ever so lonely." She made no reply, but remained closely held. Willy looked down at her, and with a tortured mental "Oh dear!", slipped his other arm under her legs and scooped her across his lap. She looked up, and was about to protest, when he stopped her mouth with kisses. She remained taut for a moment, then relaxed into his arms. "There!" he said, "you told me yesterday, it was my turn to kiss you!"

"Oh Will! You shouldn't, you know you shouldn't." But when he bent to kiss her again, she put her arm around his neck to draw his head down. In the move to place her across Willy's knees, her skirt had ridden up, and her rounded knees and six inches of thigh were there for Willy to caress, and his hand felt the magic of her bare flesh. At that she roused herself a little, and holding back, she took Willy's hand and placed it in her lap.

"I'm no prude," she told him, "but I'm not a slut either! Kissing's one thing, but petting's private, you'd have to be very special."

"I'm sorry, Pooh dear," I never thought of you as - well, as you said, really I didn't. It was just, well, you're irresistible, and (he tilted her face up with his hand under her chin) you've get a darling little pussycat face, and it's made for kisses."

Pooh sighed, "I could love him," she thought, "and I could go all the way with him, but what's the use, I'll never see him again after tonight. It was a long and very gentle kiss that followed, then Pooh moved herself. "Come on," she said, "we'd better start back, he doesn't always bother to fetch one or two people if he's in the pub. I don't want you to come back with me, over to Salcombe, we'll say cheerio at the ferry."

It was quite dark down by the stream. They walked slowly, perilously, on the rough hillside, arms tightly holding. At the stream, Willy suddenly broke from her, and diving into the bushes, reappeared with four glow-worms on his hand. Some girls would have shied off, but Pooh said, "Oh! Glow-worms! I haven't seen any since I was a kid, we used to collect them in jamjars. There were lots n the other side then, but they seem to have died cut now."

Willy took them and placed them gently on the curve of her bosom. "They're beautiful," he said.

"What are?" Pooh replied with a giggle. "All six of them," said Willy.

They reached the slipway and rang the ferry bell. It was still light enough to see the boat tied up across the narrow channel, but there was no sign of the boatman. They sat on the bench, close together, to wait.

"I suppose I ought to say goodbye now, before he comes," said Willy, "but there's no reason why I shouldn't go over with you. I told you, Jerry'll pick me up, so there's no need to leave you here."

"Yes, there is, Will. You're a dear, and I could easily fall for you, but Jerry told me you've get a girl and will be getting married soon, so it's just as well to say thanks for a pleasant evening, and goodbye, because we won't be seeing each other again. I won't forget you, I could hardly do that, after yesterday, and I'll always remember you as a very nice bloke, and when I see your articles and when your novel's published, I'll think of a camp fire and hot buttered toast and a very dear boy saying I've got a pussycat face."

Willy hugged her. "I'll always remember you too, Pooh, if only because I'm still alive."

There was a long silence. There really was no more to say. Willy rang the bell again, loud and long, then again. A figure appeared on the quay opposite. " 'ello, over there! No more ferry tonight. 'E's done for the day." The voice carried clearly over the water.

"'Tisn't ten yet," Willy called back.

"Do'n matter, 'e aint coming," came the reply, and the figure vanished into the gloom.

"Oh heck! What'll we do now?" said Willy in alarm. "You'll have to wait for Jerry to come back, then I'll drive you all around, but it'll be two o'clock or more before you get home."

After Pooh's little speech of farewell, Willy suddenly found that another two or three hours marooned with Pooh, would be an embarrassment, and he was having a few niggles of conscience about Madge.

"I bet he's compelled to take passengers under his licence," he declared.

"Not old Snodger, not when he's got a few ciders in him," said Pooh, who knew her locals. They stood irresolute for a while, then, "Well, it's worth a try," said Pooh, and taking the hand rope on the tongue of the bell, she rang a prolonged peal. Nothing happened. "Damn," she said, "Well, I suppose we'll have to wait - if it hadn't been for those glow-worms, we might have made it."

"Oh lor," thought Willy, "now she's starting to complain."

Suddenly, Pooh pointed, "Look," she said, pointing down the estuary. Willy looked, then in the light already becoming silvered by the full moon, he saw a yacht, its sails like a great moth, coming up fast on the flowing tide.

Pooh sprang to the bell again and hammered out S.O.S. S.O.S. S.O.S. Willy recognised the morse, and was aghast at her action.

"Pooh! You'll have the lifeboat out or something!"

"Good," said Pooh.

The yacht was coming closer, and the sails were being taken down. S.O.S. went the bell. The yacht was near, and going fast in the tide.

"Ahoy," yelled Pooh, in a surprisingly nautical manner. "Doctor Winstone, can you send your tender? We're stuck."

The yacht swept by, no more than ten feet from them. A figure was by the rail. "Are you in trouble?" came a voice.

"It's Win Foster, Doctor. Old Snodger packed up early and we're stuck." Pooh called back.

"Hang on for half an hour," came the reply, and the boat was gone on the hissing tide. "That's all right then," Pooh announced.

Willy laughed, "Well, of all the cheek! I wouldn't have dreamed of doing that, you could've ended up in jail or something, ringing S.O.S. like that!"

"Oh! Get out! That's Dr. Winstone's *Sea Spray*. He won't mind sending for me when he's moored up."

Within the half hour, a little motor boat came battling against the tide. The boatman said, "You didden never ought to ha' done that Miss, you don' know what you might have started, ringing S.O.S., could ha' bin anythin' - matter o'life'n death."

"Oh well! Nobody seems to have taken any notice but you, and thanks a lot. Will, can you give Charlie five bob? He's a pal of my dad, fortunately."

With that they were gone, crab-wise across the tide. Willy forgot to say goodbye again till she was in mid-stream. He called then, but he wasn't sure if she heard or answered. There were peals of laughter coming across the water. Well! What an extraordinary girl, he thought, but he felt all alone again, and fed up with himself.

Next morning, Jerry asked how he had got on the previous night, and Willy told him how Pooh had eventually got home. Jerry listened in amazement.

"Cor!" he said. "What a girl, talk about initiative! Blimey! She might have called cut the lifeboat!"

"Yes, I told her, but she only said 'Good'. I suppose, if she had, she'd have known the crew and got away with it. Thing was, if I hadn't collected those glow-worms, we'd have probably caught the ferry."

"Glow-worms! Glow-worms! You went collecting glow-worms!" Jerry, who was sitting up in his sleeping bag, rolled on the grass with glee. "You took her picking glow-worms! Oh Will, Will! They can't make many like you!"

"I don't see anything funny in that."

"No, you wouldn't. It's just having a smashing crumpet like that all to yourself, all on your own, and you go catching glow-worms!" Jerry looked at Willy in fond amusement. "Never mind, old boy, I expect it was for the best!" He went off with the bucket to fetch water, saying "Glow-worms! Glow-worms!"

That day they spent at Plymouth. It was 'Navy Week' and they toured the docks at Devonport, went aboard ships that were open for inspection, and watched various displays. Jerry was far more interested than Willy. He found the ships, especially the majestic battleships, with their vast guns, had a compelling attraction. He said to Willy, "I reckon, if I was in the navy, I'd be damned proud of myself." In the evening they went to the theatre where there was a summer variety show. The day had been well filled and Willy had enjoyed getting close to the ships that were so common a sight, riding at anchor in the bay, at home.

Jerry had been sorely tempted to visit a house he knew in Stonehouse, but decided that, in Willy's company, he would postpone the visit.

Willy had included amongst the few things that he had taken to camp, plenty of writing paper, thinking that he might have time on his hands and an opportunity to write a little, so on the Wednesday, when Jerry departed to join a boat for a day's fishing, Willy was quite happy to remain in camp to write.

Jerry was so taken with the fishing that he booked for another trip, and finding Willy quite happy with his own company, he left him to it. In the evenings they drove to the nearest village with a pub, and spent their evening there. It was a quiet inn, with a small, local patronage, and the two boys found a corner where they could sit and sip their drinks in a haze of tobacco smoke. In some ways, they rediscovered each other, and had long discussions on various items of mutual interest. Willy, owing to his years at evening school, his reading, the tutorial guidance of Mr. Watts, his experience at work and at the *Echo*, and his literary efforts, had become an articulate speaker, with a considerable range of knowledge for his age, and he enjoyed discussions almost as much as he did writing. Jerry too, in spite of having left school at fourteen, the same as Willy, and not having had the academic advantages Willy had made for himself, was, nonetheless, well able to uphold his opinions in argument. Both had retained their Devon accent. Though Willy's speech was grammatically sound and Jerry's was not, neither had retained the uncouth mannerisms of speech common to their childhood. Willy was impressed by Jerry's business acumen, initiative and breadth of vision, and Jerry was continually throwing up his hands in despair of overcoming Willy's logic. When Willy got on to his literary interests, Jerry became bored, and when Jerry began delving into a murky store of jokes that he had acquired, or led the conversation into the realms of feminine pleasures, Willy listened half-heartedly, and gave no encouragement. It wasn't that he was shocked, it was just that such talk disturbed him and he tried to shut his mind to the easy indulgence of fantasy; not that he need have left it to fantasy - that was a fear that haunted him. He knew he had only to give Jerry the slightest encouragement, and they would have been in Jerry's van, with the excited driver haring off to somewhere where they could fulfil their needs, and, since Pooh, Willy had considerable doubts of being able to withstand temptation.

The week had seemed so long to Willy. The near tragedy that had started it seemed months away, and little Pooh, with her cherubic face and desirable body, was slipping into the past. He was suntanned after a week, near naked, in continuous sunshine, and felt another man to the pale beanpole of a week ago. He had got on well with his novel too. Once started, he spent hours absorbed in writing, and his plans to explore the woods and headland were forgotten. Jerry would come back from his day's doings, throw himself down and say, "Blimey Will! Not still writing!"

It had been their intention to return home on the Saturday, but early in the week, Jerry had said, "O.K., I suppose, if we go home on Sunday? I'm seeing She Saturday night."

"Oh dear!" thought Willy, at the time. "He's a wicked devil." But all the same, he knew he would love to have another evening with Pooh.

They went home on Sunday, Willy to the luxury of a bath and the vast comfort of a proper toilet. He decided that he would not tell his mother of the drowning episode, and allowed her to think that he had enjoyed an uneventful week. Gwen beamed with pleasure at his brown face, and declared that she thought he had put on weight. He had written to Madge while at camp, and had given her a humorous account of his efforts at cooking and of their visit to the navy, and so on, but had not told her that he had nearly drowned. He'd do so later, he decided. He did not mention Pooh, either. "Better not," common sense told him. "Anyway, there was no harm done, and she helped save me." He put Pooh out of his thoughts, just thinking, as he turned to other interests, "She did have a face like a pussycat; she was scrummy!"

Chapter 19

Jerry went back to work with the intention of fulfilling the first phase of his ambitions - to include in the second block of houses, one for himself, and in so doing, provide a home for his mother whom he had determined to rescue from her involvements in Well Street. He had a feeling that she might not be willing, but nevertheless, he proceeded with enthusiasm. He had taken a larger piece of land, a cul-de-sac on the estate plan, and had ear-marked the centre house of three, at the blind end of the road, that was shaped roughly like a horseshoe, as his own. He would have to build and sell the other fourteen houses before he could finish it, but he reckoned, at the careful rate at which he worked, it would not be more than two years before he would have his home. Effie, his mother, was to remain blissfully unaware of her impending rehabilitation until then!

He continued to live in his lodgings with a landlady who had become increasingly respectful of his business success. He had two rooms in the little terraced house, a bedroom and a sitting room. He had furnished them comfortably, and his landlady was delighted with her extra income at a time when poverty was the order of the day. It suited Jerry, and as she did not object to him having a 'bird' in for the evening sometimes, it suited everyone. He had got a wireless and when he had time he spent hours combing the air for sounds. The fascination of hearing voices and music coming in from the air kept him glued to the set for hours sometimes. Generally though, he remained a solitary soul, affable and friendly to everyone, and at ease in any company, but never committing himself to anyone, except Willy, whom he was always ready to meet on a close brotherly footing that had been greatly deepened by their holiday experience, though he gave no hint to Willy that it was so.

All August, the heatwave continued. Paignton, in its marshy saucer between the hills of Torquay and Brixham, panted in the heat. In spite of the depression of trade, the unemployment and the desperate poverty in some parts, there were many who could afford holidays, and the three towns around the bay enjoyed a few months of modest prosperity.

The regattas were in full swing. The famous yachts were stationed in the bay for weeks, and the locals followed the fortunes of their rowing clubs, swimming and diving competitions and athletics meetings. The fair dominated the interest of most. It arrived at the town whose regatta was first, in a long line of brightly painted wagons and caravans, drawn by massive steam engines, all twisted brass and shining paint. Their huge ribbed wheels tore up the tarred road surface that had gone all sticky in the heat. Every child was agog and most older people felt an uplift of spirit when the gay caravan appeared.

It had long been the only holiday that the humble folk had. In recent years the influx of shopkeepers from the Midlands and other foreign parts - people who had no regard for traditions and kept their shops open on regatta days - meant that much of the fair day spirit was fading, but it was still unthinkable that anyone should not go down to the fair, even if it was only to walk around, admire the roundabouts, listen to the steam organs blaring, and spend a copper on nougat or brandysnaps, before 'oohing and aahing' at the firework display at night.

Paignton's regatta was always in the middle of the month, so at the beginning of the month, the whole procession of fair wagons came into the bay, and on to its first site, just beyond Torquay at Babbacombe, then right around the bay to Brixham, after that around the bay again to Torquay, and afterwards to Paignton. From there it left the bay for towns further afield. It was three weeks of thunderous motion as the half mile or so of wagons moved to and fro. There was not enough traffic to cause much congestion, and no matter what the inconvenience, everyone smiled a welcome as the fair came to town. It was always a bright spot in a humdrum existence.

The office where Willy worked still observed the tradition of closing on the Wednesday afternoon in regatta week. This was an extra holiday given for the sole purpose of attending the festivities and everyone did just that. The boss was sailing his boat in one of the many classes. The senior clerk had every intention of giving his family the slip at some time of the day, and satisfying himself as to the genuineness, or not, of 'the beautiful She', who was depicted as a statuesque nude, but who turned out to be a rather worn-looking woman in a flesh coloured leotard, who pranced on a tiny stage for about five minutes before being wrapped again in a cloak of ostrich feathers by the showman. One of Paignton's few police constables was stationed outside the booth, just in case something happened that the beady-eyed voyeurs were hoping for. 'Tantalus' was the name of his duty.

Willy had decided to write an account of the fair, as one of a series of articles that he was submitting as a monthly contribution to a magazine, chronicling the town affairs through a year. He had developed a good humorous style, that made amusing reading,and had had several articles accepted.

Val, never backward at coming forward, had asked Willy if he would take her to the fair and fireworks. Willy, in his role of 'Big Brother', was glad to do so. She did not arouse him now, not much anyway, but he was proud to be in her company.

The day was so hot, Willy suggested meeting about five o'clock. Meanwhile he would attend the athletic sports to 'get the flavour' of them, then go to the harbour and watch the boats and their crews coming and going. He knew a couple of boys in the rowing club, so hoped to snoop around there, to get some 'behind the scenes' impressions.

A bag of chips from a chip cart substituted for his tea, then he met Val by the bandstand, and they entered the crush and bustle of the fair. Val wanted to do it all: the golden dragons; the cake walk, chair-O-planes; helter-skelter; hall of mirrors; flea circus; coconut shies; shooting gallery; fat lady - the lot. She seemed to have endless energy and found fresh enthusiasm as Willy flagged. They had been to see an 'African Chief' who licked red hot iron and walked on broken glass, and were considering patronising 'Anita - the Smallest Woman in the World', when Jerry came upon them. He wanted to go into the boxing booth, but was waiting until the barker had drummed up more customers. The fireworks were almost due, and the crowds were thinning out.

"Come on, Will, let's have a go at this," said Jerry. "It'll fill in time till the boxing starts, or the fireworks." He pointed to a "Test your Strength" contraption, and taking Willy's consent for granted, moved towards it. It was a beam of wood, about twenty feet high, measured out in feet and inches. The customer was required to hit a stump at the foot of it with a mallet. This caused a piece of metal to run up the beam. The height it attained showed the power of the stroke. If a really powerful bang was given, the metal rang a gong at the top of the beam. Willy observed this contraption with apprehension. He knew it well, for years he had seen tough navvies and fishermen ringing the gong, stroke after stroke, but had never tried it himself. Jerry took the mallet, heaved it, and swung. The metal tongue leapt about half-way up. He swung again, hit the stump well and truly, and the metal shot up to within a foot or so of the top.

"Go on, hit it!" said Val. "I thought you'd have knocked the top off!"

Jerry grinned. "No, I'm leaving that for Will to do," he said.

Willy's heart sank and near panic seized him. A group of men arrived and stayed to watch, offering facetious advice, and making Jerry's last try most conspicuous. The man in charge, seeing an audience gathering, and looking for trade, began his "This way, gents, try your strength! Show the girls what sort of a man you are!" Jerry grinned at his audience, removed his jacket which he handed to Willy to hold, spat on his hands, and swung the mallet back and over his shoulder to hit the stump plumb centre. "Dong" went the gong, and there was a ragged cheer from Val and the dozen or so men and girls grouped around.

"Right, Will, your go now," said Jerry, inclining the handle of the mallet towards Willy. Willy knew that he should say "Not likely!", but he had grasped the handle before he knew it. He was amazed at its weight and he knew that he would make an ass of himself, but he felt he had to accept the challenge.

"Go on!" said Val, making things even more difficult. "Let's see Mr. Atlas ring the gong."

Willy grasped the handle. He had to put one hand down by the head before he could raise it, then lifting with all his strength, he got the wretched thing waist high and landed a clumsy blow on the stump.

The metal tongue just peeped out of its socket and fell in again. There was ribald laughter from the audience, and Val clapped her hands. Jerry saw Willy's mortification, took the mallet and said to all and sundry, "Come on, two more tries paid for, who's going to take 'em? There was some half-hearted chaffing from the fellows, then they turned away and left Willy to his shame. Even Val looked confused.

"Don't worry, Will, old man. 'Tisn't strength that does it, it's knack. I've been swinging a sledge on the buildings for years, or I couldn't ha' done it. Anyway, I only just got one up there."

"Well," said Willy, cheering up, "it proves you can't have brain and brawn, anyway, I never pretended to be a Sampson."

There came the explosion of the first rocket - a "hurry-up" signal to the crowds to leave the fair - and the trio made their way to the sea wall to find a good place to watch. Jerry left them after a short while to return to the boxing booth. Willy and Val remained perched on the wall. She snuggled comfortably against him, joining in the swelling sound of "ooohh" as the spectacular fireworks burst overhead. Willy put a protective arm around her, thinking to himself, "It's all right. I'm nothing to her, so it doesn't matter." But it was very nice, all the same. He did give poor Madge a thought, wondering if she would be home again by regatta time next year.

When the last set piece had spluttered out, Willy looked at his watch. It was almost ten o'clock. He looked across the bay to where the little North Star twinkled in the cloudless sky. The Plough stood upon its handle above it. "Madge," he thought. "Madge, I'm not being a two-timer, there's nothing in it between Val and me. I'm thinking of you, thinking of me, and hoping that next year you'll be home again with me." It was a sort of prayer really, and he felt better for observing his tryst.

Val was all for having another tour of the fair. Now that the crowds were swarming back from the fireworks, the fun became fast and furious. Under the dark sky, the lights were brilliant and all the stalls and booths were vying with each other for custom. Rowdy young men chased shrieking girls, thumping them with small white balls on the ends of elastic. The roundabouts seemed to go faster, the swings higher, the steam engines, humming and throbbing as they generated electricity, whooped and whistled. The rifles cracked, the barkers barked, and playing an accompaniment to the whole cacophony was the blare and beat of the great steam organs. "Just once around," said Willy, "I'm spent out!"

He took her home. As she got out of the car, she turned and said, "Thanks, Will, see you in the morning." It was an unemotional parting that left Willy cold. He was having compulsive thoughts of another girl. As Val wiggled her nice little self up her garden path, it was someone else that Willy saw. It wasn't Madge, it was Pooh. Recollecting himself, he swore inwardly. "Damn it all, it isn't fair, Madge shouldn't have gone," he moaned.

Madge wrote faithfully every week, but she was in despair to find some news to tell him. Most of her letters were comments on his letters to her. Will wrote, saying, "Tell me anything, everything that you do, so that I can see you in my mind's eye, as you go about your day."

Madge wrote back, "Will dear, what can I tell you that I haven't told you already? I look after the children, get them up, wash and dress them, see to their meals, play with them, take them walks, bring them back again, more meals, more washing, then reading them stories and then to bed. After that, I see to myself, do my mending and so on. Sometimes I read a book, then I go to bed. The only breaks I have are your letters. I look for them every day. Sometimes there is a gap, and then I get two together. I do love them, Will! It's no use me trying, I can't write like you, so don't expect me to. Sometimes I feel so happy to know that you're waiting so patiently, other times I feel cross to know you have such an exciting life compared to me, and sometimes I cry because I'm so lonely and miss you so." Madge always finished with their coded endearments and Willy read into them all that he was missing. He also felt a bit smug to know that his letters were so superbly written that Madge was enthralled by their eloquence. He disregarded her repeated warnings that he was making her a person that she could never be, and that he would be disappointed in her when she returned. Willy, with his analytical mind, recognised this and he knew why he was doing it. If he didn't concentrate so closely on Madge, relive their courtship and fantasise about their future, he knew that the charms of such girls as Val and Pooh would tear his resolution asunder. Besides, he loved writing to Madge just for the joy of doing so. He was saying things to her, in his letters, that were the near fulfilment of desires, that had never been spoken by him, or written in any of his writings. He wrote of a secret world, but was sensible enough to know its illusions. He would finish off a passionate page with his code to her and then smile to himself, thinking, "Just as long as she still loves me, it'll be all right."

Chapter 20

November came. That superb summer gave way to an early winter. Wretchedly early for the poor unemployed, who shivered in their worn clothes as they walked the unhappy trail to Torquay twice a week, to the labour exchange to receive the dole, grudgingly given, and whittled down by the Means Test, till its very asking raised a miserable fury in honest men, presenting their crushed pride in return for a pittance.

Jerry often gave lifts to some of these when he had business in Torquay. He felt anger at the sight of that continuous straggle of men, like ants, moving to and from Torquay. He employed half a dozen on his building, and worked hard himself, for in spite of what people were calling "The Slump", there was a steady demand for homes, but these had to be provided at a price that left a meagre profit. Nonetheless, for a young man of twenty-three, he was prosperous. His houses sold at £600 to £1000. The building societies advanced ninety per cent and he found ready buyers. Some builders were selling bungalows for £395, and all that was required was a five pound deposit. All the rest, and the legal fees, were advanced. Jerry preferred to build houses that satisfied his own critical judgement, building three at a time and selling them before venturing more. He had won firm approval for his industry from the solicitor and from his original backer. This guarantor had been relinquished at the end of the first phase, and Jerry had looked forward, with satisfaction, to being financially untrammelled.

A chance meeting, however, with a freelance bricklayer, had sent him out to a village called Stoke Gabriel where enquiries of an aged smallholder, ruined by the prices slump, had eventually led the man to sell thirty acres of derelict farm land and apple orchards. Jerry bought it cheap. Telling Willy about it, he said, "I'll finish this lot by '34, then the next option for thirty by '39 or '40. I'll be all clear and well stacked by then, so I'll be able to open up this estate in the forties. I'll take me time, and by 1950 or so, I'll be done there and I'll be able to pick and choose.

Depends on how things go, but I reckon I'll have a crack at public works and that sort of thing, I'll probably have a big company by then, and I'll be able to put me feet up by the time I'm sixty."

"Good for you," Willy had said. "You'll do it too! I hope you won't be too high and mighty to remember me!"

"Not likely, Will. You're better off actually than I am now, cash in hand, and by that time you'll be in the money too!"

A few weeks later, on a Sunday, Jerry arrived at Willy's home. He was driving his van, a new one, that had been bought, of necessity, as a general purpose vehicle for his business.

"Will, got an hour to spare?" he enquired. "I want you for a tree planting ceremony. Coming?"

"Where? What's it all about?"

Jerry spread himself over Gwen's sofa. "Remember you saying I ought to get myself a medlar tree? Well, I've been down to Avoncombe, and my old dear down there let me have the one her husband grafted before he died. She's giving up, I only just caught her. Anyway, I dug it up and I've got it on my lorry and I'm going to plant it on the plot I'm going to build on for myself. How about coming and giving me a hand? Bit of exercise'll do you good."

"Well, I was going to do some writing."

"Oh! Bugger your writing, get out and breathe some fresh air. Anyone'd think you were married to that bloody typewriter! I bet you take it to bed with you!"

"Yes, but a lot depends on what I'm doing, and I've only got evenings and weekends."

"Oh rot! Do a bit more tonight, and come out now before it rains again."

"All right then. I'll come and watch you dance around it and weave a magic spell."

They drove out to the buildings. The plots were already pegged out, and Jerry pointed out the first three that he had started, then drove on over the muddy, pot-holed track that would eventually become a road. It was like an elongated horseshoe, and as Jerry explained, would have a narrow belt of trees in the centre. "There's going to be a hundred and fifty trees planted there. It's not my concern, that's on the estate plan, and it'll make this crescent a bit exclusive."

They bumped their way to the top of the horseshoe, and Jerry stopped. "This is it," he said, "the middle one of the top three. See, the back garden is a triangle, sort of, with the old field hedge at the bottom. I hope to keep that. The house will be here, and I visualise a lawn or something between the house and the hedge, and I'm going to plant the medlar in the middle of it. By the time the house is built - not for a couple of years maybe - it'll have established itself."

Jerry had brought tools with him, and after pacing off distances, cut out a square patch of turf, exposing the red earth beneath. He dug a large hole, then returned to the lorry to fetch the tree. It was about ten feet high with a smooth, silvery bark. The branches were, as Jerry had said, bent at angles. "There you are," he said, "it's made its main trunk, all new young wood. As it grows older the bark gets cracked in lines and squares, like a crocodile skin - at least, that's what the old tree was like."

First, Jerry put a heavy stake in the ground then, getting Willy to hold the tree against it, he arranged the roots and filled the hole in. "Think it'll grow?" asked Willy.

"Remains to be seen. Should do, I got quite a bit of root with it. It's hawthorn, the old dear said. The graft was here, see? It's a hell of a job to kill hawthorn, so I reckon it'll take all right."

Willy was amused and intrigued by Jerry's interest. "You don't really believe you can read your fortune in it, do you?" he asked, not for the first time.

"No, not really, but somehow, the way the old lady told it, it seemed to have some sort of power. I know it's superstition, but I just feel I'd like to have it - it's a sort of good luck thing really."

"Supposing it tells you bad luck?"

"If it does, I'll cut it down, like the old lady did."

When the tree was tied to the stake, and the turf replaced, Jerry stood leaning on the spade and surveying it. "Tell you what," he said, "I'll trim off all the branches, so's the new growth'll be mine."

Willy looked at him and was about to make some remark, when he saw how serious Jerry's face had become, and he thought, "Poor old

Jerry, he's got nobody really. This has got under his skin somehow. I mustn't ridicule him." Aloud, he said, "Well, if that's well and truly planted, I vote we go home, my feet are frozen. How about coming in? Mum's got a cake, I know."

"No, can't, Will. I've got to meet some chaps at the Crown and I've got to clean first." He took Willy home, and went his way.

After Sunday tea with his mother, Willy went to his room, and Gwen soon heard the rattle of his typewriter. "Always writin', writin'," she thought. "Where on earth does he find enough words?" Gwen was beginning to realise the value of what went on in that room upstairs. She had ceased to be astonished at Willy's affluence and was beginning to become accustomed to the ease and comfort it accorded her. Willy paid for his board and lodging as if he were a lodger. That was his idea. He paid her two pounds a week, the same as Jerry paid his landlady. At first she had protested that it was too much, saying that a pound was ample, but Willy had insisted, and now she was finding that, for the first time in her life, she had a little money left over each week and was able to spend a bit on clothes and personal luxuries. Willy was generous with presents too, giving her a little extra when he had received a cheque.

There was a day, her last birthday, when she had opened Willy's present, to find he had given her a pretty little brooch. If she had received it only a year previously, she would have been delighted and flattered by his gift, but this year she felt a little touch of disappointment, because it was such a small offering after the other occasional ones she had received. She showed no sign though, kissing Willy and thanking him and saying she'd wear it with her new blouse. Then the postman came with Willy's card. He always sent one by post. Gwen opened the envelope and looking at the picture of a country cottage, with an archway of roses spelling "Happy Birthday", said, "Oh! That's pretty dear!" Then she opened the card, and as she did so a crisp, white five pound note opened itself too. Willy had pinned it so that it would open with the card. Gwen was literally speechless for a moment, then she turned to Willy, who was grinning delightedly at her surprise.

"Oh Willy! You shouldn't have, it's too much, really it is!"

"Oh, go on, it's not at all. I can well afford it. I'm really doing well now."

Gwen unpinned the note and fingered it, almost in wonder.

"Do you know, boy, it's the first time I've ever held one."

"Well, it won't be the last, I hope, and you be sure and spend it. Don't go putting it in the post office for a rainy day, buy yourself some nice clothes or something. I'll be your umbrella if ever it rains.

"Oh, you are a good son, Willy, you'm more than good to me. I wonder what your dad would have thought of you now. You're like him, you know, he had wonderful ideas in his head, a real daydreamer. I think he'd be proud of you, a posh young gentleman, with steady work, and your writing, and a car and all, and with money in your pocket. He'd be surprised to see you now, I'm sure. He'd just smile slow, like he did when he was thinking, and say 'Fancy that now, my boy a writer'."

She was near to tears and embarrassed at having made such a long speech, and talking of Dave too. Willy gave her a hug. "Well, have a happy birthday, Mum. I say! I'll buy a cake and bring it home, and I'll bring Val, and we'll have a birthday party."

"Oh no, I've not got anything ready."

"You don't need to, I'll bring it all, six o'clock. You have the kettle on, we'll do the rest."

"Willy, this Val, what's she to you?" asked Gwen anxiously. "You're not finishing with Madge, are you?"

"No, 'course not. Val's only a friend. You'll like her."

Gwen worried away, all the day, at the prospect of the birthday tea. She had heard about Val, often enough, but had not doubted Willy's word when he said she was just a girl in the office. She had seen Madge's letters arrive each week, and often wondered if the romance would survive, but had never had reason to think that Willy had begun to cast his eyes elsewhere. So many things had happened, in so short a time, and their circumstances had altered so much, that she had been driven to declare, many a time, "Well, I don't know I'm sure, perhaps it's all for the best!"

She needn't have worried. They arrived with a whirl of good wishes and a kiss from Val, who thrust a bunch of flowers into her hands, then set about unpacking a basket containing a fruit cake and some small sweet confections that her mother had made that afternoon. Gwen was a bit overwhelmed, but her protests were cut short by Val, who said, "Good Lord! You needn't worry. My Mum thinks the world of old Will, she'd do anything for him!"

"Oh dear," thought Gwen, "I suppose she's hoping he'll have her girl."

As if she had read Gwen's thoughts, Val continued, "And don't think she's after your precious son for me, she isn't, normal. It's just that Will did us all a good turn, and mum's grateful." Another puzzle for Gwen to think about. Really, she sometimes wondered if she knew anything at all about her son.

The tea was a great success, due entirely to Val, who bubbled away happily, covering Willy's natural silences, but giving Gwen chance enough to talk. She enjoyed it. She seldom had anyone to talk to, and even less often, someone to talk to her. Meals usually passed in silence. Willy often read as he ate, and either did not hear any remark she might make, or greeted it with a grunt of acceptance or a monosyllabic reply that killed the conversation stone dead. She seldom tried to talk to him, he always seemed miles away. In any case, she didn't see him much now. She still packed a lunch for him, or left something for him to warm up for himself. Most days he dashed in of an evening, wolfed whatever was going, then went out on some reporting job, or shut himself away upstairs for the evening with the typewriter that stuttered on long after she had gone to bed. She couldn't help wondering what this pretty girl thought of Willy. She contrasted her to Madge, thinking of that sturdy, four-square figure, with the round, dimpled face and loving eyes, that had become such a hope for her, and this radiant little girl, slim, vivacious, charming, frightening almost, in her sparkling personality. She was beyond Gwen's experience and she was glad that Willy had met Madge first.

"This one'd lead him a dance," was her private opinion. Still, as no danger to Willy seemed indicated, she enjoyed her company. When it came to cutting the cake, Val started up, "Happy Birthday to You," and beckoned Willy to join in, which he did with a cracked tenor voice, that sent Val into fits, and had her declaring that she wished she'd never asked him to sing. Val insisted on helping with the washing-up, while Willy was engaged on something upstairs. She did the drying, poor Gwen rushing around in a tizzy to hide her worn and holey dish cloth and getting her best one out before the girl could see it. Val chattered away about this and that, and when she said something that invited the question, Gwen asked, "Haven't you got a young man? I'd have thought a pretty girl like you would have had plenty chances."

Val was serious for once. "Hasn't Willy told you anything about us, my dad and mum, I mean, and me, of course?"

"Why no, he's mentioned you at work, and he said you'd been dancing with him, but that's all."

Val looked relieved. "Well, it's a long story, but it's come right now, and I have got a boy, only he's not a steady, but I think he might be; only he's rather well to do, and important. He seems to like me, and takes me out sometimes. Dad approves of him, and (wistfully) I think of him a lot and I think I could fall in love with him if he'd let me!"

"Well!" said Gwen, at a loss for words. "Well! I expect he will."

Val smiled, again her radiant self. "Will helped there as well, so that's why I love him too!"

Gwen looked shocked, and Val laughed. "I don't mean like that. I always think of Will as a kind of uncle, he's so serious and profound. In fact, to be honest, most of the time he's a dead bore, but he's very kind!"

"Well!" thought Gwen, lost for words again. "Willy, her little boy, an uncle to this chit, well!"

"I sometimes wonder," continued Val, "what his girl in Malta will make of him, but I suppose she knows what she's doing. Anyway, he's faithful, I know that."

"Madge is a good girl. They'll be happy, I'm sure," said Gwen, bridling a little at Val's criticism of Willy.

"Oh! Please don't think I'm saying anything against Will, he's been wonderful to us, he really has, only he's not my type, that's all, but I love him all the same - my 'Uncle Will'." She laughed as she said that, and Gwen found herself laughing too; she suddenly saw the funny side of this little minx looking on Willy as an uncle.

After that birthday tea, Gwen worried no more about Willy's possible involvement with Val. In fact, she felt warm and proud towards him because of his obvious status among his friends, and no underhand 'goings on', with the dreaded consequence of some wretched girl's seduction. It never occurred to Gwen that Willy might be the seducer. She was well aware that among the men of her times, marriage was seldom entered into, unless demanded by urgent necessity. She excluded her dead Dave from this category, remembering his protection of her own innocence, but it had not been possible to live in the turmoil of a changing world without seeing something of the broader, and less lovely, values around her. Many was the night, when Willy was out late, that she had lain sleepless, wondering what he was doing, and where. Now she was content to think that he was mature and wise, and a gentleman. She sighed with pleasure at the thought. It was just as well that she could have no knowledge of her son, deep in the bracken, with young Pooh across his lap, her willing mouth pressed to his, while her hands were busy restraining his! On the whole though, her trust was not misplaced.

Chapter 21

When Willy reached his twenty-first birthday, it was more than just an occasion for a party. He did, in fact, have a very enjoyable celebration held at Deller's, and attended by his mother, of course, and to her astonished pride, by many people whom she had never met before, including a surprising number of young people; Jerry, Val and her parents, old Mr Watts, Willy's editor at the *Echo* and others. There was a buffet and dancing. Gwen had a new outfit and she received the guests at first with some confusion but soon some of Willy's sang-froid rubbed of on her, and she began to enjoy her importance   There were photographs and gifts, and a rather naughty speech by Jerry, the meaning of which mostly passed over her head, and then Willy replied, with an ease and simplicity that made her realise just how far he had leaped from their humble beginnings. She was bursting with pride and finally wept with emotion when Willy, having said his 'thank yous', continued with "And of course, there is someone else, who unfortunately cannot be here, but whom I wish you all to include in your good wishes to me, for she soon will be here, and then I trust will remain with me till death us do part! Few of you have ever met my fiancee, though I'm sure I often bored you with my eulogies of her, so I would like to include her now in all your congratulations." So saying, he turned to the table that held the cake, and an array of gifts, and unwrapped a framed photograph of Madge, an enlargement of the one she had given to him before she went away, and placed it next to the cake.

"Oh, he is a good boy!" Gwen thought, dabbing her eye and sniffing loudly, just as if she was at home.

After his coming of age, Willy took steps to establish himself more professionally than he had been able to do before. He immediately withdrew his savings from the post office savings bank, and opened an account with Lloyds. He kept his financial status a secret, to be shared only with Madge. She was astonished when he told her that he had put fifty pounds into Lloyds and nearly two hundred into the Halifax. It was a measure of his success as a writer, and of his thrift. He lived on his wages as a clerk, and everything else, except for occasional items, went into savings. He was well satisfied with what he had achieved in less than two years and knew himself to be poised, ready to become self sufficient as a writer.

His novel was going well, though slowly. He was now a regular contributor to four national magazines, he still did local reporting for the *Echo*, and was beginning to make fairly regular contributions to the *Western Morning News*, which paid much better than the *Echo*. He was sending articles to *Punch*, but, so far; without having them accepted, and was compiling an anthology of his own poems that he hoped, one day, to have published. He was beginning to feel that he soon would not have time to do a regular job, but knew that,for the time being, he dared not leave it. The spectre of unemployment, with its hunger and distress, haunted everyone's life, and remained at the back of his mind, in even his most optimistic moments.

Willy's letters to Madge became more insistent as the months passed. "Have you heard yet when you are coming home?" was the constant query, with "Why don't you ask?" and "Tell them you must know," voicing his exasperation at Madge's s repeated, "I don't know," and "They haven't decided yet."

When the two years had at last elapsed, Willy demanded a firm date: "You can't be expected to go on and on, without any idea of when you are leaving," he told her.

"But I am expected to," she replied. "That's what I agreed to. I said I would stay with them for about two years, but I can't just come home, there isn't a bus I can get on!" she told him, with a touch of exasperation at his constant chiding. Their letters were not all like that though. Willy was making plans for when she returned, and told her all about Jerry's building, suggesting that now he was of age, and able to raise a mortgage, he would arrange with Jerry for one of the houses next to the plot Jerry had reserved for himself. "It will be all new, and we can watch the trees, they're going to plant, grow into a little wood; by the time our kids are big enough they'll be able to play cowboys and indians there."

Madge loved the 'our kids' and told him so. "I didn't think you would remember my football team," she said once, when replying to some rather imaginative love making in one of his letters. "That's going a bit strong, but oh!, I am so longing to have my own babies. I'm afraid I'll miss my little ones here till I have my own. I do love them so, and they love me; they love me more than their mother, I know they do, and I dread leaving them for their sakes, they'll miss me so'." That was something Willy hadn't thought of. "Crumbs!" he thought, "I hope she's not going to be too soft-hearted to leave them."

Then came a letter. "The master's going to Palestine. Missus is in a rare old tizzy, she doesn't know if she's going or not, but she wants to. She says she's had all she wants of Malta, but there's trouble in Palestine between the Arabs and Jews, and she doesn't know what will be decided. I'll let you know as soon as I know anything definite."

That was all that Willy could get out of her. He posted his letters two or three times a week, instead of saving them, and posting once a week, but all his protestations were met with "Don't know yet." Willy wondered sometimes if she really wanted to come home, and told her so. Her assurances that she was longing to do so, did less to reassure him, than a little bit in one letter that said, "I took the kids out this morning, before it got too hot, and was going along the road by the sea. I'd got the baby in the pram, one on the foot of the pram and the others on each side. We came to a navy lorry, parked by the road, it was full of sailors, and they all wolf whistled me. 'course I didn't take any notice, but one of them called out, 'All those yours darling? 'Who's been a busy girl then!' It was just cheek, but the sailor had a Bristol accent, and it took me right home in a flash, I couldn't help it, I cried, and the poor kids, bless 'em, crowded up to me and put their arms around me to comfort me."

Willy brooded over the scene, trying to imagine the white, dusty road, the pram and the children, and the saucy sailors. Madge had told him, so often, how lonely she was, and he could imagine how that homely voice had spoken to her spirit.

The year wore on, summer came and autumn was fading into winter, when at last the letter came. "We're coming home, Madge said, "they've decided to take the children to the missus' home in Yorkshire and put the older ones in school, then if she can arrange something with her family, she'll leave the kids in England and go on to Palestine with the Colonel. She asked me if I would stay and look after the little ones. I was ever so upset really, it'll break their hearts if I leave them, and I'll miss them so, but I said that I was going to get married when I got home. It was ever so nice to be able to say that. I think she was surprised. She said, 'Will the man you propose to marry, be able to support you?' I think she thought I might stop on, even if I was married, but I said, 'Oh yes, ma'am, he's an author and quite well to do.' (Madge did not say so, but Willy read into those words the rebuff that Madge enjoyed giving to the unthinking patronage of her mistress). "She said, 'Oh really. Well, in that case we must make some arrangements to employ another nanny!'

"It's going to be pretty awful for them, Will, for over three years now, I've been everything to them. They run to me whatever happens. They only see her once or twice a day, and they hardly ever see their dad. They won't understand, Will, and I'll miss them so much. If I didn't have you to come home to, I don't think I could leave them."

It was late November when Madge came back to England. She travelled up to Yorkshire with the family, and stayed until they found another nurse. On her day off, she spoke to Willy on the telephone. They both found it difficult to maintain a conversation. After the first few loving exchanges, there were long silences, each knowing the other was struggling to voice their emotions, but bereft of the means by the cold wire running across country joining them, and killing sensation. Willy found it hard to say the things that he wrote so fluently, and Madge, tearful at the sound of his voice, was dumb.

Afterwards Willy wrote, "If I'd have had you in my arms, I would have said much more, and between the words, there would have been your soft breath on my cheek, the warmth of you to give me solace."

She was in Yorkshire for another two weeks, then she went home to her parents in Bristol. Willy was invited up, and he went on the Saturday afternoon. He was in a strange turmoil of emotions, and in the train, pondered much on how Madge would find him. He had changed a lot, he knew. He'd grown up, and he looked on life differently. He reckoned he was as well read and articulate as any college boy, and his writing he knew, from its financial reward, was good and would get better. When he'd last seen Madge he was a gangling youth, blindly innocent of the world and besotted by his love for her. She had been far more mature than he, but sweetly innocent of guile, loving and trusting. He knew she had been lonely, a young girl away from home for the first time. They had found comfort in each other then. Would she find him still so appealing, and (he must be honest) would she be the goddess he had worshipped all their time apart.

Madge's mother was the best of mums. She made sure that her husband and sons would go to the football (they were playing at home, fortunately) and she told her daughters firmly, "You're coming shopping with me, my ladies, she'll not want us at home when her boy arrives. After all this time, they will need time to themselves, so as to be able to say what they've got to, in private."

Madge waited behind the curtains watching the road for Willy. She was all of a tremble with worry, asking herself a score of times, how did she look? Would he find her the girl he remembered, and be happy, or would he expect her to be the marvellous person he had built her up to be in his imagination? And that conundrum being insoluble, there followed another. How would he look and behave? Would she find him a stranger - different? Or would he be the same dear Will, loving and kind, and wanting nothing more than her love?

The road stretched fifty yards or so to the corner. Not many people were out. Those who had no need to be, were indoors by their firesides, the others were already gone to the football, cinema or shopping, and except for three small boys playing and squabbling over a single roller skate, the road was quiet. Twice, men came hurrying around the corner, buttoned up against the wind and bowed to meet it. Each time a little shock made her catch her breath for a moment, then relax again, as she realised that the figure she saw could not be Willy. The train should have arrived nearly an hour before, and the bus should have dropped Willy a couple of roads away, within half an hour, that was, if he had caught the right bus and got off at the right place, and if the train was on time. There were so many things that could delay him. Perhaps he'd come by taxi. Madge went to the mirror for the hundredth time and fiddled about with her hair, telling herself for the hundredth time that her brown skin, tanned by the Maltese sun, was a poor exchange for the apple blossom that Willy liked to write about.

She returned to the window and there he was, bowed to the bitter wind, but unmistakable by his walk. "Gosh," she thought, near panic seizing her. "He looks like a. bank clerk." (All bank clerks wore plus-fours to work on Saturday mornings as an indication that they were going for a round of golf as soon as the bank closed at midday. It was a concession, hardly won, from the banks, that informal dress might be worn on Saturday mornings, and thereafter it became as much a uniform as the black coats and pinstripe trousers worn, perforce, all the week. Willy, after much cogitation and advice from his mother, had decided to wear his plus-four suit, of Harris tweed. It had cost him all of eight guineas, and had taken forty weeks to pay for at Burtons.

"Oh Lor'." said Madge, "here goes'." She waited in the passage behind the front door. She saw his profile appear against the glass, and opened the door just as he reached for the knocker. They stood for a moment looking at each other, then Madge's dimple quivered as she tried to keep back her tears. Willy stepped through the doorway, and she was in his arms They went into the little sitting room and seated themselves on the sofa by the fire. When Madge had overcome her tears, and Willy too had managed to choke back what seemed to him to be unmanly emotion, he held her away from him and said, "Let's look at you." He looked long and hard, till Madge grew uncomfortable under his scrutiny.

"Will I do?" she said at last.

"Will you do? Oh Madge, I'm, sorry, I didn't mean to stare like that, I was going over you in my mind, telling myself that it was really you, just as I remembered you, only prettier than ever."

There were more important and satisfying things to do after that, than talk, if soft whisperings and little crooning sounds don't count as such. After a time, their hopes were talked about and the plans in letters made over so many months, suddenly became realisable.

"Tonight, Willy said, "I'm going to ask your dad and mum if I can marry you. I'm going to wed you anyway, but I'd like to do it properly, and to make the engagement formal. So saying he reached into his pocket and produced a little box. "Madge dear," he said, "will you wear this for me, and marry me just as soon as ever we can?"

The joy and relief of the moment was altogether too much for Madge, she wept floods of tears that had to be kissed and comforted away. Willy was taken aback by so much emotion, but he felt rather elated to think that he could command so much response to his loving. He began to think he must be quite remarkable. Before Madge had gone abroad, his love had always been humble, and a sense of unreality had made it seem hardly possible that Madge could have found him worthy of her. Now he suddenly discovered that he had a patronising feeling towards her acceptance of him, that didn't last long; he loved her too much, but the fact that it was he that was offering all, and Madge was happily accepting, took some getting used to.

The family returned with the early dusk. They had not noticed how the light had faded and Madge switched on the light when she heard the first arrivals at the door. In the sudden light, they hugged and laughed. "Whatever does my hair look like," said Madge, not caring much anyway, and then, "Oh gosh! You've got lipstick on your collar'."

"Who cares?" said Willy. "Good job I'm not wearing the stuff, or you wouldn't be fit to be seen."

They let the family assemble in the back room. Madge's mother had organised the occasion and Madge had been well briefed. They made up the fire, and sat themselves decorously on the sofa, and began to take stock of each other.

"You're slimmer," said Willy.

"Yes, thank goodness, I lost over a stone while I was away."

"It suits you, but don't go losing any more, there are certain areas, such as here, and these, that I don't want any smaller!."

"It'll be all yours very soon now," said Madge contentedly. After a short, wordless, but well occupied, interlude, Madge said to Willy. "You're ever so much more grown up, Will, and you look so important'.

Do you know, I didn't recognise you at first, I thought you were a bank clerk at least."

Willy laughed. "They're not very important, I'm better off than most of them, soon I'll only be dealing with bank managers and they'll be careful to make me welcome."

Madge looked at Willy, and wondered. So much arrogance. Where had he found it in the time she was away. "You're different Will, when I think of you, at that first dance, and sitting on that shop window, waiting, just to see me after Sunday school; it's hard to believe you're the same boy."

"You're not having doubts, are you? I am the same and love you just as much. Just a decent suit and some money in my pocket, doesn't mean I have changed."

"No, of course not," said Madge, but inwardly she asked herself, "Is he still the boy I knew?"

Any feeling of uncertainty was postponed then, by a discreet rattle of the door handle that was an obvious cue for them to be ready for the door to open, then Madge's mum was welcoming Willy, and all the family seemed to fill the house with greetings and emotions that accompanied them into the back room where a special tea had been prepared. Not a lot, apart from commonplace chatter was said during the meal. Mrs Hadden was delighted at Willy's appreciation of her cooking, and his appetite was a subject to marvel at when he had departed. Willy felt again the pleasure and excitement of being involved in a family. There was such a difference to his silent meals, taken at home, either with his mother, or alone. When the meal was done, Willy made quite a little speech thanking Madge's parents for their welcome, and then said, "Madge has something to show you all, and I hope that there will be no objection to her wearing it ."

Madge flushed and a little confused, by the unexpected manner of Willy's announcement, took the engagement ring from her pocket, opened the little box and passed it to her mother. There where the expected exclamations, and Willy said, "And I hope you will, both of you, let me marry Madge as soon as possible."

Without waiting for a reply, Willy put the ring on Madge's finger, then kissed it, and kissed her on her lips Madge's brothers hurriedly left the room and ran into the back garden, where they howled with glee. Her sisters had got the giggles, and her mother was quite overcome, telling Madge later, "Oh, I thought it was sweet of him, it was like Prince Charming in a story book."

Mr Hadden, having said nothing so far, then said, "Yes, well look here young man, it's one thing to get engaged, but another to marry. I mean, can you really look after her, and make her happy? What are your prospects?"

"Oh, I assure you, I can look after her all right. I'm doing well; for the year up to the end of last month I've earned three hundred and forty-two pounds, that' s better than six pounds a week, and I'll do more next year."

"Yes, but how secure is your job, after all, nowadays, men find themselves on the dole when they thought they were secure for life. They've sacked over two hundred from my place during the past twelve months and I can't bank on my job lasting, as I always did."

"My job isn't much, but it's safe enough, I made my money freelancing, and that's paying me better all the time."

"You're very young though."

"I' m over twenty-one."

"Yes well, twenty-one may seem old enough for you, but we're in difficult times, and you've no experience of hardship to fall back on. If you marry and then things go wrong, what can you do?"

"They won't go wrong for me, I'm sire of that. Now that Madge is home again, after all the time we've waited, I'd like to marry straight away, just as soon as possible."

"Now, now, hold on son, I'm not in favour of rushing things like that. I'm quite happy for you to have my girl, you've waited for her, as you've said, and you've done well financially, but first things first, get your home together, have a place of your own to take her to, and still have enough to live decently, then you'll have my blessing."

Mr Hadden's comments came as quite a shock to Willy. He had had little experience of parents, except his own mother, who had long since ceased to influence his behaviour, and Val's father, who he thought was an interesting nut case; so to have Madge's father suddenly laying down the law to him, was a hurt to his pride, in fact, he felt it was almost an unreasonable interference. His face made his resentment obvious, and there was a momentary silence, with both Willy and Madge flushed, Willy angrily, Madge with embarrassment, while Mrs Hadden looked anxiously towards Madge, then her husband.

He was a kindly, sensible man, who, seeing the youngsters' consternation, stepped forward, reached a hand up to Willy's shoulder and putting his other arm around Madge.

"Now let's talk this over," he said. "Come on, Mum, let's go into the front room, the girls can clear the table, and we'll have a little chat to decide what's best to be done."

He ushered them all into the little parlour and closed the door.

"Now then," he said, when they were all seated, "let me put my opinion first, then you can put yours, and we'll have a discussion to see if we can agree."

His calm, judicial attitude soothed Willy's annoyance somewhat, so he said, "I agree, go ahead and make your objections and I'll put my case later."

"Good lad'. Now'. First when you came here over two years and more ago, you told me straight out, that you intended to marry our Madge. I remember that well. I admired you for having the guts to say so, but I was a bit amused too, because, well, you were both very young. Madge was going away for a couple of years, and who knows who you both might have met, or how different you might have felt by the time she came home again. Then there was the depression, and with the unemployment and all, so there was no telling what might have happened to you. Now, here you are again. You're a man now, and doing well. You've stuck by Madge, and she to you, so nobody can say that it's not right for you to expect to marry, least of all me'. I want my girl to be happy, that's my main concern, but, and I think this is important, it's nigh on two and a half years since you've been together. Oh, I know, Madge has told us, how you've written back and forth all the time, but that's not the same as being together. You were both young kids, now you're man and woman, and, no matter what you feel now, you've got to get to know each other again. One afternoon's not enough. What I suggest is, find yourselves a house, get it furnished, see as much of each other as you can, then in six months or so, decide about when you'll be wed, and, if either one of you, or both, decide after all that it'd be better not to, then there should be no hard feelings."

As the incredible suggestion was made, Willy looked at Madge in dismay, but she squeezed his hand and nodded her head, setting the fire glow jumping through her hair. Willy put his arm around her. "I appreciate your concern for Madge's happiness, and I think she's lucky to have a dad to look out for her; but there's no need to worry on that score. We were courting for a couple of years before she left England, and we have shared our plans all the time she was away. We do know each other, it's over four years since we started going out together. Now, I'd like to tell you my plans, and I hope you'll agree that they are sensible. Mind you - I've not had time to discuss them with Madge yet, but if she's happy with them, I hope you will be too. I suggest that Madge comes down to Paignton and stays with mum and me. My mum will love to have her, she's said so, and we've got a spare room. Then we'll look around for lodgings, and, as soon as we find some that we like, we'll get married."

Before either of her parents could comment., Willy continued, "I've already got an option on a new house that a pal of mine (that's Jerry, he explained to Madge) will be building. Its a new estate, and I've got a prime plot. My firm is handling the legal side, and I've been told that I'll have no trouble getting a mortgage. The house will cost eight hundred and fifty pounds - it's a bit above the usual semi, and the repayments will be thirty shillings a week. I can also get furniture that'll cost me another thirty shillings, so I'll manage easily on my earnings. Now, please, can I talk this over with Madge, then come back to you for a verdict?"

Madge's parents looked at one another, then at the young couple so trustingly embraced. Mr Hadden stuck out his chin and proceeded to rub the bristles noisily. Then he closed his eyes, corrugated his forehead and appeared to try to iron out the wrinkles. His wife looked at him, waiting for.him to speak, but as the facial wrestling continued, she smiled half-heartedly at the couple, and motioned them to keep quiet. Mr. Hadden reached a decision at last, and rising, said "Come on, mother, let's leave the love-birds to talk it over. You and me had better have a talk too. Now you two, mother and me's going to the club, like we do most Saturdays, so make the most of your time. We'll be home 10.15 sharp. With that they left the room, and Willy and Madge got down to practicalities.

Willy was surprised that Madge didn't fall in with all his suggestions. He had not anticipated that his decisions would be questioned, and, at first, felt little piqued when Madge did so. She said, "I think dad!s got a point, Will. We have been apart for a long time. I don't know if you find me changed, but you have, you're not a bit like you were. Oh, I don't mean (she hurriedly assured him) that I love you any less. I'm sure you're still the Will I knew, but I've got to get used to the other Will, the 'William Churchward' who is getting to be quite an important man. You talk as if you can do anything, and are as good as anybody. I know you are, you always were, but you were quiet and gentle, not a businessman like you are now."

Madge didn't know how to explain how she found this dominant personality to be a little unnerving. Willy was standing by the mantel, Madge was sitting on her feet on the sofa, a small table lamp, sitting on top of the wireless was behind her, so that her face was lit by the fireglow and Willy was disconcerted by the doubt and worry that the flickering light showed. Willy's tall figure, elbow on mantelshelf, one brogue-shod foot crossing the other, was such a contrast to the gangling, anxious-faced young boy that Madge remembered, and Willy knew it.

Standing so, he was conscious of striking a pose that pleased him. "I look," he might have thought, if he had analysed his conceit, like an advertisement for some pipe tobacco, or a good sherry." To be fair he wasn't all that conceited, but he had grown used to developing a facade that he hoped impressed the local professional and political figures, with whom he became involved in the course of his work.

"Will dear," said Madge, and the anxiety she felt played a scale on her voice. "I wonder if you've grown away from me, if... if I'm good enough for you now?" Whether you should have kept this ring for a little while, till you're sure?"

Willy was dumbfounded. Madge, his Madge, the love of his life, that he had held in his heart all this time, writing to so passionately, longing for so desperately, was telling him that she was not going to be his, was that what she was saying? Was she breaking it to him slowly that she didn't want him? Madge, who has responding to eagerly to his loving only minutes ago.

He was silent so long, that Madge began to feel forced to implement what she had said. "After all, Will, if you're going to be famous, you'll need a wife who'll be able to keep up with you."

Willy found his voice, "Madge, there's never going to be anyone but you, I haven't changed, I love you just the same, really I do. Your dad doesn't know me, that's why he's anxious, but you and me - we're the same as always. I want to marry you, as soon as possible, don't you believe that? You didn't seem to have any doubts this afternoon, so why now?" Willy's complacent self-assurance had cracked wide open, and the shock sent him to Madge's side, to reach for her, to try and regain the singleness of purpose that had been theirs until then, but Madge did not snuggle into his arms. "Dad only said what I've been afraid to say myself. Oh, Willy. Don't think I don't love you, I do. I love you and love you. I've looked forward to today ever since that day up at Shorton. I want to be your wife, only now dad's put it into words, what I felt, I'm afraid, Will. I want a little time to get to know you again, so's I know that I can live up to you, and we'll be happy."

She let him lay her across his knees, her head on the arm of the sofa, his arm under her shoulder and his other hand caressing her cheek.

"You're more like my old Will now," like some young officer in mufti."

"What on earth do they look like?"

Madge's inner self would have replied, "Stuck up show-offs." she just said, "Oh, people that are not at all like you really."

After a while, when Willy's shocked nerves had been calmed by her loving, he asked, whispering, for their heads were so close, their lips almost spoke to each other. "You will keep the ring, won't you? And you'll come on down to Paignton?"

"Yes, of course I'll keep the ring, my darling, but I may not wear it yet, I want us to both be absolutely sure, not about loving - I love you, and I will for ever, and I know you love me, you've told me so often in your wonderful letters, and I can tell you do now, but we must be sure that if we get married, we'll still go on loving - I mean loving like we do now. Oh Will'. My family, the ones I worked for, I've seen their wedding pictures and they looked so happy, but now they don't seem to have any feeling for each other. She's had five kids, and she doesn't really want them. He drinks a lot, and I know she locks him out of the bedroom. Sometimes all she does is play bridge and drink cocktails. They hold parties, all smiles and 'Darling this' and 'Darling that', and then everyone's gone they have awful rows - yet they've had all those kids!. Will, that's not loving, not my kind of loving, I'd die if that happened to us."

"It won't. It couldn't. Forget all about that lot, think about us, We'll have each other for ever - and that football team you told me you wanted." At that, Madge could only hug him close to her and thank him with kisses.

When they surfaced again, Madge re-opened the subject. "I don't think it would be a very good idea," she said, "to stay at your house. I'll come for a holiday but I'll have to get a job till we marry (it slipped out she knew that they would, it was just the dread of being hurt that had made her so cautious), so it'd be best if I got a live-in job till then."

"Not on your life!" said Willy with indignation, sitting up and looking down on her, so sweet and warm and rumpled. "You're not going into any sort of service any more. If you want to get a job, it'll be a daytime one, and there's no reason why you shouldn't live with us, mum'll love to have you, you should have seen how pleased she was when I suggested it."

"Well, we'll think about that dear, but I do think we ought not to rush into it. Like dad says, wait six months, then we'll be sure."

"I'm sure now. Madge, my little lovey, we've waited so long- why go on waiting more?"

"Because I want you to know how I'm going to fit into your fine plans, that's why'."

Willy sighed with exasperation, throwing his head back and biting his lips, then he looked down on her rounded knees and little bit of thigh that showed where her skirt had rucked up, and he saw again, for the thousandth time, that mind picture, that had tortured, yet sustained his love over the time of their parting, that picture of her kneeling against the golden gorse. Now she was really there, no fantasy, under his hand. He tried no intimacies, but held her tight, crooning his desires away. Madge did not know what had gone through his mind, but she was happy that he did not make a quarrel. After a long moment, he said, "Whatever you want darling, just as long as you'll wed me in the end."

The parents came home just then, and the two roused themselves, and Madge straightened herself up a bit. The carefully rattled door handle preceded her mother's entrance.

"Oh my," she said, "you've let the fire down, the room's got quite cold." She smiled inwardly, remembering her own courting days, and happy that her girl had been too much in love to notice. "Come into the other room, dad's got some fish and chips for supper."

All the family shared the gorgeous smelling feast, then the younger ones went off to bed and Mrs Hadden said, "I'll get the bedding, Madge love, give me a hand to make up Will's bed on the sofa, there's a dear."

While they were doing that, her father told Willy that they were very pleased to welcome him into the family, but were still of the opinion that the wedding should not be hurried. "Not only that boy, but think of the girl - you go getting married all of a rush, and what'll everyone think? It isn't fair on the girl'."

"Good Lord'." said Willy "I don't care what people think."

"Well I do, it's important to me."

Mrs Hadden came back with Madge, "There, I hope you'll be able to manage, I've dropped the end down, but it'll still be short for your long legs. Anyway, I've made the fire up, so you won't be cold."

"Oh. You needn't have bothered, I'd have been warm enough."

"Right then you two take your cocoa in there while you say goodnight. Dad and I'll be off upstairs.

When they wished each other goodnight, Mr Hadden drew Willy aside. "I can trust you with my girl, can't I?" he said looking Willy hard in the eyes.

"Absolutely, Sir, I love her." It was the 'Sir' that reassured the man. He was only too aware of the temptations a warm, loving body offered.

When they were alone again, Madge said, "Mum's a brick, she made the fire up purposely, then said it was a pity to waste it, so we'd better sit it out.'

"Willy laughed happily," and your dad's just issued me a warning to behave myself." They settled themselves on Willy's bedding, all arguments forgotten.

"Just a minute," said Willy, as they were snuggling down, "I'll put a couple more knobs on the fire." It was one o'clock before a little loose soot rattled down the chimney and roused them from sleep.

"Gosh'. Look at the time, Will, I'll have to go."

Willy rubbed his eyes and nodded agreement. "You've been a dear, he said, "it's terribly hard to wait for you any longer'."

"I must creep upstairs," she said. "Goodness knows what my sister will have to say."

Her sister, with whom she was sharing a bed, awoke as she climbed in. "Hey! Have you been cuddling all this time?"

"Go to sleep and mind your own business," said Madge. She was awake for quite a time while thinking over what had happened, wishing that she could be sure, then decided to leave it all till tomorrow. "He must love me anyway," she thought, "or he wouldn't have said so over and over. Dear Will, sometimes he's just the same as he always was. He's good too, he didn't try anything on. I'm glad he didn't, because if I'd let him, it would have meant I'd said 'yes' to everything. I could tell he wanted to, poor Will. When I think of all the things that he's said in his letters - what he imagined he was doing to me, I wonder he was able not to." A little bit of doubt crept in then. "I suppose he really did want to, he could have tried... I'd have let him if he had. Oh, Lord. I hope he'll like my bosom now it's smaller'. I think I will let him, as long as he doesn't go too far."

Willy thought, "I can't expect her to let me go all the way, but soon's I get her home, I'll do all she'll let me."

The next day was fine and they went for a walk into the country that was easily reached by a short bus ride. During the morning they talked over their situation again and reached a solution. When they had eaten the Sunday dinner that Mrs Hadden and Madge's sisters had spent all morning preparing, Willy said to Madge's parents, "Well, we've agreed on what we will do, (no 'if you agree', this time) Madge wants to stay here with you for a bit - that's natural, she hasn't seen much of you for so long - then she's going to come down to me for a holiday, she'll stay with us, of course, then if she can find a job (and I've thought of a possibility already at a nursery school) she will get lodgings, and we'll be able to spend all our spare time together. I'll show her where I've booked a plot for our house, and she can see the plans and everything, then, after about three months, if she thinks I'll make her a good hubby, we'll find a place to rent and get married, and we'll move to our new house as soon as it's ready. Will that be to your liking?"

Mr Hadden had had a rough time with his usually acquiescent wife who had been all for letting the young ones do what they pleased. She thought Willy would be an excellent husband for Madge, and was living again, in Madge, all her own emotional hopes and fears of her courting days. Also, the house was none too big, and with Madge home again, there were domestic pressures that did not affect her husband, but were important to the happiness of the family, so Madge's father decided that, having made his stand, and checked Willy's impulsiveness to some degree, he would be wise to retire gracefully. "Welcome son." he said, "Make sure you do the right thing by her and make her happy." He shook Willy's hand and kissed Madge, then her mother kissed them both, saying, "I declare, I think I'm going to cry!" Her brother shook hands and said, in the way of teenage brothers, good luck mate, you'll need it" and her sister thought with satisfaction, "Good'. I'll have my room to myself. The others stood around and giggled.

Chapter 22

Willy returned home full of plans to make Madge welcome, and to make sure that she would be happy. Gwen was pleased that she would be coming to her, at least for a week or two. She had already turned out her meagre store of bedclothes, and had been juggling the sheets and blankets about to give Madge the most presentable but was very conscious of how old and worn it all was. Willy settled her fears, saying, "I'll have to buy new when we furnish our own house, so I may as well get some now." The spare room had not been used as a bedroom and was full of Willy's junk. For the next few evenings he deserted his writing to clear everything out and Walpamour the walls. He bought a bed and flock mattress, feather pillows, sheets and blankets, and finally an artificial silk counterpane and eiderdown to match. He managed to fit some cheap floor covering, that Gwen, in the vocabulary of her youth, still called oilcloth, on the floor, with a pretty bedside rug, that he took from his own room. This, he had bought in the furnishers across the road from his office for four and sixpence, and he now put it beside Madge's bed, in a sort of homage to her pretty little feet. He even thought to buy a rubber hot water bottle, for the little room was ice colt in the winter.

He kept going up to look at the room, trying to think of more ways of improving it. A tiny dressing table, and a chair, was all that there was room for apart from the bed, until he fitted a hanging wardrobe across the corner over the foot of the bed. Gwen had a piece of curtaining left over from the curtains she had made when they moved in, so she made the material up, and fitted it to the shelf. She too kept looking into the little room, delighted by what seemed to her the luxury of the furnishings, and so pleased at Willy's evident pleasure in making this room so cosy for his girl.

"I'm glad he's so happy, " she thought. "It'll be so nice having them near."

She sometimes remembered how she had dreaded the day when her little boy would be taken from her by some minx of a girl; it seemed silly now. She liked what she knew of Madge, and thought, with pleasure, of the time she would have grandchildren to spoil.

Madge arrived at the end of the week. "Oh, no wonder he loves her.'" thought Gwen, when Willy brought her home. She had grown up too, was slimmer, and her face had a golden tan, that Gwen thought very attractive. She still had a round face, but the adolescent fat had been fined away. Her loving eyes and her dimple had not changed and, anything else apart, Gwen would have accepted her on them alone. She had her portmanteau with her, still retaining the steamship labels, and Gwen thought that very impressive.

When Gwen took her upstairs to her room, (quietly motioning to Willy that it was her place to do so), Madge said, "Oh.' What a pretty little room, I hope you haven't gone to a lot of trouble for me."

"Willy's done it all, not me."

"Oh, I'll like it all the more for that." Gwen then showed her which was the bathroom, and in an undertone, with a gesture, said "The other place is just next door," as if she was revealing some unwholesome secret. That being done, she looked over the bannisters to where Willy was fretting at the foot of the stairs, and motioned him to come up. He came bounding, up in his usual style, three steps at a time, and giving Madge a hug, said, "Do you like it?"

"It's lovely, and your mum says you did it for me. Thank you Will, it's ever so cosy."

"The bed's new, you know, so I hope it will be comfy, and there's an eiderdown to keep you warm, and a hot water bottle'."

"You've thought of everything, Will."

"Yes, you're right, I thought of everything, especially of when we'll have our own room it'll be better than this - our own bit of heaven'."

"Well.'" Gwen almost said it aloud. "Well'. What these young people say these days'. Well, I don't know'."

She was shocked again when all her genteel manoeuvers come to nothing as Willy asked without any pretensions, "Mum's shown you the bogs, has she?"

Gwen still worked at the big house. She was the only domestic now. Her employers had lost heavily in the recession, and could not afford the staff they used to keep. Gwen worked five mornings a week, cooking a midday meal and washing up afterwards. Once a week a woman came in and cleaned, otherwise the family fended for themselves. This gave Gwen the opportunity to get to know Madge during the afternoons, and after the first day's reserve had been overcome, she found herself confiding in the girl in a way that she had never done to anyone.

Madge learned all about her lonely struggle to care for Willy and her heart near broke with compassion when Gwen, reminiscing, told her of the tragedy of Dave's death. She thought how brave and strong this woman was, and wondered if Willy had inherited her courage. She saw also how lonely Gwen was, though Gwen did not say so, and probed a little as to the relationship between her and Willy.

"Well," said Gwen, "I don't really see an awful lot of him. Of course, I go out before he's down, and I don't come in till after he's had his dinner hour, so I give him something to take, or leave him something to warm up. Then, when he comes in after work, it's a quick tea and he's either off somewhere or he's upstairs banging away on his typewriter till all hours."

Gwen made no complaints though. "He's a good boy, that I know. He's been true to you all the time, though he's had chances, there's plenty of young maids on the lookout for a lad like him, but he never bothered with any, so that's a compliment to you really."

Madge also did a little digging to find out what Willy was like to his friends. "Oh'. He's well respected," said Gwen proudly. "He's quite well known to all sorts. 'course, he goes to lots of functions to do his reporting. He knows all the big knobs about the bay. I expect he'll take you to some do or other, then you can see for yourself. That young girl in his office, she came here on my birthday, she speaks well of him, and she ought to know. No need for you to worry there mind - I asked her right out, and there's nothing in it, she's got a young man of her own. Still, he'll be taking you out, and you'll see for yourself."

"Does he ever take you out?"

"No, well, it's not my way. I never thought to see how he goes on. He could be anyone, and he goes anywhere, but I'd be embarrassed, I'd be out of my depth."

"Do you stop at home night after night?"

"No, I still go to the whist drive every week, and I go to the Red Cross on Wednesday afternoons, knitting and that. Oh, I'm all right. I've got this nice house. It's so much better than the old cottage, what with electric light and hot water from the back of the fire, I'm very comfortable. I've got my wireless too, and Willy pays me well, though I've not expected so much, I'm better off now than I've ever been."

"Yes," thought Madge, "but what happens when he leaves you?" As if she had read the girl's mind, as well she might have done, for Madge's expressive face was an open book, Gwen continued, "When he gets married and leaves home, I'll be all right. I've got me widow's pension, (it was only twelve shillings but she made it sound as if it was enough to live on) and me work, and of course, I get me food there so there's nothing much to pay except the rent."

Madge had no illusions about finances. She had been brought up in a thrifty home, her father had always been in regular work at the tobacco factory and got as good, or better,wages than average, but there never seemed anything to spare. Her mother had always kept them neatly dressed and well fed, but there were never any extravagances, and she saw through Gwen's situation. Quite clearly, she saw a reversion to constant make do and mend, penny pinching on light and heat, and the gradual deterioration of her present comfort. Madge remembered the poverty of the old cottage, that had been such a contrast to her own home, and realised how much Willy had done in those two years, to improve their living. She thought, "Poor woman'. She must have dreaded Willy leaving her, she ought to hate me'."

She put a hand on Gwen's arm and said, "Don't worry, you'll never have to go without, Will and I will see to that, that's a promise'."

Gwen said, "Oh'. My dear girl, don't you go thinking you got to be looking after me, I'm all right, you go ahead and make Will happy." Then in a burst of affection, she said: "I'm so glad he found you. He needs someone to love him. He never had anyone 'cept me, and I was always out to work. He missed being loved, I know he did, but I did me best, but there, he's like his dad, all locked up inside, I couldn't ever get to him, but he'll open up to you, like his dad did to me. He was a very loving man.

"Many a time I'd see him sitting there, staring at nothing, but with a little smile on his face. Stay quiet like that for ages he would. Then I'd say, like "What are you smiling at?" and he'd look up surprised, as if I'd woken him up from sleep, then he'd say, p'haps, "Was I smiling? 'Well, I got lots to smile about haven't I." and he'd give me a hug and a kiss and say something like, "Whatever would I do without you to look out for me, and to have to come home to?" We were ever so happy those two years and a bit."

Gwen had to blow her nose to stop the tears from falling, and Madge wept for her. "Oh drat it'. said Gwen, then, "I shouldn't go on like that, it's all so long ago, but you're a sweet little thing to listen. I haven't talked about Dave to anyone for years."

Madge thought to herself that she'd have to have a serious talk to Willy, about his mother. She didn't put it in so many words, but she saw how all the sterile years had gradually begun to grow a second life, with Willy's maturity, and her heart quailed at the thought of stifling the new hope Gwen must have found.

"It's true, like mum said," thought Madge, "tisn't all love and kisses, there's problems too," then she thought, "I'll see to the problems, if Will will see to the love and kisses - well. We'll do it together anyway." She had a deeper feeling for Willy that morning, her eyes grew bright as she thought of the previous night, when they had seen the fire out before going to bed, and she had let Willy take all her treasures into his loving hands, and gave all he sought for, to his lips. He had not tried to force himself on her and they had both stopped short of the ultimate. Both wanting to, but both willing to save themselves till marriage banished any shadow of guilt. Something had happened to her during that secret hour, that she had never known before, and that morning she felt a deeper love for Willy, and a wanting to be loved, that dispelled her previous doubts. "If it's love he wants," she thought, "I'll give it to him!"

Sitting the fire out, became a regular thing. Gwen was usually in bed about ten, and Willy made the fire up to make it last till well after midnight. They were happy nights, when almost all the fantasies that he had written to Madge about while she was away came true. So much so that Madge made a mild protest, that perhaps he would have tired of her before their wedding, but he murmured a scornful denial from somewhere between her breasts. Madge determined to stay with her resolve not to yield the final pleasure, and Willy doing everything but, did not object. In the evenings they walked around the town, and through the park, looking at the villa where Madge had worked, and finding a sense of unreality in remembering some of the traumas of their courtship. They went to the pictures and bought chips afterwards, all just as they had done, but the glory of it was, that afterwards they went home together, not she to the house by the park, he to the cottage. On the Friday night, Willy suggested that they went to the church hall dance as a nostalgic pilgrimage to their first meeting. Madge was dubious about what to wear. "Oh, wear anything, you'll still look beautiful," said Willy with complete lack of understanding "No'." said Madge, with a spirit that surprised him. "I'm not going looking dowdy with all the other girls dolled up!"

"We'll then, buy a dress, I'll pay!"

"No you won't, I've got some money, and I'll buy my own."

"Okay, if you want to," laughed Willy, "be independent'."

Madge spent the morning in the several ladies shops in the town and finally found what she wanted. Then she yielded to an increasing temptation that had bothered her for some days, and went up the stairs to the office where Willy worked. Madge smiled to herself at the recollection of Willy crashing down those same stairs, almost into her arms. It seemed so long ago, yet only yesterday. She was going to tell Willy that she would wait for him in the Morris, till his lunch hour, but she was really going to get a look at Val, often mentioned, but so far unseen.

There was the chatter of a typewriter coming from the office, and she thought she could hear Willy's voice. Then another voice called, "Churchward" and there was the sound of feet crossing the floor. "Sounds like his big feet," thought Madge with a giggle. She tapped on the door and entered. Val was seated behind her typewriter, facing the door. She looked up as Madge entered. "Good morning," she said.

Madge did a woman's lightning appraisal of the girl. "Blue jumper, gold chin with a tiny pendant, red nail varnish, red lipstick, hair curling in a pageboy bob, very blue eyes, real golden hair - very unusual - pretty face, good skin." It took her no time at all to absorb that information - like a camera shot.

Val had done precisely the same thing. She recognised Madge at once from the photograph Willy had shown her on many occasions and she had expected her to call at some time. She knew, intuitively, that Madge had really come to see her. In the instant of recognition, she had thought wordlessly, "slimmer than she was, old coat, her old uniform, nice face, not pretty but attractive, good eyes, not much make-up, skin looks dry - (that's the sun)."

"You're Madge," she said, coming around her desk, (pleated skirt, nice legs high heels recorded Madge's eye). "Hello'. I've been longing to meet you, I've heard so much about you. Your Will doesn't know what cloud he's sitting on since you came home!"

Madge's slight resentment of the girl, for being so beautiful, faded, as she saw the honest interest in herself, shown in Val's face.

"And you are Val, I suppose, I've heard about you too, and I'm pleased to meet you."

"Will's in with the boss, take a pew, he'll be out soon for lunch hour I'll have to get on with this draft or your chap will nag me. Make yourself at home."

Madge moved over to the window and looked out. "This is where he used to keep a look-out for me," she thought, remembering all the excuses she had made in the past to go shopping so that she might pass the building. Footsteps came, and the door at the other end of the room opened and a stout, florid-faced man came in with some papers in his hand. Snap went Madge's eye camera. "Fat, seedy, nasty eyes, horrid mouth," it recorded. The senior clerk's eye did not take a snapshot, it rather took a time exposure. "All right," it recorded, "smashing bust, good bottom, nice strong legs, then, moving up, 'come to bed' eyes, nice mouth."

"Good morning Miss," he said, advancing on Madge and unconsciously licking his full lips. "Have you an appointment?"

"Yes, I'm waiting for Mr Churchward."

"Oh, you're his young lady (his mind said 'bit of crumpet'), just home from foreign parts. Well, who's a lucky fellah then!." He shook Madge's hand, holding it much too long. "I'm young Churchward's guide and mentor you know, looked after him ever since he came here as a little schoolboy - well, well, I'm glad to meet you... ."

A bell rang as he was speaking, and he hurried to a cabinet and took out some papers. "Can't stop now, see you again I hope," he said, and hurried out of the room.

"Ugh'." said Val as the door shut, "the original dirty old man. I always feel I need to go and have a wash when he's been hanging over me, he never misses a chance. Will says he's to be pitied, but Will doesn't get crowded up in corners like I do."

Willy and his senior came in then, and Willy introduced Madge "Yes, we've just met," said: the man, shaking Madge's hand again, and holding on to it, then, putting his arm around her shoulders and saying, "and I reckon your young man knows how to pick 'em, eh!" This, with a squeeze. "Better to be born lucky than rich, eh!"

He released Madge then, his greedy eyes slithering up and down her front, appraising her contours. "Well, you make him behave himself, eh!" This, with a laugh that he thought jovial, but which sounded as lewd as a seaside comic postcard.

They went downstairs together, Val just behind them, "See what I mean?" she said to Madge.

When they got home, and had eaten the lunch Madge had prepared before she went shopping, Madge showed Willy her new dress. "Put it on," he said, "I can't see how it would look without you in it."

"All right," she said. As she went to her bedroom she chuckled to herself, "He's feeling naughty again," was her thought. When she came down, Willy was entranced. "You look lovely," he said.

The gown was low cut and revealed enough of her pretty bosom to catch even the most jaundiced eye. "Do you think it suits me?"

"Yes, of course it does - and it suits me too," said Willy, lifting her breasts and pressing them together so that they swelled above the dress and the cleavage was a deep, dark channel. "Oh gosh'. Aren't you gorgeous'." he crooned in an agony of pleasure. "Hey! You're not going to waste this dress on that crummy old church hall, we'll go to Dellers there's a dance on there tonight.

Madge spent the afternoon doing some minor adjustments to the dress. Gwen fussed about her, delighting in the excitement of having Madge to mother and help. Then after she had washed her hair, Gwen showed an unexpected skill in dressing it for her. She told Madge that she had done 'her lady's' hair for her, for years.

Madge's hair had a natural curl, and Gwen was proud of her prowess. "The only thing is," said Madge, "I haven't any shoes to go with the dress. It's long, so they won't show much, but I've only got these, except for my walking shoes, and they could hardly be counted evening shoes, could they. Oh well, I'll have to keep them out of sight, that's all'."

The old Morris came barking up the hill very promptly that evening, and Willy bounded into the house. "Hey Madge, where are you?"

"Here," called Madge from the kitchen. She came in, wearing Willy's dressing gown hitched up, and a cherubic grin on her face.

"Oh gosh!." If you only knew what you do to me, you monkey, grrr'. he said, hugging her so tight, she pleaded to be released.

"Hey! I forgot - Val says what about shoes - have you brought any with you?'

"I haven't any to bring, I've only got two pairs. '

"Well, Val says, if you can wear hers, she's size five, she'll lend you some." "Well now," said Gwen, coming in just then, "isn't that kind. Madge was saying she hadn't got any to wear."

"Right," said Willy, "what colour do you want? She's got gold, silver, black or beige. I said I thought you took fives." Madge conferred with Gwen and they decided: that silver would be the safest.

"Okay, you get the tea on the go and I'll go and get them. Tell you what, I'll bring the lot, she can have 'em back in the morning." He was back ten minutes later, with a bag full of shoes.

"It's very kind of her," said Madge, "she must be a very good-hearted person."

"Oh'. Val's all right, long's I don't let her get too toffee nosed over her boyfriend."

Gwen said quietly, "Do you know what that girl said to me? That she looked on Willy like an uncle!" Madge burst into laughter, happy that Val had no designs on Willy, and amused, that her Will seemed like an uncle to anybody. Later she did wonder at the side of his character that he must be showing to Val, a facet she did not know. "And a good job too," she told herself.

The dance was a huge success. Madge was pleased with her own appearance and proud of Will in his dinner suit. She was amazed at the number of people that he knew. Half the evening seemed: to be taken up with introductions. The men looked at her with open admiration and made sly remarks to Willy. The girls gushed a bit saying. "So you're the mystery lady Will has been hiding all this time." But they were all friendly, and she noticed that Willy was very courteous to the ladies, and seemed: 'one of the boys' amongst the young men, and was polite and at ease with the elder gentlemen.

They danced a lot too, and here again Willy surprised her. The shambling youth who had trodden all over her in the past, was now as good as most on the floor. His efforts were restricted to about three steps, but he had at last discovered that there was a beat to follow, and sometimes he managed to do so. He didn't tread on her at all. She gave no thought to the many bruised feet and laddered stockings that had unwittingly contributed to his ability. Nor did she know that, in even that friendly gathering, there were some who still fled to the 'ladies' if they saw him approaching, looking for a partner, and who in the inevitable 'Paul Jones' would watch warily, and cheat callously, when the music stopped.

Next day, being Saturday, was Willy's half day. He had tried to contact Jerry all the week, but had somehow missed him. So he drove Madge to the building site to show her where their house would be. They were standing on the site, and Willy was explaining the layout, when Jerry appeared from somewhere, 'all red mud and stick-out ears' as Madge described him to herself.

She liked Jerry. He was such a happy go lucky person, she thought, taking the world for granted and looking everyone straight in the eye. He came climbing through the mud and rubble in his wellingtons, his face a broad grin, long before he got to within earshot. Then, "Strewth, Will, you lucky old man! Madge, my beautiful! Why did I ever let Will see you? I should have kept you to myself; come here, you lovely!" He reached for her and planted a big kiss on her cheek. "Well now, come to see your future home eh! When's the happy day - don't say inside of next year, because I can't get this far for another twelve months at least, then you'll have to allow another three months, and after that, if you can, some months for the place to dry out before you move in."

"Oh lor. When'll that be then, asked Willy.

"I'd say about August '35, can't do it much earlier."

Willy's face showed his disappointment, and Madge looked a bit disconsolate too.

Jerry looked at them both. "You did know that, Will, when you picked the site. Course you could have one that I'm working on now, they're all supposed to be spoken for, but there's one, that the chap's firm looks like going bust and he may have to drop the option - come and have a look."

The house was up to the first floor joists, it was near the main road and looked up the cul-de-sac. Willy looked in that direction and turned to Madge and Jerry. "When the trees are grown we'll see a line of them right up the road from this angle, that'll be rather pleasant," he said. "What do you think?"

"It's hard to imagine it," said Madge, "could we go into the ones over there, with the roofs on, so as to get an idea of what it'll be like?" Of course, come on, I'll show you."

The first pair were almost finished, only the painting inside was left to be done. Madge liked it at once. The rooms were a little bigger than her old home in Bristol. She had got used to the big rooms at her employer's houses and felt shut in, in the little modern homes. Jerry had purposely gone for more roomy plans to attract a customer with taste and money. The appointments were better too. Oak flooring in the hall and an oak surround in the 'lounge' (not sitting room), that pre-supposed a carpet. Fireplaces were tiled, and the one in the lounge had an oak mantel and 'Devon' grate.

"What do you think?" asked Jerry.

"It's beautiful, don't you think so Will?"

"Yes, you've done a good job here. What'll it cost?"

"'These will be nine hundred and ninety pound, I'm afraid, Will. It's the garage and half cellar under. The Bridgwater will give a twenty-five year mortgage on ninety-five per cent - about two pounds weekly."

Willy's calculator was buzzing around in his brain, and to break the silence, he said, "You've got it all worked out."

"I've had to."

"How long can you hold the option, if that chap backs out?"

"As long as I can for you, Will. I'd like you to have one of these, and I tell you what, if you do, I'll make sure yours will be the best in road."

"When will it be ready?"

"Three or four months, depends on the weather."

"Willy looked at Madge, she looked at him. "I like it," she said, "but we'll have to talk it over a bit, there's things we haven't decided yet, isn't there." Willy looked puzzled. Whatever was she meaning, he wondered.

Jerry grinned at Madge. "You take your time love, make sure you get it right, just pick a moment when old Will can't say 'no'."

Madge didn't get the point of the last remark. Jerry assumed that all minds (except Willy's) worked like his own, but she knew that Willy was in danger of committing himself before they had really thought it out.

On the way home, Willy said, "I'd looked forward to living next door to Jerry but now you're here I don't think it matters. I think that house would be fine, don't you? Or have you got second thoughts? What did you mean there were things we had to decide?"

"Well, it's a big thing to do, we've got to talk about it first." Madge thought, "I came down here to decide if I'd marry him. I was all confused up at home. Now I know I can't live without him, but I still don't know what he's like when he working - after all, he's not done any work, writing, since I've been here."

That evening, Gwen went to her whist drive, so they stayed in, and on Madge's insistence, talked instead of cuddling. She asked him what his extra work entailed, how often he would be out all evening, how long he'd have to work on his book and articles. In short, how much would she see of him. When he came to tell her he surprised himself be the hours he would be closeted in his room.

"You're doing two days work each day," Madge pointed out. "It's like when dad was on shifts, he worked all night and slept most of the day. Mum never saw him, it got so bad he had to go back on days, even though he lost money."

"But it's only for a while," said Willy, I'll finish my book by Easter, I hope, then I'll have time to spare, and when it's published, I'll give up my job and write by day."

There was a pause, Madge looked at his ernest, worried face, so different from the eager one that pressed against hers by the fireside. Madge hesitated, but came out with the the question she knew she must ask. "Are you sure it will be published?"

Willy's face set hard. "No, I'm not, but I expect it to be. It's good, I'm sure it is, and it's readable. Good Lord. I've had articles and reports published for three years now! If the *Strand* will take articles, why should publishers refuse my novel?"

"I don't know, Will, I don't know anything about it, only I love you so much, it would break my heart if your work spoilt our marriage. Mum told me it wasn't all love and kisses, well it's true, though I wish it wasn't."

Willy stopped his prowling and sat beside her. "Will you marry me Madge, will you? We're engaged, surely there's no reason why not."

"I'll marry you Will, I can't live without you now, I know that, but it's when. When can we marry and be sure to be happy. I can't live to see us living without love, real love, I mean."

A miserable silence hung between them. Willy sat with his head in his hands, trying to see things from Madge's view. He knew it was true. Even now, he was behind with work for the *Argosy*. He'd given himself two weeks holiday for when Madge arrived, and had told himself that it Would be easy to catch up afterwards. He'd work late, and all the weekends. He was quite well aware that what Madge told him, what his mother had said was true. He hardly ever saw her, but surely Madge didn't think that he would treat her the same. But hold on. He'd have to, or give up his literary work, or his job.

"Crumbs." he thought, that last would be risky, and he'd never get a mortgage without a regular job and his boss's influence. Two quid a week for mortgage, say thirty bob for furniture on hire purchase, then they'd got to live and run a car - he needed that now, as he was going further afield for the paper. It was too true, what Madge said, there was more to marriage than love and kisses.

Madge sat beside him, her legs tucked under her, as she liked to do. She was so unhappy to have provoked this miserable scene. She started to move her hand to smooth Willy's head, but at the same moment he hunched further forward, as if avoiding her touch. It was coincidental, not intended, she knew that, but she felt the hurt. Dropping her hand back in her lap, she idly turned Willy's ring round her finger, thinking of the courtly way he had given it to her, then in an equally idle way she slipped it off her finger and held it in her hard, knowing that she held his love, with that ring in her palm.

Willy had come to some kind of decision and looked up. He saw Madge's hand held towards him with the ring lying in her palm. His face went quite pale with shock, as for the moment, he thought Madge was returning it to him, but she slipped it back on her finger and opened her arms to him. He didn't say anything, just breathed his relief against the warmth of her breast. However, the shock had crystalised his decision, and comforted by her warmth, he said, "What you said is true. I'd never thought of it that way, I enjoy writing so much I've never thought of it as work. Look, if I go on, as I am, earning what I do, I'll be quids in, without my novel, so, what I've thought I'll do is carry on with the *Echo* and articles, and leave the novel ticking over - just writing a bit when I've got spare time, though (leaning forward and kissing her pretty nose) when I'll ever have spare time with you to love and distract me, I really don't know."

"Your book means a lot to you, doesn't it. I mean, just the writing."

"Yes, it does. Once I start I find it hard to stop, the words keep rushing out, and I'm always surprised at what develops, I think it comes by itself."

"Will it make you miserable, not to be writing it?"

"No, not with you here. No! That's the sensible thing to do. I've got regular outlets for all I write, and a few hours a week will be enough, and I won't be writing to you! That used to take up an hour or so each night."

"Did it really? They were lovely letters, Will. I'd have been so unhappy without them. I always read, and re-read them in bed. It used to give me a lovely feeling knowing how much you thought of me, and wanted me."

"They were a bit much of it, sometimes, weren't they."

"Yes, they certainly were, but I loved them, especially the naughty bits."

"Well then, what about it? One or two evenings out for the *Echo* and you could come too, to the social ones, a couple of hours, a nights a week on my literary efforts, and all the rest for you!"

"I won't ask for more, Will dear, if you can do that. Anyway, it's not good for you to work till one or two every night, you'll make yourself ill doing that."

"Yes, I know, 'you'll ruin your eyesight', as my mum's been telling me for years. Hey! look! She'll be in soon, and we've wasted all the evening."

"No, we haven't," said Madge, "we've decided to buy a house and get married!"

How the bells rang and angels sang for them in their refound happiness. Gwen looked hard at Willy when she came in, and saw their dishevelled appearance. "'These youngsters, these days!" she thought.

During the week that followed, Willy suggested that Madge should call on a lady who ran a prep school, catering for little boys from five to seven years of age. Willy had called on this lady as a result of an advertisement she had put in the *Echo*. He made a little story about the venture in his 'Around the Bay' column and, as a result, the school had engaged several new pupils.

Will telephoned and suggested she might find Madge to be of great assistance if she were able to employ her. She was offered a position of general help and minder for five mornings a week. The salary was three pounds a month, starting after Christmas. Madge could hardly have managed on this if she had to find board and lodgings, but with Willy's insistence and Gwen's genuine invitation, she agreed to remain with them. "There's no need to feel obligated," he told her, "you'll make no difference to the household expenses and I'll see to the food, you'll be my guest."

At the end of the week, Madge went home. She intended to stay no more than a week, and would bring back what few belongings she possessed. "I daresay Dad would like me to stay longer," she said, "mum would too, but she knows how difficult it would be. They've got used to me being away, and the girls have grown up so, there just isn't room for me. Mum said she'd make the front room into a bedroom for Kath and me, but it'd be an upset and expense and they would have nowhere for anyone to go to be private. The young ones do their homework there and the others'll want somewhere to take their friends."

"Good," said Willy, "come back next day, if you can."

During the week, Willy told his boss that he intended to buy the house from Jerry, if the present option was not taken up. The solicitor was sitting at his desk. Willy stood facing him. Between them was a huge mahogany table, upon which were neat rows of files, each tied with pink tape, every one one inscribed in Willy's neat script, with the client's name, and that of the person, or property, involved in the transaction. He stood a trifle nervously, waiting for the man's reaction, but he showed no particular surprise.

"That will be Plot 8, will it?"

"Yes Sir, the one Mr Grant is having."

"And Wilkins thinks he may not go on with it?"

"He thinks that he may lose his job."

"Umm. Unfortunate. He's with Hunters, I think, and they're a subsidiary of Walker Thompson. Let's see," He picked up the *Financial*

Times, looked at the share quotations and raised his eyebrows. "Might well be'" he said, "it'll just be another casualty, one wonders if the market will ever turn up again." Folding the paper he put it on his desk, then removed his spectacles and began polishing them. Willy recognised this as an action he always used before making a statement of any importance. He used the few moments gained to marshall his facts.

"Come and sit down," he said to Willy, waving to the 'client's' armchair. Willy did so with a feeling of importance, seeing himself promoted to client status.

"Now let's see, you're over twenty-one, now, aren't you, and you've known the lady you intend to marry for some time, so we can assume that it is not simply a passing infatuation, and that you are both in agreement?"

"Oh yes, Sir."

"And you think you could afford to buy this house and support a wife?"

"Yes Sir, I do. I've worked it out and I can manage."

"Not on what you earn here!"

"No, but I do earn money by reporting for the *Echo* - as you know, and I make regular contributions to *Strand*, *Argosy* and *The Passing Show*, as well as odd bits here and there."

"I congratulate you Churchward, you've done well, and did I not hear something about a novel perhaps?"

Willy blushed, "Now who told him that?" he thought. "I have hopes, in time."

"Well, tell me, what is your involvement with the *Echo* worth? I ask because that seems to be a stable income."

"I do the column, 'Around the Bay', and I'm paid one pound for a thousand words for that, and I also do the 'Roving Reporter' column, for about the same, and I get commission on new advertising."

The solicitor looked at him with an admiring eye. "You are what the Americans call a 'go-getter', aren't you?"

Willy smiled. "It's really just that I like writing and I get paid for doing so."

"Lucky you! Tell me, have you plans for leaving this office at all?"

Willy flushed scarlet, the question caught him by surprise. He sat, elbows on the arm of the chair, fingertips touching and covering his mouth. It was his unconscious gesture to gain time before replying. "No Sir, not in the forseeable future. I hardly think I am established enough to go completely freelance."

"I'm glad you said that, because I would be wary of recommending you for a mortgage if you had no steady employment. Well, we'll wait and see if this option is surrendered, and if it is, then we will pass it to you, eh?"

"Thank you, Sir."

"Right'. Now I want the Perkins file."

Willy recognised that he had reverted to employee again, and got out of the chair and reached for the file."

"Churchward, look at those files, they're all titled by you, every one, and some go back for years. I must say I've been very satisfied with your work over the, what is it, seven years? I'm glad that you don't allow your other interests to impinge on your duties here. Ah, yes, that's the one, thank you."

Willy was dismissed and returned to his desk in the other room. He felt very pleased. His boss was a man of few words, and he seldom broke the employer/employee status. Had Willy but known it, he always made a point of reading Willy's columns of local gossip.

Later in the day, the senior clerk came out of the inner office and stood over Willy's desk pouting his lips and protruding his great belly at him. "Here, what you been up to then?"

"What? You tell me'.

"The old man's given you a rise of a quid a week, that's what'."

Willy gasped in amazement. "Good Lord. Has he?"

"Well, you ought to know, you must have asked for it."

"No, I didn't. I never thought of asking. I told him I wanted to buy a Wilkins house, and asked if he would recommend me for a mortgage."

"So he gives you a rise so you can get one. You jammy little bugger. I'd never have gone crawling."

"I didn't. I don't need to. I'm as surprised as you are."

That week was a busy one for Willy. He had to catch up with some of his magazine contributions, and go out, chasing news, every evening.

Gwen heard the familiar sound of his typewriter rattling away every night, long after she had gone to bed. By the time Friday night had gone, he felt very tired indeed. Madge was returning on the Sunday, so Willy had his Saturday's half day, and the evening left before she arrived. After his gulped-down lunch, he hurried off to Torquay to wander along the breakwater where there was a fishing competition in progress, then to the rugby ground to have a word with the local team after the match. In between, he surveyed the sea road that was being constructed. Later, in Paignton, he telephoned the secretary of the local amateur dramatic society for news of the New Year production of 'The Ghost Train'. There was a long standing dispute over moorings at Brixham that needed to be brought up to date, and a local art exhibition that must not be forgotten.

Willy did no more than note essential names and relative facts, but he found himself hard put to make up his 'Around the Bay' column. His contributions to the *Echo* were much appreciated by the Editor, who was impressed by the boy's industry. He had, long since, given Willy a key to his office, to enable him to telephone around the bay for news when he needed it. The Editor did the council news, funerals, weddings and such like when important people were involved. Most organisations sent him reports of their activities. These he only needed to pass on to the printer.

Over the past two years, Willy had introduced something more. He had an eye for a story, and developed an interesting paragraph out of the most mundane subject. The readers loved it. To have one's name in the *Echo* pleased most people. The Editor showed Willy the notifications of events to come, and reports sent in of social, sporting and political meetings, and Willy would make a telephone call to get some elaboration, or he would call on someone to get the story behind the show. In this way, he had rapidly become known in the town and, such is human conceit, that he was made welcome wherever he appeared.

That Saturday night, or rather, Sunday morning, when he had at last got his two columns done, he sat at his table in his bedroom and took stock of himself. The week just gone had been like many another in the past, except that he had not written to Madge (except for one short note that was no more than a 'Hurry back' message) nor had he touched his novel, yet he had worked solidly every night till long past midnight. He had been out most evenings, and all Saturday afternoon. He went back over the week and acknowledged that Madge was right. It was no life for them. While she was away, he had been happy to be so busy, but the fortnight that they had together had been so blissful that he knew it would be impossible to go back to his long hours of writing. He ought to do one or the other.

Some while previously, Mr Watts suggested that he should apply for a job on the *Western Morning News* or some other paper, but Willy had funked taking the plunge of leaving his job and home. He knew he could write, but he thought that he could do little else, and admitted to himself that he was afraid to try. He would have to reach a compromise over his work. "I'll have to see how it goes," he decided.

Madge thought he looked pale and tired when he met her at the station, and said so to Gwen. "I'm not surprised, I doubt if he's been in bed before two o'clock any night all week'."

"Why? Where's he been?'

"In his room, writing on that dratted machine."

Madge felt depressed. Willy had told her of his rise and she had shared his pleasure, but now she was worried. "I mustn't be too hasty, she thought, "but I will be firm, after all, money's not everything."

The weeks that followed fell into an easy routine. Gwen went off to work early, as she always did, then Madge got Willy his breakfast, and saw him off to work. She prepared their midday dinner, and had cleared away before Gwen returned. Then when Willy came in after work, the three had tea together and afterwards the youngsters retired to the front room, that had been taken over as there own. Gwen seldom used it anyway, preferring the kitchen when she was at home alone.

On several evenings, Willy went out, sometimes for the *Echo*, or to some function, but he arranged to return by mid-evening. Most evenings he had some writing up to do, but he brought his typewriter down to the sitting room and worked there, while Madge sat curled on the sofa with a book or listening to the wireless.

When work was done, the old sofa groaned and squeaked under the stresses of their combined weight. Gwen took to tapping on the door and wishing them goodnight as she went to bed at about half past ten. Sometimes she heard them whispering on the landing round about midnight, and would worry away to herself.

She needn't have worried. Madge shut her door firmly after the oft repeated 'last' kiss, and Gwen comforted herself too with the knowledge that Willy was not working on 'that dratted machine' till the small hours anymore.

Christmas was a happy time. For the first time in years, Gwen took the trouble to decorate the rooms and she and Madge made Christmas puddings, mince pies and a Christmas cake. Gwen felt rejuvenated with the presence of the girl in the house and found herself comparing their modest festivities with the even less fulsome rejoicings of her brief life with Dave. It was so long ago though, and the years had changed her life so much that it was hard to remember. They had been happy, she thought wistfully, but it seemed they belonged to another world, and only she had survived it.

In the early months of 1934, Jerry rang Willy at the office, to tell him that the sale of the house had fallen through, and later, that his boss received confirmation that the option would not be taken up. Thereupon Willy became the prospective owner.

He had managed to maintain a reasonable balance between work and leisure, and he and Madge had decided to make the first week in April the date for their wedding.

The novel was never mentioned between them, but it still lay, like a secret life, in Willy's mind. From time to time, he made notes of situations, dialogue and descriptions, for the time he would have the opportunity to return to it. His poems too became a luxury he could not afford the time for, and even his visits to Mr Watts ceased. Not that he begrudged the time lost, for it was employed in the dearest of all occupations, and his young body burned just as it was right and proper that it should. Madge was no less eager than he, and often their temptation was well nigh irresistible, but Madge would say, 'It's only a few weeks, and we'd wish we'd waited then."

As the short winter days lengthened into Spring, Willy and Madge often went to inspect their house, and as the building developed, so the longing to be able to move in deepened, and the months seemed interminable. Jerry was often there, or would appear when he saw them, and he took a lot of trouble to finish things to their liking. He would say, "Come on, girl, you tell me how you'd like this done," or "may as well get this finished so as to tone in." He usually addressed himself to Madge, saying, "You have it like you want, old Will'll be happy to leave it to you."

He seemed to take a proprietory interest in Madge, as if, because he had introduced her to Willy, he had some unusual right over her. He was well aware of her physical charms too, and never tried to hide the fact from her. Madge didn't find this offensive, she had begun to look on Jerry as 'family' and treated his admiring looks with amused tolerance. She was pleased too that he found her attractive. She never guessed how much Jerry coveted her.

It was an Easter wedding. Jerry was best man. He, Willy and Gwen went up to Bristol, where Madge had been for the previous week. Her family had found neighbours who would put up Gwen and Jerry for two nights, and the bridal pair went to Weston-super-Mare for a week's honeymoon.

The wedding was a simple affair at the ancient village church that had been engulfed by the city's sprawling housing estate. Madge, smiling a greeting to Willy through the folds of her veil, looked the cherubic virgin that she was, and Willy and his best man were resplendent in new suits that proclaimed their professional status.

The reception was a boisterous affair, held in the church hall, to which the newlyweds walked through the churchyard, Easter-decked with primroses, celandines and dandelions, shining among the multitudes of rose-tipped daisies in the grass. Madge's parents had done her proud, at who knows what cost to themselves, and when Gwen stood with them at the doorway, to receive the guests, she fairly swelled with pride to be gathered into such a happy family.

The landlady at the seaside boarding house was indulgent to the honeymooners. They were the harbingers of her summer season, and she looked forward to the several couples that she relied on receiving each Easter. She made no pretence at not recognising them as newly-weds, but welcomed them with gusto, and lost no time in telling them that if they wanted to be private, no one would bother them, and that she usually reckoned to serve them breakfast in their bedroom, and an early nightcap of cocoa or Ovaltine, if they wanted one. "You make the most of your week, my loves, it'll go all too fast, I'm thinking."

Who can describe the glory of young love offered and taken in marriage? That thing in church, and the bit of paper afterwards, that had irked Willy's desires for so long, and had seemed of such little importance when his whole body was clamouring for relief, suddenly assumed its true significance. They shared each other with a sublime joy, that was beyond just physical delight.

Next morning, when Willy awoke, and propped on his elbow, looked down on Madge's sleeping face, he knew she had been right to make him wait. He moved his hand to find the warmth of her body, then stooped and kissed her lips gently, hardly more than a brush of his against hers. She awoke, wide-eyed, with a momentary alarm, then with a sigh of content, encircled his head with her bare arms. "What a lovely way to wake," she said.

They had a few moments of whispering and caressing, then eased their ardours in happy union. Afterwards, they lay, embraced, Willy stooping to meet her kisses and murmuring all his endearments. He marvelled at the strange luminosity of her eyes. The huge pupils, that had shone like lamps while she fulfilled all her promises to him, seemed to soften with content and hold out an emotion to him that he had never seen before. He kissed each lid and said, softly, "Your eyes are misty with love. Now I understand what is meant by 'the lovelight in your eyes'."

"Aren't you glad we waited?"

"Yes, my love, I am. I thought of that last night, and again as soon as I woke up. I was so happy that we could do it without shame, or a guilty conscience. It!s so wonderful, I can't believe it'."

"I know, I'm so happy. I'm yours now and always will be, and you're mine, and we're both part of each other, so we'll never have to ask; we're 'ours'."

"I thought, yesterday, when the vicar said to repeat the promise, and I came to the words, 'To have and to hold', that he needn't think I'd ever go back on that."

"Naughty - but it is nice, I feel like another person - Mrs William Churchward - I'm so glad'."

Little more can be said of their honeymoon. Those who say that honeymoons are a mistake, have just been unfortunate. Madge honoured her promises to Willy with such enthusiasm that he was hard put to match her vitality, and he lived in a happy daze of wonderment.

Jerry had given Willy's house priority, and had got it finished in good time for the wedding. All the legalities had gone through without hinderance, and they had got their essential furniture installed in good time. Gwen was very impressed. It was a palace, compared with the dark little cottage she and Dave had moved into, yet that had seemed wonderful to her. When she had been taken, by Madge, to see the house furnished, she went from room to room, exclaiming and marvelling. There was no envy, only pride, for them. "I can't hardly believe," she told Madge, "that my Willy's done this. I dunnow how he's managed it and all with writing and that. 'Tis only a while ago he was a little scrap of a boy, with me hard put to keep him in decent clothes. I never thought to see anything like this, it's wonderful, only I do hope he hasn't taken on too much, it must have cost a mint, all this lovely furniture, and a carpet in the parlour - sorry, 'lounge', and that new kind of mattress with springs inside. I dunnow, I'm sure, but you'm a lucky girl, if I do say so myself, to have my boy, and I'm not saying he isn't lucky too with you, and I'm lucky as well to have you both, and I'm sure I hope you're going to be happy here."

"We will be," said Madge, with conviction. "And you must come and see us whenever you want to."

"Oh, you won't be wanting me around, not at first anyway."

"No, well," said Madge in her honest, forthright way. "I'll want him to myself, all I can, soon's we're married, but you and me can have nice talks together in the day, while he's at work. I'll be glad to have you to help me sometimes, I expect."

Gwen glowed with pleasure. "I'd love to," she said. "Then" continued Madge, "when the babies arrive, I'll want someone to turn to, I expect."

Gwen felt a little embarrassed by Madge talking about babies, even before she was wed, and was quite astonished when Madge went on. "Course I know all about kids, and I can manage all that, but if they come quickly, I'll have problems. I've told Will that I want lots. Years ago, I said I wanted a football team, and he's never forgotten it."

Gwen, stuck for any comment suitable for that news, said "Well, it'll be nice for me to see my grandchildren."

"Yes," said Madge, standing at the bay window, and looking out on the rubble that would eventually be their garden, "I'm longing for kids of my own. I love babies, any babies, I can nurse them, and love them, whose ever they are, but I've got such a yearning for my own, my very own, part of me and Will, it's been so hard waiting and looking after other people's. You won't have long to wait for grandchildren."

"Well, really, the things she says," thought Gwen.

When they arrived home from their honeymoon, they had a surprise. In place of the rough ground in front of the house, they found a lawn and flower beds. They were standing at the gate looking at the neat landscaping, when Jerry appeared, with his usual wide grin. "Like it?"

"Great'. Hey, that wasn't in the contract, was it?"

"Nope, but I had a couple of blokes spare for a day, so I sent 'em over and they levelled it off. The crazy paving is only some broken up concrete I had by me, and I got the turfs delivered and laid in exchange for some topsoil I let a nursery have, and they threw in a few plants as well."

"I don't know what to say," said Willy. "It finishes off the house beautifully. I'm ever so grateful."

"Oh rot. You've got the back to do anyway and I couldn't see you getting round to do the front for a while, and I didn't want the place letting down the neighbourhood."

"You're only saying that. I am grateful Jerry. Isn't it great Madge?"

"It's lovely Jerry, really lovely, and I'm going to give you a kiss." Willy didn't notice, but Madge saw that Jerry's usual brash nonchalance give way to a flushed pleasure when she kissed him, and he held her for a second too long, for such a formal salute.

"Well, get along in," said Jerry, "I'll not stop to see the bride carried over the threshold'."

Halfway up the garden path, they heard Jerry call, "I turned on your immersion, I thought you'd want some hot water" They acknowledged with a wave, and Willy took his bride indoors. Madge said, "Jerry's very considerate, isn't he."

"Oh, he's all right. He's a good bloke."

That night they revelled in the sheer joy of being in their own house, in the big new bed with the doors locked and curtains drawn, alone, the two of them, in their private heaven. After a voluptuous week, they were not too quick, the tender lovemaking was all the more delightful, and they immersed themselves in the ecstasy that came at last.

Afterwards, as they lay, still embraced, Willy said "Do you know, I make this fifteen, that's a rugby team." They laughed contentedly, and so close, that the laughter sent little pulses into both of them. "Anyway, I should think you've got your centre forward now."

Madge hugged him. "You're a darling, lots of men would have wanted to wait before starting a family."

"Well, I promised, didn't I."

"Yes, and you weigh a ton."

"Sorry, I like to stay a bit," said Willy, parting company and sighing happily as his arm encircled her and pulled her head on to his shoulder.

"Happy?"

"Umm, very." A long ten minutes passed. Willy was almost drifting asleep when Madge, with her face just below his chin, said, Willy are you very fond of Jerry?"

"Willy, still dozing, said "Yes, I suppose so, he's the only friend I've ever had."

"Yes, but do you like him very much?"

Willy's consciousness came swimming back from slumber, and he gave his wife a little hug. "Who wants to talk about Jerry tonight?" Being awake again, his free hand found something soft to hold. "Jerry's special, for a special reason, but tonight there's nobody in the world but you."

"What's the special reason?"

"Oh Madge, my lovely! What do you want to ask me that for tonight. This is our real first night, in our own bed; let Jerry be. I expect he's got someone to stop him feeling lonely. He's all right in his way of thinking, and now you've woken me up again, I'll prove it."

The next day, Sunday, what was left of the morning was taken up with doing things about the house and indulging themselves in the pleasure of their possessions, and the day went as a day should when a young couple have been married for just a week. When night came, they lay contentedly, holding close, and happy to do just that. After the exertions of the last night, they had been to bed again in the afternoon, and so were happy to lay in a languorous repose, talking, planning, and enjoying their close company.

"What's the special reason why Jerry's special?" Madge asked, suddenly.

Willy, content and at rest, did not mind the repeated question. "Well, if it wasn't for him, I wouldn't be here now."

Madge turned her face up to him.

"Tell me," she said.

"Oh'. It's quite a story, and he wouldn't want you to know."

"Never mind, tell me."

"Okay. You remember I wrote and told you that I went camping with him last summer. Well, I got caught in a current, when I was bathing, and if Jerry hadn't come in after me, I'd have been drowned. I was drowned really, Jerry hung on to me, and we both got dragged under, it was only by luck that a motor boat came along and a chap managed to get his boat hook into Jerry's bathers and hoick him up, and me.

Because he wouldn't let me go Jerry saved me. I don't remember anything until I came around on the sands, but there was a girl there, she was a nurse, and she told me afterwards, that the people in the boat said I was dead, but Jerry wouldn't give up, and in the end he brought me back to life. So that's why he's special, not only because he saved my life, but because he was willing to risk being drowned himself, rather than let me go, and then afterwards refusing to let me die, like the others would have done."

There was a silence. Madge had tightened her arms around him.

"You never told me."

"No, I thought you'd worry."

"Oh, dear God. And I was all out there, and I'd have had no one to come home to."

Willy hugged her. "I survived," he said. During the telling, something of the horror had come back to him, and he had taken his free arm away from her, and lay on his back, staring at the ceiling, seeing again the water closing over him and feeling his throat contract.

Madge held him close to her till the thoughts of what might have been receded, then she took his hand and placed it on her breast, and loving fingers traced a line down his body till her hand came to rest. "Then really, I owe Jerry; you."

"No. Well yes, but not really. You mustn't say anything to him. He asked me if I'd told you and I said I hadn't, and I promised him that I wouldn't. It's over and done with, and he'd be embarrassed. I know what I owe him, and some day, if I can, I'll do something for him, but I'm not making a thing of it."

"But why is he so fond of you? After all, saving your life was a spur of the moment act. I don't mean he wasn't brave, but other people might have done that, but he got us this house, and did it special, and the garden, all out of kindness - it's as if he loves you, like a brother, I mean."

"Well if you want to know what I think, I think he's lonely, He ought to be married, instead of 'picking up birds' as he puts it. You see, his old man was killed in the war, like my dad was, and he's only got his mother, and she's - well, they don't meet. He's very fond of her, worships her, in fact, I think, but well - she's a bad lot, and he can't get on with her. Don't ever tell him that mind. But he wants somebody to love, I suppose, and until he meets someone, he likes to be pals with me. By the way, I'll have to make sure I see him from time to time, or he'll think now I've got you, I don't want to know him any more."

"Poor Jerry, I always thought he was a happy-go-lucky person."

"He is, that's his nature, but he's got no family. That's why we got on; neither of us had a dad, or brothers and sisters, like you."

"I wonder why he hasn't married."

"Just hasn't met the right one, I suppose, and he's got a different way of looking at girls. He's a bit of a scamp really, like that. Anyway, I'm glad he introduced me to you, and didn't go after you himself."

Madge lay quietly, a question worried her thoughts, but it wasn't anything she could ask Willy.

Back at work, Willy savoured a new sense of maturity. He had broken the last link with his junior status, his boyishness. He was now a married man. Few men married, few could afford to marry till they were about thirty. Those who married earlier often had an urgent reason, forcefully presented by the bride's family. Willy felt a superiority over the callow youths of his acquaintance.

Val greeted his return with real pleasure. She was going to say, "Had a good time?" but realised, just as she was saying it, that it was an inappropriate query to make concerning a honeymoon, so lamely added, "Weather-wise?"

"Yes, glorious, it was a week in heaven, I recommend marriage to anyone. It's great!" Val's pretty face grew a little pink. She was hoping so much that her boyfriend would ask her to marry him. He was taking her out often, and had taken her home to meet his family, but he still remained casual and she couldn't make out if he had any real feelings for her.

When he arrived home that evening, and they had had their tea, Willy followed Madge into the kitchen. He stood behind her as she washed up at the sink, with his arms encircling her, his hands busy, and his lips caressing her head. She could feel him against her and protested that she would never get done if he didn't leave her alone. He gave her a squeeze and took the tea towel to dry the crockery.

"Jerry came in today."

"Oh, what did he want?"

"He said he was held up or something or other, and if you like he could get a couple of men to sort out the back garden."

"That would be a help. I've never done any gardening."

"Well, he said if you like to make a plan he'd get them to do it. He said you ought to get some ornamental trees and some hedging, unless you want to make it all for vegetables."

"No, I'll never have time. Let's make a plan now."

So they spent an hour, heads together, planning the garden. There was quite a bit of ground, and they gave the layout serious thought. "I'd like to have a tree here," said Madge, stabbing her pencil into a particular spot, "but not an evergreen, in case it makes the garden too dark in the winter."

"How about an apple tree or a pear?"

"No, I want something pretty. Remember those golden chain trees in the park? I'd like one of those."

"No'. The seeds are poisonous; I know that, and our football team would eat them and be sick."

"I think I'd like a walnut tree in the opposite corner, and a red May tree, how's that?"

"You must ask Jerry if his Medlar tree has survived. He fetched it from Plymouth you know, and planted it on the plot he's going to have."

"When does Jerry want to know?"

"He said he'd come in tomorrow morning. Is it all right if I make him a cup of tea when he comes?"

"Of course'. Make the bloke welcome!"

"I don't want to make him too welcome, I mean, I don't want him dropping in at any old time."

"Oh he won't, still, if he does, don't put him off. I expect he's glad to have a cup of tea and a chat."

"You said, last night, that he likes 'chatting up birds' and probably had someone to keep him from feeling lonely. Well, I like Jerry, he seems fun, and he's happy and good natured, but is he all right? I mean, he wouldn't try anything on, would he?"

"Madge! He's my best friend. He was my best man last week. We've been pals for years. You don't think he'd ever try anything on with my wife, do you? He's all right, he's a bit of a lad, I know, but he'd never do anything like that to me."

"All right then, only your mother told me she never trusted him, and I must say that I've noticed he's got a roving eye."

"Mum's never liked him, because of his mum, and because he lived in Well Street, but he's a true friend to me, and I'd trust him with anything, even with my dearest possession, that's you."

This conversation had come up because Madge had been a little apprehensive of Jerry after his call that morning. She had been in the kitchen on her knees, polishing the floor, when Jerry had walked in the back door. He must have seen her through the window, and opened the door suddenly, saying, "Boo." She saw at once that his eyes were on her neckline, and put a hand to her throat to hide what might be showing.

"How about a cup of tea, Missus?" Jerry had said, turning away and picking up the kettle, as if he did not doubt her welcome.

He turned back with his wide grin and she felt the compelling charm that he exuded. She liked him, he was a very likeable person, and they had a half hour's cheerful chatter, with Jerry poking fun at her about her housekeeping, and Willy, and this and that. Then he had proposed the garden, and Madge had thanked him with a genuine appreciation of his gesture. He had said, "Okay then, my darling I'll get on with it, soon's you give me a plan." And then "Don't I get a kiss today for looking after you?" She flushed. It wasn't the same as a spontaneous action, like yesterday, but she offered her cheek.

"I said, don't I get a kiss?" he said. Madge flushed again, but because there didn't seem any way to avoid complying, with dignity, she moved to kiss him. He held her loosely by the arms, and turned his face so that she kissed him on the lips. Then he looked her in the eyes and he saw her troubled feelings. She saw him flush scarlet but held her for a brief moment at arm's length, then said, "Sorry'. It was only meant in fun."

359

With that he had left and Madge found she was trembling. She had sat down and said "It wasn't meant in fun, either he was flirting, and then felt ashamed, or else he's a bit struck on me - Lord. I hope he isn't, it'll be difficult, I don't want to come between him and Will.

Jerry was quite shocked to find himself suddenly disturbed by Madge. He had never got emotionally involved with a girl before, and he felt dismayed and upset. There was something about Madge that appealed to him in a way that startled him. He was in the carefree habit of picking up girls, dallying a while, then slipping away for other game. He wasn't a bad man, there was nothing that was erotic or perverse in his behaviour. He was just healthy with a good appetite for his bodily needs. He didn't want a lasting liaison, and dropped, like a hot potato, any girl who showed designs upon him. After Dot, and his introduction to professional ladies, he realised that there was always someone ready to fill a need, either for mutual pleasure, or for profit. He found pleasure, without responsibility, an ideal way of life. Willy's fidelity to Madge had amused and exasperated him, and he refused to consider it right or sensible. He did wish, often, that Willy was not such a prude, so that he could have discussed with him his many adventures, but he had accepted Willy's opinions as being something inexplicable and foolish, but genuine. He had hoped to stampede him with the girl that Willy called 'Pooh' at their summer camp, but she had evidently not had the determined promiscuity of her friend, who had given him such a good time, or else Willy's innocence had overridden it. He had never been able to ask Willy, so he had no idea how near Willy had been to blotting his copybook, or how the girl had resisted him. It was when Madge had thanked him, on their arrival home, that he had first felt the stirring of this new feeling. At the wedding, Madge, in her bridal dress, had seemed virginal and untouchable - anyway, all Willy's, but now he was seeing Madge as a married woman, the wife of his best friend, and unattainable, and at once thought, ruefully - "Cor'. The lucky bugger, he knew what he was doing." Then, when he had gone to the house again, when he knew she would be alone, he had gone, drawn compulsively, not as he might have done to many another with the intention of a bit of slap and tickle, but because he wanted to see her, talk to her, be near her. When he had opened the door with a joke "Boo" he had done it to cover a feeling of diffidence. The sight of her kneeling, looking up all startled, with her white bosom half exposed, had confused him, and he had turned away to pick up the kettle so as to recover his composure. After that he behaved, he thought, in his usual way. But it was all an act, and he yearned to reach for her. When he asked for a kiss, it was blurted out against his real intent, and when he received it and saw how Madge was troubled, he felt ashamed, and left as soon as he could.

As he trudged away across the building sites, he said to himself, "Bloody hell. I'm in love with her. Gawd Almighty. I'll have to stay away from her, I can't do that to Will." But by the time he had reached his present work site, he was already planning how to spin out the gardening, to give himself an excuse to call again and again.

In the weeks that followed, Jerry became a frequent visitor to Willy's house. He usually managed to contrive to arrive at a time convenient for 'elevenses'. His behaviour was exemplary, or so he thought, and Madge had no reason to object. She told Willy, who said, "Good. I expect he enjoys a little break. He's got no real home to go to."

Madge got to waiting for his call, feeling disappointed if he failed to show up. He was always good for a laugh, and cheered up the day. Madge was careful to avoid getting too close to him, and was never provocative, for although he thought his mask never slipped, she sometimes caught his hungry eyes, peering through his laughter, pleading for her. "Oh. He'll get over it," she thought. "He can't be serious." She felt a little flattered too. She lavished all her love on Willy, and needed no one else.

So the months went by. Jerry's men had laid out the garden, but he still called for his elevenses whenever he could. He had come to terms with himself, and though he was still attracted to her by a great yearning, he never said or did anything to which she could object. In fact, he treated her with loving respect, like a beggar boy worshipping an unattainable princess. Madge really enjoyed his company. She would say to Willy, "Jerry's a scream, what do you think he said today?" Willy laughed contentedly from his impregnable possession of her love.

Gwen called often in the afternoons, and occasionally she found Jerry at the house. "What's he doing 'ere?" she'd wonder to herself. "I 'ope he's not up to anything." Then she would scold herself for implying that Madge would allow any 'goings on', but all the same, remind herself "He's his mother's son, and bad blood will out."

When the summer was gone, and the business of settling in to their new home was done with, Madge found the days too long. Willy had gradually slipped back into his weekend and evening work, and was seldom free until eight, or after, at night. Madge was lonely. She had made casual acquaintance with other new households, as they arrived, but had not, so far, found a friend amongst them. More and more, she looked forward to Jerry calling for a few minutes of cheerful chatter. Gwen called too, but it was quite a way for her to walk, so it was more often that Madge would visit her instead.

On one of those visits, Gwen had said something to the effect that Madge would soon have her day taken up with her baby., when it arrived.

"When it arrives." Madge had said. "How long did it take you to get pregnant with Willy?"

"Well, really," thought Gwen, who had never discussed such things with anyone before. Then she thought how nice it was to have intimate conversations at long last, and, having overcome her inhibitions she found herself happily gossiping about the only truly happy days of her life.

"We'd been married for more than two years before I conceived. We'd both stopped expecting anything to happen by then."

"So there is hope yet then?" said Madge.

"Good gracious girl, of course there is, you'll be having a houseful yet."

Chapter 23

Just at the start of the New Year of 1955, the Editor of the *Echo* caught a severe chill attending the funeral of a local bigwig. The Editor was a short, stout man with a thick neck and a barrel-shaped body. He was always 'chesty' and, having fortified himself with a tot of brandy, he had stayed shivering in his cold office, working for hours before going home, where he collapsed, wheezing and shivering. He developed pneumonia and three days later, he died.

The printers who owned and published the *Echo*, decided to run a few editions to satisfy the advertisers, and suggested that Willy should make sufficient copy to stretch the news for a week or two until they decided what to do about the paper. Faced with the challenge, Willy boldly approached his boss and asked for a couple of weeks off to make the paper viable. It may have been the confident way that Willy put his request, with the new authority that marriage had brought to his manner, but his boss agreed. Willy enjoyed producing those two editions. He wrote articles instead of bare reports. With the extra time then available, he ferreted about and found himself expanding his usual columns. The printers where impressed with what he had done, and when the second edition came up, as good, or better than the first, they called him in and congratulated him. Willy pointed out that he could not keep up the news flow with only evenings to gather it, and did not anticipate anything more than his old contribution. The next day, they contacted him again, and when he saw them, they suggested that he should take on the full time editorship. They wanted a quick decision. Willy took the news to Madge.

"Will that mean you'll be paid more, and not have to work such long hours?"

"I'll lose the money for my two columns, but I'll get three pounds more than I've been getting for my work at Luckhams, and for my columns. I'll be able to do my reporting and writing during the day -

well, most of it, so I'll have it much easier, I should think"

"You enjoy writing, don't you, and you've often said that you'd like to do nothing else, so if you feel confident, and will be happy, I say take it."

Willy made up his mind to do so, but before doing anything else he went to see Mr Watts to get his advice. The old man was pleased to see him. Willy was a rare visitor now that he was married.

Mr Watts ushered Willy into his sitting room. "Mother," he called, It's Will Churchward come to see us."

Willy gave his news. Mrs Watts listened intently, then, "I wondered what what happen to the *Echo*. Of course, it's only a local rag, but it serves a need, and it has always been a model of good journalism. Very conservative of course, none of the flamboyance of the popular press but a good paper nonetheless. It will hardly make you another Beaverbrook, but who can say what opportunities it may present. I've told you, often, that you should widen your horizons, for you have the ability to go far. Now, if you take on the paper, what will you do? Gradually become fossilised in the local tittle tattle, or will you use it as a stepping stone to one of the great dailies. That's where you belong."

"I don't think I need decide that now. The immediate question is, should I leave my job at Luckhams and take on the *Echo*? I've really decided to do so, and Madge agrees, but I would appreciate your opinion."

"There is no question, boy. Take it, and use it for your own advantage. How many men of your age, what twenty-three? How many have even a senior position on a local paper, much less the editorship!"

The next day Willy asked his boss to spare him a moment. He was waved to the 'clients' chair. His boss pursed his lip and polished his spectacles.

"I have been offered a job producing the *Echo*, Sir," said Willy, "and I've been asked for a quick decision."

"Are you asking my advice, or are you giving me your notice?"

Willy was feeling very uneasy. He had spent eight relatively happy years working for this man who had given him an unasked for rise when he married a few months previously, and had let him take the past two weeks off, for the sake of the paper. He felt a certain disloyalty about leaving his employ.

"I feel, Sir, that it is an opportunity that I should make use of."

"I entirely agree. I anticipated that you might be offered the position, when you approached me a fortnight ago. I'm not unaware of the value you have been to the *Echo*, and I've admired your industry, and I must admit, your work. In fact, you've been making a name for yourself, and I'm surprised that you haven't gone to a more prestigious publication before this. However, for a chap of your age, this is a good opportunity, and I will be happy to see you take it. When do you want to go?"

Willy was quite overwhelmed by this praise, and this glimpse of the man, behind the employer, was very satisfying.

"As soon as I may, Sir."

"Yes, of course, you'll have your work cut out to get the paper out his week. You'd better go at once. I'm sorry to lose you, you've been a very dependable clerk and now I'll have to find another, but that's my problem. Just clear up anything that you've started, then go as soon as you will. Come and see me again before you leave."

The senior clerk congratulated Willy, and, for once, made no insinuating remarks. Val wept. She was very fond of Willy and was dismayed to know that he was leaving.

"Never mind," he said, "when you get your coalman to make up his mind I'll give your wedding a two column headline - and I'll print a picture of his horse and cart!"

When Gwen heard the news, she could only gasp in astonishment and say over and over again, "Well, I never did." Her Willy becoming the Editor of the *Echo*.

The town was growing so fast, that the close community fellowship was being diluted by the many immigrants from the Midlands, and North, that having come to Paignton for a summer holiday, had gone back to their grim hometowns, sold up whatever possessions they had, and returned to buy houses, to run as holiday accommodation, or to open shops to cater for the summer visitors. There was still a solid core of professional and commercial stalwarts, who tended to look on the new residents as foreigners, and their regard was tinged by resentment of the way they attacked the unhurried pace of life in their new surroundings, disturbing the somnolent Sundays with lighted shop windows and open shops, wherever the law allowed. Some, with no more than a year or two of residence, even managed to get themselves elected to serve on the Urban District Council, where their strident accents offended the native ears like the new mechanical tools that rent the peace of the town. The old guard closed ranks, not in battle order, but to give themselves protection from the upsurge of strangers, who were having the audacity to call themselves natives.

Willy, in his new capacity of newspaper man, stepped into this arena with ease. He was born and bred in the town, and his speech had the unmistakable sound of Devon. He was known already to most of the traders and merchants of the town, and there was no society, association or club, that had not made his acquaintance. So he was welcome and accepted. He had, during his years at Luckhams, known the newcomers, through their legal business. He had grown used to the abrasive Scots voice, that had at first been hardly understandable. These folk were mostly interested in guest houses. When he first encountered a client from the border country, whose broad Geordie accent might as well have been German for all that he could fathom it, he had felt something of the Southerner's contempt. But, on closer knowledge, he found the initiative and drive of these people mildly exciting, and it amused him to see them 'putting a bomb' under the complacent backsides of some of the pompous locals.

He had already ingratiated himself into the several societies that these expatriots had set up. The Lancastrian Association, the Ebor Club, the Welsh Society, the Birmingham, the London, the Scottish, all the little groups who met in little strongholds amongst the distrusting natives. He had reported their annual general meetings, their social nights, their fundraising activities, and so found himself welcome, though at times he had felt that he should have approached under cover of a white flag. He rapidly became a well known citizen, and his paper reflected his interest in the town. He instituted a column that he entitled, "Dear Sir, I think..." in which he posed a question of local interest and invited readers to give their opinions. There was a new sports section too and angling news as well as all the regular reports of social events, council meetings, chamber of trade and so on.

After a few months, the circulation showed a considerable improvement. The paper became thicker, because the publishers made a successful advertising drive, and Willy, with ideas for expansion, requested more assistance.

Until then, he and the typist, had managed on their own. The publishers provided him with a beery individual, who had worked for the daily evening paper, published in Torquay and serving the three towns. Willy was not impressed, but at least he was able to do all the routine reporting, and was able to spend more time in the deeper waters of local politics. He and Madge were familiar figures at all the social functions, and Madge glowed with pleasure at the deference shown her as Willy's wife.

"He's a real Mr Importance." she said to Jerry. Jerry roared with laughter at some of Willy's mannerisms, and Madge laughed with him, not at Willy, for she loved him too much, but about him, in a loving way. She was immensely proud of him, and of her home, and their new car (one of the new Morris Minors) and of the social status she enjoyed. She could not help comparing him to Jerry. Jerry was doing all right. He was a prosperous builder, but still a craftsman who used his skills and saved his profits for the big one, that would come once his present commitments where done. Willy, with his good suits, his leather brief case, his well-oiled hair and highly polished shoes; Jerry with his muddy overalls, leather-beaten skin, tousled hair and clumping wellingtons.

Willy, with his well considered opinions, his precise speech; Jerry with his light-hearted banter, his colloquial phrases, his sometimes, broad dialect. Willy with his loving arms, his hungry lips, his satisfying body; Jerry, with his eyes that laughed, to hide their longings, his strictly disciplined desire. Jerry was fun. "Poor Jerry." she thought. "He's a naughty boy, but he makes me laugh." She needed laughter sometimes, for month by month, the years were passing and no family came into being, and her longing for a child became desperate at times. She took to visiting the little prep school where she had spent a few months before her marriage. She was not concerned with the meagre pay that she had received then, but found herself welcome as a voluntary child minder. She bandaged grazed knees, cuddled away the tears of forlorn little boys, and found some solace for her yearning maternity in their warm little bodies.

She had suggested to Willy that they should adopt a baby. She had done so on a cold night when they were huddled together, to get themselves warm, after bouncing into bed and kicking the hot water bottles down to the bottom. They shivered against the cold sheets and warmed their hands, under their arms, between their legs, until they could fondle in comfort.

Madge had been up the road that afternoon to visit a young woman with whom she had struck up an acquaintance. They where much of an age, and talked woman talk. The other girl had confided in Madge, that she was expecting. This had led to Madge telling of her frustration and longing. They had gone into the reasons, or non reasons, and eventually the girl had said, "Well, after three years you should have been lucky. Why don't you adopt one? They say, if you do, you conceive yourself, right away." They had got warm and done their loving, when Madge made the suggestion. She was lying on her back, staring at the moonlit rectangle of the window. Willy was drowsy and would soon be asleep.

"Will. Do you think we'll ever have a baby?"

"Eh? Oh, I expect so," said Willy, struggling out of somnolence.

Madge prodded his ribs with an elbow. "Will, it's been years now. I want a family, like we planned. It's not me, Will. I've been to the doctor and he's told me that I'm built for child-bearing. You must do something. I want children of my own. I've got to have them."

"Madge, love, what can I do, more than we've done already? It just hasn't happened, that's all."

"That's not all. It's not going to happen by the look of it. Will, could we adopt a baby?"

"Oh no, darling, not someone else's. We'd never feel the same. I wouldn't anyway."

"I'm serious dear. I'm not blaming you, or anything, but I must have children. It's what I've lived for the last ten years - a family of my own."

There was a long silence. The silence of the night was complete as though the elements were sleeping too. Willy, wide awake, felt her misery settling on him. He turned to her, slipped his hand into the top of her nightie and squeezed gently. It was an almost automatic act, and usually Madge's hand would respond, but she lay quite still, and he leant over and kissed her face. It was wet with tears.

"Oh, Madge we'll have a family, of course we will, there can't be any reason why not. I'm healthy and we do it often enough. I'll go to the doctor to see if there's anything I can do to hurry it up. Let me do that, then we'll see, eh?"

"All right. Go to sleep, I know you're tired." Willy was soon asleep. Madge lay on, wide-eyed and miserable.

Willy did go to his doctor, who sent him to the big new hospital at Torquay where he had to do something into a test tube, and pass it, shame-facedly, to a woman in a white overall, for processing. Days later, his doctor told him that there should not be any reason why he could not become a father, just to keen on trying. "Don't wait until you go to bed," he told Willy. "Anytime you both feel in the mood, is the time."

"We do," said Willy.

"Oh," said the doctor, (thinking of the couple of times a year when he was lucky). Well, good luck!"

"Let's try for a while yet," he suggested to Madge after telling her his doctor's advice. "Then we'll think about adoption."

Meanwhile at work, Willy had been inviting various people to write for the *Echo* on subjects of local interest and one such, a young medical student from Edinburgh, whose home was in Paignton, came to his office with an account of a walking holiday that he and two friends, had just completed in Germany. It was not just a diary of their walk, it was a disturbing account of the rising power of the Brown Shirts, led by Adolph Hitler, and a warning of the danger of the Nazi party flowing out of Germany to regain territories lost in the Great War, and of the writer's opinion, that a new German eagle had arisen to threaten the whole of Europe, Great Britain included. The young man had slapped the typewritten sheets on to Willy's desk, telling him that he had already been to *The Times*, the *Telegraph* and the *Express*, but none had the guts to print it. "I've sent a copy to Winston Churchill - by the look of the articles in the *News of the World*, he's the only man - who seems to see any danger. Now, you print it, I know it's only a local, but once it's in print, it will get picked up by others. Print it. Show you care for the peace of the world. Make somebody sit up and take notice."

Willy looked at the young man with the fervour of a zealot shining from his eyes. "One of these political tub thumpers," he thought. "It's an interesting article," he said, "but my paper isn't political, it's just a medium for local events and opinions about them. If I started concerning the paper with national news, it would change the whole format. People buy the national dailies for that, they don't want local opinions. Also, if the national press has returned your manuscript, it would seem they either don't consider it accurate, or they have better means of evaluating the situation themselves."

"All right, don't print it, don't bother to take your head out of the sand. When you're up to your waist in mud and blood, in another Passchendale, remember that you couldn't be bothered to strike a warning, even a feeble one, when you had the chance."

The man seemed so genuine that Willy stopped him when he began to gather up his papers. "Hang on. Look, I'll make something of it. You've got me thinking. I'll not promise to print the lot, but I'll make something of it if you will be satisfied with that."

"Okay. Look! I haven't made this up. You and I will be in khaki before the end of this decade, and God only knows what will have happened to the country by then."

Willy read the article again. Seeing through the careful apprisals, the marching armies, the persecution of the Jews, the adulation, or was it adoration, of Hitler by the besotted youth of the nation, held (he thought) not 'like greyhounds in the leash', but like wolves, ready to 'Come down like the Assyrians, on the fold'. Willy was impressed by the forceful arguments the man had put forward for preparing the nation for this new German threat. He felt alarmed too. In order to keep himself informed of current events, he read *The Times* and *Express* every day, and had noticed many articles on the same subject. None of them had been so explicit in their threats, and after reading them, Willy had disregarded them.

He took the article to Mr Watts, now retired, but still a font of advice. The old man read the article, put the sheets carefully into the folder, then looked up at Willy with a bleak, weary expression. "Oh God. Are we to endure that again," he said, more to himself than to Willy.

"Do you think there is anything in it, Sir?"

"Yes, my boy, I do. The signs are there for all to see. This young man thinks he has made a discovery. He's only seen what many have seen, and written about, before him. You can't print this. You would be laughed at, abused, and be called a scaremonger, if you did. The public don't want to know. They deceive themselves into thinking that with our Empire we're invincible, and look on this man Hitler, as a loud-mouthed idiot.

"I've read an abridged version of his *Mein Kamph*, and it's all in there. Britain will do nothing until he makes his first move, then, pray God, it will not be too late. Willy sat in shocked silence, gazing, almost unbelievably, at the old man. Do I sound like an alarmist? Well, open your eyes to read the signs. Remember those articles you wrote for *Answers* years ago. Your second series, 'A Boy in the Woods' - I came across a draft of one a while ago, telling how you tracked a badger to its holt, all the tell-tale signs you saw - well, look for signs now. Look at the River Dart. Have you been to Dartmouth lately?"

"Yes, this week."

"What did you see, or what did you not see?"

Willy pondered the question. "The Bibby Ships weren't there."

"No, but it's the trooping season, they wouldn't be there anyway."

Willy thought again, then his face lit up. "All the merchantmen have gone."

"Yes. Right'. And how many were there? Twenty, thirty, forty - or more, moored two-abreast right up as far as Greenway. Where have they gone, and why? They've been there for years, some of them. Ever since the beginning of the slump back in the mid-twenties. They've been going a few at a time for quite a while, but they're not going back into service they've gone for scrap. Japan seems the biggest market, she's desperate for steel for her conquest of China, then Germany and our own steel makers the whole world is buying steel. I read the *Financial Times*, not to watch my investments, for I haven't any, but to feel the pulse of the nation."

"How is that, Sir?"

"Will, my boy, it's money rules the world. The state of the stock market tells more of the hopes and fears of mankind than any posturing politician. There is a war brewing. Pray God it can be avoided, but the die is almost cast Germany has risen from the ashes, and degradation, of the Great War. She is impoverished, hedged in, controlled by restrictions set up at the end of the war. A new generation, your generation, has grown up and they demand freedom to expand.

"They see themselves as a nation reborn. Hitler is a puppet in the hands of the great industrialists, who see no future without conquest, and he has gathered around him a cadre of opportunists that will stop at nothing to see Germany powerful again. They are a nation of great genius too, and must be respected. Just look at their battleships. After the war a limit was imposed on the size and weight of warships that they might want to build. It was considered that anything they could build within those limits would be puny compared to our vast ships. Now look they've got what we've dubbed 'pocket' battleships. New designs, new everything, capable of matching our ships, out-pacing them, out-firing most of them; and the airforce - they're not supposed to have one, but it is thought to be larger than our own, and more modern. As for tanks, there has been so much nonsense written about wooden tanks, built to boost the morale and deceive other nations, that German tanks have become a music hall joke, but there was an article in *The Times* recently, from a very knowledgeable source, that set a figure of fifteen hundred ultra-modern vehicles, capable of out-pacing and out-gunning anything we've got, and it is thought that we have less than a hundred."

Mr Watts stopped talking. He looked tired and unhappy. Willy sat opposite him, serious and concerned.

"When do you think it might start?"

"When they're ready. The only thing that will Stop them will be for the rest of Europe to be ready too; and they're not, nor will be. France has built the Maginot Line. Nothing can cross it, it's impregnable, they say. Have they never heard of aeroplanes? Then there's Spain. Germany is already there. Spain is devastated by the civil war, she is an open base for Germany. And Italy. Italy has got a huge trained army, from the Abyssinian war. She's got bases on the African continent. What will Italy do under Mussolini? Stay neutral? Join Germany more likely'. For any pickings she can get. Then look East. Poland and the Polish corridor - Germany is itching to get that back. The more you think, the more certain it becomes."

"Oh Lord," said Willy. "I hadn't a clue it was that serious. But surely, if you can see it all, others can. What about the government?"

"Oh, they're a bunch of weaklings. There's no one of courage and valour. They think that if they do nothing, they can keep out of the argument. They cannot, of course, but there is no great statesman to rally the nation. They're afraid. They'll 'wait and see', as Asquith used to say. There is just a glimmer of sense, probably in the War Office or the Admiralty or the Air Force. They got a one thousand million for defence in the last budget, so someone is awake somewhere."

After the conversation with Mr Watts, Willy felt very worried. Was there a war impending? If so, what would happen to him, and therefore Madge? Could he be called up to fight? He felt a sudden clutch to his insides, when he remembered that his father had been killed in the Great War. He said nothing to Madge. "Let's forget it for now", he told himself. He did publish part of the young man's article. He headed it 'Local Man's Tour of Germany - Some Disturbing Sights', and made a precis of his observations, playing down the most controversial parts.

As news gatherer, and editor, Willy did not see the layout of the paper, that was done by the printers. When he received his copy that week there was, by a coincidence, an advertisement by the local council, of a course for volunteers, for instruction in air raid precautions, and the announcement that an A.R.P. organisation was to be set up.

Since his talk with Mr Watts, Willy's gloom had lifted. There seemed to be no sign of any alarm anywhere, and life went on as usual, but seeing the advertisement, all his forebodings came rushing back. He had been out on business that took him near home, so he called in, as he usually did, for a cup of tea or just a little word or two with Madge. That day she was out when he called. He wandered through the house and in to the back garden. The bulbs were nearly out and buds were showing on the bushes. Coal tits where busy on the bird table, everything was normal, but the black cloud of worry sat heavily on him. He was just leaving again, when Jerry's whistle made him turn. It was their code whistle. They had used it since boyhood.

Willy looked round and saw Jerry leaning from the window frame of an unfinished house across the cul-de-sac. Willy walked over to him. Jerry leaned out of the window. "Haven't seen you for ages. How's the Press Lord getting on?"

Willy went inside and they chatted about the progress of the buildings. The road was nearly finished, and Jerry's own house was under construction. "I dunno if I'll ever move in," he told Willy. "That'll mean having to have a housekeeper, or someone call in every day. 'course, I'd reckon on getting Mum to pack up and come and live with me, but she's not keen. He screwed up his eyes, drew in his cheeks and bit his lower lip, then sighed, and in the old, confidential way of their boyhood, said: "I wrote to her, 'cos she told me not to call, and asked her to phone what she thought. Blimey! You know what? She turned me down flat. Said she didn't want to play housekeeper to me for the rest of her life. Said she's doing all right. Cor! She's been to the South of France with some bloke, had a whale of a time. Monte Carlo, the lot She says she's quite okay where she is, stashing away enough to look after herself when she's old, so thank you Jerry, but forget it."

Jerry's mother was always an embarrassing subject between them, and Willy sought to change the subject. "Well, why on earth don't you get married? Good heavens. You know enough girls, you shouldn't have any difficulty in finding someone you could settle down with." Jerry was screwing the hinges on to a door, and spoke with his back to Willy.

"Oh, I could do that all right," he said, but I left it too late. Someone else has got her."

"Oh.' You mean the one you took to the carnival last year, and ran around with all winter - I saw her photograph recently in the *Echo*, at her wedding."

Jerry went on with his screwing, careful not to deny Willy's supposition. "Well, we all make mistakes," he said.

"Never mind there's plenty more fish in the sea - as you told me once." I can certainly recommend the state of matrimony.

"Yes," said Jerry. "I bet you can." He didn't seem to want to continue the subject further, remaining bent over the door, marking out the hinges, and gauging the recess with a chisel. Willy went to the window frame and looked across towards his home.

"Jerry, do you read the papers much?"

"When I get time, I do. I read the *News of the World* on Sundays."

"You would'. What I was wondering was, do you worry about the German Nazis."

"Naaw. That lot of tripe. It's all newspaper talk. They just like dressing up and marching about, pushing people around like old Moseley's lot here. They just want kicking up the arse."

"Some people think there's going to be a war."

Ah, you know what it is, a lot of people who want to be important, trying to stir up trouble. I don't bother with 'em.

"What will you join if there is one, Army, Navy or Air Force?"

Jerry straightened up and looked at Willy in surprise. "You're not serious?"

"Yes, I am. '

"Get out.' There's not going to be any war, why the hell should there?"

"I never gave it a serious thought till a week ago, now every day I notice something that says there will be. I feel worried. You and I both had our old men killed in the last one. I'm trying to believe it's all a scare, but I can't convince myself."

"Blimey'. You're cheerful'. Oh, forget it. There's nothing you could do anyway."

"Except get killed!"

"God Almighty'. What's the matter with you? Look, there's Madge. Go on over and get her to cheer you up."

"All right, see you again," said Willy, running down the stairs and crossing the plantation to join Madge. Jerry watched them meet, saw them kiss and go indoors together. "Hell," he said to himself'. "He's got her, and all he can do is belly-ache about there might be a war."

Willy and Madge were going through an unhappy period of their marriage. Their courtship, full of frustration had blossomed into what promised to be an idyllic marriage. Willy had prospered, and the future was so bright it had dazzled them for the first few months. Then came the constant disappointment of Madge failing to conceive a child. This grew so frustrating for her that it was robbing their lovemaking of its spontaneous delight.

Madge was convinced that Willy was to blame, and felt a resentment that made her miserable because she knew that he couldn't help it, and that she was making him feel inadequate and a failure. He was so kind and loving that his every caress was a reproach to her complaints. She was just as sensuous as ever, but was giving herself to him with the fierceness of despair, rather than the voluptuousness of love, and it troubled her a lot, and Willy too.

He had long since ceased to comment on his enforced celibacy for the few days each month, but lying beside her then, with unspoken resentment hanging like a barrier between them, he remembered only too vividly, how she used to compensate him on those occasions, and how she had not needed to be asked; it was all a part of their joyous marriage, and he felt depressed and miserable. Sometimes, if he had not known, and reached for her, only to have his hand pushed away, they would turn back to back and go to sleep without even a goodnight to each other, but both longing to turn and hold each other in their arms.

The question of adopting a baby was ever a source of worry too. Willy was not at all keen. He felt it would only emphasise his failure as a husband, and also he recoiled from the idea of fathering the offspring of some other couple's philandering. He wanted his own child. Madge was not happy about it either. She had had her fill of other people's babies and longed for her own. But she would have welcomed the opportunity, had it come, but it didn't. If she wanted to adopt a child, she would have to find it. The positive action required was hard to make without Willy's co-operation, freely given. So the matter stayed unresolved, while Willy ate and drank various nourishing foods, recommended in a book that Madge had bought.

He did exercises and tried his hardest whenever he could but it was becoming a chore rather than a pleasure and he seldom stayed to kiss the love light from her eyes afterwards. Then came the worry of an impending war. What would happen? What should he do? If he joined up, or was made to join up, what would Madge do? Had he any right to adopt a child, only to leave Madge to bring it up unaided? And under what circumstances? He said nothing to Madge about the latest worry, and when he lay sleepless beside her, she sometimes suffered miserably, thinking that his light breathing, betraying his wakefulness, was the sound of his unhappiness and she would reach out and give him a comforting squeeze to reassure him of her love. Sometimes he hadn't the heart to respond, then Madge, too, would lay wakeful in the dark.

The spring of '37 reached out to the summer that faltered, making the coming of autumn almost a surprise, when summer had hardly been known, then it was winter, and a chill foreboding seemed to lurk in its early frosts and tearing winds. For those with eyes to see, there was no doubt now of the looming disaster across the channel. Slowly, almost imperceptibly, the nation was being aroused. Article after article appeared in the intellectual papers. Questions were asked in parliament and answered with soothing phrases, but the bright boys in industry were looking around to see how they had best begin to stockpile the right things, and others were digging in, where no recruiting agency would find them. The public still couldn't be bothered to think seriously and those in command sang them a constant lullaby, while they whistled in the dark to cheer their frightened souls. The brave battled on to force the situation into the light of day. Only fools mocked Hitler. Even the most wooden headed had to believe the enormous strength of the German forces.

The popular press had found the Nazis made news, but even so a lethargy lay over the land. "It'll never come to war," was the general opinion. "Why should it? What's it to do with us?"

The old soldiers remembered 1914-18 and felt a certain quickening of the spirit. For most of them it would not be their war this time, but they were the ones that had come back, and they sniffed the martial air, and felt again their youth. The generation born since, thought little of their fathers' tales, and scoffed at the idea of hostilities. "Nobody would be so bloody daft," they said, and "we still have the navy, haven't we? Nobody's going to come over here past them. Let them get on with it. It's not our business." Somewhere though, wheels were beginning to turn, electronic miracles were beginning to leave the drawing boards for the industrial womb that would deliver them, in the years to come, in the great travail that brought victory. Britain won the Schneider Trophy, with the tiny seaplane, that would, in time, gain immortal fame as the Spitfire, and the navy started to study all the plans and schemes laid by, during the years of indolence, against the time of need.

Paignton, like any other town in the land, was unperturbed and disinterested. The local affairs ran their usual unexceptional ways. Nothing seemed to happen at all. Willy's paper grew in circulation, more because of the steady increase of population than anything else, but he was happy with it, and took pride in the diversity of its interests, and the way that he was welcomed by the town's whole society. He had extended his news columns to embrace the villages nearest to the town, and found a new fund of interest for his readers. He and Madge attended all the main social functions and together they were building up a circle of friends that seemed likely to make them popular figures wherever they went. Willy kept in touch with Val and her parents, and sometimes met them socially.

The day came when he and Madge were invited to a supper dance at Dellers, when Val's engagement was celebrated. After toasts had been drunk to their happiness, and speeches were done, Val had come over to them with her fiance, and had put her arms around Willy's neck, and kissed him, saying, "That's for all I owe you," and then, turning to Madge, said "I'll always be grateful to your Will, I owe him so much." And her young man had laughed, and said, "Well, that's all he's getting."

Madge, who knew something of Val's story, didn't feel jealous, she just thought, "He's so good and kind, everybody likes him, I'm lucky to be his wife," and then thought, "I'll be extra good to him tonight."

Next day, when Willy was at work, Jerry appeared at Madge's window, as he did most days, making a gesture with his hand, as if drinking a cup of tea. Madge called him in, happy to see his cheerful grin.

"Have a good time last night?"

"Yes, fine, they put on a good spread. All the usual crowd were there."

"She's a smashing kid, isn't she?"

"Um, yes, I suppose so."

"Go on, you know she is. I dunnow how old Will didn't go for her. You know, I used to be amazed by the way he never got anyone else while you were away. He had chances you know, I mean he took that kid out several times, and I mean to say, well, you must admit she's a humdinger. But he never even kissed her goodnight afterwards, much less try to get her into the back seat. I know for a fact, he didn't, 'cause I asked her down at the office one day. I told her she'd not have got away with it with me or anyone else. You know what she said? 'Ah, but then Willy's in love with his Madge and he doesn't see anyone else.' That's love for you."

Madge flushed with pride. She understood Willy and was grateful for his fidelity. Then a little feeling of guilt crept in for she knew that he wasn't as happy as he used to be, neither was she, but that, she thought was her own fault, and she shouldn't make Willy miserable.

"Penny for them," said Jerry, looking at her over the top of his tea mug. Madge blushed deep red, looking very embarrassed at being caught out unawares. "I was just thinking how good he is to me."

Jerry kept his face half hidden behind the mug, his fingers wrapped round it, letting the hot mug warm them. "You're not all that happy lately, are you," he stated, rather than questioned. "Have you had a row over something?"

"No we haven't and I'm not unhappy."

"Yes you are, so's Will, I can tell. Well, it's no business of mine, but I don't like to see it. You were made to laugh and love, not to mope, like you been doing lately. Whatever it is, you ought to sort it out 'fore it gets serious."

Madge had turned away while he spoke, annoyed at his impertinence, and when she turned to look at him again, she intended to tell him off for his cheek, but her eyes were tear filled.

"Oh Gawd. Don't cry girl. I didn't mean to upset you."

Madge covered her face.

"Is there anything I can do?"

Madge shook her head, and sniffed into her hands. Jerry leaned over her. "Madge, please, I'd do anything for you, whatever the trouble, you can rely on me. I'll help, honest I will." Gently, he placed his hands on her shoulders, feeling the warmth of her body. A dreadful craving came over him to take her in his arms and kiss her fears away. He stood there, stooped over her, gently kneading her shoulders, waiting for some response. Madge was very aware of his nearness. She could smell the tang of sawn timber that hung about his overalls, and felt the strength of his hands. She had heard the emotion in his voice, and had not dared to look up.

"He loves me too," she thought, I know he does, I wish he didn't." Then, after the moment's trauma, she looked up, grinned a wan smile, and stood up.

Jerry stepped away from her and smiled back. "That's better," he said:. "It can't be that bad, so cheer up, and I'm sorry I butted in."

"It's all right, I don't mind. Sometimes I think you're a part of Will he thinks so much of you."

"Oh well, we've had our times. Will's one of the best."

"I know, that's why I don't like to see him worried."

"Well, is there anything I can do? I mean it. Is it this war that he's worried about?'

"War. What war?"

"Oh, it's the Nazis'. He's had a go at me several times these last few months. Takes them very seriously. 'course, he reads all the papers. I don't get time, so I don't know. But he reckons there'll be a war, and we'll be in it."

"He's never said a word, how could there be a war? We're not involved in anything, are we?"

"I don't know, Madge, but he seems to think so, and he's worried. Still, if he hasn't said anything to you, perhaps I shouldn't have done, so forget it."

"No, please Jerry, I'm glad you did. I thought I was making him unhappy."

"How could you possibly..."

"Oh, I could and I have."

"Well make it up to him tonight. Tell the lucky beggar how lucky he is, then prove it to him."

Madge laughed with relief. "Thank you, Jerry, you've helped me a lot."

"Well, if there is anything, just ask. I'd be doing it for Will."

That evening, Willy was out reporting on a political meeting, and did not get home till after nine. Madge looked hard at him when he came in. He looked tired, she thought, and low spirited. He was past eating a meal and flopped into his chair by the fireside. Madge knelt on the hearth rug, placed her arms on his knees and rested her chin on them. Willy smiled down at her, and ran his hand over her head, threading her dark hair through his fingers, then gently pulling the lobe of her ear. "I'll have some bread and cheese and a Guinness," he told her.

Madge did not move. She looked into his face with steady eyes. "We're going to talk tonight," she said. We've been letting something come between us, and I want to know what it is."

Willy sighed. "I hope there won't ever be anything that spoils us."

"But there is, you're miserable, and depressed, and you look all lined and tired.

"No I don't, I need a shave, that's all."

"No, it isn't, even Jerry's noticed."

"Jerry'. What's he been saying?"

Madge got up. "First of all some food," she said. "Then we can talk."

When he had eaten, Willy felt, and looked, more cheerful. He moved to the settee and patted the seat for Madge to join him.

"Right then, said Madge, "what's worrying you?" Willy blew out his cheeks and grimaced.

Madge cuddled up to him "What's this about war? Jerry says you're worried, are you? Is that what it is?"

"Yes, I am, but I didn't want to worry you. It may not happen."

I've been unhappy too - if you'd noticed. I thought it was me, nagging you you about me not having a baby."

"No. Silly girl. Of course I'm sorry about that but it will happen one day. No, I'm concerned about what will happen if there is a war, and it looks as if there will be one unless someone does something. Madge, love, I've been talking to some people tonight, after the meeting. I may as well tell you, it's got to be faced. Do you know, they've even got plans for rationing food, and evacuating cities. There's all sorts of plans and preparations going on. I'm amazed. There was a chap there from Exeter and he'd got it all off pat. It's only a question of time he reckoned and there's not much of that left. He reckoned a year at most. Madge, my love, it gave me the creeps. I thought of you, and what would happen. I suppose I'll be called up and I'll have to go."

Madge had sat silent while Willy was talking, his arm around her, her head on his shoulder, her bosom soft against his chest. When he stopped speaking, she looked up, her face white with shock. She looked at Willy, her eyes beseeching him to deny all he had said, but she read the certainty in his face, and tears gushed on to her cheeks. Willy held her tight, saying nothing for a while, then, when her shocked weeping quietened, he said, "I didn't want to worry you, my precious, I wouldn't have, if you hadn't asked."

Then Madge sat up, away from him and poured out her incredulity. "Why doesn't everybody know? Why don't the papers tell about it? Why isn't it on the wireless? There's no sign of any war anywhere, everything's just the same as always. How did those men know, when nobody else did?"

"Well, said Willy, "I've read articles warning of the German threat, and all that, and some people were saying that a war was coming, but I was just as shocked as you, when I heard what was said tonight. It seems that the government doesn't want to alarm people, and doesn't want to let the Germans think that we expect them to start a war, in case they blame us, or something, and they hope, anyway, to be able to keep out of it, if there is one, so nothing is being said, and the papers are playing along.

The chap from Exeter reckoned that they're yellow, anyway, and dead scared. He reckoned we ought to have an election and get someone to take a firm line with Hitler."

There was another long silence. Madge tucked her legs under her and put her arm around Willy's shoulders, drawing his head into the hollow of her throat. She smoothed his hair back from his forehead, and traced the line of his eyebrow with her finger.

"Would you have to go?"

"I suppose my job at the *Echo* isn't that important. Not like mining, or farming, or making munitions." (A strange word that, 'munitions' It came so readily to his tongue. It brought back memories, long submerged, from his childhood. He suddenly recalled his mother, and a friend, sitting by the window in the cottage, bitterly complaining of the good fortune of the 'munition workers', that made their widowhood doubly bleak.

"What will yóu do?"

"I can't say, not yet, I must think about it."

"Will?"

"Yes love."

"I'm sorry I've been so unkind to you lately. I never thought you had any worry except me."

"That's all right," said Willy, kissing her throat, and breathing in the warm, sweet air, that rose from her bosom.

"Yes, but - Will. Oh God, Will! If you have to go, and anything happens, I won't have anything of you, not anything."

"Oh Lord, Madge - everyone doesn't get killed. I'll be back. We don't even know what'll happen yet, so we may be worrying needlessly. Anyway (using a brighter tone), we'll keep on trying, eh?"

His hand cupped her plumpness and he kissed her throat again. She took his hand and placed it between her thighs, where the satin smooth flesh cherished it. They sat a long time, in silence, then moved upstairs. They didn't try that night. Willy could not respond, and they lay sleepless for hours, thinking.

The weeks that followed, saw them regain their happiness. They were both more conscious of 'war talk' in the papers and on the wireless, but it seemed concerned with Spain and Eriteria, and neither of them related their lives, to the terrible things reported from there, and looking about them, life continued so normally, that the sudden shook that had so distressed them that night, gradually faded into an uneasy calm. It had brought them together again though, and Jerry watched their obvious affection with an empty, longing, envy.

During the summer of '38, Jerry finished building his section of the estate. He had done very well out of it, and was in a sound financial position. He had an option on another ten plots, further up the estate. Prime plots that overlooked the golf course that had been constructed on his boyhood fields of oats and wheat. He talked of this to Willy. He was sprawled in front of Willy's hearth, with a bottle of Watneys, half emptied beside him, and the inevitable Players curling smoke through his fingers. He called in, of an evening, quite often those days. He was sensible enough to call only when Willy was at home, usually ringing up first with, "Hello love, the boss in tonight? What's the chances of a bit of your cooking?"

He was living in his house by then. It had stood empty for some months, then the husband of the woman with whom he had lodged for so long, died, and Jerry had persuaded her to move in with him as his housekeeper.

"You know me, and I know you and I can trust you, can't I me old darling," he had said. She had always made him comfortable, and was tolerant of his promiscuity. Her memory stirred pleasantly at his 'goings on', and she found nothing to criticise in the various girls who had appeared, half scared, at her door; then to scamper quietly as they could, upstairs. "Good luck to 'em," she had thought.

He was twenty-seven then, and hard work and responsibility had matured him. His wide-shouldered figure, that once had towered over the shrimplike Willy, was thickening, and when he stood beside Willy, who had grown half a head taller than he, he looked years older than his slim, raw-boned friend.

Madge was not very pleased to see him of an evening. She had so few when Willy was at home, and found Jerry's company an intrusion. "He only comes because he's got nothing better to do, and then he mostly just sits there, half asleep, till I have to almost throw him out." She complained to Willy when Jerry had called the first few times.

"Well, darling, I can't say, 'Don't come'. Actually, I'm the only 'family' he's got. Be nice to him, love, he'll get married, I expect, then he'll have a wife to keep him home - like I have, eh?. A soft, delicious, seductive woman, that he'll want to grab hold of like this... and not want anyone else."

"I wish he would get married," Madge said, "It's high time he did."

"Trouble is," said Willy, "he wishes he'd grabbed you first, now you've spoiled him for anyone else."

"Oh dear," thought Madge, "I suppose that's a joke , but I wonder if he's rumbled anything? Jerry wouldn't have said anything, would he? Perhaps he has - Will never suspects anyone, especially Jerry. It's a good thing he can trust me, silly old dear'. Still, I'll never let him down."

On that evening, Jerry had been talking to Willy of his plans for the future. He liked to discuss his business with Willy who had a way of seeing problems in detail, and he was a good source of information concerning local developments and personalities. "I'm going in for something a bit better than I have been doing," he told Willy "Good, solid, four bedroomed detached villas - real class - selling for a couple of thousand or more. It'll be a nice development, all on its own, and I'll make an extra five hundred pounds just for the exclusiveness - snob value - but they'll be worth it, with the golf course running down the valley and the top of Shorton woods below and the whole bay beyond.

I've gotta good team going now, craftsmen, every one. You know the big ginger one, with the flat nose'. He' a good man, done twelve years in the navy, came out five years ago. Well, I'm going to make him foreman, and I'm going to spend more time on the office side of it. I'm fed up with having stuff all over the place. Now I'm going to find somewhere in the town for an office, perhaps, somewhere with enough room for a stock yard as well. My old shiny arse is pretty good all round with the accounts, and that, but I think I'll get a secretary as well.

"Ah ha!," interrupted Willy.

Jerry grinned, "Well, it'll make life brighter if I found a nice little bit that could add up and type as well."

"As well as what?"

"Oh shut up, Will, you're as bad as he is," Madge grumbled. "Look Jerry," she went on, "For goodness sake, why don't you get married. You're well off, successful, and no responsibilities. There must be dozens of girls you could choose from."

"Oh, I dare say, but that don't mean I'd choose any of 'em. I'd want to be very sure before I married one of 'em."

"No," said Willy, in all innocence, "I told Madge, you ought to have grabbed her, when you had the chance, instead of letting me have her."

"Nobody let me have you, than you very much, Will, and Jerry didn't have a chance before you, so don't put ideas into his head." Her voice was so angry that Willy roused himself and turned around to look at her. Her face was red and her eyes were angry - no, hurt, thought Willy.

"I was only joking love."

"Well, don't, not about that'."

"Oh Lord!" thought Willy, "what've I done now?" He looked across at Jerry, but Jerry had his face turned away while he filled his glass. The silence in the room suddenly seemed electric.

"I'll wash up" said Madge.

"Yes, better be going, I suppose," said Jerry. "Cheerio then, thanks for the evening."

When he had gone, Willy followed Madge into the kitchen. "What was that all that about?"

"Well, I didn't like it when you made it sound like I'd have gone with either of you for the asking."

"You know I didn't mean that, love. I was complementing you really. I just meant that, after you, it'd be hard to be satisfied with anyone else. I was speaking for myself really. I'd never find anyone as good as you, ever."

"I know, dear, you're a lamb, but you ought to think before you say things like that, especially to Jerry, you know how he is with girls."

"Oh well, he didn't make anything of it." ("A lot you know," thought Madge.) "Hey'. How about him coming into town, eh? Wilkins, Ltd, Contractors - gosh'. He's done well!"

"No more than you, dear. You're a 'personality' now, everyone knows you, and respects you, which is more than you can say of Jerry."

"Both of us have got on, when you think of how we started. It seems only yesterday that we used to muck about in the old fountain." Willy thought awhile "I wish I'd known that they were going to demolish it. I'd have taken a photograph of it before they did. Looking back, it seems to have dominated my childhood. Lots of others too. I bet in years to come, they'll wish they'd left it as part of the old town."

The 'Green' of the boys' childhood had lost its thatched cottages, too. There was a warehouse on the site of some, and neat little houses had replaced the two next to the church. The old cider stores behind the big house had lost the tangy reek of apples, and were used for storing furniture.

When Germany invaded Czechoslovakia in '38, it came as a complete surprise to most people. There was a feeling of shock and bewilderment. What did it mean to us? What should Britain do? asked the ordinary man, busy with his own affairs. "There will be no war," said the *Daily Express* day after day, across its front page, and on the newsagent's boards. Then came Munich, and the promise of peace. "Good old Chamberlain." cried everyone and went on with their gardening, cricketing and horse racing. The powers that be were aroused though, and plans for defence, tentatively experimented with, went into full operation.

Jerry called in one evening in the late autumn. He seemed preoccupied and after his initial greeting, said little, sitting sprawled in one of the chairs with a look of concern on his face.

"What's up? Something gone wrong?" Madge asked.

Jerry frowned. "Yes, and no. I've almost made a decision, and in one way I'm excited, and in another, I'm scared."

"You haven't decided to get married?"

"No, not likely, wait till Will comes in, I want his opinion."

Willy came in soon after. "Hello Jerry," he said. He spoke without much enthusiasm for he was not best pleased to see him. He had had a busy week, with his work keeping him out each evening until late. He knew that he would have a free evening that way, and had told Madge so. They both had looked forward to a quiet and amiable time, gossiping by the fireside, in the loving way that made them so happy in their intimate companionship. They were hours to be cherished.

"Will. Hope you don't mind me dropping in - Madge said you'd be in tonight and I wanted to ask you something."

"That's all right," said Willy. "Any help I can give, you know."

Willy and Madge ate their meal, they did not speak much, conscious of the brooding figure by the fire. Willy looked at Madge, his raised eyebrows asking, "What's up?". She shrugged and grimaced, turning down her mouth to indicate, "How should I know?"

The meal over, they sat together on the sofa, and Willy said, "Well, fire away. Are you going to buy up Bellmans, (the biggest building firm in the district) or what?"

Jerry looked across at them. "No, in fact, the reverse, I'm thinking of stopping building altogether."

"Go on, you're not, are you? What's happened?"

"You know the chap I made foreman, Sandy, the ex-navy one, - well, he's leaving me, he's rejoining the navy. Reckons there'll be a big expansion, and he'll pick up his rank, and be in for promotion in no time. Got me thinking. It's obvious there'll be a war now, leastways, it's very likely, and, well, I've always had a sort of hankering for the navy. I've got a good mind to join up." There was silence from the two on the sofa. They were so astonished, and so stunned by the sudden onrush of fears, smothered, but so real, that they had no words to say. "'course, when it comes, I could get exemption, and go in for government contracts. There'll be plenty of those about, but I can't get the sort of vision of great grey ships, that I've had for years, out of mind. You know, when they come into the bay in July each summer. I've sort of feasted my eyes on 'em. They look so majestic. All those rows and rows of 'em - battleships, cruisers, destroyers - it's as if they were a woman, showing her body to bloke, they're so beautiful. Daft, I suppose, but it's in me, somehow, and if there's going to be a war, there's where I'd like to be."

"Blimey said Willy "I never thought you'd think of doing anything like that - What about the houses up on the links?"

"I'll get in what I need damned quick now, and get the ones part built, finished, then the rest can wait."

"But you have to sign on for years though?"

"Yes, but I could buy myself out when it's over, I'm not short of dough."

Willy looked at his friend. "I thought we'd get some sort of directive, if it got urgent."

"We will, I expect, but Sandy says 'Get in first'."

"I wouldn't fancy the navy," said Willy, Nor the air force." His gentle nature quailed at the thought of savagery. "I'd rather join the air raids precautions, or something like that."

"Some hopes. Sandy says they'll have all young men out of that lot, and all the other cushy jobs." Willy had been facing Jerry, his face puckered with worry. It seemed ages ago that he had told Jerry about the Germans, and Jerry had scoffed, then nothing seemed to happen, and the fears subsided. Rearoused by the Czech invasion, they were quietened again by Munich. Now he shivered inwardly and became aware of Madge's fingers gripping his arm. He turned to her and was shocked by the whiteness of her face, and the horror in her eyes. He took her in his arms, and she cried. He felt his own tears welling up and hid his face from Jerry. Jerry stood up. "I didn't mean to upset Madge," he said, "I just wanted to tell you what I'd been thinking of doing. I feel excited'. I feel I'm going to start another life."

Jerry walked around the sofa, leaning his hands on the back, and looking down on them. He saw how pale Madge was, and the tears on her lashes, and Willy's worried face, pale too, and unhappy. "Sorry, old things. I didn't think of you, I was just excited and wanted your opinion 'course, I've got nothing to lose. It's different for you, I should have thought, sorry."

"It's all right. It was a bit of a shock, that's all. Brings it home a bit. Still, you're right. If you want to join up, now's the time. I've been told the same several times, but I haven't been able to force myself to believe it."

Jerry sat down again, and they talked awhile of all the risks and upsets that were looming ever closer. Jerry finally told them that he thought he'd give it to the early spring, by which time he'd have tied up his business, and be free to do as he pleased. He said to Willy, "You could join the Terriers, get in as a clerk or something, and you could carry on writing - you'd have something new to write about - you'd need to, I reckon, I'm told you'd only get two bob a day once you are in."

Chapter 24

When '39 came, life seemed little different, but there were subtle changes. The unemployment figures shrank as a surge of new life began to rejuvenate the factories and workshops up and down the country. Most people still preferred to scoff at the 'warmongers', and either through blind ignorance, or fearful stupidity, told each other that it would never happen. Willy, gathering news week by week, was in no doubt that war really loomed.

One day, early in February, Jerry, who had been in cheerful mood for some months, and had not since that ominous night, reopened the subject of joining up, came into the *Echo* office. He was full of bounce and saucy chaff for the typist. He put his hands on Willy's shoulders and said, "Well, I'm off, old man. I've got everything tied up with your old boss, and my accountant, and I'm going down to Devonport, tomorrow to tell 'em that Nelson's arrived, and to get going."

The friends had a few stilted remarks to cover their feelings of emotion at parting, but Jerry was so cheerful that he managed to leave Willy in a somewhat excited mood too. Left alone, Willy took a lightning decision, on a half-hearted idea he had had for some time. Without further thought, he drove to the local drill hall of the artillery company centred on Paignton.

The Sergeant Major instructor was busy forking over some ground behind his house. He was somewhat dishevelled and hardly looked his part. Willy, who had been waiting on the doorstep while his wife fetched him, found his nervousness depart and the familiar opening remarks of a reporter, ready on his tongue. "Good morning, Sir - hope I haven't come at an awkward time."

"Depends what you've come for.'"

"Oh sorry'. I came to enquire how I can join the Territorials."

"Ah well, that's a question. We got a lot applying. We're full and I've got a waiting list, so I don't think it's much good you applying."

"Good Lord'. I thought, with the situation as it is, you'd be glad of recruits!"

"Oh, it doesn't work like that. We have an establishment laid down, and that's it as far as we're concerned."

"Oh dear, that's my ignorance. I haven't a clue how the army works."

"Well, you'll find out soon enough son, but I can't help you now."

The soldier, collarless, in a ragged sweater, muddy boots and trousers, considered Willy kindly.

"Keen to join?"

"Yes, I thought I'd try and get in before I'm sent for."

"Fair enough'. Well, there's the R.E.s at Torquay, and the Devons at Newton Abbot - you could try them'."

"Thanks, I will. Sorry to have wasted your time." The sense of anti-climax made Willy feel relieved and indignant, almost at the same time. "If they don't want recruits, they can't think there's much urgency," he grumbled to himself.

Back at his office, he did some work that needed doing, but his mind was elsewhere. He had tried to take the plunge, without success. He wanted to go home, to face Madge with a fait accompli, for he knew he could never go voluntarily, if she didn't agree, and he felt he would not be able to make out a convincing case for doing so.

By mid-afternoon, he could stay no longer, and drove into Torquay. He found the H.Q. of the Royal Engineers and, bracing himself for the effort, he gave a tentative knock on a large double door, pushed it open, and entered. It was a large hall, smelling of dust and tobacco smoke. He crossed to an inner door, behind which he could hear the click of billiard balls. He knocked: and entered a smaller room. There were benches around the walls, and a bar at one end. The bar was closed, and two men were playing snooker on the billiard table, that occupied the centre of the room. Another man was marking the score. Willy walked up to him. "Excuse me," he said, quietly, (he knew better than cause a diversion during play), "any chance of having a word with who ever's in charge?"

The man did not appear to have heard him. A wretched, wet dogend of a cigarette, hung to his lower lip; he breathed through his mouth, exhaling thin, blue smoke. The dogend seemed to be hardly alight, but the man appeared to generate a haze of rank smoke from it. His eyes were on the players. "Nineteen, Charlie" he announced, and slid the marker along the board. Then he became convulsed by a wracking cough and he removed the dog-end, and threw it into a bucket of sand nearby, then hacked raspingly, and spat a revolting gob into a cuspidor placed handily near.

"Over there," he said, nodding to a door beside the bar. As he did not seem to be likely to get any more information from the man, whose attention was divided between the players and the lighting of another Woodbine, Willy knocked on the door indicated, and someone called, "Come in." He entered a room that was obviously an office, though all sorts of equipment and boxes occupied most of the space.

A soldier was seated at a table. He was in uniform but his unbuttoned tunic indicated that he was off duty. "Yes'. What can I do for you?"

"I've come to enquire if I could join the Territorials."

The man stood up, buttoned up his tunic and faced Willy. Willy felt himself being evaluated by the soldier, and unconsciously braced his shoulders and looked the other man in the eye.

"You a tradesman?"

"I'm the Editor of the Paignton *Echo*.

"Well now, we require every man in the R.E.s to be a master of some trade, and I don't somehow think we've got much scope for a newspaper editor in this unit. You see, we're 'searchlights'. We've got electricians, motor mechanics, engineers, plumbers, carpenters, all sorts. We've even got a window cleaner - after all, the searchlight's got to be kept clean. As a matter of fact, we got a waiting list of men anxious to join, and I could only take on another if he was an expert in something that was essential. Even then, he'd have to wait. We're up to establishment and we can't take and more until a vacancy comes up. Sorry lad. Nice to see someone keen, but I reckon you won't have to wait very long the way things are going."

Willy's face must have betrayed his feelings for the Sergeant Major gave him a slap on the back and said, "Why not join the Regulars. You'd have no trouble there."

"No, I don't want an army career. I just want to be fixed up in something, so that if war does come along, I know where I am."

"Look, if you're not fussy what you join, there's a new mob being formed. There's a doctor raising a C.C.S. Have you been in the St John's, or anything? No, well, it's starting from scratch, so you should be able to get in." He gave Willy the doctor's name, and advised him to phone him.

Willy phoned when he returned to the office. The doctor told him that he was only in the preliminary stages of getting war office consent but suggested that he call and see him, in the evening, in a couple of days time. "You'll be able to give me a write up, I daresay," he said.

It was the end of the month before Willy actually signed up. He was the third man in, and others came, thick and fast. The doctor had been given the rank of Lieutenant Colonel, and soon began to give Willy most of the clerical work to do. After a few weeks, he was, unofficially, the C.O.'s clerk.

There was a strange unreality about life for Willy and Madge. Everything about the town went on as normal. There seemed no urgency, or threat. The holiday boarding houses, the sea front hotels, the harbourside boatmen, were all using the Spring months as a preparation for the summer season. Saturday football was on the wireless, and cup ties were on 'Pathe' gazettes at the cinema. Local politics were wrangled over, annual dinners, balls and theatricals were all just as usual.

To Madge, Willy's joining up was just a bad dream. He hadn't got a uniform yet, so there was nothing to bring reality to his new-found interest. At first she was frightened. Frightened of what would happen to herself when Willy went away. She would be alone in the house, a sort of near widow. Frightened of how she would manage about money. Frightened of Willy not coming back. Frightened of the empty future. They talked a lot, and Willy found out all he could, which was little, to comfort her. But neither of them spoke of the cold dread of separation. It seemed that to do so would invite it's realisation.

Then as the weeks passed, and nothing seemed to happen, buoyancy came back to her and she comforted herself with the thought that it might never happen. Her friend, up the road, scoffed at Willy playing soldiers. "Men!" she said to Madge. "They're a lot of kids."

There was one thing though. Jerry had gone. They had laughed at first because, after his dramatic farewell, he reappeared the same evening. "They're going to manage without me, for a week or two," he told them. "But they've got me booked and will let me know." Three weeks later he came in to wish them 'a sailor's farewell' and was really gone. Madge missed him a lot. During the three weeks of waiting, he had spent a lot of time with her. He took her out in his M.G. and did a lot to ease her worries. He was kind and gentle with her, and sensing her fears, he kept off war talk. He never tried undue familiarities with her, and she never knew (or did she guess?) how hard it was for him to play the big brother, instead of the ardent lover.

"Dear Jerry," she thought, "He's good really, and he's wasted. He ought to be married." When he called to say his real goodbye, he kissed her, hard, full on the mouth, then he rushed away, with the vision of her eyes, wide with surprise, so close to his own. She missed him, and because she knew that he loved her, she felt a sort of maternal grief at his going

In March '39, the Territorial Army was suddenly expanded to double its size. It became the thing to be a 'Terrier'. In June, Willy's unit got their uniforms. They were over a hundred strong by then, mostly young, eighteen to twenty-two years old. Willy was one of the older men. A few ex-regulars had joined them, even one with his Great War medals. They didn't do much. Drill once a week, and P.T. to occupy the evening. When their uniforms were issued, and they began to look regimental, their Sergeant Major Instructor even took them on a march through the town. He gave them dire warnings as to what would happen to "Any bugger who didn't remember that he was representing the Corps and was supposed to be a soldier." Willy's new boots gave him blisters.

In August, the unit went into camp at Weymouth for two weeks. It was a holiday really, special coaches on the train, and a Sunday School outing atmosphere pervaded. There was not much likeness to a Sunday School in the songs and jokes with which one man vied with another, only to be capped by someone else. Willy's ears burned, and he felt his eyes must be popping. It was a revelation. Jerry often had a lewd joke to tell, but Willy had not found them funny. He, in common with many boys of that time, was very innocent and 'decent minded' as the phrase went He was not alone in his distaste for obscenities and soon found out who was who, conversationally.

While at camp, the mornings were spent in drills and medical lectures. Six local doctors had joined them and commenced the arduous task of turning the men into an efficient medical unit. They had to start from scratch and had to plumb deep into their memories of their own student days to make their lectures intelligible to the men before them. The afternoons were occupied learning how to pitch tents, fold kit and use gas masks. The evenings were free, but the town was several miles away, and there was no transport. Nonetheless, many tramped in, Willy included, to spend their time at the cinema and the pubs.

Everyone was glad when it was time to return home, though Willy had fared better than most, sending quite a lot of time in the C.O.'s 'office', sorting a mass of forms and information that the Colonel had lately received.

Willy was home for a week when, on 1 September, the announcement came that all territorials were to report to their headquarters. Willy had been working, full time, all that week, at the Colonel's house, where a room had been made into an office, so he heard the news there.

Madge was out shopping when the news came and she noticed people gathered around a car in the main street. It had been fitted with a wireless and she could tell by the look of concern on the listeners' faces that something serious had happened:. She stopped, and asked a woman what it was. "Oh, my love, they've called up the territorials, they have got to go right away!"

Chapter 25

When war was declared on 3 September, 1939 many people were astonished to find that the event had been anticipated for some time, and long laid plans were put into action. Madge, suddenly bereft of her husband, had had little time to plan what to do with herself before she was canvassed as a hostess for children to be evacuated from industrial cities, and next day, opened her door, to find a woman presenting her with family of four children, aged seven to twelve. They stood there, gazing, round-eyed and fearful, and Madge opened her home and her arms to them. They were part of a school from one of the London boroughs that had arrived in the charge of heroic teachers who had the job of billeting them, teaching them, and acting as guardians for them.

Jerry's housekeeper had decided to go to live with a sister, whose husband was a navy reservist, and who had been recalled, so Jerry's house was untenanted, and promptly requisitioned. Three mothers with young children were soon in residence.

With the care of her 'family', Madge's spirits rose and she began to feel some purpose in life. Her nights were a nightmare, at first; not only was the bed so big, and so empty, but unusual noises terrified her. Everyone expected to have bombs falling, or gas attacks, or even an invasion right from the first day, but nothing happened.

It was a beautiful Indian summer; God still seemed to be in his heaven, and, if one did not listen to the wireless, or read the papers, all seemed well with the world. It didn't stay like that, of course, but the progress of the war became the history recorded later on, and only some aspects of it touched Madge, Willy and Jerry.

Madge's 'family' went home during the 'phoney' war, and others came. Shocked, begrimed and exhausted refugees from the bomb wrecked cities, to take their place. Madge was fully occupied with the nursery school and with her 'evacuees'.

Willy's mob got licked into shape and were sent to Wales for a couple of years to deal with the sick and accidentally injured from the great training centres in that area. Then on a bright June day in '42, they sailed way from the Mersey in a great convoy of liners and, after eight weeks at sea, arrived at Tewfic transit camp on the canal.

Willy, along with thousands of others, contracted dysentery and was hospitalised. By the time he recovered, his unit had moved into Syria and Willy found himself at the R.A.M.C. depot in Cairo. From there he was posted to Alexandria, to a general hospital.

Willy arrived as a sergeant, graded Hospital Clerk 1. Most of the other sergeants and warrant officers were regular soldiers, who had been serving in Palestine when war was declared. When October came, rumours spread like wildfire. The new General Montgomery, was going into the attack. Even the Italian prisoners of war, who did nursing orderly duties, knew all about it. Willy was told by an Italian N.C.O. "Big push coming, eh Sergeant! Up the blue. Boom! Boom! Back again pretty damn quick with a mucking bayonet up the arse, eh?"

The attack came though, and the opening barrage of gunfire rattled the jalousies on the hospital windows, though they were forty miles away.

When he first left home, it was Madge who reinstated the ten o'clock North Star tryst, and most nights, Willy kept it. He spent some afternoons in Alexandria, riding in on the fast two or three carriage trams that had their terminus at the hospital gates. He ate huge meals at one of the service clubs, exploring the shops and bazaars. It was another world from war-torn Europe.

One day he went into a stationers shop and bought a ream of paper. When he got back to the mess he took a table in a quiet part of the room, far from the bar, and shielded by a card school that sat for hours, silent, except for the quiet mutter of 'stick' or 'twist', he settled down and began a precis of his novel. The he started to write, and his imagination quickened with his creative excitement. "I'll get it done," he told himself, "and I'll get it home somehow, then I'll rewrite it all when this lot is over."

Chapter 26

Jerry had not been home since joining up. He wrote to Madge once or twice without giving any news. He enquired after Willy, and sent her his love. His address was just a P.O. number, so Madge did not know where he was. She replied to his letters, wishing him well and telling him that she prayed for him every night after she had prayed for Willy. Jerry kept her letters as a sort of talisman.

After some weeks of basic training, he had been sent to Scotland, and, soon after, to a shore job in the Orkney Islands where various deep water anchorages enabled warships to lie in relative safety, while repairs and alterations where carried out. Jerry worked at his trade and, once out of initial training, was quite happy.

The severe winter of '39-'40, extra severe in that far northern place, quenched his desire for immediate sea going duties. Evidence of the terrible force of the sea was very obvious on ships that he boarded to repair, and the tales told by their crews were of nightmarish voyages.

In the early days of '41, when day and night seemed merged into one, he suddenly found himself part of a replacement for the crew of a destroyer that had come in to be patched up after damage while on convoy work. So at last, he found himself at sea. It was a cruel baptism. His ship was engaged in protecting convoys in the Arctic seas. He was sea-sick for a week, and dragged himself about his tasks, in a misery that denied any reality.

He was a sea for two weeks on that trip, and found the sensation of stillness and quiet, when they made port, the sweetest experience ever. They only stayed long enough to take on supplies, then sailed again and when they rose to the first great swell and slid down into the following trough, Jerry was prepared for it and, using the experience he had gained on his first voyage, found that life was livable after all.

As the year lengthened, Jerry's ship was sent further south and worked in less arduous waters. It was still convoy work, playing sheepdog to flotillas of ships homing in on Britain from all over the world, bringing sustenance of all kinds. His was beginning to be known as a lucky ship. It had been damaged by bombers before Jerry joined it, but since then had not suffered damage or casualties. There had been near misses but the U-boats were after the tankers and merchantmen, and seldom tried their luck on the navy.

After months of continual sea-going, the ship developed a serious mechanical fault and, for a day, lay motionless while her engineers worked desperately to make a repair. Jerry had a job to do on deck and he watched the convoy of ships sail away to disappear into the vastness of the ocean. The silence, while she lay motionless, was uncanny and unnerving as they realised that they were now a sitting duck for any U-boat that was out there.

Further trips took the ship to the Middle East and as far as Freetown and the West coast of Africa. Here, in the warmer climate, with less of a threat from enemy action, the great engines of the ship sent her scything through the sea, the great hump of white water astern, and smoke belching out to form a smokescreen.

After the third trip, the ship was in urgent need of repairs and the crew were sent to shore base for rest. Jerry had been suffering with pains in his leg, the leg he had broken years before. He went sick and had to attend hospital for x-rays and heat treatment. He luxuriated in the steady ground beneath his feet, the quietness, and the warmth.

As the long Northern days returned in the Spring of '43, the passage of ships to Russia became more and more expensive. With round the clock daylight, the German planes from Norway had the convoys like sitting ducks, so for the time, the sea route was little used. Jerry had been posted to another ship by then, and had been on convoy work in the Atlantic, but still based in the north, then the powers that be moved the ship to Devonport, where she had to have repairs carried out.

It was the first time Jerry had been 'home' since 1939. He got seven days' leave and, spirits high, set off for Paignton.

Out in Egypt, the war had moved away from Willy, and an unexciting routine of general hospital work kept him reasonably employed, perfectly safe, and in considerable comfort. He listened to the reports on the wireless, of bombings at home. 'A south coast town' was the only clue of where attacks had been made, and each time he fancied Madge with her evacuee 'family', huddled under the table with her 'Morrison' shelter to protect her.

In her letters to him Madge had told him something of this, making light of it, but in fact she was terrified at times, and found consolation in the care and comfort of the children. His mother sent him a telegram once, saying 'All well at home', and he assumed from that, that Paignton had been hit. He felt a fraud lying in the sun on the sands at Sidi Bishr, while England battled on. Word was, that there would be an invasion of Italy soon, and maybe the hospital would move there.

Madge had somehow 'grown in' to the war years. She had a houseful of children to care for, and worked some days at a nursery run by the local council, to allow mothers to do their bit for the war effort. There were many small businesses that contributed to the overall task, and, of course, the vacancies left in the trades and shops, by men called to the forces, required to be filled.

She looked forward to Willy's letters. They were the bright spot in the week. He described his leisure so vividly that she, after her experience in Malta, could almost feel the heat, and the white glare of the sun. She felt a bit envious, especially if it was a wet and chilly day at home, but she thought that he was safe, and would come home one day. Gwen called often, and helped out with the children when Madge was due at the nursery. She had been very pessimistic when war started. She saw Willy in khaki as a reflection of his father, and, privately, assumed that he would meet the same fate. As the years passed, she became resigned, like everyone else, to the hardships that came her way, and was glad that Willy was in such a remote place. She used to come into Madge's with a beaming face, and put a copy of the *Echo* on the table for Madge to see. "Look what he's got this week," she used to say, and together they would read and laugh over a humorous article, that Willy had sent home by airgraph. "Oh! Just like a blinking kid." Madge said sometimes when Willy had described setting the guard dogs baying, in the rich men's villas by rattling a stick along the house railings, so that the hubbub was taken up and spread away into the distance. Or when he described a camel, laden with corn stalks looking like a walking hayrick that had taken fright, and bolted through a narrow street, lined with barrows selling fruit, and the chaos and babel that ensued. He sent something most weeks, either true or imagined, and the two women felt a pride in 'their Willy' talking to the town from so far away.

It was on a hot day in July that Jerry came home. Madge had been busy with her housework. She was at home that day, no nursery, and was absorbed in the daily battle to keep her home 'nice', in spite of the rampaging children. She was in the kitchen when a shadow darkened the room. She looked towards the window and there was Jerry, looking in, his face beaming, his wide mouth agleam with his strong teeth, and the sunshine showing red through his stick-out ears. "Jerry!" She ran to the door with a delighted greeting. Jerry back again, after all that time.

The rush of emotion surprised her, and she had only just time to check it before she opened the door to him. She thought, afterwards, that if he had walked in on her unawares, she would have gone to his arms, almost as though he had been Willy.

"Jerry! Fancy you. Come in."

"Madge You're pretty as ever." He came towards her, but Madge half turned away to close the door. "Well, this is a surprise, where have you come from?"

"Devonport. I got seven days. First time I been south since I joined." He had almost scooped her into his arms, but her evasion gave him time to control himself. Madge too.

"Cup of tea, I suppose?"

"Yes please if you can spare it."

"Oh yes, I can, I don't do bad with the children's rations."

"Children?"

"Evacuees. I've got five."

"Good Lord'. Five, eh'. That must keep you busy."

"Oh, I do a part-time job as well."

"What you doing today?" he asked. Madge new at once that he'd got something planned. Madge had her back to him, filling the kettle at the sink, so he stayed that way, and replied, "Oh, just the usual, housework cooking, mending, shopping." She had to turn then and go to the stove. Jerry was seated at the table. He looked at her and she saw nothing but kindness in his eyes.

"Well, could you spare me a bit of time. It's a gorgeous day, and the country looks so green and good. How about coming out for a run?"

"A run?"

"An old mate of mine has been using my M.G. He'll have to let me have it while I'm home. We could go out into the country somewhere. How about it?"

Madge stood beside the stove, looking out of the window. The idea appealed to her greatly. "I was thinking about the kids."

"When will they be in."

"Half past three."

"That's okay. We can be back by then."

Madge poured the water into the tea pot. Her hand was shaking and she didn't want Jerry to see her face. "I'll ask Will's mum to come in," she said, and that thing inside her said, "Knew you would'." And another voice said, "He's all right, and I'm not going to let him do anything."

But Jerry said, "Good'. We can have the rest of the day." His pleasure was so obvious and so devoid of any look of concupiscence, that Madge laughed and her spirits rose. "It'll be lovely'." she said.

While Jerry went to collect his car from further up the road, Madge made a few sandwiches and filled a thermos to take with them Jerry was gone a long time and Madge began to fret at the delay. Then he drove up and beckoned her out. She got into the car, tied a headscarf tightly on her head to combat the backdraught, and grinned happily at Jerry. "I thought you must have forgotten me," she said.

"No, I was just having a look around my house," he replied, thinking "Forgotten you, my darling, I've never had you out of my thoughts all these years."

"Where are we going?"

"Not far love, there's only about a gallon of juice in the tank. How about down by the lake at Afton. It'll be nice and peaceful down there."

It was only ten minutes later that they were coasting down the hill to Afton. Jerry was amazed, and hurt, to find that the dense woodlands on either side were gone. The hillsides were devastated. Only the great beech trees lining the road remained. "Blimey!" he said. "There won't be anything left by the time this lot's over. I suppose they'll replant, but it'll not be the same in my lifetime."

He thought back to a day when he and Willy had sneaked through the woods and had been chased by a keeper. "Cor! Didn't old Will travel." he remembered, with glee.

There was a bank beside the lake in those days. The woods, down there, had not been cut. The lake was a lake then, with an island in the middle, with ducks and moorhens busy about it. There was a quarry just below and Jerry parked there, then led the way back to the bank. "Come on, let's sit here. Will and me used to come here when we were young and Will used to lie here for hours, reading, and I used to fish in the pond. Never caught anything. Used to catch newts, and pond skaters."

He spread the weatherproof cover from the car, and sprawled on it. Madge put the bag with the sandwiches against a tree and lay down on her tummy, resting on her elbows, and looking across the water. Jerry rolled on to his back, and looked up into the cloudless sky. "Peace," he thought, "utter peace." Two brown buzzards came into his view, soaring on motionless wings. He felt a balm soothing his nerves, stopping the jangling that made his flesh flutter and his voice shake.

A beautiful relaxation came over him. All that old familiar sound and scent of his boyhood were around him. "Today, anyway," he thought, "I'll forget everything."

He hadn't realised it, but he had been silent for half an hour. "Well!" thought Madge. "He's gone to sleep!" She turned on her side and looked at him. Looking more closely, she saw how three years of war had marked him. He looked older, and lined. The skin was tight on his bones and she noticed that his eyelids seemed to quiver. She had often scrutinised her sleeping husband, and teased him into wakefulness, by lightly kissing his eyelids. They hadn't been all jumpy like that. "I wonder what he's been through?" she thought.

Some sound, some movement, roused him. His eyes were dazzled by the brilliant sky. He blinked and frowned, then saw Madge and realised where he was. "Oh Lord! I'm sorry love, I must have dropped off."'

"That's all right. You're tired, aren't you."

"Not tired, love - exhausted more like. Still, a few nights with sheets, and I'll be okay."

"Let's have our eats, I can do with some." She shared out the sandwiches and poured the tea.

"Spam!"

"Yes, you're lucky. It isn't often I can get it. Actually, we shouldn't be eating it. It came in a 'Bundles for Britain' food parcel, for the kids."

They ate in silence, then - "You said Will was okay'. But what's he doing?"

"He's in Egypt He's a clerk in a big hospital. Seems to spend most of his time on the beach, or playing tennis, lucky chap."

"Cor blimey! The jammy bugger - sorry - he certainly did all right for himself. The lucky old devil. It's hard to think, lying here, that there's a war on. The old castle ruins up there, poking up from the trees, and the swifts in and out of their nests on the walls. What a life, eh! If we were like them, we'd come up here for the summer and then off to Africa for the summer down there. They don't take any notice of wars. There's a buzz that we're going to the Med, so perhaps I'll be there before them."

"When'll it be over, do you think?"

"I don't know, and I think it's best not to. Still, we've won in Africa and they reckon we're winning the subs, so I suppose we can begin to hope."

Madge lay down again beside him. She was a little further forward than him, so he couldn't see her face. She lay flat, with her arms under her chest and her chin resting on her hands. He was acutely aware of her nearness to him and the allure of her. They lay like that for some time, neither of them speaking.

Jerry!s eyes ran over her as she lay there. "Cor'. Don't I just wish I

405

had the nerve to make you pay," He thought. "If it had been any other woman with him, he'd have made his play long ago, but with Madge he couldn't do it. It's like that bloody Dot, all over again - I was scared then 'cause she was married, and I'd never done it. I was just a plain innocent fool then, but it's the same now. I just can't spoil it." He looked at her dark head, silhouetted against the lake, her shoulders raised, as she rested on her elbows, then the downward sweep of her back, and the lovely rounded plumpness of her bottom as it curved up again, then down to her thighs. Her dress dipped ever so slightly between her buttocks, and then between the top of her legs. She was bare-legged, and her skin shone slightly beyond the back of her knees where her dress ended.

"She's a smashing little darling," said Jerry to himself. "Just what? Nine, ten inches? And I'd have a handful'. He thought of Madge as she was twelve years ago, when he'd first seen her. She had been quite fat, he remembered, but with a cheeky, round face, with a dimple. The dimple was still there, but she was now much slimmer ("All the better," he thought), but not too slim. She still had a big bosom. ("Gosh I wish it was squashed against me, not the grass") and that beautiful bum. If he patted it, it would wobble, and then he could trace the cleft downwards, and gently slide inside. The nearness of her, and his overwhelming desire, almost made him do what his fancy had prompted. Then he rolled on to his face, crushing his wanton body into the earth. "I can't do that to her." his inner self wailed, "or to Will." He buried his face in his arms. "Oh God'. If only I'd taken her before Will." He was almost praying. He'd had women whenever he'd felt the need. He'd paid for them and hardly noticed who or what they were, and he'd teased and flattered and seduced them, with only a fleeting compunction for their distress, but Madge was something else. One apart. He'd have liked to have taken her with joy and with reverence, to really give himself, not as finding satisfaction, but to give her love.

The sun had swung around the valley and gone behind the castle woods. Madge said, "Perhaps we'd better move, the midges are biting me and they've got all inside my clothes."

"Want me to get 'em out?" said Jerry. The words were spontaneous, and as they moved their heads were close together. Madge looked into his face and saw his desire. "Don't Jerry, please."

"I won't, my darling, but I want to."

Madge's face was red and her look so pitiful, that Jerry felt ashamed. "you know that I fancy you . I have done for years. I know it's no good, but there's no harm in it, so long as I leave you alone, is there?"

"I know how you've felt about me for ages. I didn't want Will to know, but I wish you hadn't said it. I'm sorry, ever so sorry, but there's only Will for me, nobody else. Please."

"Not, even for a few days, just one day?"

"No, please, be sensible, please."

"Okay, I'll behave."

Silence. Madge began to gather up her things. She was disturbed too. No one, especially one of her voluptuous nature, could have seen Jerry's desire so plainly without being moved. She thought to herself that it was lucky that she didn't find Jerry attractive in that way.

Jerry was sitting, his chin on his knees. "You remember that tree I planted, the Medlar I got from down Avonford?"

"Yes."

"Well, those evacuees have chopped the top off and fixed a clothes line to the trunk."

"Oh, what a shame."

"I've thought of it since. Perhaps the old dear was right. Perhaps you can read your fortune in it. If so, my branch, the one that grew since I planted it, has been cut off."

"Oh Jerry'. Don't be morbid. There can't be any truth in that old yarn, it's just a superstition."

"I know, but I went up, specially, this morning, to see if there was another bend in it. I thought it might show I'd be having some good luck, but the whole top was gone, just a bare pole of a trunk left. I felt quite a shock. I thought, "That's me then, done for."

"Nonsense, you know it is. Come on, buck up. Let's go home and I'll make up something or other for tea."

The little car took the steep hill as if was level. The wind met them, then turned around and hit them from behind. Madge squeezed down in her seat and hung on to her headscarf. She looked across at Jerry. His usual happy look was gone, his face looked grim. "How thin and old he looks," she thought. They left the devastated valley below them in a matter of moments and emerged from the narrow lane into the wider road. For a moment their way was blocked by a farm wagon. The carter seemed asleep and his black and white collie dog padded along behind, a few steps to the right, then a few steps to the left, as if it were heading the wagon like a flock of sheep. Jerry squeezed past, but having slowed down, his manner changed. He turned to Madge with a smile and a jerk of the head towards the wagon. "He's all right, no call call up for him. I should've stayed in some reserved occupation too, I could've."

Now he had slowed down, Madge pulled herself up and asked the question she had avoided doing all day, but knew, after Jerry's recent outburst that she must do without any further delay. "Where are you going to stay."

"Well I was hoping to stay with you, but seeing you're full up with kids, I asked Mrs Thompson if she could put me up. He's had the use of this car, and they got a spare room. She said it'd be okay."

"That's all right then. I was thinking Will's mum might manage, but she's got an old couple from Plymouth."

Halfway down the hill, Jerry slowed the car again, then stopped. "Hop out," he said. They went over to a field gate. The field was almost gone. A road almost reached the gate where it has evidently intended to join the main road.

Suddenly, they both saw the plane. They saw it before they heard it. It came out of the mist like a ghost and roared over the town. "It's a German," said Madge, standing stiff with horror. The plane swept in a circle below them, hardly higher than the church tower, it seemed, and was almost immediately a ghost again in the mist. The explosions could be seen right below them, then came the concussion and the noise. "God! It's Well Street," said Jerry. He ran to the car, and, hardly waiting for Madge to get in beside him, raced downhill like a comet. Madge had always liked driving down that hill. Willy had shown her how, at one point, there was an optical illusion, when, because the houses at the foot of the hill blocked the view, anyone coming down quickly, got the impression that the church tower was sinking into the ground. Then, as they raced down, the whole of the foot of the hill was obscured by smoke end dust. The siren started wailing only as they reached the green, so fast had they descended. Jerry drove down Well Street, then stopped. Rubble blocked the road. Dust and smoke obscured what was beyond. "You go home," he shouted to Madge and vanished into the wreckage

Later, it was decided that three bombs had been dropped. One had fallen harmlessly in the churchyard, another into a builder's yard, the third, the middle one, had made a direct hit on Effie's little home.

When Jerry got there, people were only just collecting their dazed senses. The silence, following the explosions, was complete, until loose timbers, roofing slates and the crackle of fire could be heard above the ringing in the ears.

Jerry was there first. He was vaguely aware of whistles blowing, and voices shouting. He found his mother almost at once. He knew at first glance that she was dead. There was the wreckage of furniture all around her, and he grabbed a coverlet - strangely, he wondered at the Chinese dragon embroidered on it and wrapped it around her, then a torn sheet. He worked like one demented, hating the shame of her naked body, loving the warmth that was still hers, crying for the loss of the only person to have shown him love. He found men in tin hats around him. People trying to drag him away. He held the body in his arms. "No! No'. Leave her, she's my mum," he told them. They were local A.R.P. men, and some knew him. "It's her boy, Jerry," they said. Someone arrived with a stretcher and said he must see if she was alive. "Go to hell!" said Jerry, and staggered through the debris with her in his arms. "There's an ambulance," someone said, and he heard the tinkle of its bell. When they opened the ambulance door, he let them lay her inside, then sat beside her, holding her hand.

He did not see the knowing glances of her neighbours, or the shaking heads, or the grim jokes. The rescuers had worked hard, and there was an unseemly guffaw from one woman when an airforce officer's tunic was thrown out from the wreckage. The man was taken away in the same ambulance. Jerry hardly noticed the still form covered with a blanket. The crowd moved shamefacedly away, but there was many a coarse joke going the rounds that night.

Jerry had no clear recollection of what happened later. He was parted from his mother somewhere where they asked him a lot of questions, and filled up forms, with the answers his dulled brain gave them. Someone had moved his car to get it out of the way of fire engines, ambulances, and all the rest of the rescue operation; but for the time, he had forgotten it. Someone gave him tea to drink, and stood over him, talking with compassion, for him. They were all very kind, but he was in a state of nervous exhaustion, such as he had been more than once on the Arctic run. His frayed nerves, so slightly soothed during the last few weeks, went into shock again, jumping and jerking like puppet strings. Whoever it was, must have understood. She gave him something else to drink, and he gradually grew calm. Then he remembered. "It's me mum. Me Mum!" he kept saying. All he could see through his tears was a white shape that spoke soothingly.

He must somehow have given them Madge's address, for hours later, some kind person took him there. He was still dazed. "All right Missus, if I leave him with you?"

"Yes, I'll see to him," Madge answered bravely, and led him indoors. The children were in bed and the house was quiet. The whole town was quiet. Madge got him to the sofa and managed to make him lie down. She put a cushion under his head and took his boots off. With something to do, she became quite professional. "Now then, do you want to rest a while, or can I get you something to eat?"

He lay there, his arm across his face, and did not answer. It was hardly dark and Madge did not want to draw the black-out curtains as long as any daylight lasted. She went to the window. All was at peace. A bat kept fluttering by in swoops and twirls, it was so quiet she could hear its 'Tick, tick, tick', as it passed.

"Me mum's dead. The bastards got her. I'll get even for this, I'll see a few drown yet and laugh, the rotten bastards." Jerry started to cry.

Madge went back to the window and stood with her back to him. She knew he was in a private world of misery, and it was better to let him give way to his grief. It grew dark. She got her torch, and fixed the black--out, then turned on a small table lamp in the corner of the room, then went all over the house seeing that all the curtains and blinds were drawn. The house grew very hot. Madge opened the back door to let some air in, and in the dark, made coffee from a precious bottle of essence, and returned to the lounge. Jerry was lying, staring at the ceiling. "I've brought you some coffee."

He sat up and reached for it. "I'm sorry if I made a fuss. I don't know who brought me here. I don't remember telling anyone to." His voice was shaking, and so was his hand. "It turned me up, you know, really shook me. My poor old mum. What did she ever do to get one like that. Trust in God, the padre tells us - fat lot he cares who cops it. I wish I'd gone to see her this morning, or even phoned her. Too late now, too late to tell her anything." He began to sip the coffee.

"He told her, all right," thought Madge. "He told her there was someone who loved her."

Madge had stayed in the car when Jerry dashed into the ruin of the house. She was stunned by the swiftness of the happening. She saw Jerry reappear with a bundle in his arms, wrapped in a silk counterpane with a dragon on it. There was a mop of brilliant red hair drooped over Jerry's shoulder and a long, bare leg protruded from the covers. "Oh Jerry! Jerry!" she had cried to herself, in pity, as she realised what he was doing, and why, and flamed in fury as she heard a toothless old crone say, even in that moment of terror, "Well, 'er's got what 'er's been asking for for years, wonder her hadn't been struck down long ago." They came and asked her where the driver was, as the car was in the way. She told them, and presently someone came and drove it into an open shed nearby. Then the ambulance had come and Madge had walked wearily home.

Gwen had been agog for news. She'd been in the Morrison for an hour, though all danger to her had passed before she heard the explosions. The kids had enjoyed it. Then Madge told her it was Well Street, and that she thought Jerry's mother was dead, Gwen said nothing, but her mouth set firm, betrayed her lack of sympathy. "Poor Jerry," Madge had said. He loved her, you know, and he did so want her to love him. He's got nobody now!" Gwen had remained grimly silent. She had gone home long before Jerry arrived.

Jerry drank his coffee, then ate some pudding that Madge had left over from the children's meal. He seemed calmed and refreshed. "I've got an egg if you could eat it."

"No love, it's your rations. I don't feel hungry. Anyway, I'd better be going."

Madge felt relief at that remark. It was near eleven o'clock and she was desperately tired.

"I suppose you wouldn't let me crash down here for the night?" he asked. "They'll have given me up by now."

Madge was worried. "Will you be all right?"

"Yes, of course I will, I'll be out early, there'll be things I'll have to do?"

The moment of resurgence had passed and Madge saw him seem to collapse inwardly, his face began to twitch.

"Okay then, I'll bring some bedding and some pyjamas of Willy's "Pyjamas! Blimey! It's three years since I ever wore night clothes!"

Madge made up the bed. Jerry refused the pyjamas, saying it was far too hot.

"If I open the window and let up the blind, will you be sure not to turn the light on?"

"Yes, let some air in, please."

She let the blind run up, and pulled the window down. "It's a lovely night, almost full moon. Goodnight."

"Goodnight, and thank you."

Madge went to bed. She was in the smallest bedroom, the others being given overt to the children. She pulled the curtains back, breathed deeply of the warm night air that flooded in, and looked for their star. She was late for their rendezvous, but she sent her love and her prayer out into the moonlight with Willy in her heart. She put her torch under the pillow and slipped under the sheet. The horror of the day had taken its toll, and she felt weary and depressed. In her mind, she kept seeing Jerry's stricken face as he staggered from the wreckage with his mother over his shoulder, and the brilliant silk Chinese dragon making such an eyecatching shroud. It was the bare leg swinging free that made tears start in her eyes. "Poor Jerry." There at the one moment when it was possible to save his mother from the shameful glare of her neighbours. "At least he did that for her," she thought. Her mind then went back to the afternoon. She thought of Jerry telling her that he loved her. "Poor Jerry," she thought again, "what a dreadful day it's been for him." She felt a great pity for the man. She had seen his emotions laid bare and reflecting his tortured mind. She felt the warm maternal feeling of care for him, and wished that somehow, she could have protected him from his tragedy.

She was gazing at the window that occupied all one wall of the little room. A big, white moon had put out the stars. "A good night for bombing," she thought. "Please God, don't let them come here."

She heard the soft footfall on the landing and sat up in bed, feeling for the torch. The door that she always left ajar, pushed open. "Auntie, I can't sleep."

"Oh Shirley, you should have been asleep hours ago.

"I can't, who's that downstairs?"

"Just a friend, staying for the night."

Madge had put on a thin dressing gown, tying the belt in front. She took the child back to its bed. "Auntie, I want to go toilet."

"Well, hurry, and keep quiet, don't pull the chain."

The child reappeared and got into bed. "Can I have a drink, Auntie?"

"Oh, you don't want one, do you? Look, you'll wake the others up."

"I can't sleep, I want a drink'."

"Very well, lie down and I'll get you one."

"Can I have orange juice please, Auntie?"

"You lie down, and I'll see."

Madge crept downstairs and got the child its drink. She made hardly a sound in her bare feet. At the lounge door she listened. There was no sound from inside. "I wonder if he's asleep?" she thought. As she listened she heard the twang of a loose spring in the settee seat, (Willy had said that it had suffered undue hardship, due to their lovemaking) as Jerry moved. She went to go upstairs and trod on a shoe that one of the children had discarded there. It was only a little noise, but Jerry heard it.

"Madge, is that you?"

("Oh Lord'." thought Madge), but answered, "It's all right. I'm just getting a drink for Shirley."

"Have you got some Aspirin, please?"

"I'll get some, just wait a minute." She settled the child, then found the Aspirin. She poured some water in a cup and went to the lounge door. "Here it is," she called.

"Oh, bring it in please. '

She went in. The moon was right opposite the window, and a square of bright light fell across the settee where Jerry lay. The rest of the room was in a pale luminance that showed everything as shadows.

"Can't you sleep?"

"No, I can't sleep and I can't keep still. I'm all a-twitch. Shock, I suppose."

"I'm so sorry, Jerry. I don't know what to say that will be any comfort, but I am sorry."

Jerry took the Aspirin and the cup and drank. Madge was kneeling by his side and she took the cup to place it on a chair nearby. As she did so, her dressing gown fell away from her reaching arm, and in the ethereal light, her full bosom showed, cradled in the top of her nightdress. As she moved, little quivers showed against the thin fabric. Jerry groaned. "Madge, Madge, if you want to comfort me, please let me, just this once." She went to rise and move away, but he'd got her in his arms, his face was pressed against her breast.

"Jerry you mustn't. Let me go!"

He made no reply, just snuggled his face deeper.

She hit his head and struggled. "Let me go, please, you mustn't, let me go!"

He still made no reply, just exhaling a vast sigh of content, and held her closer still. Madge didn't know what to do. He was too strong for her to struggle free, and she was conscious of the thinness of her night clothes. "Oh dear," she wailed to herself.

They remained locked together and motionless. Madge began to feel the warmth of his breath against her, and the recollections of Willy lying like that, so many hundreds of times brought on a sudden woeful longing for him, now so long away. "Oh Will! Will!" her body called. She put a hand on Jerry's head in a light caress. When he felt it, Jerry raised his head and kissed her throat.

"Oh no'. No!" She didn't have any intention of allowing any intimacy at all. Jerry had no attraction for her, but in one strange moment of hallucination, she thought that Willy had her in his arms. It was very soon over. He had rolled off the settee and taken possession of her without protest. Then the realisation of what had happened, hit them both. Madge pushed him away, and pulling her things around her, ran from the room in tears. Jerry lay down on the settee again. His body was quiet, but his conscience was shocked. "Oh God! How could I Little Madge What'll Will do?" He berated himself furiously for his wickedness, but somewhere inwardly, his old Adam was exuberant, and his nerves felt settled. Madge fled upstairs in the darkness, in blind panic. She did what had to be done, disgust nauseating her, then she got into bed, her door locked as it had never been before, giving her the privacy that she needed.

She felt little anger for Jerry, but a fury for herself. She kept saying, "How could I let him do it?" She may have dozed towards morning but she still had not slept when dawn lightened the room. She started into wakefulness when banging on her door, and the call of "Auntie! Auntie!" fetched her from her bed.

"Why was your door locked, I couldn't come in," complained the child. Madge saw the rest of the children up, then dressed and steeled herself to meet Jerry.

"Auntie, who was in the sitting room?"

"Hush dear'. It's a friend, don't wake him up."

"There's nobody there, Auntie, I looked."

Madge crossed to the lounge and looked inside. The sheet and blanket were neatly folded with the pillow on top. On the pillow was a piece of paper. Madge took it, and put it in her overall pocket, then went to prepare the breakfast. With that done, she retired upstairs and read the note. It was written on a sheet of paper taken from Willy's desk. She read:

Madge,
I don't know what last night meant to you, but it was heaven to me. I know we should not have done it, and I am sure you feel the same. Neither of us would want Will to know. I'm going before you are up, so as not to embarrass you, and I will try not to see you again. I've got a feeling that I'm never going to see you again. As soon as I've seen mum buried, I'm going, back to Plymouth.
Jerry.

Madge's cheeks flamed at the cool assumption that she had been as willing as he, and she wept. In her mind was repeated over and over again, "But I let him! I let him," and groping through the half remembered delirium of the previous night, she asked herself a hundred times, "Why did I?" and could not find an answer. She could only remember an impression that she thought Willy was with her, back after that long, long time away.

After forlornly hoping, so long, for a child, Madge had begun to accept that none was coming, and it was only later in the day that she suddenly realised that she might have conceived. The shock turned her cold. She tried to 'pooh-pooh' her fears, but they would not go away, and she spent the next two weeks on tenterhooks of worry. When the worry crystalized she spent another miserable month before going to her doctor, who confirmed her fears.

Madge sat at home knowing her life to be devastated. How could she possibly tell Willy in a way that he would understand. What would her parents say and do? And - Oh God help her! - what would Willy's mother do, and what would she write and tell Willy? She was in despair. They'd even take her evacuees away, when they knew. She wouldn't be considered a fit person to care for them. What could she do? In all the bleak misery besetting her, there was one comfort. She chided herself for feeling that way, but whatever happened to her, there was always the knowledge that, bring what hardship and sorrow it may, she was going to have a baby. It was inside her already, her very own, what she had longed for for years. Even if it wasn't Willy's, it was hers!

She did not know where Jerry was. She had not seen him again. She had seen his photograph in the *Echo*, standing, all alone, by the graveside, when they buried his mother. 'Bomb Victim is Buried' read the caption under the Picture. She had his naval post number, and she wrote to him, telling him that she was expecting his child, but that she did not want to hear from him, or see him, again. Madge thought she must tell him, in case some awkward thing happened in the future. She continued to write to Willy, struggling to sound as happy and affectionate as she always did, but her letters became increasingly sterile, and Willy noticed it, and worried that there must be worries and hardships at home that he had not been told about. He wrote to Gwen, asking if Madge was ill, or anything.

Madge knew that it would not be long before her secret would be out, and she had to make up her mind what to do about it. On an impulse, she rang up Val, Willy's old colleague at Luckhams. Val invited her to her home.

It was a grand villa up in the 'posh' hills above Torquay. Val hadn't changed, and welcomed Madge warmly. "How's old Willy?" she queried. "Bet he's doing okay.". Madge gave some sort of reply, then Val saw the trouble and fear in her face. "He's not wounded, or anything?"

"No," she said, sitting down, "he's all right, it's me'."

"Oh, what d'you mean?"

"Look Val, you know Will, and you know me. Can I treat you like a friend of both of us?"

"'course you can, you're special, you two, what's up?"

"Me," said Madge, simply. "I'm pregnant."

"Oh, my gosh! Who? I mean, were you raped. The Yanks are a menace. I got caught in a doorway one night and had to fight like hell to get away."

"No," said Madge. It was my fault, really - look, will you try to understand?"

"Go on. I know you wouldn't play around, tell me what happened."

Madge did so. It took nearly an hour, but she managed to convey to Val all the bizarre unreality of it.

Val's husband was in a government post to do with the allocation of fuel He had turned out to be rather pompous and unexciting. Val constantly told herself that she was lucky to have a good man for a husband, and all the money she needed for a life of affluence. She was employed in his business as an alternative to being directed into employment. Her job, as the boss's wife, was not very demanding and she knew that she did little more than decorate the office. As Madge's tale unfolded, she found she had to deal sternly with a wanton spirit that suddenly possessed her, and made her sigh at thought of an unhappy sailor boy who needed comforting. When Madge had finished her story, Val was in complete sympathy with her.

They started to plan what Madge should do. They decided that they should both write to Willy and try to explain how it happened. Madge should wait as long as she could before telling Willy's mother, so that Willy would know first, and she was to tell her own mother, and enlist her help. "Of course, you can get it adopted easily enough," said Val.

"No, no, I won't. I want it myself. It's my baby. I'll never let anyone else have it."

"Well that's for you to decide, but you'll have to see how Will takes it, won't you."

"It'll make no difference. It's mine, and I'm keeping it."

They had many more discussions after writing to Willy, trying to make plans for all eventualities. Meanwhile Madge waited in an agony of anticipation for Willy's reply. Letters took anything from a week to a month to reach the Middle East forces, but were fairly sure of getting there by then, as all the North african coast was in allied control. She could but wait.

Chapter 27

It was a Saturday, and Willy was off duty. The hospital shimmered in the glare of the sun. There were great things afoot in the Mediterranean, but they were outside the area of Willy's work. There were few war casualties, except from the navy, who went their tireless way without great drama. Only a skeleton staff manned the administration of the hospital at weekends, and he was free to do as he liked. He took the tram from the terminus outside the hospital gates and went into the city. Though he had done the trip scores of times, he always enjoyed it. His journalist's eye saw constant scenes of interest. Alexandria was such a cosmopolitan city, basically French with British influences. Suburb after suburb was crossed - the French, the Greek, the Swiss, the Italian, the Jewish, all with their distinctive architecture. The street life varied too, from the affluent to the native peasant.

The Egyptian 'wogs' as they were known (that was the working man, and more especially, boys) saw no virtue in paying to ride on the tramcar. They just jumped on and off as often as they could, often running between the cars, and grinning at the ticket collector, who could not reach them. At every stop, the conductor blew on a sort of squealer, something like the ones used at parties, with a blow-out tube and a feather on the end.

Willy got off the tram at the city terminus. It was very hot, but he enjoyed the heat. He intended to go to one of the forces clubs, to have some ice-cream and strawberries, or something similar, and then go to the air-conditioned cinema.

He found a table near an open window and gave his order. It was pleasantly cool. The marble floor and tiled walls, the bubbling of a little fountain that sprayed into a pool in the centre of the room, the revolving fans, all gave an air of ease and relaxation.

Willy had finished his fruit and ice cream, and was sipping an iced orange juice, when he heard an unmistakably Devonian voice. He turned in his seat to see who had spoken. The voice was lost in a babble of talk and roars of laughter. It all came from half a dozen matelots at the other end of the room. Willy stood up. The man seated with his back to him, was unmistakable. Those two stick-out ears identified him. It was Jerry.

Willy felt a surge of delight. He walked over to him and put his hand on his shoulder. He was grinning with pleasure as he anticipated Jerry's surprise. Jerry turned, and at once truly was aware that something was amiss. "Jerry." He held out his hand. Jerry had flushed scarlet and hesitated, but when he took Willy's hand, and laughed, giving Willy a thump on his other hand.

"Christ Almighty! Will! Fancy you."

"What are you doing, are you off somewhere, with your mates?"

"Yes, well, we were going down to Sister Street.

"Oh," thought Willy, "so that was why he didn't seem too pleased to see me at first. Well, I suppose that's him, he wouldn't have changed." Jerry gave a shrug and a short laugh. "Still, no hurry Will, let's sit down for a bit." He turned to the others at the table. "This is my mate from Civvy Street - I'll see you later." He went with Willy to a balcony overlooking the street. They leaned on the balustrade, and exchanged the usual Service chat. Willy said. "Sorry to hear about your mother."

"Oh, you heard!"

"Yes, Madge told me. Sorry, it must have been rough."

"What did Madge tell you?"

"Not much really', she just said that you were home on leave, and you where close at hand, when a tip and run Nazi hit your mum's house - as a matter of fact, I've written asking, her for more about it."

"There's not much more to tell. She was killed outright. I got her out that's about all."

Willy made no comment. It was a difficult subject. He didn't know how much Jerry felt, and they had never spoken much about Effie.

"You saw Madge, didn't you?"

Jerry turned half away. "Yes, I saw her that same day."

"How was she?"

"Positively blooming. Got her hand's full of evacuees."

"It's nearly two years now, seems ages more. God knows when we'll be together again."

They both stayed silent for a time. Jerry was so conscience stricken that he found it difficult to speak. When Willy had appeared suddenly, he had been shocked, but had realised at once that Madge had not yet told him of the child. He had received Madge's short note just before leaving England, and remembering the few bitter words that it had contained, felt the shame and regret anew.

The busy street was waking up after siesta. Opposite them was a barrow, piled high with water melons, large green globes the size of footballs. They looked down on it, with its barrow boy in immaculate white galabiere and ornamental cap. "Water mel-e-on - very sheep'. George, you buy water mel-e-on?" he called to passing servicemen. "George." he persisted, tugging on sleeves. As they watched, a posse of Australians came along, and in the exuberance of their beer, they responded to the barrow boy's solicitation, by up-ending the barrow, spilling the melons, that went rolling down the street. With whoops of delight they started booting the melons from one to the other.

"Bloody shame!" said Jerry

"Yes, Aussies again, they're at the bottom of half the trouble here. You want to watch out if you're on your own. Best to keep to the main road or gang up with some more blokes, specially if you're going down to Sister Street, even more if you're half cut; they'll get you. We get a lot brought in. Hardly a night without. Can't blame 'em really. It's not their war, and the troops do abuse them.

Jerry was relieved that the hiatus between them had been joined and, managing a laugh, said, "Remember old Sally falling into her pile of oranges at that carnival?"

They laughed quietly together at the memory and then stood watching the street in silence.

"Will," said Jerry, "after Mum was killed, and before I rejoined my ship I went into Luckhams and re-made my will. I'd left everything to mum before. I thought, if I didn't come back, at least she'd be well off. But now she's gone, I thought I'd leave it all to you

"Good Lord:, don't be so morbid! You'll come through, why not?"

"Plenty reasons. Anyway, it's sensible. I've got nobody else. But anyway, I changed my mind. I thought I'd leave it all to Madge, in case you bought it too, that's possible, even if you are a shiny arse at base."

"Well, it's good of you to do it, but I don't suppose we'll collect, you'll come back okay."

"There'll be quite a lot, that land out at Stoke will be worth a packet. Anyway, it's all hers when I get mine, and I've got a strong presentiment that I'll buy it."

"You are a pessimist. What!s the matter? Anything up?"

"No, but those bloody evacuees cut my medlar tree down, and when I saw it, I got a cold sort of feeling. I thought, "That's me done for, there's one waiting for me somewhere, with my name on it, and ever since, I just found myself waiting for it - so, eat, drink and make merry, I say. Wine, women and song, 'specially women. Can't persuade you to come along, I suppose?"

"Not likely!"

"Why not? Does you good, and they're certified healthy!"

"No thanks, I don't fancy queuing up for ten minutes on some old hag."

"Old hag, be mucked, some of the birds are smashers!"

"No, Jerry, you know me better than that."

Jerry looked at Willy in a compassionate way "War gives excuses."

"Still no."

"Okay then. I'll be off or I'll loose my mates. Cheers old man."

He held out his hand. Willy took it. "Yes, but do you know how long you're here for, couldn't we meet again?"

"No idea. Here today, gone tomorrow, or next week, or any time.

"Well, I'm at the 64th. It's a navy/army unit, you can come there any time if you want to."

"I'll do that. Cheers!"

With that, Jerry left and Willy, staying on the balcony, saw him go off along the street to where, incongruously, the cathedral tower pointed the way to the services' brothels. "He's worth more than that, he's degrading himself," thought Willy sadly, "and he's got a death wish, for some reason."

Chapter 28

The next evening Willy received three letters. They usually came in bunches. There was one from Madge, one from his mother, and one that was typewritten. Being curious, he opened that one first. In it was a single sheet of paper and more sheets, sealed together with Scotch tape. He opened the single sheet and looked at the signature. "Val! What the heck!" He read the note:

Dear Will,
Madge is writing to you today. If her letter hasn't arrived, don't open the enclosed until it does, then read mine first. Sorry to be mysterious, but you'll need all your love to help you to understand, and remember that I love you and Madge too.

"Oh God'." thought Willy, in alarm, "whatever can have happened?" He put all the letters in his pocket, walked out of the Sergeant's Mess and over to the hospital office. It was deserted. He went to his desk and sat down. He took the letters out of his pocket and looked fearfully at the envelopes. First he read his mother's. It was the usual, "I'm well, hope you are too. I got some gooseberries from the house (her name for the Big House where she worked). I wish I had some sugar so I could make jam. Not so bad though, I can stew them and use sweetener tablets. More chit-chat followed. It had taken Gwen an hour to think of enough news to fill a page. She finished, "I was at your house today. Madge looks very well, I think she's put on a bit of weight."

"That's that, then," thought Willy, "Madge is all right anyway."

After that he opened Val's enclosure, and read it in growing disbelief, then anger, then shocked horror. He read Madge's letter last. Val's had prepared him, but still the very words numbed his brain. He read it again, put it down and looked at the familiar writing as though it were poisoned. He tried to think sensibly, and after a time read the letter a third time. Madge had adopted the method that Willy had begged her to use - that of talking to him. She did so, and he could almost imagine her voice. She told him all. She described their drive back from Afton, the bombing, Jerry's shock and collapse. How he came, uninvited, to stay the night, and what happened, and how it did, and why. She made pitiful pleas that he would understand how she felt him to be with her, until it was too late. How she hadn't wanted to, but had not resisted. How it hadn't been done properly. How she had hated Jerry for doing it, and hated herself for unconsciously encouraging him; and then that she was pregnant. "I know that I can't ask you to excuse me, but I do hope that you will believe me, for it is only you I love, truly. Please Will, think about it for a long time. I've thought it over for six weeks, and can't see much hope, but if the way I've loved for all these years doesn't make you believe me, then I'm sorry beyond anything, and if you want to, you can divorce me. One thing, though. the hardest of all perhaps. I'm not giving the baby up, not on any account. It's my only comfort now."

Willy sat at his desk for hours. He read Val's letter several times. It wasn't so hard to accept as Madge's. Val hadn't minced matters. She told him much that Madge had done. Going into details that would have astonished him in the normal way, and absolutely demanding that Willy accepted Madge's story. She too, finished on a note about the baby. "She won't give it up Will. She's adamant about that. She's wanted a baby for so long, and she reckons it's hers to keep."

Neither of them claimed that Jerry had raped Madge. Madge said she hated him and had warned him never to try to see her again. Val said Jerry had taken a mean advantage of Madge, and ought to be ashamed of himself. Val's letter ended, "So it's up to you, Will. You know she loves you, and you've always been potty about her, so do you want to loose her? Think about it Will. Think hard. I'll pray for you both.'

Willy was blessed (sometimes cursed, but this time, blessed) with an imagination that was capable of transforming his thinking, even his life. Gradually, after almost memorising the letters, his revulsion began to subside, and a spark of pity for Madge sprang into being. Beyond the wording, he saw her wretchedness, her distraught face. He began to see her facing the future of condemnation with the one hope that could save her. His trust in her love, ravaged, but unshaken. Willy almost fell asleep so deep was his reverie, but he woke and his heart sank as all the high-flown sentiments that had been filling his head, suddenly gave way to the fact that Madge, his dear love, was going to have an illegitimate child by his best friend. At that, a cold fury took him. A fury, that for the moment excused Madge and centred on Jerry. That was why he'd looked so queer when they'd met. Jerry, the rotten, dirty bastard. He'd used Madge, just as he'd paid his money and used the regimental prostitutes down in Rue le Seur last night. He was obscene, a seducer, with the morals of a Tom cat. Willy raged on, pacing up and down the office, swearing, thinking of all the horrible fates that might be wished on Jerry, then, worn out and mentally exhausted, he sat down at his desk and wept for the lost innocence of their love together, and he wept with chagrin that he could not wreak vengeance on Jerry. The Orderly Sergeant Major on patrol saw the light in his office and he and his runner went to investigate. It was gone four in the morning and he was surprised to see Willy, haggard and bleary-eyed, sprawled at his desk.

"Cor, blimey, Will! Never seen you pissed before. What you been having, a celebration somewhere?"

"I'm all right Chalky, I was just about to turn in."

"Turn in! It's getting on for Reveille. Do you want a hand to bed?"

"No. I can walk."

"Get on then and don't forget you don't normally drink next time!"

Willy, grateful for the N.C.O.'s assumption that he was drunk, did go to his hut and lay exhausted, but sleepless, till the O.S. came bawling through, announcing another day.

After the trauma of the previous day, Willy began to think over the situation, problem by problem. He did his work efficiently from habit, his thoughts elsewhere. By mid-morning, when one of the civilian girls, employed as clerks, came around with the 'elevenses', and he sat back for ten minutes with his tea and a cigarette, he tried to make an analysis of his feelings. At once, he dismissed Madge from any blame. He accepted her story without question. He knew how he felt about her, of the longing for her that made his body ache, and he knew very well, and admitted to it himself as a perfectly natural thing to do, that he had often fantasised making love to several of the nursing sisters, Palestinian, A.T.S. and civilian clerks, not as themselves, but seeing and feeling Madge in them. Plenty of others had the same feelings, but did not complicate things by thinking of their wives.

He remembered the girl 'Pooh' and remembered that he would have broken faith with Madge if the girl had let him. Willy had not been unfaithful to Madge, and after the first shock, he never doubted her fidelity to him. He quietly filed away a complete absolution for Madge on problem one. Problem two was Jerry. His rage of the previous night had subsided into an anger of disgust and revulsion.

How could a man get to take advantage of a vulnerable woman like that. Val had said Madge should never have gone into the room, not like that, in her nightgown, if he hadn't asked her to bring an aspirin and drink. She thought he was too exhausted and ill to help himself! Willy imagined Madge lying there, all soft curves, appealingly warm and fragrant, and ground his teeth at the other's perfidy. Then he'd had the cheek to leave her his property! Paying her off! And what would happen when the war ended, and they both went home? There'd be no living in the same town. Problem two must wait to be resolved.

Problem three was the big one. The baby. Madge said she was going to keep it, come what may. He thought, with shame, of his inability to give her children, the family she craved, her football team. All the love, and pulsating efforts of their two clamourous bodies, time after time, over the years, had been in vain, and then one hurriedly snatched, incomplete union, and Madge was carrying a child. The injustice of it made him rage anew. Then he thought of the child (he thought of it as a boy). How could he accept it. It might be several years old by the time he got home. What if he was confronted by a little, wide shouldered boy, with a big grin and stick-out ears. Jerry again in miniature. He couldn't live with it. He'd never be able to accept him as a son, and that would mean he'd lose Madge. He'd face a life of resentment that would kill joy in each other. "Think about it for a long time," Madge had written. Poor Madge. What a terrible choice she was making. He understood, to some extent, her decision to keep the child. It was what she wanted so much.

An orderly delivered a sheet of paper to his desk: medical transfers for the next day. He decided to leave his problem for the time being. Perhaps he'd be able to think more sensibly later. "I must divorce my reasoning from my emotion," he told himself. The word 'divorce' recalled Madge's pitiful suggestion. How could he divorce her. It would be like killing himself. The war was only endurable because he would one day, go back to her. Oh God! His mind went round and round.

He didn't answer the letter that day or the next. He wanted to, he wanted desperately to tell her that he loved her, and did not blame her, but every time he began to write he came up with the problem of the baby. What could he say? How could he bring himself to accept what would amount to a lifetime of reminders of Jerry's betrayal? It was a decision he just could not make. He thought of Madge waiting to hear from him. She must be going through hell. Good job she'd contacted Val. Good old Val. She'd be a comfort.

At the end of a week, he still hadn't written. It was his turn on the Orderly Sergeant roster. He thought to himself, "I'll decide something tonight, when it's dead quiet, and I'm on my own." He had the idea that he could come to some decision while on prowler patrol which took him around the perimeter of the hospital grounds, and to several outstations to check on security, making sure that the East African troops, used as guards, were awake, and that all was secure.

One place that he must visit was a house on the Corniche, where the sisters were billeted. There he could sit on the sea wall, with the surf thundering on the sand, the black velvet sky, with its incredibly beautiful stars, and the moon, twice as large as it ever was at home, seeming to hang like a theatre backdrop over the city. Then in a calm and quiet mood he could decide what to write to Madge.

It didn't work out like that. The 'Runner', who accompanied him for safety's sake, was a garrulous sick-berth attendant, who had an inexhaustible supply of dirty jokes, that he insisted on telling and who was extremely nervous about being set upon by the 'wogs', so the rounds were completed in double-quick time. Fortunately so, for there was a body to be taken from one of the wards to the mortuary.

Willy had only once before been called upon to do that duty. At the time, he was a general dogsbody, and a message from the Regimental Sergeant Major had told him to collect a stretcher party, and take a body to the mortuary.

In all innocence, he had taken four P.O.W.s from the squad, who were always on standby for loading ambulances etc., and gone to the ward with them. When he arrived, he found the Regiment Sergeant Major there already, and when he saw Willy's stretcher party, he fairly exploded. The R.S.M. was a regular soldier, and carried out his duties as if he were in a peace-time depot.

"Get these wops out of here. What the blazes do you think you're doing'. Get a party of British bearers here within five minutes, or I'll have you on a charge!"

It was one of the 'wogs' who put him right. "You go get four men from Air Raid Squad, Sergeant. We not allowed to move dead." Willy managed to press gang a party he met, just about to go into town, and returned with them, their muttered curses snapping at his heels all the way. The dead man, draped in a Union Jack, was carried shoulder high out of the ward. The R.S.M. marched in front, his swagger cane under his arm. Willy had brought up the rear, and had been shocked to see the despairing gaze of a patient, who, with eyes sunk into pallid cheeks, clearly saw himself as the next to go. He decided it was a barbarous formality, and quite unnecessary.

This time it was near midnight. He phoned the mortuary to make sure the attendant was there. This man had a room adjacent to the post mortem theatre. He answered the phone grumpily, saying he was waiting there for someone to come and identify a stiff 'brought-in-dead'.

In the quiet night, Willy took four Italians and a stretcher and went to the ward. Nobody would know, he thought, and he wasn't going to have a parade like the last time. He found the Ward Sister just about ready to let the dead man go. He was very young, and looked almost untouched by death. The Sister was gently brushing his hair and making a neat parting. "Ready Sister?"

"Yes, you can have him, I've done all I can."

As the orderlies lifted him on to the stretcher, the Sister (a young Q.A.I.M.S.) said, partly to Willy, partly it seemed to herself, "I could always weep when I send a patient away like this." (Then taking the flag, she gave Willy the other end and together they covered the body). "Not for the boy, though it always seems such a shame, but for some poor woman, his mother, or wife, or girlfriend, who's gone to bed home in England, happy, and hoping to see him again, and they won't know till the telegram comes, that he's gone for good."

Willy was touched by the sentiment, his sensitive nature responding. "They'd be comforted if they knew how kindly you'd seen to him."

"But they won't - They'll never know."

They carried the stretcher, by hand carriage, through the sleeping ward and away down the flights of stairs to the open hall. Here they paused, the bearers sweating from the difficult carry and the humid night air. Willy walked in front with a hurricane lamp to light the way through the black-out.

It was quite a long way to the mortuary, and the night was very dark, only the fabulous stars to give some little light. They passed the Prisoner of War wards, two huts in a compound. As they went, the light from Willy's lamp lit up for a moment, the figure of the armed African guard, at the compound gate, and Willy had the impression of two white eyes under the dim shape of a bush hat. The face, as black as the night itself, was invisible.

Willy's imagination dwelt on the scene as the black man must have seen it. The bier, caught in the swinging light of the lantern, the flashing colours of the shrouding flag, the measured tread of the bearers. No wonder his eyes where rolling. "I must write that up," he thought, finding relief from the worries that beset him.

The attendant let them in. A single bulb lit the room in a harsh light. "Dump it there," said the man, waving to a stone table. "Take the stretcher and the Jack back where you got 'em."

The bearers heaved the body on to the slab, the head lolled down, and the nice parting in its hair was lost.

" Right, sign here then!"

Willy signed. He was already sickened by the sweet smell of death that hung about the room. He had little experience of the tragic side of his job. In fact, he'd only seen two bodies before then.

"Hey, Serg! Look at that lot - some poor bastard of a matelot got himself shoved under a tram by some mucking wogs! Both legs gone! Makes you think, don't it. You don't ever want to go down town on your own, 'specially by the docks! Bastards!"

The body was on one of the slabs and the attendant walked over to it. Willy's stomach turned over at the sight of the mangled legs, and he was about to vomit when shock stayed the retch. He was looking down at Jerry. No kindly Ward Sister had prepared him, only the attendant's hose-pipe. His matted hair was clinging to his forehead and his open eyes seemed to gaze at Willy in reproach. "Oh God!" Willy turned away and was sick. The attendant roared with laughter. "Fat lot of good you'd be on this job! You want to be here when they bring 'em in after being in the sea for weeks!" He got busy with his hose-pipe, washing away the vomit.

"I know him! He was my best friend in Civvy Street!"

"Get out! Well, sorry mate, but I wasn't to know. Still, you can help. The buggers stripped everything off him. I just got his identity disc. Come and give me his name and so on, if you can. Hey you! (to the bearers). Muck off! You're not wanted any more."

The four men who had been talking in their own tongue amongst themselves, went out into the night. Willy soon followed them, grateful for the soft night air, fragrant with Jasmine, that cleansed his lungs of the dreadful exhalations of the dead. He found himself shaking all over. "Shock," he told himself. His bitter fury at Jerry had evaporated. He was seeing again those eyes that seemed to look right at him, as though in sorrow, or pleading. He felt an urge to go back and try and understand their message. But there was no way that he could recall the pleading of that dead mind. He would never know Jerry's bitter regret, or understand the circumstances that built towards the tragedy.

Jerry was dead, so he could never explain how he had gone ashore, after his last duty up in the Arctic, exhausted, physically and mentally. How he had eaten a hot meal from a table that was steady, and had fallen on a bed that did not pitch and roll under him, and how the sudden relaxation had released nerves held taut for weeks, that began to twitch and shudder. His teeth chattered and the very bed beneath him shook.

Then a kindly sailor came across and enquired, "Got the ad-dabs mate? 'ere, have a swig of this, you'll be okay when you wake," and passed him a bottle of whisky. "Go on, knock it back. I know how you feel, I've been out there too!" He had slept when the whisky had crept through his body and slowed the twitching down. Next day, he had collected his warrant and headed for home, longing to see the accustomed sights and the quiet land. Then he had called on Madge and taken her out to Afton, where the peace and silence had raised his spirits until he could look on Madge with longing for her love.

"I loved her Will, I've loved her ever since I met her, but never realised it 'til I saw her on your wedding day, and it was too late, but I never tried anything on, though, God knows, I wanted to. Then the bomb got me mum and I must have gone up the pole, and I don't remember much more 'til I was on your sofa and Madge was opening the black-out, and saying goodnight to me. I'd had some sort of sedative given me, I think, and I was feeling knackered, then I started to shake again, and I was scared that I was going to stay awake and see all that down in Well Street, and me poor mum.

I heard Madge on the stairs and called for a drink and some aspirin, and I couldn't, I just couldn't go to get them, so Madge came in and when she was so near, I couldn't help myself, she was all I wanted, I wanted her so much. I was ashamed afterwards because I loved her too much to hurt her. I didn't think anything would come of it, it wasn't proper, you know, so I wrote a note to brazen it out, and slipped away as soon as it was light. She had my P.O. number and when she wrote and told me, I was flabbergasted.

But, anyway I'd decided that my number was up, and I'd made a will looking after her and you if I didn't come back, now I'm glad it'll see to the kid as well. I was coming to see you Will. When you find out, don't blame Madge, it was all my fault and I'm sorry.

Willy walked on and went to the Guard Room. The runner was there, waiting for him, probably with more jokes. "Stay by the phone, I'll be at reception," Willy told him. He crossed the quadrangle between the hospital blocks and sat down on a bench outside of reception. All was quiet except for the cicadas and the distant braying of a donkey. The humid air prevented the sweat from evaporating and he felt it trickling down his chest. Jerry was dead. Not blown to bits by bombs or torpedoes, or drowned in deep waters, but by being murdered by marauding thugs. What a terrible end. No heroics to be remembered by, just a sordid finish to a probably sordid night out. ("No, that's unfair, I don't know how it happened. He might have been coming to see me and talk about it," he reminded himself).

All Jerry's hopes and plans, gone for nothing. Well, so had thousands of others. He came to realise, now that Jerry was dead, he couldn't maintain his anger and hate for him. He thought of him as he was when they roamed the woods together. He remembered how much pleasure he owed him for their childhood together, and how he owed him his very life that time when he all but drowned. He began to think how he would miss him when the war was over at last. Then, almost with a sense of shock, he realised that he was thinking, with maudlin affection, of the man who had despoiled his wife and jeopardised his marriage.

He sat still and tried to stop thinking, calling instead, as he had done on other occasions, for some spiritual initiative to come and direct him. After a time, in the vacuum of his mind, there came a great peace. He opened his eyes, and smiled at the uplift of his spirit.

Jerry was dead. Jerry's son could now be his own son. The worst of Jerry could be forgotten and the best of him would live again. "The Medlar tree's got a new shoot," he said to himself. He went over to the casualty entrance, went in, gave the N.C.O. a greeting and asked for a piece of paper. On it he wrote a telegram. He handed it in to the Unit Post Office as soon as it opened. It was to Madge, saying:

> "All my love to you and the Centre Forward.
> Letter follows. Love Will."